BAGMAN

ALWAYS LEARN FROM THE BEST

BILL PAQUETTE

BAGMAN
ALWAYS LEARN FROM THE BEST

iUniverse books may be ordered through booksellers or by contacting:

iUniverse
1663 Liberty Drive
Bloomington, IN 47403
www.iuniverse.com
1-800-Authors (1-800-288-4677)

Because of the dynamic nature of the Internet, any web addresses or links contained in this book may have changed since publication and may no longer be valid. The views expressed in this work are solely those of the author and do not necessarily reflect the views of the publisher, and the publisher hereby disclaims any responsibility for them.

Any people depicted in stock imagery provided by Thinkstock are models, and such images are being used for illustrative purposes only. Certain stock imagery © Thinkstock.

ISBN: 978-1-4917-7422-9 (sc)
ISBN: 978-1-4917-7423-6 (e)

Library of Congress Control Number: 2015912934

Print information available on the last page.

iUniverse rev. date: 08/07/2015

VIETNAM: HOW JOHN KERRY AND THE LEFT WING AMERICAN NEWS MEDIA TORPEDOD THE UNITED STATES MILITARY COST US THE WAR AND HELPED ETCH THE 58,267 NAMES ONTO THE VIETNAM WALL, AND MORE NAMES ARE STILL BEING ADDED THE WALL ON THE WASHINGTON D.C. MALL.

My leave was about through and I was anxious to get down to Washington D.C. and on to my next assignment; the 1100th Material Squadron, Bolling Air Force Base. I had no idea what I was going to do when I arrived but I'm sure that the air force would find something to keep me busy and out of trouble.

My tour of duty in 'Nam went by quickly and mostly uneventfully except for the fact that I had almost drowned when I fell through the rotted out wooden floor of a French latrine in the Zion sector of Tay Ninh Provence.

The French ruled Vietnam for a hundred and twenty-five years but then in August of 1954 the "Puddle Jumpers" got their clocks cleaned by the Viet Minh at Dien Bien Phu.

Yeah I lost some friends while I was stationed in Vietnam but so did almost everyone else who served their tour or tours of duty in country, but my most heart breaking loss wasn't in 'Nam, it was back in the "world"... home. Charlotte "Sharly" O'Sullivan was not only the girl that I loved with all my heart but she was one of the most beautiful girl that Heaven had ever created.

I suppose I'm fortunate to be returning home with my head still attached to my neck, my neck still attached to my shoulders and still in control of most of my mental faculties. I wish I could say that to about the more than fifty eight thousand dead Soldiers, Sailors, Airmen, and Marines who were sent home in body bags and for what? The American press and Television news cast made sure that we would never have a fighting chance of winning the war. And the sad part was we had them on the ropes.

When the TET offensive over and the war was about finished so was North Vietnam. They were done for and about to throw in the towel and ready to talk peace! But of course the enemy had access to the American news media and the American news media let it be known that the US forces took a horrible shellacking all over South Vietnam and that was a fucking lie! Thank you Walter Cronkite! Thank you Andy Rooney! I hope and pray that you two are rotting in hell along with the rest of your cohorts that made sure that we lost the war!

And John Kerry came home from 'Nam with the Silver Star; Bronze Star and three Purple Hearts! He accomplished all of this in less than four months! He was a disgrace to the uniform, the Navy, and the whole military that fought and died in Vietnam.

FUN IN VIETNAM

Now…let me get on with the war. I was a senior vehicle operator assigned to the 3rd Transportation Squadron Bien Hoa Airbase. The base was in the Thee Corps area of operation in the Tay Ninh, Province. I was trained as a heavy equipment driver, but the year that I spent in 'Nam was behind the wheel of a ten ton International tractor followed by a forty foot Fontaine flat bed trailer. My job was transporting supplies that would help us win the war, empty auxiliary tip tanks for the fighter aircraft, heavy construction equipment, huge dump trucks, just about anything that we could fit on the trailers with absolutely no concern that we just might to be overloading the flatbeds. If the tires were still inflated we on our way.

The truck route went from Bien Hoa south to Long Binh and then up at the Tan Son Nhut Air Base supply area and occasionally east to Zion. Zion or "The Big Red One" was where the Americal Division was fighting the V.C. who was shooting at us from the other side of the Vietnam Cambodian border.

The Special Express section of the squadron transported ammunition in five and ten ton tractor-trailer convoys from the Saigon docks up to Bien Hoa. That was an ass puckering trip.

On my last month before rotating state side, I had my windshield shield shot out. The funny or fortunate thing was that I was never a smoker, but one of the troops in the outfit, Freddie "Whitey" White's wife had a ten pound bouncing baby boy and he handed out more of his shit smelling cigars. He had to have smoked the cheapest fucking

1

stogies sold at the Base Exchange. I turned down Whitey's generous offer but he smiled, shook my hand and stuffed the rope into my fatigue pocket. I was going to heave it out of the window as soon as I drove off the base.

On my ride back to the base I was slowed down by the traffic as I turned off Highway 1 then squeezed the slow moving, empty eighteen wheeler into traffic, then onto the road that led to the main gate, I didn't get any argument from the little shit boxes that the locals drove. If I want to I could have run them into the river that ran beside the dirt that road that ran down the middle of the city of Bien Hoa.

Tech Sgt Riley Jefferson (Jeff) told the gear jammers time after time do not, under any circumstances take the exit that went behind the perimeter of the base. It's too dangerous, but it was the middle of another hot afternoon, the visibility was unlimited and I wanted to get back onto the base, have a shower and a drink. I thought while I was moving at a snail's pace heading for the forbidden outer perimeter road I would fire up the Guinea rope. While I was attempting to get some fire to the end of Whitey's generous gift, the wind kept blowing out my Zippo. Everybody whether you smoked or not carried a Zippo lighter, so I lowered my head behind the dash to try and get out of the wind, and when I finally got it lit and I lifted my head back up to see if my rig was still on the road and not in a rice patty, there was a hole the size of a silver dollar shot through the windshield! The bullet went through the windshield and exited through the rear window taking the glass and the frame with it, thank you God and thank you Whitey's wife!

As I approached the east gate that ran parallel to the flight line Air Policeman Airman 1st Class Ray Boudreau, held out his hand and signaled for me pull my rig over to the side of the road. "Looks like someone had you zeroed in, Dy." he said in his soft Cajun voice as he climbed on to the saddle tank and looked inside of the cab at my windshield. "Jeff's gonna ream you a new one, old buddy, you know how he feels about you guys taking the back perimeter road. He ain't gonna take this all that lightly."

"Yeah I know, but I was trying to light one of Whitey's shit tasting ropes a Gook took a shot at me. If it wasn't for Whitey's wife dropping a kid my head would have come right off, Ray."

"You're one lucky Mick." He said as he jumped off my rig and waved me through.

"Do me a favor will you Ray? Call Jeff and tell him I'm on my way back with half my windshield shot out?" I shouted as I put the truck into first gear, released the trailer brakes gave the big V8 a little gas and slowly let out the clutch.

"Are you sure you want me to call him, Dy?" Ray shouted back at me.

"Yeah go ahead, it'll give me some time to come up with a bullshit story!"

"You got it Dy… good luck!"

"Hey Ray, you gonna drop by tonight? Col. Davys got us a good flick from TASS Headquarters; the Carpetbaggers. It should be good. The book was."

"Yeah, I'll stop by and have a beer."

"The flick begins at seven thirty, the Col's orders." I shouted then pulled my rig into the traffic and was waved through the gate and drove down the motor pool.

Now it was time to face Jeff's wrath. I still can hear Sgt Jefferson's voice, the large black cigar chewing Transportation NCO's voice booming, even now: "I just got a call from the east gate you asshole! You're gonna pay for those broken windows! And the other windows and the frame and any Goddamn thing else I can come up with! If I can swing it I'm gonna make you pay for the whole Goddamn rig! Now how does that grab you Bagman?" My reputation followed me from basic training to as far away as Vietnam. He was waiting for me in front the maintenance building while I parked the rig, shut down the engine and climbed out. His hands on his hips and he looked as if he was going to have a heart attack. Ray called Jefferson

3

right after he waved me through. The trip from the east gate to the motor pool took about five minutes. The speed limit on the base was twenty miles an hour.

"What are you gonna do, Jeff? Keep me here in Vietnam? I'm already here! Gonna rescind my orders? You would be doing me a favor!" I challenged him back. "I about got killed and all that you can think of is making me pay for two windows that were blown out of a two year old ten ton International tractor before I got here. That shit box has more bullet hole than all the targets on the firing range! Why not send the bill to Ho Chi Minh? What do you say about that shit, Jeff?"

"Keep it up hot shit! Don't write a check with you mouth that your ass can't cash! Your big mouth is gonna get you in a world of shit I'm gonna take this shit up with Col Davys!" Col Davys was the Transportation Squadron's Commanding Officer. "How many times have I told you assholes not to use the back road and the outside perimeter fool? You know how Goddamn' dangerous it is! Go and ask Philly! He wanted to save some time to, I guess he really needed that drink didn't he? And look where it got him!"

Danny Philips was almost wiped out when his ten ton International tractor ran over a roadside land mine right near where the stretch of road that I took the KC-47 round that took out my windows. He was fortunate. Most of the explosion was absorbed by the rear of his rig, but he still has a back loaded with shrapnel.

"Come on will ya Jeff. I have less than a month to go I don't wanna go back to "World" with any dumb assed shit on my record. Give me a break will yeah? Come on, please?" I pleaded.

"Look Dy," Jeff said as he began to calm down, "You are one of my best drivers. I don't want to see any of my guys get killed. That's all. I lost Goosey Spencer, Buda Jordan, Donnie Bare-ass, (Bare-ass was Donnie Bare's nick-name), and I 'bout lost Philly Green. I take this shit personal, OK? Now get out of my face! Go take a shower, get cleaned up have a beer or a drink or whatever you want, Danny Mac got back from Saigon an hour ago with two bottles Jim Beam and a three bottles of Gold Coach gin in his locker; throw him a couple of bucks for the vodka and the Jim Beam, alright? Then get something to eat. We'll talk later, OK?"

"Okay Jeff, thanks. I can use a drink," I said.

"You guys are gonna drive me crazy with all you taking Goddamn chances! I'm gonna end up in the ward eight section at Clark!" He said slapping me on the shoulder than went back into the dispatch office. Clark was a huge Air force base in the Philippines.

The ten ton International ten wheelers were an amazingly well engineered truck. You could beat them like rented mule and they would keep on running. No other tractors that the Air Force had in the South Vietnam inventory could take that amount of abuse. They were better than the Ford cab over engines, the Ford Ten Tons, the fifteen ton white Freight Liners, and the Dodge ten ton cab over Detroit Diesels. The Ford cab over's would run over a road side mine and the whole truck would come apart, the Whites would explode because the metal used to manufacture the fuel tanks were too thin. The Dodge ten tons were good but they were diesels and couldn't get out of their own way on the other hand the Internationals would take the brunt of an explosion and so long as the wheels were still intact they would keep on going.

Pappy Scott pulled into the motor pool the engine of his ten ton was billowing smoke and it smelled like burning old tires. He shut the engine down one of the mechanics check the oil a found the engine was four quarts low on oil. That meant there was only three quarts left in the oil pan. The truck was towed into the maintenance building, the oil was drained, the oil filter changed seven quarts of fresh oil was added to the five hundred cubic inch V-8 and the International ten ton was ready for another trip.

When I received my orders for Washington D.C. that was just before Christmas, I went to talk to the 1st Sgt. and try to extend my tour of duty for another six months. The 1st Sgt forward my request to headquarters but when Col Davys got wind of my request he called personnel and had my extension request squashed. He called me into his office and gave his reason. "Airman Dyer, I want to commend you for wanting to extend you tour of duty, but I feel that another six months here at Bien Hoa would not be in your best interest or for that matter the Air Force's best interest. Sgt Jefferson told me that you take too many un-necessary chances even a bit reckless so I took it upon myself to red line your request. You will be reassigned to Bolling Air Force Base, Washington D.C. I'm sure you'll find it to your liking. Bolling is Headquarters Command USAF and only the best of the best are assigned to Bolling and the WAFs are hand-picked. Do you have any questions, Dyer?"

"No Sir," I replied. "And thank you, Sir

"That will be all, Airman Dyer."

"Yes Sir," I said flipping Col Davys a salute did an about face and walked out of his office.

Bolling Air force Base, I thought to myself. Washington D.C. and from the way Col Davys described D.C. it's a choice assignment and It's not all that far from Boston. It sounds interesting, maybe I'll like my new assignment and I already have one friend stationed there. I suppose that I'll find out soon enough. And maybe I'll meet a girl that will help me try to get over Sharly's death. There's a lot of optimism riding on the new assignment.

Two months before I was due to leave 'Nam a package arrived for me from Bolling's office of information containing a welcome form letter, a map of D.C. and all the points of interest, and map of the base. Apparently Bolling Air Force Base was expecting me.

We were outside the tents sitting on the picnic tables listening to Danny McCloud's Radio. The Christmas music was being piped in through The Armed Forces Radio and Television Services. "Pretty ain't it?" Benny Polly said as he took a pull from a quart jug of Moon Shine that his brother had brewed up special, packaged up real neat; the bottle was a plastic orange soda pop container so the chances of it breaking were almost nil and the jug was wrapped in insulation covered with masking tape boxed up and mailed out from Bogalusa, Louisiana. He was the only one drinking the one hundred and forty proof rocket fuel. Everyone else was drinking either beer or whiskey. That seventy per-cent moon shine was to heavy most of the guy's heads or livers.

Yeah the Christmas music sounded pretty and the more you had to drink the sadder you became thinking about home family and friends. This was my fifth Christmas away from home but some of the gear jammers, had a lot more time away from home then I did. Sgt. Jefferson, Tommy Stilly and Pappy Scott hadn't seen home for Christmas in years. And I still don't believe Stilly has a home, except for the military, he said he originally came from North Carolina and during the Korean conflict he enlisted. I've known him for almost a year and none of us had ever seen him receive one piece of mail, not even an advertisement catalogue.

"Maybe he's on the lamb," The CO mused.

Benny sidled up beside me and sat down. He had a real good buzz on thanks to his brother Freddie's corn squeezing distillery hidden in the southern Louisiana's back woods. "How are you doing ole Buddy, Buddy?" He asked trying to focus me with one eye closed.

"I'm doing fine ole Buddy, but don't light a cigarette or your breath will level the camp." I joked while I took a sip out of my glass of Hiram Walker Ten High rot gut Bourbon on the rocks. Whenever the booze plane from Clark landed at Bien Hoa the good stuff ended up at the Officer's club and the rest was rationed off at the class V1 store.

"Looks like you and me are gonna be stationed together down in the ole Nations Capital, Stevie. How do you feel 'bout that?"

"I feel good, Benny, how about you?"

"Well if you feel all that good about going down to Washtoning (He had trouble pronouncing "Washington" even when he was not swilling his brother's moon shine) then why did you try to extend your tour for a nother six months? Huh?" He said pointing his finger in my face. "I thought you and me was buddies." How in hell did he find out? I didn't tell anybody except for Jeff, in confidence, and I knew he wouldn't say a word.

"We are buddies, Benny but I didn't feel like I was ready to go home. I didn't know what I wanted to do but Col Davys squashed my orders."

"Well how do you feel now?" He asked as he handed me his plastic jug of 140 proof white lightning, it doesn't take all that much 'shine to get you totally shit faced but I said no to his offer, that shit will kill you.

"I'm ready to go home,"

"You gonna drive me down to Saigon tomorra mornin'?" He said as he put his arm around my shoulder looking at the side of my face; you light a match in front of his lips and his breath could level the tent area.

"Fuckin A" ole buddy," I said as tried to hold my breath. God Benny, drink something else will ya? "I wish I could drive you all the way to D.C."

"Ain't that many gas stations 'cross the 'cific Ocean," He meant the Pacific Ocean. "Shit fire, man, we'd be plum out of gas 'fore we got anywhere near Haywyre." He meant Hawaii. "We'd be plum out of gas before we got halfway 'cross the ocean."

"What you say, Benny," I said slapping on the back. "I think it's 'bout time to hit the sack. 0600's gonna come soon enough."

"Shit fire DY, I can sleep on the plane," He said wrapping his large tanned hand around the bottle and taking a healthy hit from his jug of moon shine.

"Let's go Benny, time to hit the sack," Jeff said as he leaned over the table taking the jug out of Benny's hand. "Dy's right. 0600's gonna be here before you know it,"

FRIDAY, 13 JANUARY 1967 0600 HOURS.

"Wake up Benny!" I yelled slapping him on the ass. "Time to get up, you're going home today."

"Huh?" He said slowing opening his left eye. "What time is it?"

"0600 hours Buddy, six in the AM. Come on drag your ass out of the rack. You have to be at Tan Son Nhut Ops no later than nine hundred hours," I could still smell the moon shine on his breath. "I phoned the troops at Civil Engineers and there on the way over to flush out your mouth, power wash your teeth and clean up your breath, come on."

"Very funny, Stevie," Benny said as he dropped out of the top bunk, opened his locker, took out his shaving kit, towel and left the tent stumbled down the cat-walk and stumbled into the shower tent. His summer kakis were laid out on the bottom bunk. So was his garrison cap with bill spit shined his low quarters were spit shined too and his B-4 bag carefully packed.

"Morning Dy. How's the Moon Dog doing?" Jeff asked as field stripped a Pall Mall, let the tobacco fall to the ground, balled up the paper and placed it in his pocket. Even in a war zone we took pride in a clean well organized base.

"Morning Jeff, he's in the shower tent. It took a little coxing to get his ass up, but he'll be alright once he gets some coffee and a little food in his stomach.

"I can't for the life of me see how he can drink that rot gut Moonshine, never could," Jeff remarked while he greeted the rest of the drivers as they walked out of the tent and headed for the Red Horse chow tent.

"He's been drinking that crap since he was a kid, he has to be used to it by now."

"Yeah I suppose but his liver gotta be as hard as an engine block," He lamented as he grinned and shook his head. "See you two at breakfast."

"Yeah, we'll be there in a couple."

9

By the time Benny and I left the mess tent he was feeling alright but still a bit shaky. At last count he ate a half a dozen powered scrambled eggs left over from the Korea "police action", four glasses of frozen concentrated orange juice and three cups of black coffee. Maybe I'll stop by the mess tent before we left for TSN see if I can scrounge an empty coffee can, he'll be pissing all the way to Saigon. A medic from Red Horse handed him a hand full APC's and a package holding twelve air sick pills. Benny and I walked around the motor pool while he said good-bye to the troops and shaking hands to all that were still in the area, hugged the Vietnamese girls shook hand with the Vietnamese civilian workers then he tossed his B-4 bag into the bed of the Ford F-150 climbed into the cab and drove the twenty some odd miles to Tan San Nhut Air Base. I dropped him off in front of the passenger terminal, found a parking space near the flight-line and walked back to base operations. Benny was standing amongst the two hundred or so troops waiting for the call to board the aircraft. The Pan Am 707 was sitting on the ramp the pilots sitting in the cockpit waiting for the troops to board. That's going to be me in another month and I do believe that it's time for me to go home. I had done as much as I was going to do here anyway, I'm not going to win the war all by myself and leaving the buddies I had made over the year I can handle and there will always many more opportunities to make new friends.

The buddies that I had made while in country; Benny Polly, Billy Ray Mizel, Tommy Stilly, Leroy "Pappy" Scott, Ray "Simple" Simpson and George "Goosey" Spencer were great guys and a bunch of hot shits, we all were in the same tent. We played cards, swapped bull shit stories, drank, went into town for dinner, there was a restaurant just outside the main gate that served the best water buffalo steaks I had ever eaten. They were better than any steaks my Dad grilled and Dad bought nothing but the best.

"Goosey" Spencer was the first to go home in a body bag. The Goose took AK-47 slug in the face while he was driving his rig across the dangerous outer eastern perimeter. He didn't feel a thing. He was dead before his rig crashed through the perimeter barrier and came to a stop a just short of the revetments on the west end of the flight line. His rig exploded in a huge red blue yellow ball of fire. By the time Air Police arrived at the wreck with the fire department with the medic's right behind them "Goosey" wasn't there anymore. Neither was most of the ten ton International tractor trailer. There was nothing to send home except for what was left of his jungle boots and his Seiko Watch. It had stopped at precisely 1600 hours. 4 PM.

The Air Force Honor Guard removed "Goosey's" flag from top of his closed casket that was empty except for what was left of his jungle boots, part of his Seiko watch, his dog tags and presented Old Glory to Roy's family at his grave side service at Cody Military Cemetery, Cody, Wyoming

"Goosey" enjoyed sharing his growing up days with us living in that lovely city located about two hundred miles northwest of Cheyenne. He and his friends both girls and boys loved exploring Yellowstone National Park, camping out in the winter time, waking up their tents buried in two feet of fluffy new snow. "Weren't ya'lls folks worried about ya'll being out all night sharing ya'll's sleeping bags with ya'll's girlfriends?" Benny would ask a lewd grin on his face.

"Not anymore than your folks worrying about you and your girl friends hanging around a 'shine still, drinking that crap you refer to as "Top Shelf Moonshine," He grinned.

"I understand what ya'll's saying Goosey, but it's hotter en a whore's money maker down there in Bogalusa, 'specially in the summer time so we don't need no sleeping bags."

"So what you do, Benny, romp around the fires in your birthday suits 'till you get good and sweaty then splash around in the Mississippi to cool off? You know Benny I've seen some those Southern Bells when I was stationed down at Barksdale Air Force Base, mighty nice."

"Wait 'till you get to D.C., Stevie." Benny said looking at me, "And you meet my wife. She's a lovely southern bell."

"Hey Benny," Tommy Stilly chuckled taking a hit from his bottle of VAT 69. "You know what a Southern Bell is?"

"I have no idea, Tommy" Benny said in perfect English. He could speak as eloquently as any officer or en-listed man when he wasn't drinking his brother's corn squeezing. "Tell me old friend what is a Southern Bell."

"A hillbilly whore with a dong in her."

Benny just sat there looking at Tommy with a discussed look on his face while the rest of us thought the joke was quite amusing. Stilly just shrugged his narrow shoulders and gulped down his Scotch.

Next to get blown away was Budda Jordan and Donnie Bare. Both were killed taking the short cut back to the base and Philly Green got it in the head as he tried to get out of his rig when it flipped on Route #1. He was driving back to the base from Long Bien. His eighteen wheeler flipped when the front tires of his rig were shot out.

The heavy equipment mechanics cooked most of our chow which was usually steak, chicken and pork over a 55 gallon oil barrel that had been cut in half with a welding torch, then we put the barrel half into a pickup then drove into the city of Bien Hoa sand blasted and steam cleaned, then brought back to the transportation tent area, placed on a stand we had fabricated at the base vehicle maintenance shop, half filled the barrel with charcoal doused with charcoal lighter fluid then lit it. The sand blasting cleaned out all the residue that stained the inside of the 55 gallon so the all chow the Danny Mac cooked tasted so good.

Red Horse Construction outfit, the 3rd Transportation Squadron, and the 3rd Civil Engineers were bunked out in tents at the east end of the flight line away from the base across the road from us and. when it came time for chow or enjoying a beer or a shot of whiskey we were pretty much left to our own devises and we took full advantage of our remote situation. We had a primitive outdoor movie screen made from scrounged plywood, nailed together, painted white then nailed to four 2x4's and pounded into the soft sandy ground. We had movies delivered to us from the MACV office in the main part of the base. Col Davys loved to watch out door movies while he enjoyed his Beefeater Martini. The "Old Man" had a lot of friends on base and in downtown Saigon. He spent more time hanging around MACV Headquarters (Military Assistance Command Vietnam) than he spent on running the section but he would say: "What are they gonna do? Send me to Viet Fucking Nam?"

It was a warm late August evening and while we were watching the movie "The Great Race" a mortar round launched outside the outer base perimeter, buzzed over Bien Hoa Air Base and slammed into the Long Binh Bomb Dump and the ammunition supply center. Long Binh was and Army base located three miles northeast of Bien Hoa. The concussion took down the movie screen and most of the tents plus the latrine. "God damn those gooks bastards!" Col Davys yelled as he pulled himself up from his wrecked lawn chair and wiped the spilled Martini from the front of his T shirt. "Now I'm gonna miss the movie movie and just when it was starting to get good!" The next evening the screen was rebuilt set back up, the Great Race was up on the silver painted plywood screen and Col Davys had a new lawn chair with a cup holder for his Martini.

We also had a junked out half ton Ford pick-up that Col Davys pulled out of salvage that we used to transport a 55 gallon fuel barrel that we cleaned out and filled it with ice and beer. We had the 55 gallon barrel welded to the pick-up bed of the Ford and we used it to carry the beer and ice to the outdoor theater. When the mortar took out the screen it also took out the junked out pick-up; there was exploded beer cans and ice all over the compound.

Most of the guys in the section including me had never eaten in the mess hall not just because it was out of the way but the shit they call food sucked! The crap was frozen and thawed out then frozen again and again. Have lunch in the mess hall and until you're intestines adjusted to the food, you'd be spending your dinner time in the latrine. The eggs were powered, the milk was powered and the bread bought on the local economy and was thick and doughy. The only thing that was edible was the fruits and the vegetables that were grown in country or were flown in from Thailand or Ceylon. We swapped American Whiskey and American Cigarette for the steaks that came in country from Australia and New Zeland. The tent city troops had "friends" in 8TH Arial Port so when a C- 130's came in from Thailand or Laos or an Army C-7 Caribou flew in from Vung Tau we were at the ramp ready to conduct business. The Aussies and the Kiwis were billeted in tents between Bien Hoa and Long Binh. The pork, chicken for us and a duck or two for "Ramrod" came from down town.

The Red Horse Squadron had a pet Boa Constrictor who showed up while tent city was being built. Ram Rod was now a legacy. He was use to eating rats and mice but when the troops began feeding him live ducks and chickens he became spoiled. "You're going regret feeding him ducks," Col Davys observed while the guys were sitting around the Red Horse orderly room drinking beer and watching Ram Rod feasting on his second mallard. You could hear the bones snapping as the snake coiled its twelve foot body around the duck and shipped Daffy, Donald and Daisy up to Duck cartoon heaven. "Once that slimy bastard gets used to eating high on the hog, you guys can forget about him eating anything else unless you start feeding him pigs."

Col Frank Davys was the best C.O. the gear jammers had ever served with. He'd sit down with enlisted men at the picnic table, at our make shift drive in, have a drink, he was a big time martini drinker, he would help Airman First Class, Danny Mac, cook dinner, sing along when the shit kickers from below the Mason Dixon Line ambled down to the patio area between the tents with their guitars and amps and belted out fiddle tunes for hours on end. It was Country and Western or nothing. I wasn't much of a fiddle tune fan, I liked Elvis, Roy Orbison, Motown, the British invasion groups but after a few drinks who gave a shit whether it was rock or country. They knew every country and western or country rock songs that Johnny Cash, Elvis, Carl Perkins, Wanda Jackson, Hank Williams Senior and Junior, Marty Robbins, Jerry Lee Lewis (Who was, in my opinion, almost as good as Elvis) every country music shit kicker that ever played the Grand Old Opry.

"Hey! When are you shit kickers gonna lay off the fiddle tunes and get to playing real music?" Col Davys would shout at the band after downing a Martini or two. "Play us some Beatle tunes, some Stones, how about some Elvis? you know some good ole rock and roll shit!"

In your wildest dreams Col Davys

23 FEBRUARY 1967:

The night before I was scheduled to return to the "world" most of the troops in the heavy equipment and motor pool section that wasn't on duty were sitting at the picnic tables drinking from cans of Falstaff, Hams, Olympia or Miller High Life, Tiger beer from Thailand, green bottles of Vietnamese '33 beer, or shots from bottles of Smirnoff Vodka, Ron Rico Rum, Gold Coach gin, Hiram Walker Ten High Bourbon and, on occasion, Crown Royal. The 40 ounce bottles sold at the class six store was cheap. The rot gut vodka and gin cost about sixty-five cents a jug.

The fiddle tune swingers were really wailing and Col. Davys who had a Martini or two streaming through his veins was throwing empty beer cans at them, Pappy Scott, Lou Lascano, Billy Ray Mizel and I were sitting at the picnic table throwing back drinks and talking about family and back home. Pappy, Lou and Billy Ray were due to rotate stateside next month. Danny Mc Cloud had already rotated stateside.

"Think you're gonna like DC, Stevie?" Pappy asked. Pappy, Tom Stilly and Benny was the only troops in the section that called me Stevie. We all called Leroy Scott, Pappy, because he was bald and looked older than his forty some odd years. Pappy had orders for

Randolph AFB, and he was in his glory. He was born and raised in Waco. He wasn't like any other Texan I had met and being in the military for six years I met a lot of Texans. No bragging about how great Texas was or how beautiful the girls were or how pretty the Gulf Coast was. Pappy was a genuine good guy.

"Hope so, Paps," I said as I took a pull from the can of Hams Beer shipped in from the Land of Sky Blue Waters. I was taking it easy. I didn't want to wake up on my last day in 'Nam with a hangover. "I may sound like I'm talking stupid but I'm not looking forward to going home. I'd just as soon fly right into DC. Then I thought that when I settled down at Bolling I'd drive home and visit the folks and my friends."

"Is that what you really want to do, Stevie?" Tommy Stilly asked joining the guys at the picnic table holding a bottle of Vat 69 Scotch. Vat 69 was the only Scotch that Tommy would drink. Technical Sgt (E-6) Tommy Stilly was NCOIC of the vehicle dispatch section and was on his third tour of duty. He could drink the whole squadron under the table and never slur a word or stagger when he tried to walk. Tommy said that he was not going to leave 'Nam until the war was over. If you're still over there Tommy, I thought looking at blood shot eyes. I hope you've stocked up on Vat 69, and you may be still alive Tommy but I'll bet your liver crapped out years ago.

"I don't know Tommy? You guys are my best buddies and stood by me when I really needed you. I don't know if I can handle going home by myself."

"Then take us all with you, Di. Ya'll have all the money in the world," Billy Mizel joked as he finished off the rest of his can of Falstaff.

"I wished the hell I could, guys. I really do." I said.

We spent the rest of the evening joking, talking about all the girls that we were with, most of our stories were a crock of shit; tossing back shots of Crown Royal then some of the troops from Red Horse Construction began firing up Tia Stick, it was tolerated to a certain extent but most of the heavy equipment drivers stayed away from that shit, it played with you head too much. If I was going to die for my country I wasn't going to be stoned. I'll stick with Hams Beer or Crown Royal.

"Hey Dy, remember the day we convoyed up to Zion?" Billy Mizel said with a laugh, "And when we pulled our rigs into the Army base you jumped out of your rig and yelled that you had to piss like a race horse and an Army Corporal pointed to an old rotted out French latrine?"

"Yeah, that was the day after you ran over the ARVN slope head," Pappy had to remind me. (ARVN was the Army of the Republic of Vietnam).

"Yeah he came out of nowhere and ran right in front of my rig. I tried to stop you know."

"Yeah, it took you a hundred feet to get your rig stopped," Col. Davys said as he walked out of the latrine buttoning his fly. "You sure killed him Di. Some of that poor, unfortunate bastard's hair is still in the grill!"

"Yeah, and the next day you crashed through the rotted out floor," Pappy chuckled. "I had never seen a look like you had on your face. God Damn, that was funny. You were up to your waist in a pool of shit and hanging onto the rotted floor for dear life."

"Fucking "A"," Billy said laughing his ass off. "Get me the fuck out of here! You screamed. I don't want to sacrifice my life for my country drowning in a vat filled with frog and gook shit!"

"Someone say vat?" Tommy said looking around the picnic table his eyes wide open looking for his forty ounce bottle of VAT 69, found it and took another pull from his jug.

"I said vat, Tommy," Billy chuckled. "Anyway, Benny and Philly threw you a rope and we all pulled you out, then you stripped off your clothes and then some army grunt hosed you down with a fire hose and then they gave you a set of Army jungle fatigues that had been previously worn by a big fat ass hippo, a pair of olive drab skivvies with the crotch eaten out and "T" shirt with the no arm pits."

"Yeah, I saw him when you guys dropped of your rigs. I thought you lost some weight," Stilly laughed as he put the bottle in front of me. "Go on Stevie, take a hit. It's your last night."

I looked at Tommy then looked around the picnic table at the guys I had just spent a year with, looked at the half full bottle of Scotch and said what the hell, it's still early and my flight out of TSN wasn't leaving 'til noon. I picked up the bottle toasted the guys and took a pull that almost emptied Tommy's bottle. "I'll get another Stevie, don't go anywhere," he said as he hurried back to our tent.

"How you doing, Di? Saying good bye in style?" It was Jeff.

"Trying not to, Jeff. I want to be in shape for the flight home."

"No sweat Di. We'll get you there with time to spare," Jeff assured me as he opened a bottle Tiger Beer. "I'm having Tommy Stilly and Pappy drive you down to TSN."

"That should be an adventure, Jeff. They're both half shit faced."

"That's all right, Kid. I'll make sure they be sober," he said then went on. "You know your assignment to Bolling was a gift from Col Davys. He's DC connected. He knows people that can do him favors. When your girl died and how bad you were taking it he thought of breaking a few regs and sending you home on emergency leave but I said forget it Col, Stevie Dyer's here for the year. He'll turn you down flat. Was I right, Stevie?" That was the first time the motor pool NCOIC had ever called me by my first name.

"To tell you the truth don't know if I would have or not then, I'm having trouble with the thought of going home, but when the CO turned down my request to hang around for six more months, I realized I'm through here and I want get the fuck out of here and on to my next assignment.

"You'll find your way, Stevie," Jeff said as he putting his arm around my neck and squeezed. "So not to worry. Now, where's crazy Stilly with the jug?"

It was a nice going back to the world party. Danny Mac fired up the grill and Col Davys threw the food on the grate over the hot charcoal fire. There was chicken, pork and water buffalo. The food was great and everybody except Tommy Stilly stayed pretty much sober.

SATURDAY: 27, FEBUARY 1967

Today was a hot, humid, typical duty day for everyone stuck in Vietnam. It was 0530 hours when I rolled out of my rack; good bye bunk, good bye locker, so long rats, so long Mamma San. I showered, shaved, brushed his teeth, dressed in summer tans, went to morning chow, returned to the tent, grabbed my B-4 officer's bag and walked down the motor pool. Tommy and Pappy were standing beside our one and only 1966 blue Ford station wagon car with the factory standard 289 cubic inch V8 and a three speed on the column and drove the twenty miles or so to Tan Son Nhut Air Base. This was the only time that the wagon had been driven off base. It was mostly used to pick-up the brass or dignitaries that flew into Bien Hoa Air Base and would pick by one of the motor pool vehicle operators and driven to the VIP quarters, head quarters or the officer's club. The car had less than six hundred miles on the odometer. On the drive down to TSN, I was sitting in the front seat beside Pappy. Tommy Stilly was stretched out on the back seat. The VAT 69 drinker was feeling a bit under the weather.

While Pappy was driving we were joking about Stilly and his hang over he wasn't paying that much attention to the road and before he could avoid the crash ran into a zip peddling his bicycle with a bunch of bananas loaded into basket tied to the rear fender. Pappy wasn't going that fast but fast enough to knock him backward off the bicycle ass over tea kettle and he and the bananas landed off to the side of the dirt road. "Holy shit, Pappy," I exclaimed as Pappy pulled over to the side of the road, stopped the wagon, shut off the engine and climbed out of the wagon.

"Why are we stopping?" Stilly asked as he sat up and looked out the window at the local who was now sitting on his ass on the side of the road his bike crashed against a tree. "Is he dead?"

"Naw, he's alright just a little shook up is all," Pappy said.

"What do you wanna do?" I said as I jumped out of the station wagon and ran over to the stunned papa-san who was sitting on his ass.

"Are you okay Papa san?" I asked as I knelt down beside him. He looked at me like he had bubbles coming out of his ears.

"Is he dead?"

"No, just a little fucked up," Pappy answered looking into Papa San's eyes. "But he'll be alright."

"Then give him some money for a new bike then let's get the hell outa here," Stilly said his head sticking out of the back door window.

"How much?" I asked.

"Enough to buy him a new bike," Pappy replied as tried to help the old boy to his feet.

"What's a new bike cost?"

"Beats the shit out of me," Pappy said shrugging his shoulders still looking at the gook who was still in shock. "How much you got?"

I reached in my pocket and took out all the money I had, two hundred and fifty dollars in MPCs, (military payment certificates).

Pappy snapped all my money out of my handed and handed the money to the injured papa-san. "That's all the money I have, Pappy!" I exclaimed looking at Pappy then at Papa san. He still had bubbles coming out of his ears. "Give me fifty dollars so I can pick up some booze from the class six store when we lay over in Guam."

"You wanna go home, Stevie?" Tommy asked, still looking out of back seat window.

Pappy picked up Papa san's hat placed it on his head, took my money out of his shaking hand, counted out two hundred dollars handed him the cash then helped him to his feet. We all shook his hand then climbed back into the sedan and left the gook looking at what used to be most of my money t Pappy had so generously handed over to him.

I looked at Pappy, Tommy now sitting up looking at both of us with a grin and we all began laughing. "Fuckin' Pappy," I said laughing my ass off, "You almost screwed me out of my flight back to the world.

"Did you see the way that skinny slope bounced when he hit the ground?" Pappy said. "I thought for sure I killed him!"

"To bad you didn't, Pappy," Tommy said from the back seat. "You would've saved Stevie two hundred dollars."

On our ride to TSN, Stilly insisted that we stop at Flash's Truck Stop which was half way between Bien Hoa and Ton Son Nhut for a final drink. Flash's Truck Stop was a Bomb Dee Bomb stand that sold beer, liquor, weed and the finest young virgin whores in all of Vietnam. "Hey GI, maybe you want fucky, fucky Baby- San? She still cherry girl and she only twelve year old."

Not today zip, not ever, this GI's going home.

Pappy and Tommy had a beer but I ordered a Coke. I didn't want to show up at base ops and to be pulled out of line because I had alcohol on my breath.

All returning troops going back to the world were required to go through inspection to make sure we were not bringing any contraband back home with us. There was a trash can near the inspection area where you could dump any of the shit that you were thinking about taking out of the country, no questions asked. Articles such as hand held weapons, ammo, drugs, liquor, pornography, (Pornography was easy to find in Saigon or Bien Hoa. Hell it was sold right out on the streets. "Hey GI you want maybe to buy number one fuck suck picture of me and my sister? Who took the pictures Zip? Your number one Mamma San? Everything had to be thrown out and if you were caught trying to smuggle the shit through the inspection area your tour of duty in 'Nam would be extended and you could end up doing bad time in Long Binh. There was a stockade there referred to as the LBJ…Long Binh Jail. You did not want to go there.

I said good bye to Pappy and Tommy hugged them both and told them I'd be in touch, turned in what was left my MPCs into green backs check my bag, climbed aboard the big Boeing Pan American Airlines 707 and with one hundred and eighty or so grateful souls, grabbed a seat in the rear of the 707 and flew out of Vietnam. As the 707 was leaving the ground, the pilot bank the plane and aimed it toward the South China Sea all the returning troops began applauding even the officers who were sitting up in front rendered the pilot a round of applause. The Pan Am 707 made four stops, Clark AFB in the Philippines, Guam, and Hawaii then finally into Travis AFB. Travis was north east of San Francisco then we all boarded a shuttle bus that took us from Travis to SFO and from the twenty four hours from the time the troops flew out of Saigon was aboard a big TWA 707 heading east to Boston. The nonstop out of Frisco took five hours and there at the gate were Mom, Dad and Aunt Louise. The flight landed precisely at nine PM. I hurried down the stairs, ran across the ramp and into the concourse. It was twelve degrees and I was wearing my short sleeve tans and a raincoat. My three sets of winter blues three sets of light weight blues and his overcoat were still hanging in my bedroom closet. I only took my 1505 tans and four sets of fatigues with me. Vietnam was a jungle, and so I thought, why weigh myself down with clothes I won't be wearing?

Our first stop on the seventeen hour flight across the Pacific was Clark Air Force Base in the Philippines. The air craft was re-fueled than we sat on that damn flight line baking in the hot sun for two hours waiting for a Navy admiral to show up. Everybody on the aircraft was pissed. There were one hundred and eighty GI's sitting in the air craft waiting to go home and that shit head seaweed never arrived. The Clark Air Force Base Commander called base operations, and ordered, "Get the aircraft in the air and out of here, right now! I don't want a plane full of dead GI's rotting away on the ramp." The ground crew brought out the ground power unit, fired up the four jet engines and we flew out.

Next stop, Guam, we were allowed off the plane and stopped by the "Class 6" store for duty free, inexpensive booze that was in the airport, but we were only allowed bring home four forty ounce jugs. They had the bottles conveniently packaged in a four pack. Four different brands to take home with them but they were sternly warned that there was to be no alcohol consumed while were aboard the aircraft. And although the aircraft was commercial it was a military contract flight the military did not allow alcohol consumption aboard the plane. The cost of the four 40 ounce jugs was less than four dollars. It didn't make any difference to me what it cost, I only had fifty dollars and I would need the money when we arrived at Travis. I was one of the richest GIs in the military and I couldn't afford to buy a dollar and a quarter bottle of booze.

When we arrive at Travis I'll call Rosie and have her wire me the money to get me home. I can't believe what had happened to me. I'm worth enough money to by the whole fucking island but I don't have the money to buy a cheap bottle of Gold Coach Gin!

The flight from Guam to Hawaii was the longest part of the trip. Eight hours from Anderson Air Force Base, Guam to Honolulu International Airport, the one hundred eighty weary sleepy eyed soldiers, sailors, airmen and marines climbed off the 707 to stretch their legs a quick fuel up and finally on the last leg of the long flight back to the "world".

On the flight from Hawaii to Travis I sat between two Navy Chiefs that boarded the Boeing 707 at Clark, they were stationed at Subic Bay. I told them that my brother was stationed at Subic.

"What's his name?" asked the chief sitting next to window.

"Lieutenant Dyer, Tom Dyer."

"Yeah, we knew him. He's in subs, right?" the chief sitting next to me said.

"That's my brother." I proudly replied.

"Yeah, he told us that he had a brother stationed in 'Nam. You Steve?"

"That's me." I proudly replied again.

They introduced themselves. Chief Petty Officer Tommy Lally a tall red headed Irishman from 'Frisco and Chief Petty Officer Melvin Barnes from Panama City, Florida. Melvin was a large colorful career Navy chief with a laugh that came from way down low in his stomach. They made the long trip from Hawaii to the States quick and funny. They both had over twenty four years in the military; World War Two, Korea and now Vietnam. During the war they both served on battle wagons in the Pacific, Tommy was a gunner's mate almost drowned when his ship was hit by a Kamikaze, Melvin a cook (surprised?) spent a week in a rubber life raft with a Texan and Cracker from Atlanta. "They both wanted to use me for bait. They heard that shark was very tasty and sharks weren't all that prejudice; those motherfucking sharks will eat anything," With a terrified look his eyes wide open. "I hated those two mule lopers. They had me do all the rowing."

"Rowing? Rowing to where?" I had to ask. "The Pacific's one large ocean you know."

"No shit, Man! I do believe if we were out there any longer I would had rowed us right smack dab into Tokyo Harbor!" Mel exclaimed. "What ya think Pan Am is gonna serve for chow."

"I believe its sushi this evening, Mel," Tommy said with a straight face.

"What the fuck is sushi?" Mel asked.

"Raw fish."

When we finally came into Travis I phoned Coyle and Ianotti Racing, Rosie answered the phone and when she heard my voice she couldn't believe that it was me.

"Good morning, Coyle and Ianotti Racing," Her voice sounded more mature then it did when we were all living in Waltham. She sounded professional. "How may I help you?"

"Good morning Rosie, it's lovely talking with you again," I tried to sound casual but my heart was racing like a 426 cubic inch hemi crackling on nitro.

"Stevie?" Rosie whispered. "The Stevie Dyer I grew up with, went out with who loved to rest his face in my tits, joined the Air Force went to Vietnam and now talking to me on the phone?"

"You got it Rosie. I finally made it home."

"Oh thank God Stevie! Where are you? Are you alright?"

"Yeah I'm fine," I said. "I'm out here at Travis Air Force Base and I need a favor."

"What do you need Stevie?" She asked. "What can we do for you? Anything, all you have to do is ask."

"I wanna play with your tits again," I joked as I whispered into the phone.

"Sorry Stevie, I'm still in love and still married to Frankie." She said chuckling. "Same ole Stevie."

"Aw shit! Okay I need five hundred dollars wired to the Western Union Office here on the base, Rosie," I explained. I was beginning to settle down. "I had a little problem on my way to Saigon. While a couple of buddies were driving me to Tan Son Nhut Airbase to catch my flight Pappy Scott hit a local who was riding his bike, the old boy had a bunch of bananas tied to the bike's rear fender. He wasn't all that injured but to keep him from going to the white mice I gave two hundred dollars. He needed a new bike and now I need a loan."

"What are white mice," She giggled.

"Vietnamese cops. Their uniforms are white so the troops began calling them white mice." I explained to her. "Can you help me out Rosie?"

"You have to ask Stevie?" She said. "I'll drive into Riverside right now and just to be on the safe side I'll wire you a grand, okay? Now where do you want me to send your money?" She said.

"I knew that I could count on you, Rosie."

"Oh Stevie," She cried. "We're all so very sorry about Sharly. She was so beautiful and we all loved her. I'm so sorry, Stevie. We all know how much you really loved each other."

"Thank you Rosie," I said feeling my eyes begin to mist up. "Everybody took Sharly's death so hard. I wish I could have been there for her wake and funeral."

"Every one that knew her took her death very hard, Stevie. Even Fudgie and Frankie Rosa were there to say good bye and lend us their support."

"I know, Rosie, everyone was there but me." I lamented.

"I'm so very sorry, Stevie." Rosie cried.

I filled her in on what she needed to do, the address where to wire the money and a couple of hours the thousand had arrived at The Travis Base Operations Western Union office that was beside Base Operations where I was handed the money then caught a taxi and was driven to San Francisco International airport, I bought a plane ticket on TWA and was on my way home: Thank you Rosie. You are... just like your chest... a real treasure.

My Mom and Dad and Aunt Louise, were in the TWA lobby waiting, they looked the same as they did when they dropped me off at Logan a year ago. The only person missing was Sharly and Charlotte's mother. For some incredibly stupid reason I thought that maybe Sharly's death was only a dream and she would be running across the ramp and falling into my arms. No matter how hard I tried to find her in the crowd of nameless faces, I finally realized that she wasn't going to be there after all. "Come on asshole, let's get real," I told myself.

It looked like they were still wearing the same clothes they were wearing when we were all at Logan to see me off but the difference from last year now they were all smiling: Except for me. Mom smiled through the tears in her eyes, Dad was happy to see me, but the smile Aunt Louise was wearing turned to sadness because she knew that I was going and see the sad, two family home that sat across Dix Street.

"Welcome home Dear," Mom said as we embraced, I shook hands with Dad. They all was happy to see that I made it home alive and Aunt Louise who never hugged anyone took hold of my hand and patted the back. That was how she showed her love. Hell, Aunt Louise patted every body's hand. She was the Saint in the family.

"Steve, when we get home you'll need to call Charley or Billy," Dad said. "They've been phoning every day for the last week. Billy was wondering if maybe you got zapped but I assured him that you were fine and would be home within the week."

"Thanks Dad." I said patting him on the shoulder.

Billy Toye can be a real pain in the ass at times but a great and sometimes a brilliant business partner. "Did Billy mention how the business was doing?"

"No he didn't, He and CJ only wanted you to know that they were relieved when your mother told them that you would be home soon," He said as we all hurried across the windswept parking lot. (The airline pilots said that Logan International was one of the more difficult airports to bring in plane in due to the cross winds blowing across Boston Harbor). Dad opened the Lincoln's huge trunk, I tossed in my B-4, and we all climbed into Dad's Continental and headed home.

"That's good," I said looking at the well lit Sumner Tunnel entrance. "I'll call them in the morning."

I looked at where Scollay Square used to be while Dad tooled the big Lincoln onto the Central Artery. What a rotten shame! I said to myself. Gone was the heart of Boston's historical district and in its place stood Boston's Government Center. Boston like every other major city needed to progress I suppose but I grew up hanging around the West End and the "Square", I had so many happy memories in this part of Boston but when it came progress, memories do not count for all that much to the people that destroyed this historic part of the old town. All they could see was dollar signs.

We were flying past the arsenal before I brought up enough courage to ask about Mrs. O'Sullivan and how she was holding up.

"Anne's doing just fine, Dear, thanks in part to her husband and Charlotte and Barbara's step Father." Aunt Louise replied in her soothing Irish brogue. "But we all miss the lovely Coleen. She had a beautiful soul, Stevie a beautiful saintly soul."

"So tell me Steve now that you're home for a month, what's your plans?" My Dad asked as we went past the Gore Estate past Saint Jude's Church hung a left on to Willow Street. Lots of memories in the Gore Place parking lot, I thought: Rosie Beanbags, Sharly, so many good memories. "Oh Sharly," I whispered to myself as my eyes began to well up with tears. I was glad that it was dark and I was sitting in the front seat

"Well Dad," I finally trusted my voice to answered him. I wouldn't want the old man hearing my trembling lips or shaky voice. "First thing I'm going to do is to go across the street and visit Sharly's mother, then visited Sharly's grave, placed a dozen roses beside her head stone say a Hail Mary and then catch the bus and go over to Bill Mitchell's West End Chevrolet. I'm in the mood to spend some money."

"The bus?" Mom said. "You're talking silly, Steven. You haven't taken the bus since junior high school."

"I'm joking, Mom. I'll take Dad's Lincoln, Okay?"

"I'll drive you, Stevie. I'm not going into work tomorrow, Joan's father has been pretty much running things and besides you're apt to use my Lincoln as a trade in," The old man chuckled.

"Thanks Dad."

"Think you that you can handle seeing Mrs. O'Sullivan, Steven? Maybe you should wait to get settled in first," Aunt Louise suggested.

"No, Aunty. If it wasn't so late I'd go over right now."

It felt good being home again, I said to myself as Dad opened the back door and we all walked into the kitchen of the large five room Cape style house. Dad mixed up a pitcher of Manhattans, I put my shit into the bedroom, took my shaving kit into the bathroom took a leak, brushed my teeth to get the stale taste out of my mouth, shaved, took a quick shower, then changed onto jeans, a sweatshirt and sneakers then joined the family in the kitchen. Dad poured me a large hooker with bitters and a cherry, Mom began heating up leftover meat balls and spaghetti. Mom cooked the best meatballs and spaghetti this side of the North End. She even made her own sauce from scratch as she patiently watched the sauce bubble as she spooned the residue from the top of the sauce. Her sauce was better than any of Italians cooked from this side or the other side of the Charles River.

While I was sipping on one of Dad's signature Manhattans and waiting for Mom to finish heating up dinner I called CJ and Billy too let them both know I was still alive all my vital parts were still in working order and I would like to schedule a meeting with them both as soon as I was settled down in Washington DC.

"Why don't we all meet in Boston Steve?" Billy asked. "You're going to be home for a month."

"I don't know Billy," I said trying to sound sincere. "But I want to crap out, get some rest, put on some weight, spend some time with my family and friends and get used to being back in the world. Give me a little time, alright?"

"Yeah that sounds good Stevie but as soon as you get settled down in DC, call us, alright?"

"I will, Billy," I said. "Talk to you soon."

The next morning I walked across the street and visited Mrs. O'Sullivan. Anne O'Sullivan made a pot of coffee and placed a plate of sweet rolls in the middle of the table and we had a nice visit. We talked about and laughed about us kids growing up in the Bleachery, but she was having a hard time getting over Sharly's death. So were her husband and the girls step father. But the person I had never expected to be taking Sharly's death so bad was Billy

Ryan. Mrs. O'Sullivan told me that at her wake funeral mass he was inconsolable. I never thought that he loved her that much, but Mrs. Sullivan told me the reason he began dating Babs was to be able to stay close to Charlotte, his first love.

"Mrs. O'Sullivan, now I want to visit Sharly's grave. Could you tell me where she's resting?"

"It's easy to find, Steven," She answered with a sad smile. "It's close to your family's section."

"Okay," I said looking into Mrs. O'Sullivan's deep green eyes.

"Well as you face your family plot look over to your left and four plots away is where Charlotte's is resting."

"Thank you so much, Mrs. O'Sullivan."

I finished my coffee and rolls, hugged Mrs. O'Sullivan asked her to please stay close to my Mom and Dad then drove Mom's Ford Fairlane 500 over to Jimmy Brandt's Garden and Florist Shop on Main St. across the street from Wilson's Diner bought a dozen roses then drove the short ride to Calvary Cemetery and had a quiet visit with Sharly. As I approached her grave I felt a peaceful feeling that I had never experience before in my life. She was there with me as I stood over her grave and said an Ave Maria, told her that I never forget her and the love that we once shared. I could feel her presents as I knelt at her gravestone and cried my eyes out. "Oh Holy Christ Sharly! Why did God take you away from your family your friends and me?" I wept. "You were perfect. You gave me all the love in the world and I loved you more than life."

"Stevie," I felt a whisper from the gentle February breeze. "I'm with God now and at peace. You will always be my greatest love but I'm now I'm with our Creator and His Son our Blessed Mother Mary and Joseph and my Dad. We will be together but not for a while, so now go and live your life, fall in love, raise a family and be the great man I always knew you are going to be, but never forget the lessons you learned in Vietnam and be so very careful my Darling Steven: You have not yet seen the last of that unfortunate war and that sad country. Please be careful my Love."

As I slowly walked away from her grave I felt alive and at peace. It was now time move on and that's what I intended to do. What the hell I was only twenty-four years old and a multi-millionaire to boot. "Thank you, Sharly," I said as I looked back at her grave but I should be concerned over Vietnam? For me that chapter of my life was finished. Or was it?

It was Saturday morning and after coffee and a cigarette, Dad was still smoking his Camels, we boogied over to Bill Mitchell's West End Chevrolet. I bought a brand new right out of the box Marina Blue 1967 327 cubic inch 350 horse power four speed Corvette. "How do you want to pay for the Corvette, Steve?" The sales man asked as we walked around the blue beauty parked in the showroom. As soon as I had seen the car in the showroom window, I knew right away that I was going to buy it. The 'Vette came equipped with four wheel disc brakes, AM-FM radio and red stripped tires, posi-traction rear end and a side mounted exhaust system. "Is the Corvette for sale?" I asked as the sales man approached me with a huge grin on his face and with his hand out. I gave him strong firm handshake that almost brought tears to his eyes, then I introduced my Dad then the salesman introduced himself. "I'm Eddie Newman and every car in the show room and the parking lots are for sale?" Eddie said as we walked to his desk. "Even mine," he joked.

"You don't say? What's your ride?" I said as I looked over my shoulder at my new Corvette.

"I have a new, right out of the box '67 Camaro Rally Sport 350 with four on the floor, front disc brakes and an AM FM stereo."

"Oh yeah, I had seen them advertised on television when I went through San Francisco International."

"It's the Cranberry red sport job parked outside the door. You can see it through the window," He said pointing out the dark red beauty. "They're a real popular car, and they're out selling the Mustangs if you can believe that. We can't get enough of them. We get a truck load on Monday and by Saturday we're all sold out.

For every one Corvette that goes out the door we sell a twenty-five Camaros."

"You don't say," I said looking out of the window and spied the new Camaro. "That's a nice looking car, I'm impressed. Maybe I'll pick one up when I get down to DC. Will you take a corporate check, Eddie?" I asked reaching into my old World War Two flight jacket inside pocket and took out the corporate check book. No sense in using my own money.

While I was attending to heavy equipment school in Cheyenne, Wyoming I picked up the old Army Air Corps flight jacket in an Army Navy store outside of the city. It was out of issue and wasn't authorized to wear as a part of my uniform, but it sure kept me warm.

"Is it drawn on a local bank, Steve?"

"No the Chase Manhattan Bank in New York City."

"That's no problem, there's a Chase Manhattan Bank in Boston," He told me.

"You don't say, where in Boston?" I said as I began making out the check

"They're in the financial district on State Street," he said.

Most of Black Gold's money plus CJ, Billy and my personnel accounts were held by Chase Manhattan. I'm surprised that CJ or Billy didn't tell me. "How long has Chase Manhattan been in Boston?"

"Almost a year, Chase bought out Old Colony and took over the first three floors of the Chase building. It was a shock to the Old Colony heavy hitters and old Boston yankee's."

"I'll bet it was. How hard did they get hit?" I asked Eddie while Dad was staring at me with a surprised look on his face. Dad didn't know shit from Shinola about Black Gold Investments and what the company was worth. Maybe he didn't want to know. Dad never asked how I was making enough money to lend Tommy the bread to buy his '56 Victoria or how I scraped up the money to buy and build my '51 Mercury Monterey, or my '40 Ford Coupe. But Dad and

Mom knew what I was doing thanks to his brother-in-law my Uncle Eddie who knew everybody in town and had an Irish gift of gab and a little diarrhea of the mouth so he kept Mom and Dad posted. But as long as my marks in school were good and no detectives or IRS Agents show up at the front door Mom and Dad played it cool.

Eddie looked at me and shrugged his shoulders. "I can't really say, Steve. But it was a legitimate buy out. Not a ah… what do they call it when a bank or an investment company goes in and takes over another bank or business assets?"

"Yeah a hostile takeover," I answered.

"Yeah, that what I heard, anyway, everything been settled, most of the depositors were covered by Federal Depositors Insurance but the heavy hitters? They got their heads handed to them."

"Why don't you drop by the day after tomorrow and pick up your car." He grinned. "It'll be ready."

"It'll need to be registered."

"We'll handle all that. Who's your insurance company?"

"Liberty Mutual," Dad said. "We've been dealing with Liberty Mutual for the last twenty-five years."

"What do you do for work?" Eddie asked as sat back in his chair lit up a cigarette. He offered Dad and me a Marlboro. I turned him down, so did Dad, he reached into his pants pocket and pulled out a crumpled half empty package of Camels.

"I'm in the military, the Air Force, and also I own a third of Black Gold Investments and another start up endeavor; Executive Airlines but for the next thirty days or so I'm home on leave."

"Steve just returned from Vietnam," Dad proudly announced as he looked at me then at the salesman.

"Well, welcome home, Steve," the salesman said as he reached across his desk and shook my hand. "I didn't think you got the tan laying in the February sun."

"Not here in New England," I joked

"How was Vietnam?"

"It was an adventure that I would not have missed for the world, but Christ, you're on a 365 day 24 hour long adrenaline trip," I said. "But I made it home no worse for the wear."

I wrote out a check for $5371.25, signed the sales agreement, Eddie told me to give him a call before I came over to pick up the 'Vette. He wanted to make sure that the car was ready to go and it was Bill Mitchell's policy that every new car leaving the lot was washed, the interior was vacuumed, the windows sparkled and the car had a full tank of gas. We all shook hands then Dad and I left the dealer ship, walked across the used car lot and climbed into Dad's Lincoln. "You know, Steve, I've never asked you about your business because it's really none of my business, but it appears that CJ, Billy you have done very well. Now you can tell me to mind my own business if you want, but just for shits and grins how much are the three of you worth?" He asked as I turned on the radio and dialed in WRKO to catch the Dale Dorman morning program. He was the best and most listened disc jockey in the Boston area. Dad usually listened to The Jess Cain morning show on WBZ. Dad wasn't all that crazy about rock and roll.

"Well let me see, Dad," I replied as I did a little put on fake counting on my fingers. "Well...More than enough for you to retire and buy Rockport Country Club. CJ wrote to me a few months after I had arrived in country and said that Rockport was up for sale and so was The Sun Coast Country Club in Boca Raton and a nudist resort in Tarpon Springs that's up for sale too and that would leave me with a balance of around five million dollars in my personnel saving account."

"You're shitting me, right?" Dad said looking at me his eyes in a squint then out of the windshield just in time to bring the big Lincoln to a screeching halt. He almost rear ended a Waltham police cruiser. "And a nudist resort to boot?" He asked looking at the cops in the cruiser looking back at us. "I don't think your mother would approve."

"No was just kidding about the skin resort. Dad; Black Gold Investments and our other holdings gross out at around a hundred million dollars and the reason Billy and CJ wanted me to call them as soon as I got home was they want to start up a charter airline service with the home office in DC. They even came up with a name: Executive Airlines. Do you think it will fly?" I chuckled at my attempted pun.

"Yes, I heard you mention something about that to the salesman but is it something that can be done? Something like that can run you out of business is it doesn't pan out. Jet planes are expensive."

"Oh yeah, Dad. It's a done thing."

"So you want to buy me my own golf course?" He looked at me as if to say 'you're full of shit.'

"No not just one, you're going to be the owner of two country clubs; one in Rockport and the other in Florida. Hang up your apron Dad, as of today you're now going to be mingling with the elite."

"I don't think that you Mother wants to leave Waltham," He said lighting a Camel.

"Do me a favor will you, Dad? Will you finally drop the butts. We all want you around for a long time. Those damn cigarettes will kill you."

"Alright," He said crushing out his butt in the ashtray, took the half smoked pack of Camels, crumpled up the package, opened the window and dropped them on the street and never smoked another cigarette again.

"As I said Dad, CJ he wrote me and told me about the country clubs and where they could be found. I wrote him back and that he would go ahead and buy them before they're off the market. That was about the same time that Sharly wrote and told me that Maxie Gold had passed away. He had a massive heart attack while he was playing golf in Florida with his brothers and he was dead before he hit the ground and the sad part was that he was only forty-five years old Dad but he had a bad heart since he was in his early thirties. If he didn't smoke he would maybe still be alive." I said. "Wanna stop off for a cup of coffee?"

"What time is it?" Dad asked.

"Almost twelve-thirty," I said looking at my new Rolex watch.

"Let's drop by The Three Sons, I'll let you buy me a drink."

"OK, and you know? The place is for sale; how about I buy it for you and Mom."

"What in hell are we gonna do with a Dago restaurant?" Dad asked while Carlo placed our drinks on a coaster in front of us and took the ten from the bar and returned my change.

"We'll let Mom run it," I joked. "She's the best Irish Dago cook this side of the North End… and you can wash the pots pans and do the dishes."

The Dad and I sat at the bar, Dad sipping his favorite drink, a VO Manhattan and I was sipping drinking new vodka that just came out on the market from Sweden. Absolut Vodka.

Carlo one of the Three Sons tended the bar, Leno ran the kitchen and Carman was the maitre d'. When the bar got busy Carman helped with at the bar.

This was the first time that Dad and I ever stopped off for a drink. When I was home on leave Sharly and I spent some of our free time having dinner in Boston's North End or eating dinner at Durgan Park or eating at one of the many fine restaurants in Waltham or once in a while having dinner at home.

"Steve? Your Mother and I knew how you made all your money? You mother know how you started out and your Uncle Eddie kept your Mother and me well informed and up to date."

"How come you never called me on it, Dad?" I asked I know that Mom and Dad discussed everything.

"I had a business to run, Stevie so as long as you stayed out of trouble, got good in school I wasn't going to interfere."

"Well Dad, it's an interesting story."

"Well so long as you forced me into retirement, Stevie" Dad said as he sipped his Manhattan. "Fill me in. Just how in the hell did you

CJ and Billy get that rich? I don't want to pry into you business but I am curious now."

"I'd be curious too Dad," I said and began to fill him in. While we sat at the bar, I explained everything from buying a section of open range out from under the oil company up to inauguration of Executive Airlines. Dad kept saying, "No Shit!" Dad had another Manhattan, I ordered another Absolut and tonic, we finished out drinks and Dad drove us home.

Eddie Shea and Billy Harrigan were still working out of the back room of Harrigan's Restaurant and when The Boston Redevelopment Authority demolished Scollay Square Fudgie Iaconio moved his operation to South Miami. It was time to work on the Cubans. Eddie, and Fudgie who were cordial to each other and had known each other for years said the only time he had ever saw Fudgie show any real heartfelt emotion when he lamented, "Who the fuck decided it was alright to destroy my home and my neighborhood, huh? Who? It was bad enough that they tore down the West End and put up ugly apartment buildings now this!"

Eddie said that it was probably Cardinal Cushing and his gang bead jigglers. "Why don't you get a contract out on him and have him whacked?"

"If he wasn't a Cardinal and a man of God with his red beanie he would, right now be hanging by his thumbs from the Mystic River Bridge!"

Fudgie did well in Miami. He bought a sprawling ten room ranch with an Olympic size swimming pool, a four car garage where he could park his three Corvettes and Frankie could park his Caddy and it was all just a short walk to the Atlantic. He got over Scollay Square real fast.

Now I think it's time now to take red hat down from The Mystic River Bridge Fudgie.

Once settled in, caught up on some sleep took delivery of my 'Vette I called Richie Brady and Pauly Whelan and made plans to meet for lunch. They were both doing well, Richie, owned Brady's Television Sales and Repair Services on Lexington Street and Paulie bought Scott's Surplus and Supply. He began working for Scott's Surplus when he was fifteen and when the owner, Henry Schofield passed away, Paulie was right there with his check book ready to write a check for the down payment. Hell he rarely spent a dime of his own money. He was always begging for gas and cigarette money and when the gang drove over to Richard's Car Hop he sat in the back seat of my Merc or Richie's Ford and never gave us a dime for his burgers, onion rings or shakes or gas money. And that's probably how he could afford to buy Scott's Surplus and Supply. Paulie Whelan was the only two or three Gentiles who owned a retail business on Moody Street. All the other retail stores were owned or rented by Jews.

We all met at the Peking Garden Restaurant on Main Street across from the city hall. Patty and Richie were married and had a young son, so were Paulie the Catholic and Lily the Catholic/Jew.

They were still childless and it was doubt full that they would ever have any children. According to Paulie, "Kids cost too much and when you get old they end up trying to put the screws to you!" If only their children took after their penny pinching father. But Lily saw things a little different. She made Pauly a father three times. They have two boys and a girl.

We reminisced about the fun times that we all had growing up in the Bleachery, but I shied away from talking about Vietnam. Kuckie Cohen was working in radio. That was something he wanted to do when he discovered that he would never make in adult movies. His nose was too big and his dick was too small. Kuckie graduated from the Emerson School of broadcasting, and picked up a disc-jockey gig in Toronto, Ontario, Canada married a local who worked at the station, she was a copywriter, and as far as anyone knew he was doing well. I wondered if Kuckie's mother knew that her Jewish son that could maybe be the next Messiah married a Catholic. Billy Ryan and Barbara O'Sullivan were still going together. They had been engaged for six years but they didn't want to rush into anything. I still had my '51 Mercury Monterey and my '40 Ford coupe'. I leased space on the first floor in the old Waltham Watch Factory. The place was perfect for my cars and Tommy's '56 Ford Crown Victoria. The large stall had climate control and an oak floor. I had them all up on jack stands. Across from my stall was a large auto body shop that had been there since the watch factory closed and the owner, for a generous price said that he would take care of my cars. I handed him a Bank check for twenty-five hundred dollars and handed him the keys to the cars and to the door of my stall. "Call me if you need anything, alright?" I said.

"You got it, Steve," He said as looked at the check.

"Stevie," Patty said as she took my hand. "We are all so sorry that Sharly can't be here with us. We all still miss her so much. Sharly was such a warm beautiful and classy lady. Everybody who knew her loved her."

"Yeah, I know. When I landed at Travis all I had was fifty two dollars, fifty in bills and two dollars in change. I was in a real bind so I called Rosie and asked her if she could wire me five hundred dollars so I could buy a plane ticket home. She wired me a grand. I sent her a check for a thousand, I wanted to pay her back but she mailed the check back to me with a thank you card, but in the course of our conversation Rosie said the same thing. Thank you Patty," I smiled as she caressed my hand with her hers. "She was a loss for not only for me but for all of us, and you know something stupid? When I had heard of her death I wanted to extend my tour in Vietnam. I didn't think I would be able to come home but being here with you guys, friend I grew up with well I'm glad I did come home. It's good that we all here could together again, it's help me a lot being here with my friends."

"Okay, Mr. Money Bags you who has more money than God, why did you have to put the bite on Rosie so you could catch flight home?" Lily said choking back her drink.

"On the ride to Saigon we had a little accident and I had to buy off the gook whom we hit while he was riding his bicycle. If we hung around I would have missed my flight so I gave him most of the money I had, two hundred dollars then we got the hell out of there."

"So tell us, Stevie," Paulie said changing the subject. "How's business?"

"It's incredible Pauly beyond my wildest dreams," I said fanning away the smoke from his smelly twenty- five cent rope. "I should feel guilty doing so well and not doing all that much. I have two partners CJ Wilson and Billy Toye. They run the company while I idle away my time in the Air Force, but, you know, that's the life I've chosen, but things are going to change when I go down to DC."

"Why, you getting out?" Richie asked.

"No, Black Gold Investments is going to inaugurate a charter airline service out of Washington National Airport."

"That's in Virginia," Lily said.

"Yeah, Lily. Northern Virginia, just across the Potomac River from DC," I said ordering another round of drinks. "We're going to lease two World War Two hangers from Washington National airport and we'll get the pilots from the Air Force and Navy. Some when they pilots leave active duty and some from the reserves"

"How come you chose the military pilots, Stevie?" Richie asked.

"Because they are better trained and better disciplined. Most of the pilots that fly for the commercial airlines are reservists or former military. And that's where we're going to get the aircraft mechanics and maintenance guys too."

"You'll be able to while you're still in the Air Force?" Patty asked. "The Air Force will let you run an airline?

"Yeah, so long as it doesn't interfere with my duties, but most of the company operations will be handled by the company's staff. I'll be nothing more than a figure head."

"Stevie," Lily said as she put her arm around my neck and gently pulled me close to her breast, the two stingers were beginning to get to her. "Say that the four of us decide to take a trip to Florida or California or whatever, what would it cost us, you know, for the flight down?"

"Nothing, Lily, it won't cost you guys a cent. We'll fly you all where ever you wish to go for nothing. Just call me collect and I'll have a charter pick you all up at the Bedford Airport, fly you all where ever you want to go and when you ready to come home, let me know and we'll fly you all back and it will all be first class, food, drinks Cuban cigars and that also goes for Kuckie Cohen and his wife, Billy and Babs, and Sharly's mother and step father."

I ordered another round of drinks, and we did a little more reminiscing from hustling papers for Joe Gagnon, my job running bag for Eddie Shea, building the engine for my '51 Merc in my Dad's cellar, Waltham was a great place growing up, then we toasted Sharly's memory, I picked the tab then we left the restaurant and promised to stay in touch. And we did…at wedding, wakes and funerals.

BOOK TWO

BLACK GOLD INVESTMENTS INC.

Billy Toye, C.J. Wilson and I took our basic training together and then we were assigned to the 389th school squadron, Francis E. Warren AFB, Cheyenne, Wyoming. It was a twelve week course in heavy equipment operations. I never realized that there was so much to learn when it came to driving a truck. We trained on five ton, ten ton and fifteen ton semi-tractors pulling forty foot flatbed trailers, forklifts, warehouse tugs, twenty four cubic foot dump trucks, front end loaders and loading and off loading equipment from C-124 Globe Masters, C-97s C-47s C-119s and C-123s and the all new four engine jet powered C-135 cargo transporter. The Warren Air Force Base flight-line and base operations that was located across the flight-line from Cheyenne's Municipal Airport. The base was constructed in 1867 and at first was named Fort Russell as protection for the new Union Pacific Rail Road. The Indians in the Wyoming Territory were in a foul mood. First came the "Iron Horse" then came the pale faces who slaughtered the buffalo. If I was an Indian I'd be in a foul mood too.

Then in 1947 the base came under the auspices of the Air Force and turned over to the Air Training Command and was renamed Francis E. Warren Air Force Base.

On the weekends when we were off duty we would picked-up our passes from the orderly room and drive into town. Billy and Chuck owned a 1958 Chevy Impala. Billy, Charley and I would head into Cheyenne in Billy's Impala to do go shopping and grab a bit to eat. It was the first time that we had ever seen a McDonald's fast food restaurant. You could eat a hamburger, French fries and coke for twenty-five cents. On a monthly salary of $85.00, a twenty five cent hamburger dinner that tasted good (it was better than the mess hall food) and was one hell of bargain!

"Hey, Stevie, Billy," CJ said. We were sitting at the bar in the F.E Warren AFB beer garden, (The Snake Pit) in the basement of the base laundry, the bank and the base credit union building across the street from the rear of the enlisted men's barracks. We were listening to the David Roses band belting out "The Stripper" on the juke box and enjoying a 3.2% Coors. You would drink 3.2% beer all day and night and all you would do is piss... every ten minutes. You could time it with your watch. It was a fun place to drink beer and shoot the shit with your buddies. Some of the guys were really funny, especially the rednecks and the city kids. We would listen to the juke box, drink cheap beer, play the pinball machines and on Tuesday night watch the Bugs Bunny Road Runner hour on television. I was amazed how many cigarette smoking beer guzzlers you could fit into two rooms, one of the rooms held the bar where you could sit or stand and watch TV and the other room was the lounge, both rooms were about the size as a large living room. When last call came around you couldn't see across the rooms because of the all the cigarette smoke. As soon as I got back to the barracks the first thing I did was to strip off my smelly fatigues and jump into the shower.

"Uh huh," They said in harmony and in unison.

"What say we take a trip north tomorrow and see what the Open Range looks like?" I said as I ordered another round. CJ was a tall, good looking, curly haired sandy blond quick with a joke, Irishman with deep green eyes and physique of a foot ball lineman. He was a good natured easy going guy with a great sense of humor. Good thing because CJ was the 1960 heavy weight Golden Gloves Champion from the western part of New York State. His fighting weight was a gaudy two hundred pounds and he stood six foot three inches tall.

"Why the fuck should we?" Billy asked. "I don't give a fuck what the fucking Open Range looks like!" (If Billy didn't use the "F" bomb at least ten time in a sentence he really wasn't trying). Billy was a little shorter than CJ and me. He had short, thick, black hair and deep black eyes. It was obvious that he was Italian, but the family patriarch changed the family's last name from Scarmazzi to Toye to keep the family patriarch from getting "wacked". You know; two in the hat?

From what Billy told us about his family, they originally immigrated from Palermo, Sicily, settled in Chicago's South side but in the middle part of the 1930s left Chicago and moved to the Queens Borough in New York City. When Queens became a bit too hot for Papa Scarmazzi he moved Mamma Scarmazzi and the three little Scarmazzi, Billy, Bobby and their sister Beeboe to upstate to Buffalo. Beebo had to be a nickname I thought, no mother and father in their right mind would name anything Beeboe except the family pet... I thought wrong. "You have a sister named Beeboe, Billy?"

"No just Beeboe. Not Beeboe Billy." He said as he lay on his bunk flipping through the pages of the current Play Boy magazine Beeboe had sent him wrapped in a plain brown paper bag.

"How come your sister sends you Play Boy, Billy?" CJ asked as he sat at the desk in our room writing a letter to his girlfriend Karen Grayson, the future Mrs. Charles Joseph Wilson. "Why don't you buy one when we go into Cheyenne?"

"Beeboe has a subscription." Billy explained while he held up the center fold for us to admire.

"She does? Is she a dyke? You know a muff diver?" I asked him.

"No! She ain't no fucking dyke, you asshole!" Billy yelled throwing the magazine at me.

"I can't wait to meet her," I said.

"She's a knock-out," CJ said looking up from his half completed letter. "She looks like her brother."

"Really? She looks like Billy?" I asked.

"No her other brother; the one with the beard."

"Kiss my ass CJ!"

"Why not? Don't you want to see where they filmed most of the cowboy movies from the 30's and 40's?"

"It sounds like fun," I said. "I'll even throw in some gas money."

"Don't forget to bring your camera, Stevie," Billy said with unexcited yawn.

The next morning after having breakfast at the mess hall, we filled up the 348 Cubic Inch Impala with high test Phillips 66, checked the oil, added two quarts poured some water into the radiator then headed north on route 87 through Casper, picked up route 20 west then north through Shoshoni and there it was the open range. I was looking around the open range when I spied a crew surveying a large section of land. Billy pulled the Impala off the highway, and we all climbed out of Billy's car. I took my Polaroid from the case and then we approached the surveyors and asked them in a curious way, so as not to arouse any suspicion why they were surveying the open range. They explained that they were contracted by Wind River Oil. They had dropped some test well to see if it was worth the money to drill for oil.

"Was it?" CJ asked as Billy snapped some pictures with my camera.

"Oh yeah. As soon as I turn in my survey report, Wind River Oil was going to begin drilling."

"Well, thanks a lot fellows," CJ said as we all shook hands. "We gotta get back to the base."

"You guys stationed at Warren?" the survey boss inquired.

"Yes, Sir" We all answered in unison. "We're all from the east and had never seen the open range before. It sure is desolate."

"That it is, fellows, but it's loaded with "Black Gold"."

On the ride back to the base we made our plans. I had a little over twenty five thousand dollars in the bank Billy had taken eight pictures of the parcel number and the surveying crew and Monday when classes let out for the day; usually around 1400 hours the three of us were going to the Western Union Office, pick up the check, then walk over to the Wyoming State Land Office to buy a thousand acres of Open Range.

When we returned to the base I phoned Sharly explained to her what we had in mind and instructed her to wire me fifteen thousand dollars. I needed ten thousand dollars for the land and five thousand dollars just in case. I asked Sharly to wire me two separate money orders, one for ten thousand and the other for five thousand dollars.

After classes the three of us drove to the state house, located the land office and bought parcel 409, signed the title and was handed the deed.

"It's none of my business, young fella, but why are you buying a thousand acres of open range?" The land office manager inquired.

"We're gonna shoot a cowboy movie," Billy replied as I signed over the ten thousand dollar Western Union check to the State of Wyoming.

"Well, whatever. But keep this in the back of your mind Mr. Dyer, you have a year to improve the property or you could be fined or worse; forfeit your land and your investment, all right?"

"What constitutes an improvement?" CJ asked.

"You can begin by sinking a well."

"You read our minds, Sir." CJ winked.

"You know, Stevie? As soon as Wind River find out about you buying the land out from under them the shit is going to hit the fan," Billy said on the ride back to the base.

"Find out what?" I was playing with Billy's head and that wasn't all that hard to do.

"Cut the shit! You know what I'm talking about, Stevie," Billy said looking at me through the rear view mirror. "You just bought a Wind River oil field right out from under their ass. What if they tell us to take a flying fuck and take their baseball bat and go home?"

"They won't," I replied grinning back at Billy.

"They won't? What makes you so sure?"

"According to the photos you shot with the Polaroid, Wind River will begin drilling on the first of February, snow or shine." I chuckled showing CJ the photo. The work order said that the surveying has to be completed no later than January 15th 1962. That's tomorrow.

"Hey Dyer!" The school squadron First Sgt shouted as he walked out his office and approached us as Billy, CJ and I walked into the barracks. A week went by and we hadn't heard a thing from the Wind River money men.

"Yes, First Sergeant."

"You got a phone call from a lawyer that says that he represents Wind River Oil. He would like you to call him ASAP," he said handing me the name and phone number.

"Well, it's about time. Thank you First Sergeant."

"What kind of shit you in, Dyer?" the tall, thin, Negro, 1st Sgt asked, his hand on his hips a king size Pall Mall hanging from the side of his mouth.

"I'm not in any kind of shit, Sergeant. It's just business." I answered without showing my hand.

"Might I inquire what type of business, Airman?"

"It's what dreams are made of, First Sergeant and dreams like these come around only once in a lifetime."

"Use the pay phone in the day room," he said, then turned on his heel and went back into his office.

I returned the call and was connected with Wind River's lawyer, Melvin Radner. I assumed that Mr. Radner was of the Jewish faith. I worked for a Jew when I was in high school and I had a good friend that was a Jew so I wasn't the least bit intimidated. "Yes, Sir, Mr. Radner, this is Airman Steven Dyer."

"Yes, Airman may I ask you a personnel question?" he said getting right to the point in a soft non threatening voice.

"You want to know why I bought a thousand acres of open range right where you company is planning to begin drilling for oil, is that correct, Mr. Radner?"

I could hear him groaning through the phone. "You're a very perspective young man, Airman. It wouldn't be a coincidence now would it?"

"No it wasn't, Mr. Radner," I replied getting to the point as well. "So how about we make a deal."

"I don't have the authority to make any kind of a deal with a sneak thief."

"I'm sorry that you regard me in such negative terms, Sir. I was only taking advantage of a situation that presented itself to me. The Rocky Mountain Standard Times printed a story in the financial section, I also have the Wall Street Journal delivered daily and I do follow the market, so anyway I followed up on the article, took a chance and I think that maybe I made a financial coup'."

"And how did a young man such as you acquire such a large amount of money?"

"Out on the street, I worked for a bookie From Boston's North End and he told me never let a good deal get away from you. They don't come along all that often."

"Good advice. You'll be hearing from us shortly, Steven. We'll see what kind of a deal we are able to work out," He said as he hung up the phone. He called me Steven so the future might just be looking up.

The following Saturday afternoon Billy CJ and I were called into Wind River Oil conference room and we were seated in our class "A" uniform re-telling my story to Sam Meany how we purchased some acreage of Open Range. Mr. Meany was wearing a blue suit, grey shirt a string tie and cowboy boots. He was the general manager of Wind River Oil. Mr. Meany flew up from the Denver office to talk with us, he was friendly, but he wanted to know how my friends and I could have pulled the wool over the eyes of a large corporation such as the Wind River Oil Co-operation.

I explained to him that I loved playing the horses. That was how I learned to value the power of making money. "When I was ten years old," I started to explain, "I was selling news paper at the Raytheon, a large defense plant outside of Boston, I handed my life savings, one hundred and fifty dollars to one of the guards who was my mentor and the head bookie at the defense plant. I handi-capped all the races that I was going to wager on, he took my money, put down my life savings on the daily double, three exactas and the super-fecta and Monday afternoon when I arrived at gate five Eddie Shea, my mentor and friend handed me, after his cut, fifteen hundred dollars. By the time I was eighteen I had Twenty-five thousand dollars sitting in the bank."

"I see," he said as he leaned back in his chair and lit a cigarette. He offered me a Lucky Strike but I said no. I never smoked. "So you're a crap shooter and an extremely resourceful young man. How old are you, Steven?"

"I'm nineteen, Sir."

"And you're stationed at Warren, I believe?"

"Yes, Sir. Until April, and then Billy, CJ and I are being transferred to March Air Force Base outside of Riverside, California."

"Alright Steven, Mr. Radner, sighed Wind River will be in touch with you shortly. I think we can come up with something that will be equitable to all concerned."

Wind River was more than generous. That was when, CJ Wilson and Billy Toye and I formed Black Gold Oil Investments. They were financial wizards. I was good at handi-capping horse races but when it came to finances I was a financial neophyte. Or as Billy Toye would say: A fucking rookie!

The deal was this. Frontier offered Black Gold Investments one hundred thousand dollars per year for each section of land for the mineral rights. There were ten sections and one dollar per barrel for each and every barrel of oil pumped out of the ground and after five years an option to buy our land. I signed the agreement then had Billy and Chucky name put on the deed and another agreement stating that all profits would be equally split.

When we received order transferring us from Warren AFB to March Air Force, California we had received our first check from Wind River Oil for a million dollars and another check for a three months advance covered from the net profits earned for the first three months. Wind River was doing very well and so was Black Gold Investments Inc. Wind River Oil Inc earned more money in an hour than Black Gold earned in a year. Who cares? Wind River had to pay, nationwide, more than ten thousand employees. Black Gold Investments Inc? Our payroll was three employees.

CJ and Billy were incredibly resourceful when it came to investing. They could smell out a stock deal that would require an investment of one hundred thousand dollars, hold on to it for ninety day then roll it over and reinvest the principal plus the ten grand profit. And so long as the profits were reinvested Black Gold Investments avoided paying capital gains taxes. At the end of our enlistments Black Gold Investments was worth better than seventy five million dollars. And that was only the beginning.

March Air force was a great place for three young, well off, successful flyboys to be stationed. The duty was good, driving eighteen wheelers across the Mojave seventy mile north to Edwards AFB picking up plane and jet engine parts and returning them to the aircraft maintenance hangers for repairs or rebuilding. March had a better repair and maintenance department than Edwards. March AFB was a SAC base and Edwards wasn't. They could do small simple repairs but when it came to the involved and difficult repairs March was the go to base. The duty hours went from 0700 hour to whenever the drivers got back on the base. Sometimes it was too late to cross the dessert so we let the section know that we were going too bunked out at the VAQ and headed back at first dawn. It wasn't smart to drive the dessert after dark. You didn't want to break down, there were too many curious dessert critters looking for a broken down tractor trailer to check out. The equipment we drove was five, ten and fifteen ton Fords, GMCs and International tractors with twenty-five foot Kentucky and forty Fontaine trailers. The equipment was meticulously maintained. The vehicle mechanics were the best trained in all the military, and they could pull an engine out of a tractor in the morning have another engine dropped in and have the rig back on the road that afternoon.

On our off duty hours the we would go to the base theater, bowling alley, swimming pool or visit the beer hall drinking Coors shooting pool, eating beef jerky, or pizza slices, playing the pin ball machines and watching television. On Friday nights the four charcoal grills were fired up and there would be hamburgers, cheeseburgers and hot dogs all sold for twenty-five cents. And on the weekends we would go to the drags in Riverside or up to Pomona or hit the beaches and do some surfing. I got to be pretty good, Charlie was a born surfer but Billy went to the beach only to ogle the girls. But being GI's and we were easy to pick out, due to regulations we had to wear our hair short and of course most of the guys didn't have their own surf boards they had to rent the beat up boards at two dollars a day. Charlie and I had our own boards, the best that could be purchased from the Big Kahuna's Surfer's Shack in Malibu.

Yeah we all stuck out like sore thumbs and our chances of attracting the bikini clad beauties was almost non-existent. Hell most of the guys couldn't afford to date them anyway, so it was just to watch the free show and the bikini babes knew it. They would prance about the beach giving us a show but that was all. It was the shaggy haired beach and volley ball bums that picked-up most of the action.

We were at March for about a year when we thought that it was time to give Billy's Impala a rest, the 348 was tired it had over a hundred thousand miles on the odometer, was blowing oil and the clutch was beginning to slip so we all sprung for something more suited for our financial position. Billy stored the Impala downtown then bought a dark blue a 1962 Chevy Impala SS 409 with dual four barrels, four on the floor and dual exhausts. Billy's car was fast very quick off the line. I picked up a new bright red Ford Galaxy

500 hardtop with a high performance 406 with pretty much the same equipment as Billy's 409 but his 409 could blow the doors off my 406 without working up a sweat but when we reached the end of the quarter mile my 406 would catch up with Billy's 409 and I would fly by him like a rapped ape with a roman candle up its but.

CJ being a bit more conservative bought a 1962 deep blue Pontiac Bonneville drop top automatic with a 389 cubic inch engine. His idea was that one of the corporate officers should be seen driving something other than a hot rod. Black Gold oil Investments has an image to uphold, but how did the three of us with only one stripe on our sleeves who had been on the base for less than six months were driving brand new high performance muscle cars questions were being asked, did we come from money? No! Are we crooks? No! Are we rich? You fuckin "A" we are rich mothers!

"TAK IT UP. . . GET YOUR HAT 'CAUSE BUDDY GONNA SHUT YOU DOWN!"

MAY 1964

Yeah we were rich and getting richer. Besides raking in millions a year Black Gold Investments we also sponsored a double AA fuel Hemi powered dragster. Billy and I were driving back to the base from Los Angeles where we attended a Beach Boy concert. CJ picked up tickets for Billy and for me, but he was on duty and missed the concert, (Sorry CJ). Billy pulled into the Conoco gas station and garage about three miles east of the rear entrance of the base to fill up his Chevy Super Sport. Now Billy was driving a 1964 427 Chevy Impala and I was driving a 1963 1/2 Ford 427 Galaxy. Both cars had all the high performance shit that could be bolted onto the engine, but my 427 still couldn't take Billy in the quarter mile but after the quarter mile I would catch up to Billy's Impala and take his ass down town.

While the young olive skinned wetback was filling Billy's Chevy with 103 octane Conoco High Test, I climbed out and walked into the garage and fired up a conversation with two young "gear heads" that were putting together a Chrysler hemi-powered dragster. "Nice looking car you got there, guys." I said introducing himself. "My name is Steve Dyer."

"Thanks," the tall, slim, tanned grey eyed, dark haired mechanic, dressed in a dark blue tee shirt and a pair of tight fitting Levies and work shoes said as he climbed to his feet. "I'm Artie Coyle, and the gear head lying under rear-end is my brother Eddie. We're twins." They sure do look alike I said to myself as I walked to the back of the machine and looked down at Philly, the Coyle brothers looked to be in their early twenties.

"I've a twin brother too." I said. Artie didn't appear to be all that interested.

"How ya doin," Eddie waved up at me from his position under the tubular frame that was mounted on four jack stands. He was trying to weld a good bed on the push bar.

"Looks good so far guys, what's it gonna be when it grows up?" I joked as I did a tour around the well equipped garage and shop. "You have a nice set-up here."

"Well, hopefully a blown injected 392 cubic inch, Chrysler powered double "A" nitro-methane fuel burning dragster." Artie said as we both looked at the partially disassembled hemi that was resting in the engine bay bolted onto the frame.

"What's up Stevie?" Billy asked as he walked into the garage his hands in his pockets.

"This is Artie Coyle and his brother Eddie. He's laid out under the rear end. They're putting together a double A fuel burner. What do you think?"

Billy didn't say much right away. He walked around the garage first looking at the engine, GM-671 blower that was sitting in the work bench, the fuel injection system that was sitting beside the blower and the two Harmon-Collins distributers with coils. "Well I'd say that you guys were off to a good start. You have a nice set-up here."

"So we've been told," Eddie's voice resonated from under the dragster.

"Unfortunately we are... you know..." Artie stammered.

"I know, you're about out of money," Billy said filling in the blanks. "Almost broke, right?"

"Just about," Eddie said from under the long from being ready to burn up the quarter mile dragster.

Billy and I looked at each other, grinned then Billy asked, "How much you guys gonna need to get your project finished?"

"I don't know… about twenty-five thousand, thirty thousand maybe more," Eddie said as he grabbed hold the dragster's push bar and rolled himself and the creeper out from under the dragster and slowly climbed to his feet. "Why do you ask?"

"You guys have a sponsor?" I asked.

"What do you think?" Artie asked his hands on his hips looking at me as if to say, I can't believe that you're for real.

Billy looked at me then asked. "Who's the driver?"

"Eddie's the driver," Artie said as he looked at his twin brother. "He drove The Coyle Brothers Willys gasser up in Pomona, Lyons, Famoso outside of Bakersfield and right here at Riverside. We hit every drag strip in southern California."

"How did you do?" I asked.

"We did alright but never made a lot of money and hock shops don't pay much for trophies."

"You still have the gasser?" Billy asked.

"No. We sold it to get the money to start building the double A, but we spent most of dough and we're still not half way finished."

"Think CJ will go for it, Billy?" I asked.

"Yeah, he loves to see the Black Gold Investment's name on anything," Billy chuckled then looked at the Coyle brothers. "Stevie, CJ and I own an investment company The Black Gold Corporation with an interest in Wind River Refining Corporation, and a major interest in The El Royale Hotel. We're always looking for a challenged and maybe you guys can give us the opportunity to make and investment and have some fun."

"And we're stationed out at March," I said.

"You gotta be me shitting me! You guys own Black Gold and Wind River Petroleum and part of The El Royale?" Artie exclaimed his eyes wide open. "We've seen your ads on television."

"Yeah and in the newspapers too," Eddie chimed in.

"You have?" Billy said. "I didn't know we were advertising in Southern California. There's way too much competition in this area."

"I didn't either. CJ had to have bought some air time without telling us. CJ doesn't tell us everything he does, but he generally makes us money."

"Yeah, Black Gold's ads are on during the evening news casts."

"Okay, here's some of our business cards," I said as I took four of our gold embossed business cards that said "INVEST IN THE WEST".

"You guys must be crazy to ever want to take a chance on sponsoring a dragster," Artie said as he studied one of our cards.

"Or nuts," Eddie chimed in.

Billy and I looked at each other and grinned, "You have no idea." I replied. "And we're not nuts, a little on the dopey side of the curve maybe but were not nuts."

"If we weren't crazy Stevie would never have put up the money and faked Wind River Oil out of their oil soaked jock straps then proceeded to pick up one thousand acres of open range in central Wyoming right from under their eyes."

"You guys know anything about building racing engines?" Eddie asked looking at Billy and me.

"Some, I've built flatheads, Billy knows Large and small block Chevys…"

"But CJ? He doesn't know shit from Shinola about building engines," Billy corrected as he pointed a finger towards the ceiling trying to make a point. "But he does know how to drive and he does have a driver's license and he's the best investment broker in the country. That's why we keep him on the payroll and pay him two million dollars a year."

"And he's up for a raise," I added.

"You guys are full of shit," Eddie said looking at Billy than at me. "Nobody makes that much money, not even the president."

"We do," I said. "So I guess President Johnson is grossly underpaid."

"The three of us all make the same meager salary," Billy said.

Artie looked first at me and then to Billy. So did Eddie. "And you guys are out at the base?" Artie asked.

"Yeah, Chucky drives a '64 Pontiac Catalina," I said. "Billy and I both drive high performance; Billy drives a '64 Impala 427 SS and I drive a 63 Ford Galaxy 500 with a 427 under the hood."

"The '63 didn't come with a 427 hot shot," Artie challenged me. "The only engine you could get in a '63 was a 406."

"Sorry guys it's a 63 1/2."

"If you have enough money," Billy smiled. "You get any engine you want dropped into any car you want. That includes stuffing a General Electric fan jet engine from a KC-135 into the trunk."

"How about dropping a 427 into a Fairlane 500?" Eddie asked. "Can something like that be done?"

"Oh its do able, Guys. It'll take a few modifications in the engine compartment, the shock towers and the frame but it's going to be done and Total Performance is going to do it." Billy said. "It's going to be called the Ford "Thunder Bolt.

"How do you guys know what Ford's gonna do?" Eddie asked Billy

"We just know," Billy explained. "And if you guys want to sign on with Stevie, CJ and me…"

"By the way, who in hell is CJ anyway?" Artie said.

"Charles Joseph Wilson, he's the third business partner and the brains behind the outfit. We've been in the investment business for a little over three years and we've done rather well," Billy pointed out.

"Alright, what's the deal?" Artie asked coming to the point as he handed Billy back the business cards. He sounded skeptical.

"No, no, you keep them, we have plenty more, and we're serious," I said. "You'll need the phone numbers. And we told you, we're all stationed at March but we have offices in Riverside and San Francisco and we also have offices in, New York City and Boston, Massachusetts."

"Look guys, we'd like to sponsor you and all that we ask is that you advertise our company on the side of your "Double A" fuelie and on the side of your maintenance and vehicle transporter. We'll give you the money to finish the project and to update your operation, cover your expenses and supply you the resources you'll need to transport your ride and whatever extra tools you'll need."

"What's with you guys?" Eddie said looking at Billy then at me. "Why would three high rollers like you guys want to sponsor a couple ham and eggers like Artie and me? What if we don't come up to your high expectations, you know, we don't win, blow the engines and cost you more money than you want to spend?"

"We like ham and eggs," I replied with a smile. "And the money we earn came from hard work and risk. Billy CJ and I all come from hard working blue collar middle class families and nothing was ever handed to us. And all we ask is for you guys to do your best and by all means have fun and see that nobody gets hurt, OK?"

"Yeah, okay," Artie answered stuffing his hands in his pockets.

"Where do you guys do your banking?" Billy asked.

"Coyle's Racing and Service Center do our banking with Southern California Federal Savings and Loan in Riverside," Artie said.

"Yeah we know the bank. We do business with Southern Cal too," Billy said as he wrote out a check to Artie and Eddie for a hundred thousand dollars then Billy, the Coyle twins and I walked out of the service center, shook hands and that we would be in touch.

Artie and Eddie did a good job building the 392 but were having a tough time trying to get the cars fuel injection system dialed in so I asked them if they would mind me calling in a ringer to lend you a hand.

"That's going to cost you a bundle, Stevie," Philly said.

"I don't really give a fat rat's ass. So stop worrying. It's only money. And it takes money to make money. And when everything gets together you guys are going to be the best racing team in the country."

"You think so?"

"Everything that Black Gold Investments and Wind River Refining touches turns to gold, Eddie," I said slapping him on the shoulder. "Our little store is worth over eighty million dollars."

"You're kidding," Artie said. "You gotta be kidding us! They ain't nobody in the country got that kinda money."

"We do and so will you guys and Artie?" I said looking at him. "And please do me a favor will you?"

"Yeah, whatcha want me to do?"

"Speak proper English Artie, please. You're going to find out when dealing with the public and the proper use of the English can open a lot of doors, okay?"

"He's only funning with you, Boss," Eddie said chuckling. "Artie can talk real good American."

I phoned Frankie in his Rhode Island Operation and asked if he could take a week or so off, fly out to Riverside and help the guys get the dragster fired up. He said that he and Rosie would be out in a couple of days. Frankie said that he wasn't all that busy right now and that Rosie and he could use a vacation.

The plane tickets will be in the mail in the morning.

I couldn't wait to see Rosie. She was so funny without trying to be funny. We had great times at the Natick Drive-in playing blind man's bluff in her cleavage. I wonder from time to time if Frankie had as much fun with her tits now as I did eight year earlier. If I know Rosie, I'm sure Frankie's having a hell of a good time with her major leaguers. Rosie will make sure that Frankie's having fun with her fun bags.

When I had finished talking with Frankie I phoned Sharly, to let her know what was going down and if she could get time off why not come on out. "I'll be there, Honey. How are things going?" Her voice sounded so good even if we did talk to each other four times a week. When I was first stationed at March I asked Sharly if she would want move out to the west Coast and go to work for Black Gold but she said no. She didn't want to leave her job at Cronins and her modeling career but she would be out here as soon as she finished the monthly audits and let her department know that she would be taking time off.

Sharly and I weren't ready to marry yet. Neither were Charlie and Billy. The company was still growing, Billy and Charlie were getting out of the Air Force in the fall but I was staying in for another hitch. My decision really pissed off Billy and his Italian short, passionate fuse.

Black Gold arranged for American Air Express a charter airline to pick up Sharly from Bedford Airport then journey down to Providence, Rhode Island to pickup Rosic and Frankie then a five hour flight out to Los Angeles.

While Frankie was out in Riverside helping Eddie and Artie put together their fuelie, Billy C.J. and I pulling ten hour duty driving across the Mojave Desert, Rosie and Sharly were having a wonderful time drinking in the warm southern California sun, the beautiful sandy beaches and drinking the fine California Rose' Wine and shopping at upper class stores on Rodeo Drive and dinning in the very expensive restaurants on Hollywood and Vine.

Frankie was a master magician when it came to tuning the temperamental big and ugly Enderle Buzzard Catcher mechanical fuel Injection system. Artie and Eddie were totally blown away when Frankie and the newer and more efficient fuel pumps that were needed to get enough fuel to the injectors arrived. When I call Frankie and explained the problem I explained while the engine idled it ran rough because of the full race Isky cam and Keith Black aluminum heads but when the engine was tacked up it would fart, back fire then sputter and finally stall. Frankie thought that it's probably the fuel pumps and he'd bring out two new fuel pumps for the fuel hungry blown injected 392 cubic inch hemi.

Billy picked Sharly, Rosie and Frankie up at Los Angeles International Airport and checked them into the El Royal Hotel penthouse. The El Royal was a five star hotel a few miles South of Riverside. It was wonderful seeing Sharly, Frankie and Rosie again. I was in my glory. Billy was off duty having worked the weekend so I sent him to LAX in The Black Gold's company Caddie. After Billy dropped everybody at the hotel he drove Frankie to the Coyle Brothers Service Center and introduced everybody all around. Frankie was like a doctor impatiently waiting to see his sick patient so the bullshit stories would have to wait. He nailed the problem right away. The fuel pumps on the car weren't up to the task of pulling the nitro-methane from the tank to the fuel hungry engine. He also replaced the Harmon Collins distributers to the newer and much more expensive Spaulding Flame Thrower ignition and a Vertex magneto. Later that night while we all were having after dinner brandies in the hotel bar, I told him not to spare any expense getting the Coyle Twin's dragster up and running. Frankie took my advice and ordered ten pairs of Mickey Thompson racing slicks and rims a starting system that connected to the front of the blower and plugged into a wall 220 volt receptacle that was wired to the support truck press the start button and the motor spun the engine over. That way you eliminated the starter and battery and took off another fifty pounds.

"OK Eddie, fire her up!" Frankie shouted over the noise coming from the starter. Eddie turned on the nitro-methane fuel switch, hit the ignition switch and within five revs the big two thousand horse power hemi fired up. The rear wheels were jacked up from the floor in case there was a problem. No one wanted to see the dragster popping wheelies across the shop and through shop door. Everything that Frankie did while he was setting up the engine was written down, every question asked; every question answered. The Coyle Twins had the quickest double "A" fuel burner in Southern

California and eventually the rest of the USA and Canada. The Black Gold double "A" nitro bomb tore up the quarter miles from Calgary to Edmonton and tore up the strips in Vancouver, British Columbia and Winnipeg, Manitoba. It didn't take long for Frankie realized the opportunities the west coast had to offer so he discussed his plans with Rosie, she said "WHEN CAN WE LEAVE!?!? Rosie loved Southern California and a month later they moved the whole operation, lock, stock and barrel to Riverside and went partners with Coyle Racing expanded the size of the building, hell there were about a hundred acres of dessert behind the garage and as it was said "the rest is history". Coyle and Ianotti Racing became the leading drag racing team in North America. Black Gold Investments invested over a million dollars in Coyle and Ianotti Racing and the returns were tenfold. From their humble beginnings Coyle and Ianotti built and raced ten updated versions of the original AA. T.V. Tom Ivo phrased it best, with the big Black and Gold logo on the side of the fueler now with the hemi now sitting in the rear of the machine scaring the shit out of the competition, he said that the competition was the potatoes and Coyle and Ianotti Racing were the potato mashers and they mashed the shit out of us!

The first time out of the garage the double A fueler ran seven second flat two hundred thirty two MPH and went on to win the Summer Nationals at Pomona and the team never looked back.

Coyle and Ianotti Racing was an American Icon. They remained in racing and building engines for thirty five years. The team had won five Winter Nationals, Six Summer Nationals, New England Drag Way Summer Nationals and the Mid Atlantic Challenge Series held at Aquasco Drag Way that was about twenty-five miles outside of Washington DC in Eastern Maryland.

In 1989 the team called it quits. They did about everything there was to do in the field of drag racing. They all were worth millions of dollars from racing and endorsements, their own line of racing equipment and performance parts and besides; they were all getting up there in age. Artie and Philly were crowding fifty and

Frankie was almost pushing sixty and they all wanted to enjoy their families and all their money they earned so Coyle and Ianotti Racing Incorporated including their massive real estate holding was sold to Black Gold Investments for twenty-five million dollars and we sold the company to another up and coming racing team out of Atlanta, Georgia. Executive Airlines arranged for the financing.

Now let's go back to July 1965. The three of us were promoted to Airman First Class, (E-4) and still driving the eighteen wheelers the seventy miles between Edwards and March. Billy and CJ had nine months to go but I was staying in. CJ was non committal when I discussed my plans to him but Billy was clearly upset. He went out of his way to convince me that making the Air Force a career was an incredible dumb mistake. He even went over to Coyle and Ianotti Racing and pleaded for Frankie and Rosie and the Coyle Twins to try and talk me out of re-enlisting. "Come on please," Billy cried. "You've been friends for a thousand years! And I've heard from reliable sources," which was a bullshit story, "That he's sure to be sent to 'Nam."

"Sorry Billy." Artie said while he and Frankie were getting the Black Gold fuel burning machine ready for week-end racing program at Lions Drag Way. "Stevie's minds made up."

"Artie's right, Billy," Frankie spoke up as he wiped his hands on the rag he took out of his cover all pocket. "His allegiance is to the country that made us all rich. Let him alone, Billy. I don't want to see Stevie going to 'Nam any more than you do, but that's his call, OK?" Frankie said as he looked at Billy then turned back to the blower and fuel injection system.

"Christ, Stevie, we're rich! We did our duty and did it with honor!" CJ, Billy and I were sitting at the bar at the El Royal Hotel having a drink. "Now it's time to put our service behind us and start to make some real money!"

"Start making real money? Christ Billy, what in hell have we been doing for the last four years?" CJ exclaimed his hand wrapped around his Dewars and soda ice filled glass. CJ loved his scotch. "Selling skin flicks out of the trunk of your Impala? We haven't been exactly going broke for Christ's sake!"

"Yah, yah, yah, I know, CJ, we're rich but It won't be the same without Stevie along with you and me," I thought Billy was about break down. "He's the only one in the company that has an ounce if common sense! He knows how to place a bet!"

"So when I write to you Billy; that's when I have nothing better to do, all my letters will be written with Thomas Paine quotes, alright?" I quipped.

"You don't write letters to anybody, you phone Sharly almost every night and your folks a couple times a week and there's another thing you selfish bastard Steve! We'll never get to see Sharly anymore. She spends more time here in Riverside than she does back in Boston…"

"Waltham," I corrected him.

"Boston, Waltham, who gives a rat's fat ass! She is a breath of fresh air in a world of making money just to pay our monthly bills."

"Huh?" CJ said as he looked at me with raised eyebrows then shrugging his shoulders. "What monthly bills?"

"I know she will appreciate that when I talk to her, Billy," I chuckled looking over at CJ.

Sharly would take her vacation the first week in September fly out LA. I would take a week's leave and we would check into the El Royale Hotel south of Los Angles luxuriating in the penthouse. During the day we would lay on one of the countless Southern California beaches wearing her bikini and laugh her ass off while watching me busting my ass trying to hang ten over the side of the surf board. It took me over a year before I finally began to improve, but I got pretty good hanging five or walking the nose and I could ride the pipeline or shooting the curl without too much trouble, but what I really loved about surfing was the music. The Beach Boys, Jan and Dean, The Surfaris, Dick Dale and the Daletones. Dick's guitar riffs were incredible but the best of the all time instrumental bands: The Ventures.

CJ and Billy wanted me to see if I could talk Sharly into moving out to the West Coast and work for Black Gold but I knew that she never would, so don't even think about it, not without a wedding ring. And no matter how much she loved being with us and fun we all had, her home was Waltham and with family, friends her job which she loved. She was a now a department head and Cronins made it worth her while to stay put. And her modeling career was another reason she didn't want to move. She was working for an agency in Boston modeling new lines of clothes that were sold in top line stores such as Bergdorf Goodman in New York City, Hollywood Fashion in Los Angles, Nudies in Hollywood, Macys and Filenes in Boston and Park Snows, Sterns and of course Grover Cronins all in Waltham. I asked her if she would consider moving out to the coast, but she said no and I knew where she was coming from and I respected her loyalty to Cronins Department Store and posing for the best glamour photographers on the east coast. I would never want her to leave a job that she loved.

When Karen, CJ's girlfriend, a tall strawberry blond beauty with a set of tits that would rival Rosie Beanbags, came out for a visit, Billy never suggested that Karen move out here. Billy liked Karen, we all did and when Charly and Karen were out here we all had a wonderful time at the beach, surfing, shopping in Hollywood, going to the drags all over southern California, Beach Boy concerts at the Hollywood Bowl, enjoying the L.A. night life and checking out the wackos in San Francisco. There were real strange looking folks sitting in the small park at the corner of Haight Asbury, but they were friendly pot heads that hung around the neighborhood wearing flowers In their hair, reciting poetry, singing folk tunes, popping acid, smoking weed and protesting the war. Most of these pot heads couldn't find Vietnam if they were handed a map of Southeast Asia even if it had a red circle drawn around the country. Vietnam was a war, the protesters thought, not a country.

Billy finally fell in love for real. He met a tall, well built, long haired Chinese-French American beauty, Lee Ann Ming. Lee Ann's Mother, Martha, a French Beauty from Polynesia and her Father, Anthony Ming a Chinese American who was born and raised in Hawaii. Lee Ann's mother and father met while they were attending college in San Francisco. Her father was a retired Air Force Full Bird Colonel. His last duty assignment was the Base Commander at Vandenberg Air Force Base near San Diego. Lee Ann was a civilian working for the procurement department on March and worked part time at the base library. She was the only one of us with a college degree. Billy met Lee Ann at the library where he was doing research on a Swiss medical company that was based in Zurich with branch offices in New Zealand, Malaysia, England and the USA; Mettler Toledo/Ingold had just completed developing a pure water test sensor and it was ready for the marketing phase and a viable company that Black Gold Investments would be interested in investing in, but before investing any capital Billy and Charley did a thorough investigation and as usual Billy and Charley hit it at the right time and another ten million dollars went into Black Gold's coffers. Billy and Charley were so good at marketing and investing that the two could smell out a good investment the same as Eddie Shea could look up a horse's ass and see if it was worth betting on or claiming. I was trying my best to catch on and I was doing fairly well, but when the big investment event went down I could only stand by watch and count the profits.

Whenever Billy and Lee Ann could find the time, which was almost every night they spent it in the pent house at The El Royale Hotel. Hell Black Gold owned the whole top floor. "I really love her you know," he grinned following their first evening spent together shacked up at the EL. "And you know how much I love shrimp egg fu young, right? Well her honey pot has the delicious odor of shrimp egg fu young." Billy's sexual descriptions rivaled the Kuckie Cohen's descriptions when it came to describing the many sexual acts.

Egg fu young must have agreed with Billy Toye. Following a year of dating, Lee Ann and Billy were getting married. "A piasan marrying a beautiful French-Asian from Hawaii," Frankie Ianotti said shaking his head looking at Rosie and chuckled. We were all at the engagement party held at the El Royale Hotel. Billy rented one of the hospitality suites and I flew in Sharly, Barbara and Billy Flynn, Richie and Patty Brady, Paulie and Lily Whelan, Kuckie Cohen couldn't make the wedding, he nailed a radio D.J. position in Toronto and he wasn't on the job long enough to have any vacation time on the books. CJ flew in Karen. It was nice having all the friends together.

"My folks are happy, Frankie, very, very happy," Billy said looking first at Frankie, Rosie and then at Lee Ann. "They'll be here tomorrow afternoon the whole family, Bobby, Beeboe, Mom and Dad. I can't wait to see them again; it's been a long time since I seen the folks. Your all gonna love them."

"Billy?" Rosie said. "Isn't your Dad still on the witness protection program?"

"Don't say that loud, Rosie," Billy said chuckling. "You never know whose listening."

"We're not worried about your folks, Billy, we're only concerned if her folks will accept you into the family," Rosie laughed while she sipped her wine. We were really giving it to Billy, but he knew it was all in fun.

"It will be a beautiful Catholic wedding," Lee Ann said as she gently kissed Billy on his olive skinned cheek. "I only hope that I can get him to go to confession."

"I didn't know that you're Catholic, Lee Ann," I was really surprised. You don't run in to a hell of a lot Catholic Asians, but her folks being Roman Catholic Lee Ann was brought up in the Roman Catholic Church.

"Oh yes Steve. My Uncle My Sin Ming is a Catholic Priest," She proudly smiled. "He will be performing the wedding ceremony."

"You have an Uncle named My Sin Ming who's a Catholic Priest?" Rosie asked her eyes wide open in disbelief.

"Yeah, Father Ming My Sin," Lee Ann answered back. "You ought to go to confession to him. He's wonderful, and very forgiving."

"With a name like Father Ming My Sin, he should be," Sharly laughed as she put her arm around Rosie's shoulder. "Yes he should be."

Later that night Sharly and I went up to our suite showered together and enjoyed a glass of cognac before retiring. It was Saturday night and the next day we were all off duty. "Stevie?" Sharly asked as she rubbed my chest, we were stretched out on the king sized bed watching an old John Wayne western.

"Uh huh?" I answered looking into her violet blue eyes while I caressed her ample breast.

"Do you know Rosie's going to have a baby?" Sharly said as she looked up at me and smiled.

"No I didn't know," I replied.

"That's alright, Frankie doesn't know either," She said as she put gentle kisses on my cheek.

"I'll let him know first thing in the morning. Right after breakfast," I joked as he continued to watch her.

"Like hell you will, Stevie! You breathe a word and I bite it off," Charly threatened as she slid down my naked body and displayed her pearly whites at my manhood.

STUTTERING STEVE

Charlotte and Judy Marsh, were crossing Moody Street when they were both hit by a drunk driver. They had just finished dinner at the Waldorf Cafeteria and were returning to work. Judy was lucky, she was hit too but managed to roll out of the way of the car but Sharly wasn't that fortunate.

On Moody Street back in the fifties and sixties there was a traffic cop standing in a booth about three feet of the ground at the intersection of Moody and Crescent Streets directing traffic. After the drunk hit the booth and almost killed Eddie Gaudet the cop who was directing traffic. Eddie was born and raised in the Bleachery and was one of the best cops in Waltham, anyway the drunk kept on going his car still out of control and struck Judy and Sharly. Sharly was dead before the ambulance arrived. In mere minutes the tragic news went through the Bleachery like shit through a goose.

My folks were there with Ann O'Sullivan-Grady and her husband Rick Grady, Babs, and Billy Flynn, from the emergency room at the hospital to Sharly's Last Rights and her wake that was held at Bobby Joyce's Funeral Home then to the funeral mass celebrated at Saint Jude's Church where all her friends including me, made our Confirmation to Sharly's burial in Calvary Cemetery. Babs wrote me a beautiful letter gently telling me about the celebration of Sharly's life. Bobby and Frank Joyce had their place open past mid-night to accommodate all of the mourners.

Richie, Paulie, Billy Ryan, Tommy with Joan, and now Lieutenant Junior Grade Thomas Dyer was home on leave from New London Sub Base when the accident happened, Frankie and Rosie along with Artie and Eddie Coyle arrived from California, Billy and Lee Ann Ming Toye flew in from Denver and CJ and Karen arrived from New York City. It was a sad wake, a sad funeral and a sad burial. Ann O'Sullivan-Grady was speechless. She had no idea how much her daughter was loved.

Fudgie Iaconio, Frankie Rosa was there dressed in their go to wake and funeral best. Eddie and Edie Shea were there so was Billy Harrigan; Billy's wife Ellen and Emmy were there and so was Kuckie Cohen. He flew down from Canada. He had a disk jockey gig in Toronto but took three days off without pay to pay his respects.

Everybody was there but me. If I hadn't re-upped and signed on for Vietnam she would still be alive and we would have been married. But that wasn't to be. And I remember my Grand Father in his infinite Irish wisdom telling me that everything on God's green earth happens for a reason and God never put any more weight on a Man's shoulders then the Man can carry.

Sharly and I had been dating since our junior year in high school and planned to marry but Sharly, not being part of my immediate family I was denied permission to attend her wake and funeral.

"I'm really sorry Di, I tried my best," 1st Sgt Gordy Simms lamented. "I asked Col T if he could let you go home but he said that he was so very sorry and to extend to you his heartfelt sympathy for your loss but the regulations says no dice. I'm sorry Kid."

"Thanks Top, thanks for trying and thank you and Col T for caring," I said as I walked out of the orderly room tent my head down, tears in my eyes and went back to my bunk where my best buddy had a forty ounce jug of vodka. Vodka wasn't my first choice, at that time I was partial to Jack Daniels but Benny was pouring and I was drinking. I'm glad that he didn't have his favorite, a plastic jug of white lightning distilled from his brother's still wrapped and shipped to Benny's post office box. "Just don't get caught, Moon Shine," The guys in the mail room would warn Benny Polly when he showed up at the post office to picked up his mail.

THERE OFF!!!

Most of the guy and girls from Waltham High School worked on either Moody Street or Main Street in the retail or in the radio and TV repair services, pumping gas, waiting on tables at the Moody Spa or washing dishes and bussing tables at the Monarch, Jim Harts or Wilson's diners. We all knew each other and we were all friends. My real job was working at the Sport Mart Trophy Company and when five thirty and work was finished I was one of Eddie Shea collectors. I was earning pretty good money for a kid my age, a lot more than I was earning delivering papers news papers. I started out working for Eddie while I was hustling news papers for Joe Gagnon's News Service. I hustled the Boston Herald, Globe and the Waltham News Tribune at gate five at the Raytheon. Eddie was one of the top security guards that kept the bad guys from storming the Raytheon's gates and sabotaging the defense plant but his real job was the Raytheon's go to guy whenever someone felt lucky or had a few extra bucks that was burning a hole in his pocket.

Eddie's position gave him the "in" that he needed so he could walk through the huge manufacturing facility taking bets and making payoffs. He drove to the Raytheon in a new Lincoln Cosmopolitan. His wife drove a new Caddy convertible. Not bad for a security guard and a purchasing clerk.

Edie worked for the Raytheon in the purchasing department. They both went to work for the Raytheon right after the war. Edie and Eddie were a made for each other Edie was a short slim dark Italian beauty with a fine body, humongous set of knockers and a great sense of humor. (What was with the Italian women and their big tits?) I overheard Eddie telling another guard that she loved to have Eddie bang her in her cleavage and blast pop flies into her mouth.

Eddie was a tall slim Black eyed, chain smoking, Irishman who was a natural when it came to handi-capping races. He could look up a horse's asshole and tell if the nag was worth betting on or should be shipped off to the glue factory.

When I first met Edie I thought that she and Eddie were brother and sister. But as soon as Edie opened her mouth I could tell right away that Edie Sabatini hailed from the Bronx. Eddie met Edie when he was in the Navy stationed at the Brooklyn Navy Yard. He was a machinist mate and Edie was a civilian working in the Navy Yard's purchasing department. Eddie would say that when Edie was walking toward you all you could see was her eyes and her tits.

The year was 1952 and I was a naive ten years old kid and I was total in awe of Eddie's expertise. Just by doing a little research on the racing form he could smell out winner. Eddie taught me the science of handi-capping the nags, what a claiming race was, an allowance race, how to bet the perfectas, trifectas, past posting, and most importantly...how to bet wisely. He took me under his wing and taught me everything he knew. I couldn't understand why the young man, me, with the warm smile and a terrific sense of humor who couldn't put two words together without stuttering. I was known in the Bleachery section of Waltham as "Stuttering Steve".

Howard "Kuckie" Cohen the neighborhood's token Jew and local clown would say for all to hear, "Don't worry about Stevie taking our girls," What girls was Kuckie talking about, I thought. I may have a terrible stutter but Kuckie was homely as a mud fence. "With Stevie's stutter, the only thing he'd be able to attract would be farm animals, ya know what I mean, pigs, sheep, and for a real Saturday night treat...a Shetland pony!"

"Hey Kuckie, what did the butcher do when his Kosher store caught fire?" My brother Tommy shouted across the paper office. We were all there folding papers, drinking sodas and eating peanuts bought from the machines that Joe had set-up in the paper office. Tommy, Paulie, Boogie Monaghan and Donnie Tierney were the best at telling jokes.

Gagnon's news was set up on one side of an old grocery store. There was twelve eight foot paper folding tables that were placed against the walls and were doubled up going down the middle of the the large room. The ceiling was sixteen feet above the wide wooden floor, the fluorescent lights hung about eight feet above the tables with large store front windows.

On the other side of the store was an old Greek cobbler that worked about a hundred hours a week sewing shoes, replacing heels and soles and I had never seen him sit down. Not even when he was having his lunch. And for ten cents he would nail a set of taps onto the bottom of our shoes. The steel taps would last about a day of two, the nail heads would wear off and we would hand him our shoes for rework. He would look at the suckers, chuckle, nail on another set and we were good for another two days. He was working on volume.

There were paper girls working in the office but that made no difference when it came to rotten jokes. The girls would laugh their faces in their sleeves that included Charlotte Louise O'Sullivan.

"How in hell should I know, Tommy," Kuckie said as he continued folding his news papers. If Joe Gagnon was in the office Kuckie Cohen would be on his way home for the day and another paper boy or girl would deliver Kuckie's papers. Joe didn't put up with any shit from any of his paper boys and girls. He nailed my brother when he called Chink Richards a stupid Motherfucker. Chink just laughed and flipped Tommy the bird. "One more time Tommy and you're gone for the day, you got that?"

"Yeah Joe," Tommy said. "Sorry."

"He grabbed his pork and beat it!" Tommy said laughing his ass off. So did everyone else.

"We can't Kosher pork!" The Kuckie yelled throwing a folded up Waltham News Tribune at my brother's head. Tommy caught it on the fly and threw it back hitting Kuckie squarely in the nuts.

Everyone in the paper office but Richie Brady, Paulie Whelan; my two best friends and Tommy and Sharly O'Sullivan thought that Kuckie's comments were funny. I would chuckle a little bit, but I wasn't about to start a fight. I could kick his skinny Jew ass all the way downtown and back. I was fourteen years old and bigger than most of the guys my age, I was six feet tall and weighed in at one hundred seventy pounds and if I felt so disposed, could kick the shit out of every one in the neighborhood, but I had a gentle soul that would rather laughed off Kuckie's rag time comments then to start a fight with Kuckie Cohen

Everybody in the paper office including Joe Gagnon knew that I was bagging for Eddie Shea but they didn't know how much my brilliant money making machine was pulling down and finally when a route opened I was all done humping papers at the Raytheon and was promoted the best route in the Bleachery. Joe Gagnon's ran his paper office like a union shop. The paper carriers were promoted not only on merit, but by seniority. As soon as a route became available I was handed my own burlap newspaper tote bag with the Boston Herald logo on the front and the back and mounted my bag on the front of my Columbia fat tire bicycle and a route sheet.

When I told Eddie that I had a route on Bright Street he was as happy as a pig in shit. Except for River Street, there were more Italians on Bright Street than on any other Street in The Bleachery. My route had fifteen of Eddie's best losers. Six of his high rollers were police officers and another was a State Police Officer. So was the chief of police. I know for a fact that Eddie wanted me off the gate and out on the Bright Street route. I also knew that Eddie put in the fix for me. Joe was one of Eddie's best customers. So was Joe's fat assed old man "Porky".

There were fifteen paper boys and four paper girls working at the paper office and Joe Gagnon was an equal opportunity employer. Paulie and Richie worked for Joe too. The both tried to help me with my incessant stuttering. Mom sent me to elocutions lessons, speech therapy, but nothing worked. Sharly tried explaining that the reason for my stuttering was because my mind was thinking so fast that by the time my brain sorted out what you wanted to say it came out as a stutter. Nice try, Sweetheart but my brother said it best. He pulled me aside and said, "Stevie, we're almost fifteen now and if you keep talking like Porky Pig you'll never land a girlfriend. While all us guys are out with our girls making out in the back row of the Embassy you'll be spending Friday and Saturday nights watching television with Mom and Dad." That was the day my stuttering began to subside and within a month or two I could finally begin to carry on conversation without sounding like Porky Pig. Tommy's shock therapy gave me a jolt into reality and to this day I've never stuttered again.

"Hey, you shit head! I hope that you noticed that my stutter's about gone away?" I said as I grabbed him by his skinny, boney arm as he was walking into the paper office. "You ever get a girlfriend, you skinny little shit, watch out! I'll be banging her and you'll be banging farm animals!"

He grinned, gave me the finger and suggested I go and do a sex act with my body that is virtually impossible.

Mom believed that she was sure it was all her Novenas to Saint Jude that cured his stuttering. My Mom was devoted to the Catholic Church and Dad? Well let me put it this way. Dad loved God but loved golf too and when the Catholic Church decided to change the rules and allowed their flock to attend Saturday evening instead of Sunday morning, that's when my old man's golf game really took off.

ROSE LYN "ROSIE BEAN BAGS" LEONARDI

FRIDAY; JUNE 1959:

I was in my sixth year working for Eddie Shea and getting a bit too old to be hustling papers so I thought that maybe I should probably try to secure a legitimate position, in the Moody Street retail work force. Dad knew that I was running book for Eddie Shea, my mother's brother my Uncle Eddie Cohan let my Dad know what I was doing but he didn't know how much I was pulling down. Uncle Eddie owned Cohan's TV sales and repair shop and a hobby shop on Main Street near Central Square, and he knew everybody in the city including all the cops and was a good friend of Eddie Shea. Uncle Eddie along with my mother and my aunt Louise had the typical Irish gift of gab, but so long as I stayed out of trouble and maintained an A-B average in school, my Dad let me alone but kept an eye on me so I wouldn't get in over my head.

I'm sure neighbors was wondering how in hell I was earning enough money hustling papers to buy the '40 Ford coupe from Frank Ianotti, one of New England's top engine builders and worked his way up to become one the top engine builders in the country. The three hundred and fifty dollars I dished out to buy the coupe then another two hundred and fifty dollars I sunk into the 239 cubic engine flathead engine installing dual carburetors dual exhausts, a new Mallory coil and distributor and as set of Auburn three electrode spark plugs. I did most the work myself. Richie helped me with wiring; he was really good, and all the modifications were done in my Dad's carport. Dad would look over my shoulder from time to time to see how I was doing but he mostly wanted to look at a full dressed flathead with all the chrome and polished aluminum Edlebrock High compression heads.

Most Fridays on my lunch hour, I would walk down Moody Street meet Richie in front of Swanson's Appliance Sales then we'd walk over to Goff's Hot Rod Supply and Speed Equipment and gaze at all the Speed and Performance parts hanging on the walls, in glass counters and on the floor at Goff's Speed Shop and what we wanted in the way of new go fast goodies for my '40 Ford Business Coupe or Richie's fifty Ford 2 door sedan. I really loved that little coupe' and even though I didn't know it at the time, so did Rosie "Beanbags" Leonardi.

At the ripe old age of thirteen, Rosie went from sporting a tee shirt to strapping on her first bra a 32 B. A year later she graduated to a 36 C and by the time she reached sixteen she was up to a 44 double D.

(How did I know her bra size? She told me). She had to have the largest knockers in Waltham. I had been to the Casino in Scollay Square with Richie, Paulie, my brother and Kuckie Cohen, ogling the big breasted women that had trod their high heels across the boards of the strip joint but Rosie had them all beat, except for the biggest tits of them all, the great Virginia Bell, who bettered Rosie by a paltry four inches.

An early summer Monday evening after we all got off work and finished dinner, Pauley, Richie, Tommy, Kuckie and I were sitting in the folk's back yard listening to WMEX on Dad's portable. The battery that powered Dad's radio was almost as big as the battery in his Lincoln. I was scanning the Herald's entertainment section. My eyes drifted to the Casino add. "Hey guys, listen to this" I said putting down the paper and announced: "Rosie Beans bags is stripping at the Casino!"

"Who is?" Kuckie asked looking at me giving me a "Yeah you're full of shit" look.

"Sorry, Freudian slip," I said. "What I meant to say was that VIRGINIA BELL is stripping at The Casino!"

"Anybody interested?" Paulie asked looking at each of us.

"Let's go and check out Ginny's great forty eights," My brother said jumping to his feet.

The five of us piled into Kuckie's 1954 Olds 88, stopped at the Merit Gas Station in Watertown Square, put in two dollars worth of the cheapest shit gas in the world then flew up Arsenal Street to Storrow Drive exited onto Cambridge Street and into scollay Square, parked the car on Howard Street which was a ghost town and walked down to Hanover Street and onto our final destination… the Old Howard Casino.

The rules were clearly defined and posted on the box office window, all customers needed to be at least eighteen years old and if you didn't look like you were eighteen than have your draft card in your possession before you were allowed to enter the theater, but as long as you looked old enough and were tall enough place your buck and a half on top the box office window the cashier handed you ticket to paradise.

First out danced Georgia Southern, she had seen better days but with the lights down low and the spot light shining on all of her and not just on her face she looked alright. Then out came the baggy pants comedians who were always funny, next out; Taffy O'Neil. She had breasts that fell almost to her belly button, but she was a tall, gorgeous bleached blond with a great sense of humor. She really needed a sense of humor because she was the main attraction in a skit with slapstick comedian, Bobby "Mountain Top" Wyoming. Bobby was a midget that planned a trip while he was on a step ladder through the Rocky Mountains using Taffy's breasts to plan his trip over her breasts then through her cleavage. He was funny. He used three crayons to map out his Journey. He had the bald headed old men rolling in the aisles. Next Lily LeBlanc a ballet dancer that put on a show dancing to classical music; another comedian that looked like and talked like Groucho Marx and then out came the incredible miss Virginia "Ding Dong" Bell. She was the main attraction. She waltzed out with her million dollar smile, her makeup was perfect. The spotlight proved that. She began to remove part of her costume swaying to a lively Cab Calloway composition: "Minnie Moocher". She didn't take off that much before the red curtain closed. When the red curtain reopened she was back out dancing to a hard rocking crotch grinding Elvis song. She stripped to "Heart Break Hotel" then with Eddie Corcoran's "Come On everybody" with more hip moves than the "KING". Now she began taking it all off, the full house was whooping and clapping and now she was down to her "G" string and pasties.

When the song ended she glided to the back of the stage and the red curtain closed. When the red curtain re-opened the band was beginning to play Ray Charles' classic "Georgia On My Mind" Virginia came out onto the stage her smile radiating, her tits bouncing all over chest and a spot light shining on her sandy blond neatly trimmed bush and except for her high heels, she was totally nude and the baldheaded regulars sitting in the first five rows had their jaws dropped down on their chests. Then the whole audience was on its' feet including five horny teenagers from Waltham. She was on stage for twenty minutes with the spotlight still illuminating the sandy blond haired triangle between her legs.

"That's a fine looking bush you got there Ginny Ding Dong!" Kuckie yelled out at the top of his lungs. "Very edible!"

She completed her act and strutted around the stage the spotlight now shinning on her completely nude body clapping her hands to her standing ovation. Miss Bell had it all but so did Rose Lynn "Rosie Beanbags" Leonardi.

BIRTH OF THE BAGMAN

Eddie Shea and Billy Harrigan had been the best of friends since they were kids. They had grown up in the same two family house across the street from Bill Mitchell's west end Chevrolet. The Waltham Police Department bought all their cruisers from Bill's Chevy dealership.

They both had served in the U.S. Navy during World War Two. Billy owned Harrigan's Restaurant and his eatery was a front for Waltham's largest gambling operations and Billy Harrigan was one of the best known bookies west of Boston. He had half the police department including the Chief of police plus Monsignor McCabe of Saint Jude's Church and Monsignor O'Connell of Saint Mary's Church and in his back pocket. Billy couldn't get arrested if he drove drunk and blind folded the Museum of Fine Arts. Eddie also had a friend that was a lawyer and he was better than good. It was noted that Larry Fishman was in so many the politician's back pockets that he could get Ray Charles a driver's license. "Whiplash" Larry Fishman was always there if Eddie, Billy or any of their cohorts ever landed in jail.

I met Larry while he and Eddie were having lunch at Harrigan's. On my lunch break I phoned in my take out, picked up my tuna fish sandwich a bag of chips a pickle on the side and an Orange Crush. Being Friday and me being a semi-devout Catholic I observed the Friday sacrifice and refused to eat meat. Mom always knew. She said she could smell a hamburger or a hot dog on my breath.

Billy Harrigan casually mentioned to Eddie that Maxi Goldman was told by his doctor that he had a heart condition and he was advised to take it easy, so he was looking for someone to work part time afternoons after school and all day Saturday working in Maxi's store and would I consider doing something legit, like having a real job. Of course I said yes and Eddie took me across Chestnut Street and introduced me to Maxi. Before Maxi explained to me what my duties were, he handed me a dollar and sent me over to Harrigans Lunch for a cup of coffee and to get something for myself. And there behind the counter was Rose Lyn "Rosie Beanbags" Leonardi. "Hi Rosie," I grinned looking at her 44 double 'D's". Rosie had a set of knockers that would make your eyes dance like dice on a Las Vegas crap table. Rosie was from the Bleachery but didn't hang out with us and she didn't work for Joe Gagnon. She lived in the Bleachery near the Bemis section of Watertown and spent her week-end evenings babysitting.

"Hi Stevie!" she squealed as she ran out from behind the counter and gave me a warm and passionate tit drilling hug. "How are you?" She squealed again as I felt the thrill of her major leaguers sending horny signals to my sixteen year old over sexed libido.

"I'm fine, Rosie how about yourself?" I said trying to catch my breath. I could feel her balloons smashing against my chest through her white, immaculately clean, starched, cotton, waitress uniform.

"Good, Stevie, good. What brings you into Harrigan's?" She said as I broke off our embrace.

"I'm working at for Maxi Goldman," I told her. "I started today."

"What happen, Stevie? Eddie Shea get busted?" She joked, her beautiful eyes sparkling.

"No, no; nothing like that, Rosie," I replied. I couldn't bring myself to calling her Beanbags. She didn't look like a beanbag. She was a pretty, young, Italian with an incredible body and a beautiful smile "I needed a regular job so people mind their own business and won't have to wonder how I come up with the bread to buy…"

"Yeah I know," Rosie interrupted, "Your nice looking candy apple red '40 Ford coupe, right?"

"You've been watching me Rosie?" I said giving her a wink and a smile.

"All the time," she smiled at me looking at me.

"Maxi takes his coffee black," she said walking back behind the counter. "What can I get for you, "Big Guy"?" She asked still looking at the front of my pants.

"I'll have a glass of water with a lot of ice." I said thinking that I may need the ice water to pour down the front of my pants.

She poured the coffee, filled a plastic cup with ice and water and placed them both in a brown bag, returned the dollar that I placed in her hand and she said. "The first one's on the house, handsome. So ah… what time do you get through work?"

"Five thirty I believe, why?" I asked.

"Maybe we could take a ride?" She asked as she folded her arms beneath her massive breasts.

Now I was curious. "A ride where?"

"I don't know," She was playing it cool, "Maybe a nice place quiet and private. There's something that I really need to show you."

"You do? Why not show me now?"?" I asked looking at her chest then into her deep blue eyes.

"Not now, Stevie, later and maybe we can get each other off when we get off work," she smiled as she leaned over the counter and gave me a mouth watering view of her knockers. What in hell did she have in mind? I asked myself. We didn't know each all that well.

"OK," I said shrugging his shoulders. The only thing I could think of was she wanted to show me her ample major league tits. "My coupe's parked in the Chestnut Street parking lot. I'll see you around five thirty," I said then turned and left the store with Maxi's coffee and my iced water.

"See you around five thirty," She said from behind me.

I walked back to store taking my time waiting for the front of my trousers to cool off, then walked into the Sport Mart took Maxi's coffee out of the bag and handed it to him along with the dollar that Rosie handed me back and took out my water. "What did you think of our Rosie?" Maxi asked as placed the cup over the waste basket slowly and carefully removed the cover from his steaming cup of black coffee then dropped the cover in the waste basket.

"Wow she hugged me like I was a long lost relative," I replied "When we get off work I'm giving her a ride home."

"Think that you can handle her, Stud?" Maxi asked, flashing me a lewd grin. "There's a whole lot of Rosie Beanbags there."

"I'm only giving her a ride home, Mr. Goldman, nothing more," I wasn't sure when I could begin calling him Maxi.

"Uh huh," he said looking at me and then said, "Come on I'll show you how to engrave."

"Okay; what's engraving Mr. Goldman?"

"See all the trophies?" he said as he pointed to the rear of the store. "They're the wooden statues with polished brass plates screwed onto the fronts. They're all over the back of the store. You can't miss them. There's also a shit load of trophies down in the basement the need to be assembled."

"It sounds like a job I can handle." I said as I looked around at all trophies mounted on the shelves that were mounted on the peg board walls and benches.

"Of course you can Kid, if you can read, write, do simple math and use a six inch ruler; you can write I assume?" Maxi asked grinning.

"Yeah I can write. I can read too." I thought I'd throw that in to impress my new boss.

"Good. That puts you ahead of some of the college professors I've had working for me including my two brothers. Come on, it's simple." He said placing his hand on my shoulder and guided me to the rear of the store.

"I about made the honor roll the last three quarters Mr. Goldman, but this year I'm going to do it, if I can just get past French," I thought that I would throw that in too for good measure.

"That's good, Steve, good," Maxi didn't seem all that impressed. "And call me Maxi, Steve. Mr. Goldman was my Father's name."

"Yes, sir," I said instantly regretting the yes Sir.

"Sir? That's a first, He chuckled.

Fifteen minutes before closing Maxi showed me where the cleaning stuff was and how he wanted the store cleaned. "First we sweep the floor then we dry mop behind the counters and wipe the finger prints off the glass counter tops. We'll do it every afternoon before we close up, alright? The Windex and the paper towels are in the counter under the cash register."

"Gotcha," I said as I went into the bathroom, grabbed the broom and began to sweeping the floor, but when Maxi referred to us as "we" what he usually meant was me.

"Hi Stevie," Rosie smiled her deep blue eyes twinkling as I approached my '40 coupe. She was leaning on the passenger side door her right foot on the running board. She had changed out of her cotton blouse with Harrigan's Lunch iron on patch over the right side pocket and a name tag over her left side pocket the tight skirt and changed into sleeveless cotton blouse with no bra, her knockers hanging low on rib cage, her large nipples pressing against the fabric, Bermuda shorts, and sneakers without socks. She was a cute, full figured olive skinned Italian complexion with a gorgeous smile straight pearl white teeth long, dark brown hair, and as mentioned; deep blue eyes, and a sense of humor that could get down and dirty. But I could care less, "all the guys and dolls" from the Bleachery, except Sharly, could get down and dirty too.

"Hi Rosie," I grinned smiled as I admired her chest. "Have a busy day?"

"Yeah, it's always busy at Harrigan's Stevie. But I like working for Billy and Emmy. Billy's nice to all of us," She smiled while she took my face in her hands and kissed me gently my lips. "And Emmy keeps us all loose and laughing with his funny sometimes corny jokes and he has a new joke every day like this gem…ready?"

"Go ahead," I said as I folded my arms cross my chest and grinned.

"Okay: Why did Walt Disney have Minnie Mouse thrown in the nut house?"

"I don't know; why did Walt have Minnie Mouse thrown in the nut house?"

"Because she was fucking Goofy!" She said laughing out loud while she clapped hands together. Don't clap your hands to close to your chest, Rosie, we don't to bruise those chest rockets now do we?

"Let's go," I said still laughing while I opened the passenger side door of my coupe' and helped her in. When she was comfortably seated she lifted her sleeveless loose fitting blouse and allowed me to gaze at her magnificent golden brown nipple fun bags. Before I knew what I was doing I was running around to my side of my '40 Ford Coupe' opened my door, jumped in slammed the door and looked lovingly at her major leaguers.

"Go on Stevie," She said she grabbed me by the back of my head and buried my face between her huge, soft, Naa, Naas. "Enjoy!"

"Come on, Rosie," I said still chuckling at her Minnie Mouse joke. I gotta tell Tommy that joke so he can enter it into his large joke repertory. He knew more jokes then most comedians. You give him a subject and he could tell you a joke.

I started the car, pulling the floor shift down into first gear slowly releasing the clutch. If I let the clutch too quickly I end up boiling my oversized brand new fifteen inch Firestone tires. That's how much torque the little flat head could develop. "Where do you want to go?"

"How about we check out the Gore Estate?" She said while she ran her hand up and down my inner thigh.

While we were heading over to the Gore Estate, Rosie still tickling my inner thigh, the five thirty traffic was slow and a real pain in the ass. Back in the late fifties Waltham, Watertown and Newton had a huge manufacturing base and all the blue collar union workers punched out at the same time and were anxious to get home or stop off at the many bars and taverns scattered all over the three city area.

Unfortunately, except for Wednesday and Friday when the retail stores closed at nine-thirty; the rest of the week the stores closed a five-thirty so driving home from Moody Street you were caught up in all the five-thirty traffic.

"Okay, my folks are staying in Rockport 'till tomorrow," I mentioned to her as we passed the Louis B Conner's Memorial Swimming Pool on the corner of Newton and River Streets. My Aunt Anna would say that at the end of a hot humid day the pool would be down to five percent chlorine, five percent water and up to ninety percent piss. She was probably right. By the end of a hot July or August day it did have an unpleasant order but what do you want? It only cost a penny and you could spend the hot humid summer's day swimming in Waltham's newest ccsspool. But make sure that you take a hot shower and wash your hair before getting dressed and use the foot bath before diving in. Athlete's foot ran rampant.

"It must be really nice having a summer place on the ocean, huh?" She said. "The only time I ever went to the beach was when my Uncle Guido and Aunt Bunny were having a cook out in their back yard."

Uncle Guido was Rosie's Dad's brother. Aunt Bunny and Uncle Guido had a house on Revere Beach Parkway just down the street from the amusement park and a mile or so from their ocean front cottage was Wonderland dog track. Uncle Guido spent more time at the track then he did home.

Fudgie never bothered with the Greyhounds. "They were too unpredictable. Your dog would be way out in front, a sure winner and he decides to stop squat down and take a crap while the seven other dogs run right past him!"

When Rosie introduced me to Aunt Bunny, Aunt Bunny wanted to know if I was Italian. With a last name like Dyer? I said. You gotta be kidding me. Then she told me to go fungu myself and walked away. What in hell did I do?

How in hell did Uncle Guido put up with her shit. If I was Uncle Guido I would have set up a hit on her and had her put away. Aunt Bunny was a short, fat assed, screaming Guinea that really didn't like the fact that her niece was dating an Irish Boy, not her own kind, a grease ball Guinea Goombah and Aunt Bunny let me know in no uncertain term. How in hell did she get the nick- name Bunny? She looked like a miniature Godzilla with a hairy wart on the tip of her nose and a hump on her back.

"Yeah Rockport's OK but it can be boring at times, I'd much rather be here working and running numbers. There's nothing to do in Rockport but lie on the beach and ogle the girls who were strutting past the flesh admirers adorned in their Bikinis their knockers bouncing all over their chests. I'd rather be busy making money," I told her as I looked out of the corner of my eye and watched her boobs bounce as I shifted through the gears of my spring loaded floor mounted gear shift lever.

"Maybe we can go to Rockport some time and when it got dark I could walk on the beach wearing nothing but a smile. How does that sound?" She giggled as she sat up close to me and tongued my ear. And me being close to seventeen years old, with a twenty four hour passion for the ladies, a tongue in my ear drove me nuts. My eyes would start to water and my throat would feel like I had swallowed a fur ball.

"Oh yeah I'm sure the old folks would love to see that," I said as I tried to clear the fur ball out my throat. "In a month you'd see nothing but for-sale signs. You'd wipe out the whole enclave at Pigeon Cove!"

"What's an enclave?"

"An enclave is a cultural or social unit."

"You mean something like a witch coven?" she asked. "And you know, Stevie, witches cast spells while they're dancing around their fire and they are totally naked! I'll bet you'd love to see all those naked witches dancing around a campfire wouldn't you?"

"Why do you talk like that, Rosie?" I said. "You know that I don't like it!"

"Ya you do and you love it," She said as she ran her hand across my stomach.

"Who told you that?"

"Told me what?"

"About the naked witches dancing around the camp fire."

"Paulie. He said that he had seen pictures in National Geographic of a witch coven on an island in the English Channel and all the girls were totally naked! Can you believe that?"

Leave it up to Paulie to come up with a bull shit story like that. "But he's wrong. These people don't try to cast spells or run around a roaring fire; they just hang around the fire swapping wives."

"Swapping their wives?" She asked. "Swapping them for what?"

"Nothing I just made it up."

"Oh."

The Gore estate was a historical site where the eighth Governor of Massachusetts, Christopher Gore built his mansion and lived there until his death in 1827. The grounds were a gorgeous, immaculately manicured lawns and gardens. There was a parking area between the mansion and the barn that once housed the horses and the carriages now used for grounds keeping equipment. The parking area was usually empty unless there was a function in the main ballroom. There were tours of the mansion by appointment only, but during the day public was allowed stroll the grounds and admire the view.

I turned the coupe into the parking lot, shut off the coupe', but kept the radio tuned into WMEX. Jerry Lee was pumping out Great Balls of Fire on the piano and Rosie Beans was kissing my cheek. I was amazed that she was even interested in me. We knew each other but not that well. We were in only two classes together, English and French and she sat on the other side of the room.

When I was thirteen years old I was in love with Carol LeClair. (When Kuckie Cohen first met Carol he gave her the nickname "Twat". No one knew what twat meant but the name sounded funny. He gave everybody a nickname. He was the first one that began calling Charlotte Sharly and calling me Stuttering Steve).

I would have eaten the beans out of Carol's doo, doo just too lovingly gaze at her behind. She lived across the street from me, but with my stutter, I had a better chance of goal tending for the Boston Bruins then gazing lovingly at Carol's tight round ass.

Sharly O'Sullivan lived in the house next to Carol the "Twat" but they were never friendly and they never even tried to get along. The "Twat" didn't hang out with the crowd nor did she work for Gagnon's News Office or playing boy girl base ball or skating on the frozen tennis court down at Lowell Field. She was too good to be seen with the guys and girls who delivered news papers or baby sat and though she lived in the Bleachery with the rest of the ham and eggers. Her father was an engineer in research and development. Peddling papers or babysitting was way below her status and dignity. I didn't know why Sharly and Carol clashed. Sharly got along with everyone. Christ was I in for a surprise!

"You know Stevie," Rosie said as she ran her hands through my hair. "I'm really stacked you know. I imagine you've noticed them from time to time and that's why I wanted to show you my big, soft bra stuffers."

"Rosie, let's not, we don't know each other all that well so maybe we ought to cool it for a while before we get into trouble. Yes you have been blessed but be careful, there are guys out there that would think nothing of taking advantage of you attributes and you could get hurt but thereis a compliment in order: I do believe that your knockers are as big as Virginia Bell's..."

"You mean Virginia Bell, the stripper?"

"No, Virginia Bell the Plummer, she takes care of the bathrooms at the Casino," I joked as I took her in my arms and hugged her.

"You've been to the Casino?"

"Yeah once or twice," I said as I squeaked out a little white lie.

"You go by yourself?" She asked me. "I'll bet you sit up in front so you can have a good look at her humongous fun bags."

"Come on Rosie!" I said looking at her shaking my head. "That's not my deal!"

"I'm sorry, Stevie, I was only kidding," She said while she ran her hand all over my inner thigh. God she was hot.

"As I was saying'" I said with a sigh, "I didn't go by myself, Paulie, Richie, Kuckie, Tommy and I have been there five or six times checking out the flesh parade," I said looking at her face in the rear view mirror.

"You don't have to go to a cheap burlesque show to see a nice set, and if I get the chance you play the music and I'll do a strip that will make Virginia Bell look like she's a cripple!"

I put my arm around her shoulder and gently drew her to me. Her warm soft body felt so good. "Rosie, please don't talk like that, and you're not cheap, you're a classy lady and we'll have plenty of time to spend together, but let's just get to know each other a little better, but I'll tell you this, Rosie, you are a beautiful girl that any guy would be proud to be with. I just got lucky."

"So you still want to go out with me?" She said with a surprised look on her face.

"Yes I want to go out with you, and why not? I really like you and not for your physical attributes, and like I said, you're very pretty, and we could a lot of fun together, you know, going to the drive-in, the movies, Revere Beach, the fun house, roller skating, bowling…"

"Bowling and roller skating? You have to be kidding me, Stevie, bowling and roller skating is not high on my list of fun things to do," She said squeezing my upper thigh.

"I don't know why you wouldn't want to go roller skating, Rosie," I said as I kissed her cheek.

"Why?" She asked.

"If you fell down on your knockers you would bounce right back up on your wheels."

"Very funny, Stevie, there's ten thousand comedians out of work and you're trying to be funny," She chuckled.

"Ok. Screw the bowling and the roller skating, we'll do something else," I said as we both burst out laughing.

"Do you really think I'm pretty, Stevie?" she smiled as she turned in narrow coupe front seat, faced me and put her arms around my warm, sweaty neck. "No one ever told me I was pretty."

"Take a look in the rear view mirror and tell me what you see," I said while I positioned the rear view mirror so she could admire her beautiful face.

"You're right Stevie," She said smiling into the mirror putting her straight white teeth on display.

"Rosie, you have more than just a beautiful face," I explained. "You also have a beautiful soul and you are very intelligent. I know that that you are going to have a wonderful future and with the right guy."

"Promise?" She said batting her long eye lashes.

"Come on, Honey, let's sit up," I said as I turned down the radio and began talking about what we're going to do when we finished school but she changed the subject and began talking about a part of my life that I really wanted to forget. She had to bring up my unrequited first love, Carol the "Twat" Leclair, her name raised its ugly head. "She couldn't stand you, you know, Stevie?" Rosie said as she placed her hand over mine. "She told me that you and Porky Pig had the same mother and father."

"I know how Carol felt about me, my stuttering drove her crazy," I said.

"How come everybody calls her, "Carol the twat?" Rosie asked.

"I don't know, Honey, ask Kuckie, he gave her the off the wall name. Just like he began calling you Rosie Bean Bags"

"Yeah, I know," She sighed. "But what's a twat?"

"It's slang for a woman's private area," I said.

"You mean Nancy's private area?" She said. "Like what's between her legs?"

"That's what I mean, Rosie."

"Twat, twat, twat," She said saying the twat word with a giggle. "It sounds like a friendly name for a woman's pussy. It sounds like something you wouldn't mind eating," She said while she kept on giggling.

Then she changed the subject: "But you don't stutter anymore. In fact you have a very nice speaking voice," She complimented me while she ran her fingers up and down the inside of my thigh then continued up to about an inch from my crotch then she stopped "And you don't have that high pitched annoying, squeaky, nasal, New England accent," She said.

"Thank you, Rosie. That's very nice of you to tell me that, but I still get the shakes when it comes to reading or speaking in front of the class. That's when my stomach starts rocking and rolling and my ass begins to pucker."

It was so nice the both of us sitting in the front seat of my 40 Ford coupe' talking with Rosie, she wasn't the beanbags that Kuckie and Paulie made her out to be. She was smart, articulate, had a beautiful smile but she did have a love affair with her breasts and she wanted share that affection with my hand, my face and my lips.

"See you tomorrow?" I said as I pulled my coupe' in front of her house folk's house set the parking brake and shut down the flatty.

"Yeah," She answered as I walked around my car and opened her door for her and walked her to her back door. "I'll have Maxie's coffee ready and what would you like, Stevie?"

"Oh I don't know, Rosie," I said as I rubbed my chin. "Surprise me."

"Thank you for being the voice of reason and for putting up with my raging hormones," She said while she hugged me back. "I feel so warm and comfortable when I'm with and you always treat me like a real lady, but one of these days I'm gonna wear you down, big guy."

"I really like you, Rosie," I said as I broke off our embrace.

"Give me some time with you and you're really gonna love me."

I kissed her softly on the lips, then she took hold of my hands and tried to put them under her sweatshirt, she was persistent but I finally managed to get my hands away from hers and said that I would see her in the morning at the restaurant. She hinted that maybe I could pick her up in the morning. I began work at 9:30 she started at 7:30. "I'll see you in the restaurant, Rosie." I said as I kissed and hugged her goodnight walked down the drive way hopped into my coupe' and headed for home.

Tommy and Debbie Logan, his girl friend since the seventh grade, was sitting at the kitchen table when I arrived home. They were sharing a large Three Sons pepperoni pizza. "Have a slice, Stevie," Tommy offered. There was four slices left. The Three Son's restaurant had the best Italian food west of the North End. Diners with large appetites would drive from Boston's North End to enjoy The Three Sons with the restaurant's epicurean delights then on weekends there was live entertainment by three blind musicians who call themselves "The Night Winds". The boys came by bus all the way from Cambridge, played until last call then caught the last bus back to Cambridge. They were a fixture at The Three sons for twenty-five years. During the base ball season they worked in major league base ball. They were umpires.

"How is your job going? How do you like working in the real world?" Tommy joked. But he was right; running a bag wasn't like having a real job. It paid well and took up some of your time but it wasn't a respectable way of making a living but as the old saying goes "Cash Is King". But hey…I enjoyed every minute of it and hanging around with the characters that worked for Fudgie. They were a bunch of nice guys but don't get on their bad side. They could be nasty if pushed too far. When I first began working for Fudgie I felt a bit intimidated because with a name like Dyer I was never going to be a Pisan but one by one they took me into their loop because I could be trusted but I would never be an equal.

Frankie Rosa was Fudgie's club manager and Fudgie's operations cover was his club the "Italian Men's Social Society" told me for an Irishman, I was a nice guy. And if an Italian says that you a good guy you were in.

"Good, Tommy. Maxi's funny. He started me off down in the cellar so the only way I can go is up. He wants me to try to get the trophies straightened out and inventoried. It's really a fucking mess down there" I said as I wolfed down my first slice of pizza while Debbie gave me a discussed look. I had better watched my language. Debbie doesn't go for the four letter cuss words.

"Sorry Deb," I said through a mouth full of pizza.

"How's your engraving lessons coming along?"

"It's real easy. It's like writing on a thin brass plate with a diamond tipped pencil," I explained swallowing the mouth full of pizza. "But how did you know I was going to Maxi's engraving school?"

"I was talking to Emmy Harrigan. Rosie told him."

"Well trying to get the basement cleaned up and the trophies put in order, I don't have much time to spend learning the engraving trade," I said taking a bottle of Black Label out of the fridge. "Maxi waits on customers and does the engraving."

"One thing at a time, right?" Debbie said. She was a tall, thin Irish beauty with long jet black hair and large deep green eyes. Joan's father Mike Logan worked for my Dad. Dad and Mike met during the war while they worked at the Watertown Arsenal. They worked the same shift, 0700 hours to 1900 hours, twelve hours on and twelve hours off six days a week. They became great friends and when the war finally ended, my Dad took the money he earned from war bonds and opened a small machine shop in Waltham. Dad bought a house and barn in the Clemantis Brook section in Waltham. The house and barn were on Beaver Street. (you had to love that name) and built a cement block flat roof building that was attached to the barn and with the used machines that he bought from auction or a company who was updating some of their older equipment. Some of the machines he picked up didn't cost him anything. All he had to do was haul them away. The old man did very well.

"Yeah Maxi wants to keep it simple," I said tearing into my second pizza wedge. I didn't realize that I was so hungry. I had to have burned up a lot of calories wallowing in Rosie's cleavage. "With his bum ticker he needs to take it easy, doctor's orders, so I'll be doing most of the heavy lifting."

"What do you call heavy lifting?" Tommy asked.

"The fifteen boxes of trophy hardware that arrived today. Three of them weighed seventy five pounds."

"How do you know how much the boxes weigh?" She asked me.

"A trucking company drops the trophies on the sidewalk in front of the store and the weight is written on the top of each box."

"You don't say."

"That's how they know how much to charge Maxi for the shipping charge."

"Stevie," Tommy said as he climbed to his feet, opened the fridge and helped himself to a bottle of Black Label. Dad usually kept a couple of six packs in the refrigerator for company. Every now and then Tommy and I would have a beer but we would never take advantage of Dad's generous nature. If we did he would shut us off right away. The old man didn't screw around when it came to Tommy and my drinking his beer. But Dad never drank beer. He would say only peasants drink beer. My Dad was a VO Manhattan drinker but he kept the Black Label and Little Nicks handy for all his peasant friends.

"Uh huh," I said as I took a napkin from the napkin holder and wiped my mouth.

"You know that white and powder blue '56 Ford Crown Victoria Frankie Ianotti has on his lot?"

"Yeah, it's nice, he just finished rebuilding the engine and replaced the piece of crap Fordomatic slush box with a new Ford half ton F-150 three speed on the floor and a hydraulic clutch," I nodded as I picked up another slice of pizza from the box. "Why? You wanna buy it?"

"Yeah," Tommy answered. "He'll let me have it for a grand and a half and I was kinda hoping that you can see your way to loaning me the money? I really like the car and Frankie said that he would give me a year warranty on the engine, clutch and transmission."

"Yeah, sure," I replied. "Drop by the store tomorrow morning, around nine-thirty and as soon as Maxi opens the store I'll run up to the bank and draw out money."

"You mean it, Stevie?" Tommy said his eyes wide and a huge smile on his face. "I don't know when I'll be able to pay you back."

"You can pay me back when you graduate from the Naval Academy," I grinned looking at Debbie. "Give him a call and let him know you're good for the money; now, before he sells it out from under your ass alright?"

Tommy took Frankie's business card out of his back pocket, hurried out to the hall way picked up the phone and made the call. I stayed in the kitchen and talked with Debbie while Tommy made the deal with Frankie.

Frankie bought most to the cars on the cheap in with the body in good condition but with engines that were shot and needed some work to a total rebuild or to be yanked out and be replaced with a factory short block or a good engine in a car that had been totaled. The Ford Vicky that Tommy was going to buy was one of Frankie's rebuilds, the body looked like it just came from the factory but the 312 Y block was blowing oil from both exhaust pipes and the Fordomatic transmission was shot.

Frankie would buy a car for short money around two, three hundred dollars then put a couple hundred into the engine and unload the beauties from five hundred up to three grand. He could rebuild an engine with a bag over his head. He had a machine shop in his garage and he could re-bore and clean up the cylinders walls, mill the heads and the block deck, align bore and replace the worn out main bearings, Frankie could did it all. His engine work was the best on the East Coast. He also built engines for the dragsters and gassers drag racing out of Sanford Maine and Charlestown Rhode, Island. Both drag strips were former Naval Air Bases flight lines. Ford and Mercury Flatheads, huge blown Chrysler Hemis, small and large block fuel injected Chevys. He was so good and he didn't mind if you walked into his shop and watched him working. He would explain to what he was doing and why he was doing it. Walk by his shop on a Saturday afternoon and he would have five or six kids in his shop watching the master mechanic as he showed them how he performed his magic.

During the war Frankie's father, Vito was an aircraft mechanic stationed in England and when the war was won Vito was discharged from The Army Air corps he bought Vinnie's Moody Street Garage from his brother Vinnie's family. Vinnie an Air Corps Fighter Pilot was killed flying a support mission over Japan. When Frankie graduated from trade school, he went to work for his father then took over the shop when his Dad died from lung cancer. Vito like my father like his cigarettes but unlike my father didn't know when to give the cigarettes up. Vito's Camels decided when Vito's time was up.

"Tommy and I ran into Emmy Harrigan in the Chestnut Street parking lot and he mentioned something about you giving Rosie Beans a ride home," Debbie said with her elbows on the table and her hands under her chin, batting her eyes. "Is there a romance brewing or are you only going out with her because you admire her physical attributes?"

"I like Rosie and we enjoy each other's company, Debbie, and I'm not all that shallow," I replied batting my eyes back at her. "And besides, she's real fun to be with. May I pour you a glass of wine Miss?" I asked trying to act sophisticated.

"A glass of wine would be nice, Sir." Debbie answered me a formal tone in her voice.

"Lighten up on Rosie, will ya Debbie, she has a nice set we all know that but I like her, okay?" I said pouring her a glass of merlot from a bottle that Mom kept in the 'fridge. Mom likes to have a glass of wine with her dinner. Mom would say that she wouldn't want to see Dad drinking alone.

"Come on Stevie, don't be so defensive. Rosie's a real knocker out," Debbie said as she folded the pizza box in half and placed it into the trash can. "But tell me, how did she get the name "Bean Bags", was it because of her va va vooms?" Debbie said as she placed her hands at arm's length in front of her breasts to make her point.

"No Debbie. Kuckie tagged her with that name. The only book that he had ever read was "The Amboy Dukes", and one of the characters in the Irving Schulman novel was a girl that had the nickname Rosie BeanBags. Her boyfriend's name was Larry Tuna Fish. It was a funny, and for 1948 a very sexy book. You can borrow it if you want."

"You don't know it but there's beautiful girl living right here in the neighborhood who is crazy in love with you, Stevie. She's been love with you since you were both twelve years old," Debbie told me as she sipped her wine.

Now she had my curiosity aroused. "You don't say. Can you give me a hint?"

"Well it's not Nancy "The Twat", whatever twat meant," I couldn't believe that Debbie didn't know what he word "twat" meant.

"She would have if she and her family didn't moved," I said while I listened to Tommy talking to Frankie. The deal was made. I was happy for Tommy. He was driving a turd brown 1951 Plymouth piece of shit four door woody that rattled so badly that it sounded like an ancient coffin being opened in an old horror movie when he drove it and was constantly blowing head gaskets, blowing oil out of the tail pipe, leaking oil and the clutch had a chatter that would rattle your teeth. I would laugh my ass off watching Tommy backing out of the drive way, the car would be bouncing down the drive way and Tommy would be shaking like a dog shitting razor blades. He got his money's worth, though. He bought it a year ago for a hundred fifty dollars from Kuckie's Uncle Milo. Uncle Milo owned a used car lot on Commonwealth Ave in Alston. Alston is just outside of Boston.

Milo's "Bend Over and Grab Your Ankles" Used Car Lot sold used cars on the cheap. Milo's prices started at around five hundred dollars and went down.

Tommy's '51 Plymouth needed a head gasket the day he bought it and it needs a head gasket now. The flat head six would go through a head gasket like shit through a goose. It was an easy fix, all you had to do was to unscrew the twenty or so head bolts, remove the cast iron head, pull off the blown out copper clad gasket replace with a new copper clad head gasket and screw the head back onto the engine block, torque the bolts and you were back on the road. Of course if Tommy had me install a new head he would have saved himself enough money to buy the '56 Vicky with his own money.

Tommy came back into the kitchen with a broad smile. Everything was set. Frankie told Tommy he would give him a fifty dollar trade in for the Plymouth than he would re-build the engine put in a new clutch, have some body work done, paint the car and put it up for sale. "Tommy, take along a couple of gallons of water in the event the head gasket blows," I suggested handing Tommy his half empty bottle of Black Label.

"It's only a couple of miles, Stevie."

"Yeah I know Tommy but take the water along anyway you know just in case."

As soon as Maxi arrived at the store I let him know where I was going then hit the bank. I jogged across Moody Street up to Hall's Corner went into Waltham Saving and Loan drew out the grand and half hurried back to Harrigan's handed Tommy the envelope with the money and told to hold onto the extra fifty Frankie was allowing for the trade- in and take Debbie out for dinner. Tommy grinned, we shook hands, Debbie gave me a hug but the high light of the morning was when Rosie quietly walked up behind me and grabbed my ass with both of her hands left her finger prints on my butt cheeks.

"You scared the shit out of me, Rosie!" I shouted as I turned and faced her giving her a, what in hell is wrong with you look. "Are you trying to kill me?" I said through clinched teeth waiting for my heart beat my breathing returning to normal. Both Tommy and Debbie thought it was most amusing while I stood there my face beet red!

"I'm sorry Stevie I wouldn't want you to crap out front of your brother and Debbie," Rosie said as she kissed me, gently on the cheek then smiled at Debbie and Tommy and said good morning to them. "You coming in Stevie?" She asked me.

"Yeah. I'll see you in a minute, Rosie," I said finally cooling down. "I want to say good bye to Tommy and Debbie."

"OK. I'll have Maxi's coffee ready, and what would you like, handsome?"

"The usual I guess," I said looking at the rack on her chest.

"Lemon or lime?" she asked.

"Both, Rosie with whipped cream. I'll see you in a minute."

"I'll make sure that I give you all the whipped cream you can handle," Rosie winked than went back into the restaurant.

"Now it's Honey?" Debbie said giving the evil eye then patted my cheek then asked, "But what's with this; all the whipped cream you can handle? How much whipped cream can you handle, Stevie?"

I looked at Debbie then Tommy then down at my tennis sneakers, shook my head and broke out laughing. "Rosie's a real pisser."

"Come on Debbie, let's get going," Tommy said as he took her arm. They were both still giggling. "I want to pay Frankie, get a bill of sale and register the car."

"OK, Tommy, see you guys later," I said then crossed Chestnut Street and walked into Harrigan's. Rosie had the coffee and the lemon and lime Jell-o bagged and sitting on the counter. She also gave me a large cup of whipped cream on the side. "I know I gave you a lot of cream but I'm sure that you can handle it, okay," She whispered looking up into my face. "And now what are you gonna do for me, huh?"

"I'll let you drive my car."

"Hey Stevie," Emmy shouted from the opened kitchen door. "How ya doin'?"

"I'm doing good Emmy. And you, how ya doin'?" I said grinning. How ya doing was how our Italian friends greeted each other.

"The old man's beating me like a rented mule," Emmy complained. "Rosie told me you're working for Maxi now."

"Ya. I started a month ago." I don't get to see Emmy all that much. He usually works the dinner crowd then spun pizzas at the Chateau Italian Restaurant on School Street. The Three Son's and The Chateau, were the two best Italian eateries outside of Boston. Waltham had a large Italian population and the two restaurants served the community very well.

"Really? That long?"

"Yup."

"What about Eddie Shea? Still running bag for him?"

"Nothing's changed Emmy," I answered him trying to act nonchalant.

"It was nice seeing your brother and Debbie and she's very pretty," Rosie smiled showing her pearly white even teeth. "God they've been going out for ever."

"They met in the Waltham Hospital's maternity ward, and they grew up together changing each other's diapers," I joked as I hand her a couple of dollars and picked up the goodies.

"Do you think they're, you know, fooling around Stevie?" Rosie said as she stood up close and talked in a low voice. "She does have a nice set, but there's not a nice as mine are they?"

"I don't know Rosie, Debbie hasn't shown me hers yet, but I know Tommy and Debbie want to hold off until Tommy graduates from the Naval Academy. If Tommy gets her pregnant he's out on his ass and he will be spending four years in the Navy swabbing decks."

"I don't mean if they're actually having sex," Rosie said. "You know, maybe they do what we do; ya know, a little touchy feely?"

I never really thought about Tommy and Debbie touchy, feely or doing anything else. Tommy and I rarely ever discuss what we do in private. "I don't know Rosie. And I'm not really interested in what Tommy and Debbie do when there alone nor do I care."

"Why don't you stop in for lunch? I'll make you up today's blue plate special."

"Alright, what's the blue plate special for today?" I said sticking a dollar tip down the front of her heavily starched blouse.

"Spaghetti with meat balls Italian bread and for desert… and two heaping mouthfuls of the nicest looking set of knockers you ever laid your head on," She winked while I looked at her golden tipped mountains of love crushed behind her heavily starched uniform and an over worked bra.

"Do I get one meat ball or two meat balls with lunch, Rosie?" I asked as I grinned and raised my left eye brows. Just like Elvis.

"I'll make sure that you get two of the nicest, biggest and softest set of meat balls that you have ever seen and maybe a long hot sausage placed in between the meaty treasures on a bed of steamy angel hair pasta covered with the richest tasting sauce that you had ever put in your mouth."

"Rosie, come here please," I said then I whispered in her ear. "You have a filthy mind and a mouth like a sewer."

"Yeah and you love it."

"Ya," I said.

"Almost as much as you love me," She winked as she seductively wet her lips with her tongue.

With the bag of goodies in hand, I walked across Chestnut Street and entered the Sport Mart. Maxi was sitting in his office writing out checks. I handed him his coffee took my Jell-o and whipped cream out of the bag and went out on the floor to greet the first customer of my retail career, a classy looking lady I'd guess her twenties. She was looking over the golf clubs. I approached her and I asked, "How may I help you, Ma'am?" I asked trying to sound professional and not letting her know that I was a sales rookie.

"Ma'am? I'm too young to be called Ma'am," she said as she raised her eyebrows and looked at me. "Show me what you have in the way of expensive putters," she said.

"Will you be purchasing the new putter for your husband or yourself?" My attempt at humor went over like a fart in a space suit.

"If you need to know young man the new putter is for me, I'm not married." She was wearing khaki colored shorts, a sleeveless white blouse with a collar that buttoned up the front, white socks and sneakers, and her strawberry blond hair was done up in a pony tail. She was dressed like she was going from the store to the country club. She came off like the country club type. She looked too good to be playing with the ham and eggers on a public golf course.

"How much would you want to spend for your new putter?"

"I don't know, twenty…maybe thirty dollars, I don't really worry that much about how much things cost and I probably never will."

"Then follow me," I said as walked her over to the Pings that were the display stand that I had just set up. "My Dad plays golf and he swears by the new line of golf clubs that just came onto the market. We began carrying the golf clubs about a year ago: Pings." Of course I was stretching it a little while trying to make the sale. I had no idea how long Maxi was carrying Pings.

She stared at me with an interested smile. "Pings? I had never heard of Pings. What a strange name for golf clubs." She said glancing at me.

"I think you'll like them."

"What do you friends call you?" She asked smiling.

"Oh…yes, Steve… Steve Dyer."

"Jean Sagan," She said offering me her hand smiling.

"Ping golf clubs; woods, irons and putters," I said gently shaking her hand than taking one of the putters off the display stand. "See that thin slit about a quarter of an inch from the face of the putter?"

"I've never seen a putter with anything like that. Is there any reason for that oddity, Steve?" she said as I handed her the club and she looked it over.

"Oh yes," I said my confidence improving with by the minute. "When the ball is struck by the putter the face sings out a "ping" tune, almost like you were striking a crystal goblet with your finger nail."

"You're joking!"

"I never joke about golf, Miss Sagan," I said as I handed her a ball from the bucket full of rewashes that Maxi buys on the cheap from the area golf courses "Here…Try it." I suggested handing her the putter. "I'm sure that you will find this putter just what you're looking for, and after playing with it, the putter I mean, and if you find it not to your liking we will present you with a store credit for the amount purchased. Make sure hold onto you receipt."

The sale was easy. She handed me a two twenty and a ten, the sale was rung up and I handed her a nickel change, put the head of the club in a bag, handed her the putter and receipt, she smiled thanked me then turned and walked out of the store, another satisfied customer who had a beautiful smile and a nice body.

"Because it sings out a PING tune? Like a crystal goblet?" Maxi said, staggering out of his office. He was laughing his ass off. "You are a hot shit, Steve. I'm gotta to call my wife and tell her that one! Jesus, you should be selling cars!"

"I'm not kidding, Maxi, here, let me show you," I said grabbing another putter from the display stand, picking out a rewash, placed the ball on the rug in front of one or the display cases and putted the ball; "PING".

Maxi was still laughing when he took the putter from my hand, placed it back onto the display stand and walked back to his office. An hour later he left the store, took a PING putter from the display stand and headed out to the links with his brother Frank.

The day was busy for a warm, late in the month, June day. I didn't sell any more pings, just a cheap baseball glove. Maxi picked up twenty cheap gloves that were made in Japan; they weren't all that bad going for ten bucks, a tennis racket, a tether ball set and a set of weights to a fifteen year old kid that couldn't have weighed more than a hundred pounds. I had to help the skinny, young, future Mr. America place the weights into the trunk of his mother's De Soto, than had the luncheon special at Harrigans, talked to Rosie and Emmy while I ate then returned to the store.

That afternoon I took and order for sixteen trophies for The Pushrods Hotrod Club. They were having a rod and custom show over the Fourth of July, than I swept out the place, locked up the store and I walked over to Harrigan's and talked to Emmy while I waited for Rosie to finish her shift and changed her clothes.

While I was waiting for Rosie to change into her shorts and blouse, Ginny Sinclair, another one of Billy Harrigan's girls made me a lime rickey; on a hot afternoon it tasted refreshing. While I was sitting at the soda fountain talking with Emmy, Eddie Shea walked out of the restaurant's "back room" and sat down beside me. Emmy got up, slapped me on the shoulder and went back to the kitchen. "How's your real job going, Stevie?" Eddie asked lighting a Lucky Strike.

"Those cigarettes are gonna kill you, you know?" I said waving the smoke away from my face.

"I've been smoking Camels since I was fifteen and I'm still alive, Kid, so don't preach to me, alright?"

"I'm not preaching Eddie," I said. "We're friends and I care about my friends."

"Alright, alright, I get the message," I usually pissed him off when I preach to him about the dangers of smoking cigarettes just like I pissed off my Dad when I preached to him about smoking. "So how's the job going?"

"I can't complain, Eddie. It's been over a month now and I like working in the store. I've met some interesting people, but I still want to stay with you. With my life style I couldn't afford the drop in pay."

Eddie looked relieved. I knew that he didn't feature driving into the North End two nights a week and late Saturday afternoons. When Maxi hired me I told him that I could work on Saturdays but needed to be in Boston no later than four thirty. I told Maxi that I had a part time job making deliveries, he said that it wouldn't be a problem."

"Good… very good," Eddie said as he squeezed my knee. "Look Stevie, Friday night around ten o'clock, I want you here. There's someone I want you to meet."

"He can," Rosie said from behind the counter. "He's meeting me here Friday night when he gets off work, right, Stevie?"

"I'll be here, Eddie, whether I was meeting Rosie or not," I assured him. "Now with whom am I meeting?"

"Does the name Cosmo Iaconio strike a familiar note?" he asked.

"Yeah, Fudgie Iaconio, the heavy roller from the North End," I said.

"Yeah and he wants to meet you," Eddie said putting his butt out in the glass ashtray that was placed on the lunch counter. He usually just grinds them out on the floor. Maxi refers to the floor in his store as the biggest ashtray on Moody Street.

"Why me, Eddie?" I asked. Fudgie Iacinio was one of the highest profile gamblers on the East Coast. He had all of Boston in his back pocket from the State House, to the City Hall; the police the fire department, to the crooked unions, the two dollar ham and egg gamblers on the streets of the North End, to the East Boston gambling parlors; Scollay Square, the priest that heard your confessions and whom you received Communion from at Saint Anthony's church in the North End to the priest that Baptized your babies: Fudgie had a long reach.

"Because you're honest, Stevie, you can be trusted."

"How does he know that, Eddie? He doesn't even know me."

Eddie grinned slapping me on the back as he got to his feet. "Fudgie knows who can help him and who can hurt him. He just wants to talk to you, alright?"

"I'll be here Eddie," I said watching him walk back into Billy Harrigans "back room".

I dropped Rosie off after work, and said that I would see her around seven thirty.

It was seven thirty when I arrived back at Rosie's house, parked in front of the house, climbed out of my coupe' walked up the front steps and knocked on the front door, Rosie met me with a smile and a hug then invited me in and introduced me to her Mom and Dad. They were both very nice. Her mother was a full figured beauty: I can see where Rosie got her fabulous knockers. Her father was a tall thin Italian who owned a barber shop on Arsenal Street, just outside of Watertown Square. Vic and Sylvia were your typical hard working, blue collar family. Rosie's brother Danny was in the Army, stationed in Korea. What a shithole Korea was. If you were suffering from constipation, join the military and volunteer for Korea. That rat hole will have you cleaned out in no time.

Rosie and I were sitting in a booth at Howard Johnsons sipping sodas and listening to the juke box. Roy Orbison was singing "Candy Man", if Roy had Elvis' looks people would be saying, Elvis who? Roy had a voice that was so smooth and so real but he wasn't motion picture handsome like Elvis. Roy made one movie in his singing career. "The Fastest Guitar in the West". It sucked. I looked into Rosie's deep blue eyes and smiled. "What's funny, Stevie?" Rosie asked as she flipped through the remote juke box mounted to the wall between the table and the window sill.

"You are," I said as I gazed lovingly at her breasts. She was wearing a loose fitting cool summer blouse but no bra.

"I am? Why do you think I'm funny, huh?" Rosie said as she sat back in her seat. Her arms folded under her breasts.

"The way you smile, you always make sure that you always look pretty, your funny way of laughing. It's hard to explain, but I really like being with you. You make me feel so good." I was now searching for words.

"That's just three of the sixteen reasons why you love me," Rosie grinned singing the Connie Steven's song, "Sixteen Reasons Why I Love you".

"You have a nice voice Rosie," I said.

"How about you and I drive over to the Gore Estate and I'll let you look at what makes you feel good and you can place warm wet kisses all over my center of attractions," She whispered. "I know you'll like making love too, as you call them, my major league yaboos. How come you refer to my breasts as yaboos, Stevie?" She asked while she continued flipping through the juke box menu.

"Ask Paulie. He came up the name," I said. He and Kuckie have very active imaginations when it comes to naming individual body parts and assigning nicknames.

"Those two are always coming up with off this off the wall shit. How do they think all this stuff up?"

"I don't know Rosie but the next time you see them make sure you ask."

"I will but it sounds like they have way too much time on their hands." Rosie admonished them sarcastically. She wasn't happy about her breasts referred as being called yaboos.

"I know Kuckie has, he spends most of his free time looking at girly magazines," I said as we walked over to the counter and paid the bill.

The trip to the "estate" took about a minute. Ho Jo's was across Main Street from the Gore Estate. Rosie and I found a parking space beside the maintenance barn and parked beneath one of the bright spot lights that were attached to the side of the building. Let there be light I thought to myself as I admired her tits. I shut down the flatty but kept the radio on listening to Arnie "Woo Woo" Ginsberg who was playing rock and roll on WMEX while Johnny D was singing

"The Language of Love". Rosie and I were sucking on each other's tongue, her lose fitting sweater was in back package storage area and she had her 44 double D's smashed against my chest and my golf shirt was laying on top of hers in the storage area, but my chinos were kept belted around my waist and the fly zipped. She began stripping off her top as soon as we drove out of Ho Jo's parking lot and by the time I had the '40 parked under the spot light she was crawling all over me her skirt hike up around her waist while she was dry humping my leg.

"Come on Stevie," she whispered as she guided my hand under her skirt. "Touch me."

"Come on Rosie let's cool it, alright?" I said as I let go of her hand. "I'm not ready for this, yet and neither are you. I just don't want to do something that we are going to regret later on. Let's just take it easy."

"I thought you liked me!" she whined as she broke of our embrace, reached behind the seat retrieved her blouse and put it on.

"Come on Rosie. I do like you but more than that I respect you. And I don't ever want to lose that respect. Let's just take it easy…"

"You already said that, Stevie!"

"Yeah, and I still mean it. I would never want to do anything to screw up our future just to get in your draws!"

"Who said I want to get laid, Stevie? I just want to fool around! I'm not about giving up my cherry without a ring on my finger!"

That was a relief. I wasn't about to knock up Rosie or anyone else for that matter. I wanted a future that didn't include a pregnant sixteen year old. I knew the feeling and the freedom of having money and now I was spoiled. Tommy and I grew up in a family that didn't know hard times. Yeah, we lived in a hard working middle class neighborhood where the old man went to work while Mom stayed home and raised the kids and everybody drove Chevys and Fords. The only thing that made Tommy, me and our family different from the rest of the neighbor; the old man drove Lincoln Continental. He bought a new Lincoln every year.

Rosie said that it would be fun to walk down to the grass in front of the Gore Estate I had a blanket behind the front seat and look at the stars. Why not I thought it was a nice evening. Not to warm and not that many mosquitoes. We both put our tops back on, I grabbed the blanket and in the dark we found our way around to the front of the manse walked down the slopping lawn, spread out the blanket, removed our shoes and socks, Rosie took off her top and we stretched out on the blanket on our backs and gazed into the star studded sky. "I love it here, Stevie, not a soul to bother us, a cool zephyr of a breeze cooling our bodies and a wonderful guy that I love laying beside me. What say we take off all of our clothes and we can enjoy each other's gifts from Mummy Nature.

"Let's not Rosie," I said. "There are other couples besides us strolling about the grounds. We don't need any surprises."

"Where's your spirit of adventure?" She asked as she sat up, rolled onto her side and kissed me. "No one's gonna see us, it's too dark. Come on," She said as she kissed me on the cheek.

"You know Rosie; you're the most beautiful woman in the world and I would love to get naked and go crazy but we're taking a chance."

Rosie said something that I'll never forget. "Stevie, I would never do anything that would take anything away from you because I love you too much. I know that we may not have a future together, you want a life and so do I, so we'll be careful, hold each other close and always be best friends.".

As Eddie Shea promised the meeting with Fudgie Iaconio was set for Friday Night. Maxi's brother Frank who was a window dresser for the Bell shops worked with me on Friday nights and Saturday afternoons had locked up the store said that I would see him in the morning. I walked across Chestnut Street, and entered Harrigans, greeted Rosie and Emmy, climbed up on a stool at the soda fountain, ordered a Pepsi while I anxiously waited for Eddie and Fudgie Iaconio to show up. I was fidgety as hell. I wanted to get this shit over with, then take Rosie to the Gore Estate and bury my head between her soft, large, milky white, fun bags.

"Come on Stevie, relax," Rosie said as she walked from behind fountain and sat down beside me and took hold of my hands. "I've seen Fudgie lots of times he's a real nice guy. Just don't try too hard to impress him, alright?"

"Thanks Rosie. You're a big help! Now I feel much better."

"Rosie's right, Stevie, Fudgie's cool." Emmy chimed in. "If he wasn't interested in you he wouldn't be wasting his time driving his Corvette all the way from the North End."

"Fudgie drives a 'Vette?" I asked Emmy. "That's one of my favorite cars." Maybe I'll be able to afford a 'Vette one day, ya think?"

"Then why don't you pick up two of them, Stevie," Emmy smiled from behind the counter. "I like 'Vettes too."

"I thought you said that your '40 Ford coupe' was your favorite car," Rosie reminded me.

"Yeah, so is a 1951 Mercury Monterey two door. I love them all," I said as I got up and walked over to the front window and looked out onto Moody Street. Nobody! Nothing but the closed darkened store fronts on Moody Street. Maybe some music will settle me down I thought as I went over to the juke box dropped a quarter into the slot and punched up five tunes; three Elvis and two Jerry Lee Lewis.

"Think of something pleasant," She whispered as she came up behind me and placed her arms around my waist and drilled her major leaguers into my back. "Like, ya know, going to the Natick Drive-in, parking in the moonlight row wrapped in each other's arms my crotch grinding the front of your chinos while we dry humped out brains out?"

"Rosie...cut it out will you, will ya!" I said under my breath as I turned around and faced her, my teeth clenched together, my jaws tight. "I don't want to meet Mr. Iaconio with a lump in my pants. He might get the wrong impression."

"Picture yourself standing in front of me, me on my knees your jeans and skivvies wrapped around your ankles…get the picture, Stevie?" She whispered as she tongued my ear.

"Rosie!" I said through my clenched teeth looking over her shoulder to the back of the restaurant just as Eddie and Fudgie walked out of the back room of and approached me. I gently moved Rosie aside and looked at them. I felt my bowels begin to rock and roll.

Fudgie wasn't the sort of a high roller I had expected to meet. I was expecting to meet someone that looked and dressed like Al Capone showing up wearing a black tailor made suit, black silk tie, red silk shirt, black shoes, black hat and beady black eyes. He couldn't be any more incorrect! Fudgie looked like he just walked off the golf course. He was wearing dark blue Bermuda shorts a light blue Polo shirt, a hat that advertised Pebble Beach Country Club and sandals and no socks. Emmy hurried over to the juke box and yanked the plug out of the wall and the first half of Elvis' first song came to an abrupt end.

"My good Irish friend tells me that you are an honorable young man who can be trusted. Is he telling me the truth or is it only silly stories?" He wanted to know. "I realize you've been friends and have known each other for many years and he taught you the many ways to earn easy money?" I was caught off guard. The high roller came right to the point. Fudgie Iaconio does not fuck around!

"No Sir." That was all he could think of saying. "I've been with Eddie since I was nine years old and I have never given him any reason to mistrust me, Sir."

"He's right, Fudgie. I wish I had more people like this young man handling our money." He said as he nodded his head toward me.

"Good," he said as he offered me his hand. He had a grip that could have broken my hand if I tried to screw him. "Eddie will let you know what he wants you to do."

"Yes Sir."

"Steven… my friends call me Fudgie. OK?"

"Yes Sir."

"By the way, Steven, are you a good student?"

"I'm a solid A-B student except for French. I have to struggle to make C," I sighed looking into his eyes. "But other than French I do well and find my subject easy. I'm an alright student."

"There's nothing wrong with blowing your own bugle, my young friend, I find it an admirable trait but why not forget French, and study Italian? It's the language of love," He smiled as he kissed his thumb and fingers.

"Italian's not offered as a major subject, Fudgie," It felt strange calling him by his nickname. Too bad his name wasn't Vinnie or Vito or Rocco, but Fudgie? He sounded like the good humor man.

"I'll have Frankie Rosa make a call to... where do you go to school, Steven?"

"Waltham High school."

"There will be some changes made," he said as he said good night to me and asked Eddie to come with him. There were a few changes made at Waltham High: Fudgie had my Alma Mata add Italian as an elective subject.

Eddie told hang around while he and Fudgie went back into the back room. He wanted to give me instructions on how and when to collect the bags and when to go to Boston. It will be Saturday afternoon, no later than six o'clock and Wednesday night no later than ten o'clock. "If you have any problems that you can't handle, your car won't start, you're sick, you and Rosie wanting to play hide the salami, no matter what, you call me and I'll make other arrangements. You read me Kid?" He asked.

"Yes I do and I won't let you down, Eddie," I said as we looked each other in the eyes. "And that's a promise."

"I know you won't. Now take Rosie to the Gore Estate and bury your face in her tits," He winked.

How in hell did he know what Rosie and I had planned for the evening? Rosie had her magnificent attributes drilled into my back her arms around my chest and she was speaking in a whisper; "How in hell does Eddie know what we do? What do you two talk about?"

"I tell him nothing, Rosie. What goes on between you and me stays there. I don't tell nobody nuthin', he just knows."

"I believe it should be; I don't tell anyone anything." She corrected me.

"I know, Rosie, but if I'm gonna be working for the Italians from the North End I need to learn the correct vernacular."

"Vernacular? What does vernacular mean, Honey?"

"It's a neighborhood dialect," I explained. "It's kinda like... how yah doin? Or... What's going on?"

"Is there anything that you don't know, Stevie?" She asked me. "You never fail to amaze me. You're smartest person I have ever known."

"So are you and the rest of our friends and you wanna know why?"

"Tell me, Stevie...Why?"

"Because we all come from the Bleachery section of Waltham," I said smiling while I kissed her gently on her pale moist lips.

Rosie changed into her street clothes and on the trip to the Gore Rosie asked me if I intended to make a career running numbers. I told her and I was adamant that I had no intention of working the numbers game. I just wanted to see how much money I could put away in the two years remaining before enlisting.

"I didn't know you were planning on signing up, Stevie," she looked surprised. "I thought that you wanted to go to Boston College."

"I thought it over but I want to get out of Waltham for a while and do some traveling then maybe I'll go back to school. I just want to see what the rest of the world looks like." I said while I park the Ford coupe in our usual parking space put the shift lever in first gear shut down the flatty but turned the key to accessories so we could listen to the radio. "Stick Shift" by the Duals was rocking out of the radio.

"I'm glad to know that you have enough smarts not to get to deeply involved with the shit bums that live off the other suckers misfortunes. Bookies are parasites, Stevie. I know I've seen enough of them working for Billy Harrigan and hanging around my Dad's barber shop on Saturday afternoon when I was a kid."

I looked at Rosie and asked, "Your Dad's a bookie?"

"No, he's a barber but his shop is a front, like Harrigan's is a front for Eddie Shea but don't tell anyone I told you."

"Thanks for the tip, Rosie, but I had already had them pegged."

"Well they're not all scumbags. Fudgie's a nice guy, but if you tried screw him or his machine as Emmy likes calling it, he'll think nothing of having your legs broken or all your teeth pulled out with a pair rusty of vise grips. You piss him off he'll be your worst nightmare and that's no shit!"

"Yeah, I know?" I said as I raised my left eye brow, just like Elvis. I knew what these goons were capable of doing and if you screwed up bad enough they would think nothing of blowing your brains out of your head. You know? Two in the hat?

"He wouldn't do it himself, you know; he'd call in one of his leg breakers or one of his dentists that never practice medicine and when you wake up," She said snapping her fingers. "You're sitting in a wheel chair your legs in a cast drooling talking like Gabby Hayes."

"Yeah, he sounds like a nice guy," I said as wrapped my arms around her waist and kissed her.

While we were in each other's embrace wearing the skin from our lips, who in hell shows up knocking on Rosie's side of the windshield? Paulie Whelan! What In hell did he want? "What in hell do you want Paulie?" I said while Rosie closed her blouse. He could be a real annoying pain in the ass not only to me but everyone else that knew him. Paulie was always puling that shit. He and Lily would park on the other side of the lot and he would sneak across the grounds and scare the shit out of the heavy breathers with his dopey antics. Even Lily thought, although she loved him, he could be an incredible asshole, but that was Paulie Whelan. He could be a real pain in the ass and he was a slob to boot, but if you were in trouble, needed a hand up, he was the first on line to see what he could do to help you out. You really had to love the guy.

"Well old buddy, while Lily and I were driving into the parking lot listening to the same radio station that you and Rosie are listening too I noticed the windows of you '40 Ford Coupe' were getting a little steamy and the way your '40 coupe was shaking around like Elvis' hips' in your front seat so being a concerned friend and neighbor, I only wanted to see if you and Stevie needed anything; you know something in the line of rubber protection product perhaps?" He said as he took a box out of his pocket and showed us his line of Trojans. "They're only fifty cents but in the long run the fifty cents spent to-night will save you a bundle in the future. Those little nippers can become a real expense. I'm sure that you both are aware of the consequences of having sex with-out the proper protection. Now what can I get for you?" He smiled taking a drag from his Marlboro.

And Rosie would give him the business, "Paulie you asshole, why don't you take your rubbers, your salesman bullshit and anything you want to unload on us and stick them up your ass!" Her eyes were blazing. "And get that crappy smelling cigarette butt out of our faces!"

"One of these days someone's gonna shoot you, Paulie!" I said looking into his eyes.

Paulie was like an old school lawyer and no matter how hard we tried we couldn't insult him. He would only grin, treat us to a discharge of his endless supply anal gas from his frank and bean dinner and strolled back to his car.

It was an unusually warm late in the month of June, the moon was high over the Cambridge Water Basin, the water was sparkling and Rosie and I were parked on the shores of the "The Res". She suggested that a walk through the woods would be nice and give us a chance to cool off and get away from the cars and go in for a dip but before I could object she was already out of the coupe' and into the woods and by the time I reached the shore she was standing beside the water's edge

"Hey Stevie! I have a great idea!" She exclaimed as she began removing her clothes. "Let's go skinny dipping!"

"You gotta be kidding, Rosie," I said as I looked out over the water.

"No, listen to me, it's dark and the dry humpers aren't going to be watching us."

Why not I said as I got naked took Rosie by the hand as we slowly entered the water. It was cool for a warm late June night, the water was calm and we were in each other's arms the water up to our waist and who should show up? Paulie and Lily. How in hell did they know that Rosie and I were there?

"How ya doin?" Paulie asked bubbles slipping out of his rectum and exploding when they reached the surface.

"What are you doing, Pauly?" I asked as Rosie and I ducked up to our necks.

"Same as you guys, skinny dipping," Paulie said popping out another gem.

"That's right," Lily said as she reached down and grabbed me. It wasn't so dark that Rosie didn't see what Lily's hand was doing.

"Take your hands off Stevie, Lily or I'm gonna beat the shit out of you!" Rosie whispered as she yanked Lily's arm out of the water her nose about an inch from Lily's face.

"Think there'll be a fight, Stevie?" Paulie asked as we both watched the confrontation starting. "I love to see women fighting. They're worse than men when it comes to kicking ass and the language is brutal."

"You two aren't skinny dipping, you both have bathing suits on!" I exclaimed looking at Lily's chest. She had a bikini top and I reached down and felt Paulie ass, he was wearing cut-off jeans. "Come on Rosie, let's get out of here!" I said grabbing her arm and leading her towards the shore.

"We'll get naked if you insist," Paulie said.

"Oh no we won't!" Lily blurted out. "We are only kidding, guys, we were watching you walking down to the beach, get naked and walk into the water. It was all Paulie's idea."

"What in hell do you do, Paulie, follow us around so you can get your kicks?" Rosie said. "Wanna see my tits up close?" She said as she stood up giving him an eye full.

"Oh God, Rosie, they're beautiful," Paulie said as he approached her, his hands out in front of him. "Even in the dark they're lovely."

"Cut the shit Paulie!" Lily said real anger in her voice. "Before I knee you in the nuts, let's leave them alone so they can get dressed."

Rosie and I made it to the shore, waited until we were dry enough to dress then made it back to my coupe'. "That was a surprise." Rosie observed as she dried her legs and off with a towel that was in the package compartment behind the front seat.

"Paulie can be a stupid shit when he wants to, you know," I said starting the coupe. "I hope that you weren't too embarrassed."

"If it was any one but Paulie I would have but knowing Paulie, forget about it."

I took my time driving Rosie home. I really liked Rosie but it was time to make a change. It wasn't going to easy.

Rosie and I dated for another month than went our separate ways. It was cool fondling her massive yaboos at the Natick drive-in or the Gore Estate, but I was more ambitious, I wanted more from life than making out with Rosie in the front seat of my '40 coupe' beside the Cambridge Water Basin or the drive-in, but even after we had split up we still remained friends.

ALONG CAME FRANKIE IANOTTI

Frankie was a regular at Harrigan's, he would stop by every morning on his way to his machine shop and garage for his coffee. When Rosie and I split up Frankie began dating Rosie. He was seven years older than she was but Rosie didn't care, she really fell head over heels in love with him. Everyone was happy for Rosie and Frankie. But no one was happier I was.

"Is there someone else?" Rosie asked as she choked back her tears. "I know plenty of girls that would love to go out with you."

That came as a surprise to me. The only girl that I was close to was the girls in the neighborhood and most of them were going with the guys in the neighborhood. "I doubt that, Rosie, I just want to concentrate on earning as much money I can for the next couple of years before going into the service. Save as much as I can and try to make some profitable investments."

"Good bye Stevie." She said as she opened the door and climbed out of the coupe' and before closing the door she turned and said, "I wish you all the luck in the world. But don't be a stranger. I'll have Maxi's coffee and your jell-o ready in the morning."

"Bye Rosie," I said as I watch her turn and walk up her drive-way and into the darkness of her back yard. "Good bye Rosie's and your majestic tits" I whispered softly then put the '40 coupe' into gear into first gear, let out the clutch gave the Ford some gas and drove home.

JULY 1959:

"Hey Stevie, there's a young lady here to see you," Maxi shouted down the cellar stairs.

"I'll be right up," I yelled up to him. I hoped that it was Jean Sagan, the real nice looking babe I sold the Ping putter. She would stop by the store every couple of weeks or so to replace all the golf balls she sliced into the woods, blasted into the water or hooked out of bounds.

AND NOW MY WAKE UP CALL!

"Hi Stevie," Jean would sing out as she walked into the store. It was the middle of July and the store was hot as hell. "When in hell is your boss going to put in air conditioning?"

"Keep slicing the golf balls into the woods and it won't take all that long," I joked.

"Are you still seeing the young lady with the large chest?" She asked while she looked over the golf clubs.

When Jean visited the store to replace the golf balls she sliced into the woods, Rosie could see her through the restaurant window, she would shovel some lime and lemon Jell-o into a plastic cup, spoon some whipped cream on the top and hustle her firm round ass across Chestnut Street, walk into the Sport Mart and would hang around until Jean became self conscience and left without buying anything..

"No, not anymore," I said looking at her. "We broke up."

"I didn't think she liked me hanging around the store talking to you," She said reaching in her purse and took out a pack of Salem and handed me her lighter. I lit her nail then handed Jean her lighter. I tried to tell her that smoking cigarettes wasn't good for her health but whenever I tried preaching to smokers I was usually told to mind my own business and that was the nice guys that said it. The Pisans that work for Fudgie would tell me to fungoo as they rendered me the Italian salute, the back of their fingers across the bottom of their chin.

"Hang around?" I said as I took the golf club out of her hand and place it on the rack. "You don't hang around the store, Jean, you're a valued customer and maybe before the season is thru I may be able talk you into buying brand new set of Pings."

"You're a nice guy, Stevie," She said as she gently kissed me softly on my lips.

"Thank you Jean," I said my face flushing.

"I wish I was ten year younger, handsome."

"I wish I was ten years older, gorgeous."

"Let's play around sometime." She grinned as she ground out her half smoked cigarette in the ash tray on top of the glass counter.

"I beg your pardon?" I said raising my left eyebrow and the corner of my mouth, just like Elvis did.

"I'm talking about golf, Stevie," She said.

"I'm not all that good, Jean. I just don't have all that much time to play. I've only play nine or ten times a season and I really didn't do all well not even with my father's expert instructions. My twin brother Tommy is good. He shoots in the mid to high eighties." I bragged up my brother. But I give credit where credit is due and he does shoot a fair game

"And you mentioned that your father's a good golfer also?"

"Oh yeah he shoots in the mid seventies."

"Why not meet me when you get through work?" She said. "It'll be fun and won't be too hard on you."

"All right, Jean, let's play Pine Meadow?"

"Yeah, Pine Meadow sounds fine and it's only a few mile away," She agreed.

"Great, I'll see you there around six o'clock."

"Maybe we could play with your Dad and your brother some day," She said.

"I'd like that, Jean," I grinned. "So would my Dad and Tommy."

"Does Tommy look like you?" She said looking deeply into my eyes.

"No, he's the good looking twin," I said returning her gaze.

"I still want to play around with you," She said kissing me again on the lips this time with feeling.

I left at the store usual time, locked the front door and motored the '40 over to Pine Meadows. I liked playing Pine Meadows. The nine hole course had water hazards, woods and real nice greens. It was one of the better golf courses in Massachusetts. My Dad would take Tommy and me over to Pine Meadows when we first began playing golf. Tommy picked right up on the game but with me it was a struggle. I could really launch the ball but I had no idea where the ball was going to land, usually deep in the woods or the middle of a swamp. And now years later with the best sticks money can buy I'm still not very good. Dad would say that "if you suck with cheap golf clubs you're going to suck with expensive golf clubs" and even with all the money I spent taking lessons I still couldn't play worth a shit.

Jean was waiting for me in the club house. I was surprised to see her there, I thought that maybe she was playing with my head, that's why I left my clubs in the coupe, but she was there in the club house waiting for me wearing khaki Bermuda shorts, a white, short sleeve blouse, white sox and white golf shoes. She had already paid for the round of golf and the golf cart.

"Where's your clubs?" She asked.

"They're in my coupe," I answered. "I wasn't sure you if was serious about playing with me so before I carried them to the club house, I wanted make sure you were here."

"Steven," There was a hint of irritation in her voice. "If I say I will be somewhere I'll be there, alright?"

"I apologize, Jean. Forgive me? Please?" I said looking into her blue eyes.

"Come on, Stevie," She said patting my cheek smiling. "Let's play around."

"How much do I owe you Jean?" I asked taking a hand full of bills out of my back pocket.

"It's on me, Stevie. I'll let you pay our next time out, Okay?"

"You sure?" I asked putting my money back into my back pocket: The next time? This was beginning to sound promising

"I'm sure. Now where are you parked?" She asked as we walked out of the club house climbed the golf cart and I directed her to where my '40 coupe' was parked.

"What a beautiful car," She remarked while I took my clubs out of the trunk, loaded my Pings onto the back of the cart. "I always thought the 1940 Ford Deluxe Coupe was one of the most beautiful cars that ever came out of Dearborn," She said while she gently ran her hand over the hood. "You have a real nice car there, Stevie."

She didn't strike me as someone that admired fine looking custom cars. She was more the Cadillac, Lincoln, Corvette crowed. She had way too much class for the gear heads.

I gave her the ten cent tour around my coupe then we proceeded to the first tee.

"You're up first," She smiled. I teed my ball up and hit my drive about two hundred and fifty yards right down the middle of the fairway. I had never hit a golf ball that far or that straight. I was amazed at the quality of my first shot!

"Nice shot, Stevie," Said smiled as she teed up her ball from the man's tee and blasted a drive that stopped about a foot behind mine.

"Nice shot Jean," I said returning the compliment then we climbed into the golf cart and drove down the fairway. This was the first time I had ever rode in a golf cart. My old man would say: "If you can't walk the course then take your wife shopping!"

We played nine holes. Jean shot a Forty-five and I came in with a forty-nine. Not bad for a hack golfer.

"You played a good round for a hack golfer you know," She joked as we sat in the club house. Jean was having an Orange Crush with a slice of lemon and I was drinking a Coke with a lime. "You know if you played more you could become a good golfer. Your form and swing are good and you have a nice draw, but your short game could use a little work." She said as she stirred the ice in her soda.

"Yeah, I know but I really don't have that much time, Jean, you know. The store keeps me busy and…"

"…and working for my Uncle Cosmo?" She said grinning like The Cheshire Cat. "I believe he's better known to you as Fudgie."

"Huh?" I said while I passed a mouth full of Coke through my nose. Jean laughed as she handed me a napkin.

"And he's not just my uncle, Stevie, he's also my Godfather," She said while she stirred her soda again with her finger then she put her finger in her mouth.

"You gotta be kidding me, Fudgie's your Godfather?" I said my eye's the size of saucers while she watched me mopping up the soda that I blew all over the table and ran onto my lap.

"Oh yeah. Uncle Cosmo and my Mom are brother and sister. Uncle Cosmo wanted me to invite you to play a round golf with me. He wanted to see if you played an honest game."

"Aw damn!" I said. "And I thought today was gonna be my lucky day."

"Stevie," Jean said taking my hands. "Uncle Cosmo thinks that you are an honorable young man, but if you're going to be working for him he has to know that you can be trusted. And you did just get lucky. I'm going to give Uncle Cosmo a glowing report. And whatever you do for the rest of your life you'll be part of the Iaconio family… And Uncle Cosmo always means exactly what he says."

"Does that mean no more playing around with you? Golf that is?"

She looked at me, smiled, pushed back her seat stood up kissed me on the cheek said that she loved me almost as much as she loved my '40 Ford Coupe' then she walked out of the club house not looking back.

I guess it does. I said to myself while I watched her walk across the parking lot, climb into her speeding ticket red 1957 Ford Thunderbird convertible and drove out of my life.

That was too bad. She was older than I was but that didn't matter I liked her even though she smoked, but Rosie was out of the picture and I was back in the world ready to begin dating again but Jean threw me a curve. I guess now it was just my '51 Mercury Monterey dream car and me.

But fortunately I was mistaken.

NOW BACK TO MY MYSTERIOUS VISITOR.

"She's really cute, Steve," Maxi said. "With long blond hair, whet blue eyes and she says she lives across the street from you."

"I'll be right up," I yelled up the stairs. It had to be Sharly I said to myself as I hurried up the stairs that led into the back of store. I walked passed Maxi's office and out onto the floor. It was Sharly and she was talking with the boss.

"Hi Sharly. Lovely to see you again," I said with a curious smile. Maybe she's here for a ride home I hope, I hope.

"It's lovely to see you too Stevie." She said her violet blue eye sparkled as she looked up at me.

"Does your lady friend have a name, Steve?" Maxi asked, looking her from head to toes and he's enjoying the trip. "Or is it going to be twenty question already?"

"Oh yeah, I'm sorry. Charlotte O'Sullivan, this is Maxi Gold, the boss, Maxi, this Sharly O'Sullivan."

"I'm very pleased to meet you," Maxi said giving her an approving smile as he offered her his hand. "You wouldn't be Jewish wouldn't you?" He kidded as he walked back to his office. "No you can't be. There's not many Jewish women with blond hair, blue eyes and a turned up nose."

Sharly blushed then thanked him and we both watched Maxi as he went back into his office.

"What brings you up town, Sharly?" I asked shyly smiling looking into her beautiful violet blue eyes. "To see me I hope."

"I'm always happy to see you Stevie," She said giving me back a warm smile. "There's nobody I would rather see than you."

"You need a ride, I hope?" I asked trying not to sound to desperate.

"I'm glad that I caught you before you left for the day," She said. "And yes, Stevie, I do need a ride home. Billy phoned me at the store and said he wouldn't be able to pick me up."

"That is not a problem Sharl, I have an engraving project that I've been trying to get finish and I was down in the basement cutting some brass inserts that's why I'm staying a little later than usual." Now I was running off at the mouth.

"I'm not taking you away from anything am I?" Sharly asked

"No you're not," Maxi shouted from his office. "If you don't give her a ride home, you putz, or I will!"

"What's a putz?" She asked me.

"It's another way to spell Steve Dyer," Maxi shouted again. "Now will you two get the hell out of here so I can lock up and go home!"

"Let's go." I said taking her hand and walked her out of the store. "My wheels are parked across the street."

"I know. I could see your car from the store, that's why I hurried up here before you left."

I opened her door and held it while she slid and I noticed that while I was walking around the car she reached across the seat and opened my door. If a girl did that I heard that it meant she was interested in you. When it came to realizing how Sharly felt about me, I had my head so far up my ass I could look out of my belly button and still not see anything!

"I hope I haven't screwed up your plans, Stevie, but I really don't like taking the bus. There are too many weird people," She said as she turned and faced me. "I wanted to call the store but I don't have your number and I didn't want to take the chance of missing you."

"When we get home I'll give you the store's phone number, okay?"

"That's alright, Stevie," She said. "It won't happen again. But like I said I don't like riding on the bus."

"I hope it does happen again," I said looking into the rear view mirror at the traffic behind me while I approached the Moody Street Bridge. "Whenever you need and ride or anything else, don't hesitate to ask me," I explained as I took a right onto Carter Street then drove past Jim Hart's 24 hour Grill, (The only day during the year that Jim Hart closed his grill was Easter Sunday) then past the Boston and Maine railroad depot. "I'll always be here for you." I said taking a right onto River Street.

"Thank you Stevie. You're so nice and I really do like you," She said as she placed her hand on my shoulder and kissed me on the cheek.

"Stevie tell me, how come you're still not dating anyone now?"

"Well after Rosie and I broke up I really wanted to concentrate on working and trying to locate a 1951 Mercury Monterey that wasn't a junk yard angel lying on her roof."

"I hope you get everything you want, Stevie," Sharly said looking at me with I love you written all over her beautiful face. "And someone that would really love to love you."

"Can you give me a hint? I do like a level playing field." I smiled while we were stopped on River Street waiting for the light to change when I turned my head and faced her. She was a lovely blond haired blue eyed beauty. Maybe, just maybe if she gave Billy Flynn his walking papers…then maybe not! I'm not that lucky.

"Someone real nice, Stevie," She said as she placed her hand on mine. "There is someone that loves you and loves you like you can't believe."

"Someone like you I hope," I whispered under my breath as we waited for the traffic light to change.

A short while later I pulled up in front of house got out, walked around the car opened the door and her out of my coupe', she smiled and kissed me again softly on my lips and I swear she whispered, "I love you, Stevie," Then she hurried up the porch steps, opened the front door turned and waved then went into the house. I made a u-turn in front of the folk's house and drove into the driveway. I do believe that Billy's days with the beautiful Miss O'Sullivan are numbered and rapidly coming to end. I could feel it in my bones

MY 1951 MERCURY MONTERY COUPE'

From the age of twelve I wanted to own a 1951 Mercury Monterey coupe'. I had seen one in a Life Magazine add while I was sitting in Dr. Zola's office waiting to have another tooth yanked out.(Dr. Zola was a butcher. When I was thirteen of fourteen I visited to his office after school with a tooth ache he pulled out a wrong tooth). And right there and then I made up my mind, as soon I he was old enough to drive and had the money which I now have I was going to buy one.

Emmy Harrigan was the one that turned me onto my dream coupe' he let me know that his Uncle Leo owned a '51 Mercury Monterey that he wanted to unload, the car was parked in his garage in West Newton and I could have it for short money. It was a pearl white Monterey, with a grey mohair interior, radio, heater and almost new Firestone white wall tire. Everything worked but the engine. It was seized tighter then a bull's ass at fly time. That was rare that a flathead would lock up like that unless you ran it out of oil or there was a factory defect. The 255cubic inch flatty was a tough dependable engine and when treated right the old girl was good for a hundred thousand miles before the rings had to be replaced, the valves and crankshaft reground and the cylinder walls cleaned up. The flatty in my '40 coupe' had over sixty thousand miles and even with the mild speed equipment she was still tight, the oil pressure held at around 40 PSI and I made sure that I changed the oil and filter every two thousand miles. The filter canister was an aftermarket add on that added another ten thousand miles onto the flatty.

As soon as lunch time rolled around I locked up the store went over to Harrigan's and met with Emmy. "How much does your uncle wanted for the Mercury, Emmy?" I asked watching Emmy as he expertly flipped the burgers.

"You can have it for a duce and half, Stevie, but you know that it gotta to be towed. The engine's seized tighter than a bull's ass at fly time," Emmy said looking up from the grill. Rosie was working in the kitchen but came into the restaurant when she heard Emmy and me talking.

"Hi Stevie," Rosie smiled as she wrapped her arm around my waist.

"Hi Rosie," I said as I wrapped my arm around her shoulder and kissed her on the top of her head. I still had a soft spot in my heart for her and her tits. She smiled at me then went back to the kitchen. This was going to be her last week working for Billy Harrigan.

I turned my attention back to Emmy and said, "Great, I have the money," I said counting out the two fifty and then putting the rest of my money back into my back pocket. "How about calling your uncle Leo and let him know that you sold me the Merc? I wanna buy it before someone else snatches it up."

"Not much chance of that Stevie, it's been sitting in my uncles garage for six months."

"I don't want to take any chances Emmy, okay?"

"He's probably still at work but not to worry, I'll call up to Auntie Zoot and let her know that you just bought Uncle Leo's car. By the way, do you always walk around with that much money?"

"I always carry a few bucks, just in case."

"Just in case?" He said. "Just in case of what?"

"Just in case a cherry 1951 Mercury Monterey comes along."

"Looks like you just got your wish ole Buddy," Emmy chuckled. He was one of the real nice guys living in Waltham's south side.

"Thanks Emmy," I said then walked across Moody Street to Scott's Surplus and looked up Paulie. He was sitting on his ass in the office smoking a Marlboro and thumbing through an old Play Boy Magazine. Paulie had the same type of boss that I had. He came in on Monday Morning, made the bank deposit and in the summer time he went off to play golf and during the winter he would travel back and forth from Sudbury to Florida. There were always three Eastern Airlines Electra flights a day leaving out of Boston and flying in and out of Miami.

I wanted to ask if he and Richie were up for a flathead engine rebuild. I couldn't do the whole re-build alone. Richie was the best at wiring and Paulie was good for everything else including breaking wind, smoking cigarettes and hanging around fetching sodas, handing us tools and changing the radio station. But I'll give him credit, Paulie knew more about flathead engines than anyone else except for maybe Frankie Ianotti. Paulie could go way back to the early thirties to the early fifties and tell you anything you want to know. If Frankie had a question or a problem with the temperamental flathead he would call Paulie Whelan for some direction. Frankie would rather work on the more up to date over Head valve Fords, General Motors and Chrysler engines. When it came to building a Chrysler or Dodge Hemi, Ford or a Chevy engine Frankie was the best; all the other engine builders came in a distant second.

"Yeah, why not Stevie, I'm always up for a flat head rebuild" Paulie said as he ground out a cigarette but on the floor.

"Why don't you use the ash tray, Paulie?" He could be really disgusting at times. Like after Saturday night dinner of franks and beans. We could never understand why Lily put up with his shit. "They're all over the store you fucking reprobate!"

"Who sweeps the fucking floor, Stevie, Huh?" He said as he picked up the butt and flipped it out the door and onto the sidewalk.

"Alright, Paulie," I said rolling my eye balls while he chuckled, "Think Richie will want to throw in?"

"Call him at the store when you get back from lunch," Paulie said, "When you gonna buy the Merc?"

"I already have. I gave Emmy the money and, as soon as I get back to the store I'll call Frank Ianotti and see when he will be able to tow the car."

The following Sunday morning Frankie put my car on the hook, towed it to my folk's house and dropped it onto the part of the driveway that ran beside the folk's garage and car port. With another car in the driveway my '40 coupe lost her parking space. Sharly said that I could park the coupe in her mother's driveway. Mrs. O'Sullivan's driveway had enough space for six cars. Frank did the tow job for nothing which was nice of him. Tommy and I had bought our cars from him, so did Richie and Paulie. Richie picked up a nice clean deep maroon 1948Ford four door, "woody" station wagon and Paulie went for a grey 50 Chevy. Even tight ass Kuckie Cohen went for a robin's egg blue 51 Olds Rocket 88. Lily, whose father was Jewish and mother a Catholic, told Paulie that Kuckie's old man sprung for the money to pay for his car. You know what the Jews believe? That they're waiting for the Messiah to arrive and Louis Wolf Cohen, Irving and Millie Putz's only son could be the next in line savior… Jesus Christ. Fat chance! Kuckie would have to clean up his act real quick. He had to have at least a hundred nudist and girly magazines and porno pictures stuffed in his closet. His mother knew he had them but she said that it was the next Messiah's hobby. Yeah, and on Saturday nights sitting on the toilet girly magazine in one hand choking the chicken with the other hand! That was a hobby?

Later that afternoon after I got home from making the drop in Boston and picking up my cut I was in my folk's back yard looking over the engine with Richie and Paulie. I thought that maybe I could jump start the Merc with my Dad's '58 twelve volt Lincoln but it wouldn't budge. Emmy was right. The engine was cooked. Dad thought that if I put a socket on a breaker bar then put an iron pipe over the breaker bar handle and try to turn it over with large nut that connected the harmonic balancer to the crankshaft. "Not a chance Dad, It ain't going to happen, the engine's seized tighter than a virgin's twat."

"Christ Stevie, don't let you mother hear you to talk like that, all right?" Dad said, "She would swear to God that you heard that crap from me."

"I did Dad," I chuckled still looking at the engine.

That evening, Paulie and Richie picked up Lily and Patti LeBlanc then drove into Cambridge to get a burger at Richard's Car Hop. They wanted me to go with them, but I didn't want to be the fifth wheel. What I really wanted to do was to stay at home and checkout the white elephant and to determine how to approach the problem. I had a drop light in hand shining into the engine compartment checking out the motor wishing and hoping that maybe I could, if I was lucky enough to figure out what caused the engine to seize. I drained the oil and found it clean, pulled out the oil filter and ran my finger across the bottom of the filter container. The oil was like new, so that meant that probably the crank shaft and the main bearings weren't damaged. There were no leaks from the rear or the front seals. I'd know a lot more once I pulled the intake manifold and the heads then drop the oil pan. The flat head had less than thirty thousand miles and you could almost eat out of the engine compartment. Emmy's Uncle John on his mother's side of the family drove the Merc the three miles to his restaurant in Newton Centre but when the engine crapped out he had it towed home and parked it behind his garage and knowing that Auntie Zoot wasn't going to let Uncle Leo drive her Buick even though he bought it for her he went out and bought a six year old used bright red Caddy Eldorado from Frankie Ianotti. If Frankie didn't have what you wanted on his lot he went out and found you the car you wanted.

What's with the Italians and their Cadillac's? The only Italian that didn't drive a Caddy was Fudgie Iaconio. He drove a Corvette. He bought a new 'Vette every year and donated his used 'Vette to one of his many charities. Most of the fat assed Dagos were too big to slide behind the wheel of a 'Vette but Fudgie was in good shape for a forty year old World War Two Italian American Veteran.

Fudgie came home from the war with ribbons and medals from D Day and the Battle of the Bulge. He never talked about his two Purple Hearts or his Silver Star. "I'm no hero, you got that!" He said looking at Frank Rosa who was tending the half full bar. "I just happened to be in wrong place at the right time. "Besides nobody had no money to bet so I left my Racing Form back in England, all right? Now let's concentrate on making all of us rich, including me: And by the way…I'm very generous to my family and friends!"

I was so deeply engrossed in my thoughts on a game plan as to how I should approach the rebuild that I didn't see or hear Sharly O'Sullivan standing behind me.

"Hi Stevie," she said in her, soft voice. She looked like and angel dressed in light blue Bermuda shorts, sleeveless white blouse and low top tennis sneakers. She looked like she had just stepped out of a beauty magazine. "Very nice," she smiled looking at the white two door Mercury Monterey.

"Oh hi Sharl," I jumped, startled. "I didn't hear you."

"I'm sorry, I should have cleared my throat or grabbed your ass," She chuckled. If it was Paulie, I said to myself, he would have cut a fart to warn us that he was leaving his house.

"I saw Frankie towing your car into your Folks driveway. It looks brand new," she said as she stood beside me starring into the engine compartment. "What's wrong with it?"

"I think the engine's probably seized up."

"What does that mean?" She asked.

I looked up from the engine and gazed into her violet blue eyes. "The engine won't start, it won't even turn over, could be that a piston cocked in one of the cylinders or a connecting rod seized on one of the crankshaft journals but hopefully with some help from Richie and Paulie and a bit of luck I believe we can get the thing running. If not then we'll replace the engine with another flathead.

You know something Sharly? Maybe that's not a bad idea, just buy a good engine from Benny Katz and drop it in."

"I'm sure you'll do fine, Stevie," She said smiling. "Just like the work you did on your Ford Coupe.'"

"Sharly, be sure to thank your Mom for letting me use part of her driveway. It's really nice of her."

"She's only too happy to, Stevie," Sharly said. "And there's plenty of room."

"Yeah I know." I said with a funny look on my face. Why would Sharly's mother do something like that for me? I knew that she liked me and Mrs. O'Sullivan my mother and my Aunt Louise were the best of friends. So close that Sharly's mother was beginning to speak with a Brogue. Maybe Mom an Aunt Louise could teach Ann O'Sullivan to speak Gaelic. "Why?"

"Because she wanted to, Stevie," Sharly said looking deeply into my sea green eyes. "Mom really likes you, and I like you more than Mom does. I wanted to tell you that when you gave me a ride home the other day."

"So that's what you whispered in my ear before you kissed me on the cheek?"

"Uh huh," She said as she looking at me. "I wanted to say it out loud… I wanted to scream it out, but being a lady I kept my voice to a whisper."

"It Saturday night, Sharly," I said changing the subject. "How come your not you out with Billy, or should I be minding my own business?" I said looking back down at the green shit the bed, flathead engine. I didn't wish to venture into unfamiliar territory asking her what had happened. It really wasn't any of my business.

"I broke up with him last night, Stevie. When you gave me a ride home the other day I made up my mind to tell Billy that it was all over. I couldn't go on seeing him when I'm in love with someone else and that's you Mr. Dyer." She said she as tapped on my nose with her finger to make her point. "I've been in love with for a long time you know."

Sharly just said that she was in love with me? I'm flabbergasted; Billy and Sharly had been going out for two years while she was in love with me? "I thought you and Billy were in...ah...like? I am sorry, Sharly," I said but I didn't mean it. I'm happy that she broke up with Billy Ryan. She was too good for him. Hell she was too good for everyone except me.

"Don't be, Stevie," She said shaking her head. "And not only because I was in love with you. I just couldn't take anymore of his stupid jokes and sexual innuendos. And you know, ever since he got his license and bought that pee yellow Buick Road Master from Bennie Katz he couldn't keep his hands off my body. He thought that I was an easy mark and now that he was driving his own car all he wanted to do was go parking at the Ducks or the Gore Estate, or making out in the back row at the Natick Drive-in."

"Are you sure you're in love with me?" I asked.

"Of course I'm in love with you, you dope. Everybody knew it but you. I'm surprised that your brother or Debbie Logan never mentioned it to you."

"She did drop a hint in a roundabout way,"

"Anyway it took me some time to get up the nerve, but when he called me a f-u-c-k-i-n-g c-u-n-t," She spelled out the words, "I knew I had enough of his crap."

"Why did he call you a...you know?"

"Because, when he made a play for my chest I slapped his hand away. He got upset and called me the "F" word and the "C" word and a teaser. I told him to take me home or I'm going to get out and walk!"

"Where did this drama take place, Sharl?" I asked. Now her story was getting interesting.

"We were parked at the Gore Place. He wanted to go to the Natick Drive-in but I told him I didn't feel like watching a stupid Elvis movie or a Godzilla flick."

"It a good thing your fight took place at the Gore, Waltham is a long walk to Waltham from Natick." I mused smiling.

I had to chuckle. Rosie and I spent many happy evenings parked at the Gore Estate my head resting on Rosie's pillows but I had never seen Billy's '52 piss yellow Buick, with the rotted out rocker panels parked there. The Buick looked like it was painted with a whisk broom. The Benny Katz, one hundred dollar junkyard special was as ugly as a mud fence but you could bone an elephant in the back seat of Billy's straight eight.

"So now that Billy's out of your life do think you would want to go out with me?" I asked looking at her.

"What are you talking about, Stevie?" Sharl asked looking at me with her hands on her hips. She looked as though she was about to slap me. "Think? I don't have to think about it, I've been in love with you for years Christ sake!"

"Okay, Sharly; I'm sorry for my poor choice of words," I apologized. "That was a dumb question."

"Yes it was, Stevie, but I still love you," She smiled.

"And I love you too, Sharly," I said as I took her in my arms and held tight against my body feeling the warmth of her breasts against my chest. I think I got lucky.

"Now where do we go from here?" I said gently kissing her on her warm soft lips. "Maybe we get married?" I joked.

"Not right now, Stevie, let's wait until we graduate, but I thought that maybe I could give you, Richie and Paulie some help with your car," Sharly said. "I could sneak you guys a beer from your Daddy's 'fridge," She giggled. "But I just want to be with you, even if it means being beside you in the front seat listening to the radio."

"After our friends go home and we wash our hands and clean up," I smiled. I wouldn't want to get grease on the front of her blouse I thought; wishful thinking on my part.

I felt a warm feeling in my stomach and my eyes began to water "I'll tell Paulie to clean up his mouth and go easy on the franks and bean on Saturday Night."

Sharly broke out laughing while I was trying to get my feet back down on the ground. She was a little shy and her face would turn bright red when she became embarrassed, but whenever Kuckie or Paulie told an off color joke she would laugh right along with everyone else. And when you worked at Gagnon's News Service you had to be one of gang and be opened minded.

Joe Gagnon would try to keep the swearing to a minimum at the paper office by fining us a nickel for every "fuck you"," you're full of shit". "You cocksucker" or a "mother fucker" would run you a dime. He was getting more money out of the girls than the guys! Some of the neighborhood girls from Grove Street or the upper part of Willow Street knew every filthy word ever muttered by the human race and when they were upset or when one of the guys would walk by and pat their ass they would begin cussing the guys out until Joe put them in their places. "Keep it up girls and you gonna find yourselves changing diapers for two dollars on a Saturday Night instead of making three times that much working for me."

Most of the girls hated babysitting. It meant instead of going out on Friday or out on Saturday night to the movies or dances at the Boy's Club they were stuck in a house watching some snooty nose kid at fifty cents an hour. On a good week babysitting one of the neighborhood girls could pull down three bucks. Working for Joe you were good for at least six dollars a week plus three bucks in tips.

"I love you, Stevie," Sharly said as she dropped my hand and embraced me. "And I've loved you ever since the seventh grade. But you were trying to make it with Nancy Le Clair; too bad you wasted all that time because she hated you worse than acne and the sad part was you didn't know it. I was so happy when they moved."

"You know Sharly, the old stutter," I said. "Love is blind."

"Yeah, and when it concerns you…love is dumb too," She said as she moved out of our embrace and took hold of my hands then continued. "Next to come down the Stevie Dyer turn-pike was big mouth Rita Falcone. She had to be the worst gossip in the neighborhood and everybody was her target. I had never heard her say a good thing or give a compliment to anyone including you. She thought that everyone was a jerk, and then who came along? Rosie

Beanbags with the chest. I can't for the life of me figure out how she could stand up straight with knockers as big as hers but I didn't want to come between you two, because I knew that your relationship with Rosie was going nowhere, but now that you're finished with Rosie Beans and Billy is color me gone…"

"Color me gone?" I said with a puzzled look. I thought that I heard them all. "That's a new one, Sharl. I had never heard color me gone before."

"Oh it's an Air Force term that the pilots used when there fighters went into afterburner mode. In a matter of seconds their air speed doubled," She said. "I heard my Dad use Color Me Gone when he had his pilot friends out to our quarters for a cook-out or for a few drinks."

"When the Merc's finished I may just paint "Color Me Gone" on her rear quarter panels. Thank you Major Timothy O'Sullivan."

"I know he would be very pleased, Stevie."

"You know we both wasted a lot of time with girlfriends and boyfriends while we both lived right across the street," I said as I gently squeezed her soft hands. "Now it's our time and when and if we go parking at the Ducks or the Gore Estate, the movies at the Natick drive-in or the back row of the Embassy Theater, and if I begin to take liberties you have permission to slap me silly."

"We'll see about that, Silly. I never loved Billy but I always loved you" She said as she put her arms around my waist again and gave me a warm gentle embrace.

"You know I really liked you but with my stutter, I knew that my chances going out with you were less than zero."

"You're wrong, Stevie, so wrong. When the guys at the paper office would tease you my heart would go out to you. I wanted to take you in my arms and let you know that everything was going to be alright." She said as she laid her head on my shoulder and kissed my neck.

"We wasted a lot of time didn't we?" I lamented.

"Yeah, we did," She lamented back. "But now I know that you love me and that means a lot."

"Yes I love you but your looks always intimidated me. I never thought that in my wildest dreams that you ever wanted to go out with me."

"Well you're handsome but your looks never intimidated me," Sharly as she pulled me hard against her body then gave me a long, warm, deep, open mouth kiss tongue and all.

O God, Charly, slow down, I can feel myself re-acting to her embrace. I don't want you to think you're ready to handle my erection so soon and I don't feature creaming my jeans in my folk's back yard and I don't want to have to do my own laundry.

"God Stevie, maybe we had better take it easy," She whispered. "I can feel your, well you know... Oh God I love you so damn much!" She cried as she reached down and ran her hand over the rise in my Levies.

While we were parked out in back yard sitting in the front seat of the 51 Monterey listening to the Arnie "Woo Woo" Ginsberg rock and roll radio program (the battery was new, I replaced the old battery in hopes that a new battery would spin the engine over; wrong again!) I had my arm around her waist her blond hair resting on my shoulder, when Richie Brady and Patti LeBlanc pulled into the driveway. It was later than we thought it was, but time does fly while they sitting in the front seat of my car making out listening to Elvis, Roy Orbison, the Everly Brothers, and the best rock and roll singers that ever came down the rock and roll turnpike. Richie and Patty walked up the driveway and though it was dark I didn't want to climb out of my Merc with the profile of my erection pressing against my tight fitting Levis.

"Aren't you getting out, Stevie?" She asked as she opened the passenger door the interior lights flooding the inside of the Merc.

"I will as soon as my muscle relaxes a bit," I answered as we both looked down at my lap.

"Did I do that, Stevie?" She asked looking at the front of my jeans.

"Well it wasn't Woo Woo Ginsberg." I said as Sharly closed the door, the interior lights went off and she move up close to me and laid her hand gently on my right leg about a quarter of an inch from my nuts.

"How was dinner?" Sharly asked Richie as Patti and Richie approached the Mercury. They made a nice looking couple. Richie was a tall, blond well built blue eyed Irishman. His mother and father came from London; the Irish section? Richie was soft spoken, funny, with a dry sense of humor. Patti was a tall, thin, blue eyed blond hair Canadian beauty from Montreal. She came from Quebec with her Mother and Father and her older brother James. James was an officer in Army Intelligence assigned to MACV headquarters, Saigon, Vietnam. He was a military advisor and a French translator. James spoke both Canadian and European French and understood some of the Vietnamese language if one he was addressing didn't talk to fast. This was when Vietnam was just a country, not a war.

Many of the Vietnamese could speak and understand the French Language due the French for over a century owning Vietnam, but most Americans would ask: Where in hell was Vietnam???

Patti had a beautiful French accent, and spoke perfect English. That's more than I can say for the rest of the "IN" crowd. On the opposite side of the coin was Paulie O'Neil. He was a rude, crude, tall, chain smoking skinny Irish kid that thought mother was half a word. But we all put up with him and his addiction to Marlboros. Lily would slap him on the back of his head every time he dropped a mammy jammer or stunk up the area with flatulence that originated from his somewhat questionable diet. But yeah, we all knew if someone put a "T" bone steak, mashed potatoes and a vegetable or a plate of franks and beans in front of him he would choose the franks and beans. Paulie had absolutely no class but we all loved him. But what really puzzled us, Paulie Whelan came from a good family. His father was a senior engineer in the Research and

Development Department at General Electric and his mother was a nurse at Waltham Hospital. He was an only child. Kuckie reasoned that once Mommy and Daddy Whelan took a look at their first born Baby Whelan they decided right then and there that Pauley was going to be an only child. "Then what was your folk's reason for having just you, Kuckie?" Paulie asked.

"Only one Savior to a family at a time," He came back at me.

"Not bad. The food at Richards is pretty good," She said then she looked inside the Merc. "Nice car, Stevie."

"Merci, Patti," I said as I tried out my junior year of high school French. I really sucked when it came to foreign languages.

"Not bad, Mon Ami," she said as she smiled at Sharly. "No Billy tonight? Is there problem maybe?"

"No Patti, we're through! Fini," Sharly said as she took my hand and raised it too her cheek.

"Are you serious?" Richie asked as he looked at Sharly then at me.

"Yeah, Richie," Sharly replied.

"We all knew that it was only a matter of time before you gave Billy the hook, Sharl," Paulie said coming out of nowhere. He and Lily parked across the street and walked around the lawn side of the house.

"You could have dropped a stink bomb to let us know that Lily and you were here." Richie said.

"Not with Sharly hanging around. She has too much class." Paulie joked as he took out his handkerchief and blew his nose. If the girls weren't here he would have blown his nose in his hand and wiped the snots on his pants. "Oh by the way, what's the difference between meat and fish? Anyone?" he asked shrugging his skinny shoulders. We all shook our heads. "Have you ever heard of a guy beating his fish?"

"Come on Paulie," Richie said laughing now we were all laughing. "Not in front of the girls."

"Okay, How about a clean one? How many niggers does it take to shingle a roof?"

"Will you cut the shit, Paulie!" Lily said bitching him out.

"Alright, alright. Okay, how many negro's does it take to shingle a roof?" He reiterated.

"Okay, Paulie," I said. "Tell us how many of our colored brethren does it take to shingle a house."

"It depends on how thin you slice them."

"I believe the word is thinly, stupid," Lily corrected him.

"Alright Lily: It depends on how thinly you slice them."

"How many Jewish jokes do you know, Paulie?" Lily asked. Lily was half Jewish and half Catholic but she put up with Paulie's Kike jokes because she liked him but she only put up with his rude and crude sense of humor.

"What's the difference between and Jew and a pizza?"

"Come on Paulie," Kuckie said as he finally arrived with Cookie Freidman. Cookie was Maxi's niece. "You told us that joke years ago at the news office."

"Oh hi Kucks," Paulie said as he spied Kuckie and Cookie walking up the driveway. "Where've you been for the last week?"

"We've been helping her old man," Kuckie said lighting an Old Gold filter tip. "He put in a new two ton refer unit in his store and we've been helping him move his meat."

"That reminds me of a Jewish meat joke," Paulie said wrapping his arm around Cookie's shoulder.

"Kiss my Jewish ass you dumb Irish Catholic asshole!" Cookie said pushing him away giving him dirty look.

"It was gonna be clean, Jewish meat joke, Cookie."

"No it won't be you friggin' reprobate!" She spat at him. "You wouldn't know a clean joke if came up and bit you on your Irish Eyes Are Smiling foreskin!"

"I ain't got no foreskin, Sweety," Paulie said. "I got snipped when I was born.

"I hope the doctor had his glasses on." Cookie said giving Paulie a sarcastic toothy grin.

"He did," Lily said winking at Cookie.

"What did Cookie's father do when his butcher shop burned down?" He said as he looked around at his audience for a reply. "No one?" He asked.

"He grabbed his meat and beat it." Cookie said supplying the punch line.

"Are you sure that you and Paulie aren't related?" Lily asked looking at Cookie.

JULY 4 1959:

"Sharly, why don't you drop by the folk's house tomorrow morning and we can drive over to the Common together, Mom, Dad, Tommy, Debbie and Aunt Louise was spending a few days over the 4th up at Rockport?" I decided to house sit. I was staying home so I could open the store the day after the 4th. Maxi and his family were spending a week on Long Island…the Hamptons.

"What time is good for you?" Sharly asked as we lay down facing each other on the sofa on the screened in front porch listening to my Dad's portable radio. She had a bare leg placed across my hips. We were both wearing shorts and I had my tee shirt wrapped around my neck.

"Around ten or so," I said running my hand up and down her smooth, firm thigh. "I'll leave the front door open."

"I love you, Stevie," She said caressing my cheek. "And you have no idea how much I love you. You're everything I had ever dreamed of. I still have to pinch myself every time we're together and I still can't believe we're here on your folks porch stretched out on the lounge chair."

I pulled her close feeling her large soft breasts pressed against my bare chest her hand now massaging my back. We were both sweating. "I can and if I wasn't such a putz…"

"What is a putz, Honey?" Sharly asked as she was now caressing my ass. "I heard Maxi call you a putz."

"It's Yiddish. It means that you're an asshole and maybe I was a putz but we are together and I love you more than God. And I will love you for the rest of my life. I promise."

"Don't say you love me more than God, Honey," She said looking at me. "I am the Lord thy God; thou shall not have false gods before me."

The First Commandment just kicked in, "Sorry God."

"Promise me that you'll keep your promise?" She whispered in my ear her crotch pressed hard against my thigh.

"Yes I promise, Sharly. I'll always be here for you."

The next morning I climbed out of bed; it was eight thirty, dressed in faded cut off jeans, sneakers, a tank top then drove down to The Sandwich Shop for a Boston Herald and a large cup of coffee, drove home, took the paper and my coffee into the bathroom took a crap, read the paper finished my coffee then went back to my room, removed my clothes, grabbed a clean towel from the hallway linen closet wrapped it around my waist, brushed my teeth, shaved and jumped into the shower. I had a half hour before Sharly was due to arrive so I was taking my time. With my shower finished I dried myself, hung the towel on the towel rack and left the bathroom. There was no reason to wrap my towel around my waist there was no one home. Wrong! I walked out of the bathroom and there was Charly walking up the hallway that led to the kitchen and the bathroom. When my Dad designed the house he didn't want guests coming thru the living room. That's how he had the house built so the front door opened into the hallway. I smiled and said good morning and I was so glad to see her that I didn't realize that I was standing facing her stark naked.

"Good morning, Stevie. Lovely to see you again," She smiled looking down at me. "And it's lovely seeing you for the first time too." She said as she gave me a gentle pat.

"Oh Christ," I said looking down at my naked frame. "I'll be right back."

"I'll be in the kitchen, Honey," She said as she stopped in front of me, wrapped her long thin fingers around my soft, droopy young man hood, gave it a gentle pull, let it go, smiled then walked into the kitchen.

I dressed in tan Bermuda shorts, a light blue Polo shirt sneakers and then walked into the kitchen feeling a little self conscious. Sharly was in the kitchen leaning against the counter giggling into her hands her clothes thrown over the back of one of the kitchen chairs. She was nude.

"Okay, Honey, we're even. I only wanted to show you what I have for you," She said as she slowly walked around the kitchen giving me an incredible eye full. "And I just wanted you to see me in the nude. I hope you liked it; I don't often get this brave."

"God you're gorgeous, Sharly" I said as I gazed hungrily at her beautiful nude body. "Thank you."

"So are you, Stevie" She said as we embraced. "And thank you too." She said as she slowly dressed never taking her eyes off me.

We both laughed as we talked about what had transpired in the folk's kitchen as we drove over to the Waltham Common. "Yeah know, Stevie? When I walked into you folks hallway and saw you naked and the look on your face I about broke out laughing. You looked so funny, like a deer with its eyes in caught in the headlights, but you looked so surprised when I wrapped my hand your "thingy" then walked into the kitchen."

"My "thingy"?" I had to laugh at way she put my "thingy" into perspective. "That's new but cute."

"Alright, your manhood," She replied.

"You know, what you did to my "thingy" felt great. Maybe we should have hung around the house naked" I smiled. "But you showing me your beautiful body in the kitchen, well that had to take a lot guts."

"Some, but I wanted to do something to please you," She said as she put her arm around my neck and placed her right hand on the upper part of my thigh. "I really love you and I wanted you to see who you're going to be making love to and what I have to offer to you."

"I really love you too, Sharly," I said as I felt her hand moving further up my thigh. "But let's take it slow. You can keep doing what you're doing, and when it seems right then I'm going to enjoy loving you too, but let's try not to make any dumb mistakes. I want only the best for you because you deserve only the best."

"Oh Stevie," She sighed as she kissed my cheek while she ran her hands over the front of my Bermuda shorts found my wee, wee and gently traced its outline with her long thin fingers. "I really love you, Stevie. More than you could ever imagine."

We were all on the Waltham Common along with the rest of Waltham, enjoying, the 4 July celebration. It was a carnival and a show that came up from New Jersey that set up the rides and a penny arcade. The carnival looked like that it was something that came out of the early thirties. The rides looked like they were picked up out of a junk yard loaded on three flatbeds and hauled up the east coast to Waltham. The rides were rusty, the paint was peeling off the metal, the seats for the Ferris wheel ride were ripped but when everything was all set up it looked okay, especially at night when the ride was lit.

We were all sitting around a large round picnic table enjoying one of Paulie's favorite foods; hot dogs smothered with chili, onions, relish with side orders of French fries, onion rings, hamburgers, cheeseburgers, fried dough and huge bowl of re-fried beans. I had never had eaten or even heard of re-fried beans, neither had anyone else.

"Well dig in," Paulie announced as he munched on his first chili dog. In a rare show of generosity, he sprung for the whole spread. "Before it gets cold, try the re-fried beans, they're to die for!" I wouldn't want to be around Paulie later on. He finished all the leftovers including all the re-fried beans and the chili dogs.

He also paid for the Cokes, the Pepsi, the root beer, and the orange crush. The spread had to have run him ten dollars.

After our gourmet dinner we wondered about the common trying to decide what ride we would trust with our lives. Paulie and Lily chose the Ferris wheel, so did Richie and Patti. Kuckie and Cokie pitched pennies at the arcade, Tommy and Debbie finished their chili dogs and re-fried beans and headed for Prospect Hill for a hour or so of necking, they'll be back, and Charly and I opted to watch the rock and roll band that had set up on one of the forty foot flat bed trailers. The band, Jimmy Eller and the Little People drove all the way from Washington D.C. in two station wagons and a Dodge pick-up truck and were they good. Jimmy Eller was about six, six and the rest of the band the "Little People" were short. The shortest was the base player who was about six two.

The band did everything from rock to country rock to blue grass to gospel and to what we now we refer to as soul. Sharly and I sat on the ground for two hours watching the "Little People" and enjoying every minute of their concert. By the time the concert was in full swing there was standing room only. Central Square was closed to traffic on both on Main Street and Moody Street. The crowed spilled out onto the four streets surrounding the Common.

The next night there was another concert provided by Jimmy and his band on South Street between Brandies University and the J.L Thompson Manufacturing Company then at mid-night was an incredible fireworks display. The show lasted an hour with enough aerial displays to give everybody who was in attendance walking or riding home with ringing ears.

The Fourth of July morning, Waltham hosted a parade that began at Banks Square and marched down Main Street hung a right onto Moody Street and finished up in the Grover Cronin's parking lot. The parade featured politicians, Cub Scouts, Boy Scouts, Soldier, Marines and Airman from local bases marched in the parade, so did the little league, pony league, American Legion Band and the VFW. Then Came the Hot Rod Clubs from all over New England, New York State, New Jersey, Pennsylvania and even Canada. There had to be over two hundred cars from all over the eight states and our friends from the north. The monster V-8 engines that had enough energy to power a third world country sounded great, low rumblings from the headers and the Hollywood muffled straight pipes.

And on the Independence Day morning there was a doll carriage and a decorated bicycle parade then a breakfast served in the Hovey Hall hosted by the Elks, the American Legion and the VFW. For fifty cents you got juice, coffee, bacon and eggs, pancakes and toast. The chow line went all the way past Wilson's diner. It was the only day of the year that Bobby Wilson closed his restaurant.

Before anyone in our crowd had our driver's license, most Friday nights we would all walked uptown and go to the movies. We would arrive at the movies early so we all could get the last row of the Embassy Theater and do some serious making out. Back then Sharly was going out with Billy Ryan, Tommy was going out with Debbie Logan, Richie was with Patti, Kuckie was going out with a real farm animal; Freda Ross, They went out for a year or so, then Freda and her family moved down to Florida and Kuckie took up with Cookie Friedman.

I was still in love with Nancy the "Twat" LeClair, but I was going out with Rita Falcone. (Mom really wasn't all that happy. She wanted me to go out with a nice Irish girl not a Dago). Rita and I liked each other and she never criticized my stutter. She was the first girl in the neighborhood to wear a bra, (That was before Rose Lyn Leonardi came onto the scene). It seemed that most of the Italian girls began to develop knockers when they were in their early teens. Rita worked right along with the rest of us hustling news papers for Gagnon's News Office at Raytheon's Gate 6.

And there was Gail Hartwell who also worked for Joe Gagnon. Gail was tall, thin nice looking girl with a strange sense of humor but she was a wonderful artist who liked to draw farm animals with pen and ink; especially horses and she didn't leave anything to the imagination. If it was a stallion then she had the jewels prominently put on display and if the dog she was painting was sitting and had a red chubby on display she made sure the dog's dick was on the canvas. There was a rumor going around the neighborhood that her brother posed for her in the nude when he was sixteen or seventeen.

Unfortunately her Dad, who worked for the Raytheon took a position with Martin Marrietta Missile Division so Gail and her Mom, Dad and her brother Jason pick-up stakes and moved to Georgia.

But Paulie with his franks and beans addiction would sit in the middle of the row with Lily and fart. Not thunder coming out of his ass but SBDs. Silent but Deadly. The old one cheek sneak. "Christ Paulie," kuckie would hiss. "Take that shit outside, will you? What are you trying to do, empty the theater?" How Lily put up with him, only she and God knew.

"When are you going to start pulling the engine down?" Richie asked as Paulie lit a Marlboro then gazed into the engine compartment.

"Tomorrow morning right after eight o'clock Mass," I replied as I smiled at Sharly. "You two gonna be around?"

"Yeah," Richie said. "I'll be here around ten."

"Paulie?"

"I'll be here, right after a hearty breakfast of five or six hard boiled eggs and beans soaked in beer and six or seven bangers." He said showing us a toothy smile. With all the shit he ate and all the butts he smoked he still had nicest teeth in the neighborhood.

"How about you Kuckie?" Paulie asked. "You'll be here right after Mass I assume?"

"Yup, right after eight o'clock Mass at the Temple Shalom!" The Kuckster said grinning, his sizeable honker placed about an inch from Paulie's turned up nose.

"Now make sure that if you bring Cookie along," Paulie said grinning back. "And if she gets bored, I'll bring along a box of Milk Bone dog biscuits, take her off her leash and toss the dog biscuits around Stevie's Dad's back yard. She'll love it."

"Kiss my Jewish ass you thick Irish Mick!" Kuckie shouted. I thought that Kuckie was going to punch Paulie out but he just looked at me then at Richie gave Paulie the finger turned and walked down the driveway. I followed him to his car, I was as pissed at Paulie as Kuckie was but I wanted try and cool him off. "Come on Kuckie, cool off. Paulie's like that with everybody, hell we've all been friends for years. Remember my stutter?"

"Yeah, Stevie, I know you got over your stuttering but I can't stop being being a Jew."

"Look Kuck," I said as I placed my arm around his shoulder. "We're all friends, okay? If Paulie wants to be an asshole which he usually is, his offences carry their own punishments, then get over it. We all know what kind of a jerk Paulie can be and we can't force him to change."

"Okay, Stevie, let's go back and check out your white elephant."

"Thanks Kuck," I said. "Let's go."

When we got back to my folks back yard, The Kuckster walked up to Paulie reached all the way back from Maggie's shit house and punched him in the mouth and when Paulie raised his hands to his bleeding split lips Kuckie kneed him in the nuts. Paulie hit the ground like he was shot.

Kuckie knelt down beside Paulie, it was obvious that he was in pain, one hand over his split lip the other holding his nuts. "I'm sorry Paulie," Kuckie said as he once again belted him in the mouth. "But you've been asking for this since I've known you… sorry."

"Alright," Paulie moaned. "Alright Kuckie. I'm sorry too, but I never thought you'd call me out. Christ!" He said trying to crawl to his feet. "We still friends?"

"Yeah, Paulie we'll always be friends." Kuckie said as he helped Paulie to his feet.

The next morning after Mass at Saint Jude's with Mom, Dad, Tommy and Debbie; Sharly was there with her mother and Barbara. The engine tear down I hoped was about to begin. I changed out of my Sunday Go Too Meetings and put on Levis, tee shirt, tennis shoes and went out to the back yard and looked over project Mercury. While I was leaning into the trunk of my '40 coupe' lifting my tool box loaded with Craftsman tools which are the best tools in the world as far as I'm concerned, Sharly walked up the driveway. She was wearing jeans, a short sleeved sweat shirt, black and white high top sneakers and her hair tied up in a pony tail. She looked great. "Hi Stevie, how are you?" as she greeted me with a smile and a quick kiss on the lips.

"Hi, Sharly. You looked nice dressed in your Sunday best," I said admiring her beauty. "How did I get so lucky," I whispered under my breath as I knelt down in front of red Craftsman's tool box.

"Because I made it happen," she said as she knelt down beside me, looked at me and said. "I love you Stevie."

"That's when I was at the height of my stuttering," I joked. "And you loved me even though I…"

"You had the most beautiful green eyes that I had ever seen. I loved your handsome face; every time I saw you chasing Nancy the stuck up little bitch with your tongue dragging on the ground or when you dated Rita or Rosie with the big ones, I would say to myself 'It's only a matter of time'."

"I was only across the street, Sharly…"

"I know, Stevie, but a lady doesn't go chasing after a gentleman no matter how much she loves him."

"Are they words from Mother O'Sullivan?" I grinned as I removed the socket tray from the tool box and looked at wrenches.

"No, Father O'Sullivan," Sharly's Dad was a USAF fighter pilot shot down over North Korea at the beginning of the "Police Action". The Major's body was never recovered. Sharly was only eight years old when she lost her Dad. Her sister Barbara was a year older. Barbara and Sharly could pass for twins. The only difference was that Sharly was two inches taller than Barbara and Barbara had larger breasts. But who noticed…right?"

We climbed to our feet, smiled and began charting out a plan of action. I borrowed Chilton's repair manual from Dad's brother-in-law my Uncle Bill. The manual covered automobile repairs from 1946 to 1956. The book explained, step by step how to tear down and rebuild engines, transmissions, rear differentials, repair brakes, steering, everything that you needed to know when it came to repairing Ford, GM, Chrysler and every other automobiles manufactured in the U.S. and Canada.

The engine rebuild didn't appear all that complicated I said to myself as we both looked at the chapter on the flathead engines. The engine in the Merc was a little different from the flatty that was in my '40. The heads and the intake manifold had been modified, so was the position of the distributer changed. It was moved from the crab like design that was mounted in front of the engine to the side of the engine block. It was easier to change the points and set the timing.

"What are we going to do first Stevie?" Sharly asked as we stood close, my arm place around her waist and drew her close to me. "I want help out if I can."

"I don't really know where to begin, Honey. We play it by ear maybe but it looks like the first thing we do drain the radiator and flush out the block, then we can remove the throttle linkage, and oh yea, the battery. Ready?"

"You're the boss, Stevie."

"I hope you don't mind getting your hands dirty; a little grease under your finger nails?" I asked taking her hand and looking at her long thin fingers.

"Well, I can hand you the tools and read from the mechanics manual," She reasoned, "While you, Richie, Paulie, and Kuckie do the dirty work."

"Looking beautiful?" I said looking at her beautiful face and body.

"I'm not beautiful, Stevie," She replied then pretended to ignore me while she thumbed through the service manual.

"Yes you are, Sharly." I said. "So get used to it."

"You only say that because you love me," She said as she continued to flip through the pages of the service manual. "Right?"

"Everybody that we know says you're beautiful, because you are."

Sharly closed the manual, placed it on the fender of the Merc, turned to me, wrapped her arms around my neck and gave me a wet, tongue down my throat kiss while she pressed her gorgeous body hard against mine. I could feel myself reacting to her passionate kiss, so could she Sharly. "You feel good, Stevie; too good," She said as she backed off and looked down at the front of the rise in my Levis and smiled. "Let's cool it in case the guys show up early."

"Maybe they won't show up at all," I said as I placed my arms around her waist and held her in a warm loving embrace.

It was after one o'clock when Richie and Paulie showed up at my folk's house. Paulie looked as if he had been in a slaughter on Tenth Avenue brawl. Both of his lips were split, his nose was swollen and his eyes were black. "Christ Paulie," I said looking at his beaten to a pulp face. The Kuckster did all this with only two punches. "You look like hell. How do you feel?"

"Like I was shot at and missed shit at and hit. That fucking Kuckie had a right cross that could drop a horse!"

"Sorry Paulie," Kuckie said as he walked into my folk's back yard.

"You done good, Kuckie," Paulie remarked as he rubbed his nose. "Real good."

All the guys took their own cars. Richie had to leave at 3:00, to pick Patty up for dinner. The four of us didn't accomplishing all that much except for going over the repair manual and the tools we needed and that was about all we did. It was a nice, warm Sunday afternoon and none of us really felt like getting dirty or sweaty pulling apart a frozen flat head engine so we all sat in back yard on my folk's lawn furniture talking about what was the best way break down the engine. And from there we began talking sports; how the

Red Sox were doing, The Bruins just picked up a first draft choice from Toronto, and Boston was going to get a football franchise The Boston Patriots. Sharly excused herself stood up and began to walk home. I followed her hoping that she didn't feel as though she was being ignored. I caught up to her as she was crossing the street.

"Is everything all right, Honey?"

"I don't want you guys feeling inhibited with a young, pure as the driven snow, lady listening in on your guy talk but how would you like to do something maybe after dinner, Stevie?"

"Yeah, let's," I said as I walked her across the street holding her hand. "How about we take a ride into Boston and I'll show you where I work my second job."

"Oh yes, Steven, you must tell me all about your second job," She said as we climbed the porch steps and she faced me. "I believe you collect and transport money for a gentleman named Fudgie, I think that's what Patti referred to him as ah…Fudgie? What an unusual name."

"Fudgie's not his real name, Honey," I said. "No self-respecting Italian would name their son Fudgie."

"I'm just funning with you, Stevie," Sharly giggled while she gently patted my cheek with her long slim fingers. "Yeah a ride into Boston with you sounds like fun. I haven't been "in town" since Babs and I were little. That was when Dad was stationed at Hanscom Air Force Base. Mom and Dad would take us into Filenes and see the Toy Land Christmas display."

"Yeah, my Mom and Aunt Louise would take Tommy and me in there too. I'm surprised we all didn't run into each other."

"If we did then I would have fallen in love with you six years sooner."

"Yeah," I chuckled, "And we would have probably been married by now with three or four kids."

"You think?" Sharly asked.

"Say I pick you up around five, alright?"

"Five's good for me," She smiled than kissed me, gently, on the lips. "See yah, Stevie."

"See yah, Sharly."

After Sharly and I finished making our afternoon plans I returned home and back to the project at hand. Paulie, Richie and Kuckie were standing in front of the Merc staring into the engine compartment. "Well guys," I said leaning on the front fender looking at my friends. "What do you think?"

"You make a lovely couple," Richie said his elbows on the front fender holding up his head.

"No Paulie, the car. Think it's worth the time and effort?"

"Hell yeah," Paulie said. "If you don't run out of money."

"Not much chance of that happening, right Stevie?" Kuckie winked.

"As long as people keep on gambling," I said grinning.

"But you and Sharly do make a good looking couple," Richie said again. "And I can't believe that you never knew that Sharly had feelings for you?"

"No I never did."

"That's because our old buddy Stevie was too busy wallowing in Rosie's Bean Bags 44 magnums," Paulie said lighting a Marlboro. "A nice set of tits with a pretty face and a nice ass to go along with her yaboos is sorta hard to ignore, right Stevie?"

"Yeah, Paulie, Rosie was built," I agreed. "But I wanted someone who I could really fall in love with." I said as I smiled at Paulie then turned and looked down at the painted green seized engineering marvel.

Sunday dinner was New York sirloin steaks cooked on my Dad's outdoor charcoal grill. That was before outdoor grilling was popular. My dad picked up a grill from my uncle and Dad's brother-in-law's store. Eddie Cohan, Uncle Eddie was Mom's oldest brother and the owner of Cohan's TV and Radio Sales and Service and Cohan's Toys and Hobby Shop. Uncle Eddie and my dad were probably the first in Waltham to own a television set. The new TV sets were seven inch Philcos that weighed a ton and an optional magnifying glass placed in front of the screen. It made the picture looked grainy and distorted. The magnifying glass made all the TV personalities look like Bugs Bunny. That was the days when we could only tune in two stations, but the old man didn't give a shit. All he wanted the TV for was to watch the Red Sox and the New York Giants.

Sunday afternoon, my Dad would be out in the car port with the radio on listening to the Red Sox, his Manhattan on a doily on the hood of my mother's two tone green 1955 Ford two door Crest liner, the sirloin steaks on the grill. Dad was in his glory. He wasn't much of a drinker. He would have another Manhattan with his dinner and then it was off to the living room to fall sound asleep while the Red Sox or the New York Giants were on the box; that was before the Patriots came into the NFL. The Pats arrived in the fall 1960. Thank you GOD!

After dinner I walked across Dix Street, or as it was pronounced by most of the inarticulate; Dick Street. "You live on a street that was named after some guy's Wang???" I showed up at the O'Sullivan house hold at 5 o'clock sharp and me being a gentleman that I was, rang the door bell instead of climbing the stairs and knocking on Mrs. O'Sullivan' second floor apartment door. Sharly's Sister Barbara came down the stairs and opened the door. "Hi Stevie, come on up. Sharly's helping Mom with the dishes." I followed her up the stairs admiring her ass as it twitch beneath her thin, white shorts. It didn't look like she was wearing any underwear. Barbara was a year older than her sister but was just as pretty. If you didn't know better you could mistake them as twins. They looked more alike than Tommy and I did and Tommy and I were twins.

"Hi Sharly, Hi Mrs. O'Sullivan," I said as I followed Babs into the kitchen.

"Hi Stevie," Sharly smiled as she wiped off her hands.

"Hello Steven, how are you, dear?" Mrs. O'Sullivan smile. Mrs. O'Sullivan and my mother wanted nothing more than to see Charlotte and me together. Especially when Mom found out that I was seeing the beautiful, amazingly built Rose Lyn Leonardi

"Now you listen to me Steven," Mom would say in her rich Irish brogue. "I'm sure that Rose is a very lovely young lady, and your father and I know Vic and Winnie from bingo at church and they're lovely and so kind to the poor, but with the lovely Coleen Charlotte O'Sullivan," and the emphasis being on O'SULLIVAN! "Living right across the street, well Steven…"

"Mom, please listen to me, please! Sharly's going out with Billy Ryan…" I tried to explain.

"But," AND the emphasis was on the BUT, "She's not at all happy with her situation. Mrs. O'Sullivan and I are close and we do discuss our children."

"I would say your close. Mrs. O'Sullivan has a richer brogue than you do." I joked.

"Watch your silly mouth Boyo or I'll give you a clout with the back of me hand," She threatened me then broke out into a smile, her deep velvet blue eyes sparkling. Mom was an inch or two above five feet tall and Tommy and I were an inch over six feet tall. She'd need to get out a step ladder to give us a clout with the back of "me" hand.

"Mary; this is Anne," Mrs. O'Sullivan said excitedly over the phone. She called my mother right after Sharly and I left her house. "Barbara just told me last night that Charlotte broke up with Billy Ryan. Steven and Charlotte just left my house and were driving into Boston."

"Are you sure, Anne?" Mom breathlessly inquired.

"Sure as the day you were born, Mary Dyer." Anne O'Sullivan proudly announced. God she talked like she was born and raised in County Galway.

The trip was a pleasure now that Sharly was riding into the city with me. I took the regular route to Boston; that was before the

Mass Turnpike Extension was constructed. We traveled east along Main Street into Watertown Square, then onto Arsenal Street, to Storrow Drive, a right onto Cambridge then into Scollay Square, a left onto Hanover and a right onto Blackstone and parked across the street in front of Iaconio's Italian Social Club. "That, Sharly," I said pointing across the street, "Is where Fudgie Iaconio has his office and that's where I make my drop every Wednesday night and Saturday afternoon."

"You're not you afraid driving into this part of Boston with night coming on? The people walking the streets look, well you know kind of…well scary. The streets don't look all that safe to me," She said looking over her shoulder.

"Yeah, some are, but while I was running book for Fudgie, Richie, Pauly and I would drive into the square and walked the streets and the alleys and no one would bother us. We'd walk up Hanover Street

Then onto Cambridge Street and have a hot dog and a Coke at Joe and Nemos," I continued as I climbed out of my side of my coupe, then going around to her side and opened her door. "Come on, Sharly, I'll show you all the hot spots." I immediately realize that, that was a poor choice of words.

"What hot spots, Steven?!" Sharly asked as she stopped dead in her tracks and looked at me menacingly with raised eyebrows her hands on her hips.

That sounded like a fair question, now I needed time to come up with a credible crock of a bull shit answer. "Ah, you know; the where people go and have fun have a drink. Things like that." I tried not to sound too vague.

"Alright, I'll buy your story but hold my hand, please. And don't let go, pleeeese!" She cried as she looked at the ancient brick buildings that made up the Scollay Square section of Boston. "This is the oldest part of Boston," I said as we walked north on Union Street and turned right onto Salt Marsh Lane. "Right here is where the old Boston Lawyers had their offices before they relocated to Pemberton square. Go there now and the buildings are still standing," I explained trying to reassure her. "There's nothing to be afraid of, Honey. The street people won't hurt you. I know a few of them and they're all right."

"Are you sure?" She asked squeezing my hand.

"Yeah, I'm positive, now come on," I replied while we walked back to Hanover Street and then continued west toward Tremont Street.

"Is that the Old Howard?" she asked looking into the front door of the Casino Theater.

"No, Honey, the Old Howard is on Howard Street. The Casino is also called The Old Howard Casino to make the out of town tourists believe that they had actually been to the original Old Howard."

"Have you ever been inside the Casino, Stevie?" She said looking at the promotional pictures of the latest strippers and the coming attractions in their scantily attired levels of dress. Taffy O'Neil; Taffy had a set of knockers that were long and thin and she could probably throw them over her shoulders, then there was Lily lay, Peachy Keen and Busty Moran. Virginia Bell was appearing over Labor Day Week-end. Maybe I can get Richie, Paulie, Kuckie and Tommy to take in the show. The last time we made it to the Casino; Virginia was the feature attraction and the last ten minutes of her show she pranced across the boards wearing nothing but high heels and a smile. I'll spring for the tickets.

"Yeah, once or twice," I admitted, I didn't want to begin our relationship with a lie. But the truth be known, Richie, Pauley, my brother and Kuckie I had been to The Casino Theater many times. Paulie didn't want to go to a strip show alone. He'd feel funny and he said that he didn't like driving into Boston by himself but we knew he was a cheap bastard and didn't want to spring for his gas or any of us thinking that he was a pervert. No; Kuckie was the neighborhood pervert.

"Do you enjoy watching strippers doing what they ahhh, well you know?" She asked as she still looking at the posters.

"I'd rather watch girls taking off their clothes than guys taking off their clothes," I joked, my attempt at humor to defuse the tense situation went over like a fart in the confessional. If looks could kill I'd be laying on the side walk.

"How much do they take off?" She asked still staring at the pictures of the other scantily clad, full breasted exotic dancers. "Do they take everything off? Like right down to... hummmm... naked?"

Wow, another tough question. Maybe we should go back to my car and head on back to Waltham. I can't get into this much trouble back home. "No not really, you see more skin at the beach," I casually said as I hustled her along. "Beside I go there to listen to the music."

"You do?" She looked at me while she crinkled up her nose. "What kind of music do they play?"

"Snappy tunes like, ah, music to strip by; dancing tunes." Now I was really shoveling the shit. It was time to yank the boots up a little higher.

Next we visited Jack's Joke Shop that was located a door down from the Casino and looked at all the tricks and gags, the fake vomit, fake dog crap, wooden matches that when you light them they smell like someone had just broken wind. The matches really smelled rotten, dribble glasses, whoopee cushions, fart makers, cigarette loads that you stuffed into the cigarette and when the stupid asshole lit his cigarette it exploded destroying the butt and smokers eyebrows, but the and the best joke of all, the dead mouse in the water bottle that looked so damn real. I put one of them in the refrigerator to try and fake out Mom, but she was too smart to fall for something as juvenile as the dead mouse in the water bottle. The dead mouse in the water bottle sat in the back of the fridge until Mickey totally rotted away.

Once a month usually on Saturday night, before Tommy and I made the scene, the folks would drive into Boston and go to The Old Howard Theater with Uncle Eddie and Aunt Mandy. They loved driving into Boston, first dinner at Jacob Worth's in the theater district, a trip to Jack's Joke Shop was on the itinerary, Uncle Eddie was always looking for a good seller in his TV Sales Repair and Hobby and Toy Shop then a walk through Scollay Square, onto to Howard Street and a show at the Old Howard. Uncle Eddie would tell Tommy and me all about the comedians and the beautiful "dancers" going into detail about the shows. The Old Howard the best entertainment north of New York City. He would describe into detail, puffing on his Camels until Mom finally told Uncle Eddie to stop corrupting my son's souls.

"The store was amazing. I can't believe there are people out there that think up all these tricks and jokes," She mused as we walked out onto Hanover Street.

I had to laugh. "Where do you think they find these clowns?"

"I'm not sure I want to know," She said looking across the street at the Kelly and Hayes Gym.

"Right in neighborhoods like the one we live in. It's called street humor. One Bozo the clown tries to be funny and there're always trying to outdo each other. The competition is brutal out there!"

"Guys like Kuckie Cohen, your brother, Boogey Monaghan and Paulie?" Sharly said as she watched the people hurry by.

"Yup, just like Kuckie and Paulie and the rest of the street clowns. Come on, Sharly. The Old Howard is just up the street," She was still holding my hand but now it was out of affection, not from being worried that we would be attacked, mugged or raped.

And there we were, standing in front of a theater that was known all over the country and most of the civilized world. It was training ground for most of the comedians from The Marx Brothers, Milton Berle, Phil Silvers, Larry Storch, Sammy Davis Junior, Abbot and Costello, the Marx Brothers, Fred Allen, Red Buttons; the list goes on. "You know Sharly, in front of us stands the only building in

Boston that was closed by the Watch and Ward Society because they didn't want the good people of Boston viewing obscene performances or risky jokes. Right now we see more on the beach, but back in 1933 it was considered un-Christian."

"How come you know so much about Scollay Square and The Old Howard?" She asked as she looked at the front door.

"I've always been interested in the history of Boston and Massachusetts," I answered. "There's a lot of history in this section of the city."

"Can we go inside?" She asked now she was getting brave. She dragged me up the four granite steps and we both yanked wrought iron handles that were attached to the huge front oak door. "I don't know if can get the doors opened, Sharly. They've been closed for a long time." We tried again tugging on the door handles until the doors groaned and then relented. It took all our strength but we finally got one of the doors opened enough to slip through the opening and found ourselves inside the darkened box office. "Where's the light switch?" Sharly asked looking about the dark lobby.

"Around here someplace but we won't need it, the power and the water's been off for fifteen years," I explained as we gingerly walked up the stairs then through the opened doors that led to the aisle that ran through the center of the theater and up to the stage.

As our eyes became use to the dark we explored the theater walking between the moldy rotting seats and ended up in front of the stage. "Help me up on the stage, Stevie, I'll make believe I'm stripping for you and let me know if I'm doing it right," She giggled. "You're the expert."

"It won't just be for me, Sharly," I said looking at my finger nails trying to act nonchalant.

"Huh?" She said as she took hold of my hand and held it against her cheek.

"There are street people living up in balcony's seats of this Temple of Burlesque, Sharl. The homeless drunks, pot heads, voyeurs that would like nothing more than to see a beautiful, well built, young blond removing her clothes not only for me but an audience of perverts that haven't been with woman in years. Still wanna show them your goodies, Gypsy?"

"What's a pot head?"

"It's a person that smokes marihuana."

"You mean dope?" She asked.

"You got it, Love." I said.

"Let's get the hell out of here, Stevie," She said still holding my hand and both of us running up the aisle and through the doors leading to lobby. Panic is contagious.

Once we were outside and her breathing returned to normal she asked me what that rotten odor was? It smelled like a toilet. "The stink is from the vagrants that sleep in the seats. They use the floors for their own personnel bathrooms. They go out, beg a few dollars, buy a cheap bottle of wine, grab a couple of fifteen cent hot dogs from Joe and Nemos crawl their way up onto the balcony, eat their food, drink their bottle of cheap wine and pass out."

"How do they get up to the balcony, Stevie, through the front doors?"

"No, they climb up the fire escape and enter the building through an unlocked fire escape door."

"How do you know all this, Stevie, from working with Mr. Fudgie?" She asked looking towards the cracked opened doors that lead back into the dark abyss that was once an entertainment theater that brought laughs and enjoyment in a time that Boston needed a place to go for a laugh and a good time. First we had the great depression, than World War Two.

"No, not from Fudgie, Honey," I said as I turned Sharly away from the front of the old theater and strolled up Howard Street and then went right onto Stoddard Street, as I continued going over the history of The Old Howard. "My folks and my Uncle Eddie and Aunt Mandy would tell stories about the Square. At one time Scollay

Square was the place to be when you were looking for a place to have a good time and a few laughs."

"From what I've read in the Herald or heard on the news, Scollay Square's days are numbered."

"Yeah, you're right," I said with a lamenting tone in my voice. "Three years from now all the buildings in Scollay Square will be demolished to make way for the new government center. Two hundred years of Boston history gone because the Square doesn't fit in, in the new Boston's future. This place is the oldest part of Boston and this is where all of Boston's early history took place!"

"I didn't realize that you were so passionate with Boston's history."

"Look at what they did to the West End," Now I was getting worked up. "They said that they were going to replace the rundown neighborhood with new and up dated apartments, but did they? No! They move the people out tore down their home and built expensive hi-rise apartments. Too bad folks! Enjoy the rest of your lives!"

"Take it easy, Honey," Sharly said trying to sooth my pissed off attitude with a gentle kiss on the cheek.

I told her that I was sorry, I just felt sorry for the people that the BRA had kick out of their homes.

"Isn't this the way we drove into Boston, Stevie?" she noticed as we turned right and walked out onto Cambridge Street and stopped in front of Joe and Nemos.

"Yeah, this is Cambridge Street. This is one of the few streets that'll survive the destruction of The Square. Every building from where we stand to the harbor except Faneuil Hall and Quincy Market will be gone. That includes The Old Howard, Tremont Row, Hanover Street, Cornhill and Brattle Street. All of it gone in a heartbeat." I was beginning to get hot under the collar again. Slow down shithead, I said to myself. It's too late to change what's going to happen in the Scollay Square section of Boston.

"Don't take it so hard, Honey," Sharly said as she soothed me with a smile and kissed on my cheek again. "Maybe they'll change their mind and build the government center someplace else."

"Yeah I'm sure they will, right on the banks of the Charles River and right in the middle of Grover Cronin's parking lot."

"You think that'll happen?" She chuckled as she turned and faced me.

"No not really," I answered then kissed her on her soft, warm, full lips."

Before leaving for home I acquainted her with rest of Boston, from News Paper row on Washington Street then onto Tremont Street, right on Park Street, left on Beacon Street. We paused in front of the State House. Sharly told me she had never seen the State House, most people that lived outside of Route 128 had ever seen the state house. Then we turned left onto Arlington Street and right on Commonwealth Avenue. "I didn't realize Boston was that small," she said as we cruised through Brighton, Watertown and back to Waltham. "I had pictured it the size of New York City."

"Actually Boston that we have now is about three times larger than it was when the Pilgrims landed."

"Yeah I know, I read the story about Boston's history from some of many books in the history department in the base library. That was while Dad was stationed at Hamilton Air Force Base. There were three books about how and when they filled in the Back Bay. It was amazing that they could fill that much tidal basin and swamp with such rudimentary implements.'"

"Good old Yankee ingenuity I suppose," I mused mostly to myself.

"What else would you like to do, Sharly?" I asked as she slid across the narrow seat and placed her head on my shoulder.

"I don't know, Stevie," She said as she nuzzled her face in my neck. God that made my eyes feel funny and caused my throat to itch. Rosie never made me feel the way Sharly made me feel and Rosie and I did a lot of nuzzling.

"How about we begin tearing down your Merc's engine?" I teased as she rested her hand on my right thigh about an inch south of my gonads.

"Not tonight, Steve. I have something a bit more romantic in mind."

It was almost dark when I drove the coupe' into the Gore Estate parking lot. Except for the sight seers we were the only couple who was not looking at the scenery. I didn't want to come across as a horny teenager making a play for her tits, though Sharly had her hand on my lower stomach; She had way too much class for me or anyone else thinking about groping her. I glanced at her profile as she looked straight ahead. She looked like she was in deep thought, probably wondering if she was stuck with another Billy Ryan. I hoped not. I had to much respect for not only her but for myself. Sharly was no Rosie Bean Bags. She wasn't the type to lift up her blouse and show me her tits.

"Is everything alright, Sharly?" I asked laying my hand over hers that was about a half inch north of my teen hood. "Would you like me to take you home?"

"No Stevie, I don't want you to take me home," she answered turning abruptly and faced me. "I want you to take me in your arms and hold me, Honey. Just hold me. I've waited so long for right now. I love you Stevie," Her eyes tearing.

"I love you too, Sharly," I whispered into her ear as she melted into my arms her lips searching for mine.

While Sharly and I were making up for lost time who shows up? Kuckie Cohen and Cokie Friedman arriving in his two door white and turquoise Olds Rocket 88. Kuckie brought his white walls to dusty, abrupt, all four wheels locked up halt. The crazy bastard almost ran into the barn.

Aw shit I said to myself. This was their first time we were alone. "Now what in hell does the asshole want?" I asked looking at Sharly. I was clearly upset.

"Stevie, Kuckie's your friend!" Sharly scolded me. "Watch you language!"

"Sorry."

"Stevie," Kuckie shouted as he climbed out of his car and walked around to the driver's side of my '40 coupe'. "You have a problem old Buddy, Billy Ryan's looking for you. He saw you and Sharly leave for Boston!"

"Yeah, so?" I said

"Yeah, so he's aiting waiting in Rah Tracy's back yard," Kuckie replied his breathing came in short spurts as he look at me his eye the size of saucers looking scared. "Rah asked Billy what he was doing in his back yard and he told Rah as soon as you brought Sharly home he was going to beat the sh… I mean take care of you for moving in on his girlfriend!"

"Where and when does he want to try to beat the shit out of me, Kuck?"

"Anywhere you want but Rah told Billy, not to screw with you, because you could take his fat ass down town and back before you knew what was happening!"

"This is not what I had in mind when I broke up with Billy; two guys fighting over me! I never wanted this happen," She cried looking at Kuckie than at me.

"I'll handle Billy, and there's not going to be anyone fighting over you," I assured her. "Billy's just talking mad. I'll cool him off than talk with him. Besides I never had a fight in my life."

"You haven't?" She seemed surprised. "You look like you could take care of yourself. Especially with all the years that you stuttered and all the teasing that you had to put up with."

"I suffered in silence and because I don't like fighting. Yeah I could take him down town but I wouldn't want to." I said trying to reassure Sharly. If it came down to snapping assholes like a couple of fools, I could mop the street with Billy's chubby ass.

"He's really hot to trot, Stevie" Kuckie said looking at Sharly then at me. "Rah told Babs and me that Billy was really pissed, sorry Sharly, mad. But just stay cool, Stevie, and let things work out." Kuckie said as he turned and walked back to his Olds.

"Come on Stevie, take me home. I want to talk to Babs."

"Let's go."

"We'll be right behind you." Kuckie shouted as he hurried back to his Olds.

I brought my coupe to a screeching halt in front of the O'Sullivan home Sharly opened her door jumped out. Babs was sitting on the front porch talking to Billy Ryan. When Billy spied Sharly and me jumping out of the coupe' and heading for the front steps, I was on the run, he held up his hands. "I don't want to fight with you, Stevie," he said; he was scared. "I was mad, I don't like losing, but I acted like a jerk and I'm sorry, Charlotte! I won't bother you no more,"

"Anymore," I corrected. My hackles went up when someone butchered the English language.

"Anymore," he said.

"Billy," Babs chimed in. "If you want to begin dating me, you're going have to learn to control your temper, you got that?" She was scolding Billy like he was a five year old. "And you need to take off some weight!"

I looked at Sharly then at Babs and then at Billy. "I don't believe this crap!" Sharly exclaimed. She has to be pissed. Sharly would'nt say crap...even if she had a mouth full. "You went from wanting kick Stevie's ass to asking my sister out and all this in less than three hours? You work fast Billy! Do you know that my sister's two years older than you?"

"Actually she's one year older than me, Sharl. I lost a year when I transferred from Saint Charles to Waltham High," The medium height hefty red head explained.

"Then you're eighteen?" Sharly asked.

"Yeah, I'm a year older than you."

It was a match made in Heaven. Billy and Babs hit it off right away, but she made it clear that she wasn't going to take any of his shit. Billy was always a wise ass, smart mouth tubby bastard and he wasn't even from the Bleachery! He grew up in the south side of Waltham and would get his ass kicked on a regular basis. His problem was he didn't know when to keep his mouth shut. You'd think he'd learn. One good thing about getting hit in the head with a baseball bat, it feels so good when it stops.

The south side guys were tough but as long as you weren't looking for trouble you were cool. In fact I had friends from the South Side but not Billy; he'd upset one of the guineas and his fat ass would end up in the gutter. None the guys in the Bleachery or the South Side could ever figure out what Sharly had had seen in the fat assed Billy Flynn. She was so pretty and he was a cute but pudgy jerk. Well Barbara turned him around. He lost weight, took up running and swimming, at the Boys Club, worked out in the gym and after six month of exercising and getting himself in shape, nobody but nobody wanted to screw with Billy Flynn. Not even me. He dropped his wise assed attitude, and though he was a year older than the rest of us and came for the South Side, we all made friends with him. If we were friendly towards him than maybe some of Barbara's class and intelligence would rub off on his wise ass. I was right Billy spent most of his free time either at work, the gym or with Barbara O'Sullivan. It definitely was a match made in Heaven. And nobody from the South Side ever screwed with Billy Ryan again because thanks to Barbara O'Sullivan, he was never there.

TUEDAY,
MAY 17, 1960
GRADUATION DAY:

The prom was last Friday night and it was a night never to be forgotten. The Waltham High school parking lot looked like a Rod and Custom show. I had my Mercury Monterey shining like a wet dick in the moon-light, Tommy's '56 Crown Vick looked like it was just driven off the show room floor, and Kuckie's Olds Rocket 88 was sporting a new candy apple red paint job. Yeah the senior prom was the place for the guys to show off the iron and girls to show off their looks. Even the buffalo's looked good. Sharly of course was the most beautiful girl on the dance floor, but Rosie caught most of the attention. Both the guys and girls looked at her with stunning approval or maybe a little envy. She was wearing a spectacular light blue satin gown that displayed some of her physical attributes. Stay away from rock and roll, Rosie we don't want your tits jumping out of your low cut evening gown. Yeah Rosie was the center of attention but Frank didn't seem to mind and he looked good in his tuxedo. He spent part of the evening talking with Vocational School auto repair and auto body teachers and students.

Now at last graduation night rolled around. The graduating class of 1961 had been assembled in the Embassy Theater lobby then all three hundred and thirty-five graduates were led, dressed in blue caps and gowns to our respective seats, and on the stage sat some of the Waltham's dignitaries; the mayor, superintendent of schools, the high school principal and the governor of the Commonwealth of Massachusetts. What in hell was the Governor doing giving a speech to a bunch of seventeen and eighteen year olds who couldn't vote? Out stumping? Anyway, the speeches were brief, but someone had to wake the mayor and let him know he was on next. Austin Rhodes had to be in his eighties. John McDevitt, the School Super was also brief. He needed a drink, but the best speaker was Bill Gallagher, the high school principal. All the students loved Mr. Gallagher. He would greet the students by name, ask how the folks were doing, did I finally get the Merc running. He made it his business to get to know all of his "kids". Mr. Gallagher had the smile that would light up any room that he walked into, but if there was a student that was always in trouble or acted like an asshole, he'd come down on you. Yeah, he'd be fair, give you a plenty of space, but don't push him or you'd find yourself trying to explain to your Mom and Dad why "Mr. G" wanted to see them with the offending son or daughter as soon as possible.

Following the graduation ceremony we all went to the graduation parties that were held across the city but the best party was held in Mr. Carol's back yard. John Carol was the physical education teacher and the Waltham High School football head coach. Mr. Carol was the toughest so-of-a-bitch to ever come down the pike. He stood six feet six inches tall and weighed in at a lean raw boned two hundred and twenty-five pounds. He graduated from Holy Cross and went on to play football with the New York Giants and when the war broke out he enlisted in the Army Air Corps as a private. Following basic training he went to OCS, graduated and went on to flight school. He flew B-17's out of England, was shot down over Germany spent two years in a POW camp and when the war was won he went on to teach American History at Waltham High and when the Phys Ed position opened with the retirement of Jack Leary who was a lush Mr. Carol became the Phys Ed teacher. John finally retired in 1988.

From John Carol's party we drove over to Judy Marsh's folk's house and that's where Paulie got hold of a bottle of Mr. Marsh's Crown Royal picked up a large glass in the Marsh family pantry poured the better part of a full glass of booze knocked it back and proceeded to get shit faced. We all could handle a couple of beers but now asshole Paulie put the glass down was swilling it right from the bottle. Judy's folks were home but were not paying that much attention to the graduates, they were having another party in their back yard and they all were drinking too. Paulie went right from sober to shit faced then right to sick, puking his guts out all over sidewalk in front of the Judy's folk's house. "Come on Paulie," Richie said as he tried to get Paulie into my Merc. Trying to move Paulie, who was sitting on the sidewalk puking between his legs turned out to be a real mess and he smelled like shit.

"Let's see if we can get a garden hose from Mr. Marsh and wash him down," Richie suggested as he looked at Paulie and shook his head.

"Good God, Stevie," Billy Ryan exclaimed as he knelt down beside Paulie with Babs looking over his shoulder. Babs really encouraged Billy to clean up his mouth. So far it was working.

"Why, what's the matter Billy?" I asked looking down at Paulie. "Did he die?"

"No, Stevie," Billy groaned, "But he shit fucking his pants!"

"Billy!" Babs said giving him a slap on the back of his head. "Watch your South side mouth!" Once in a while Billy would slip and fire off the "F" bomb.

"Sorry Honey."

"Aw shit!" Richie said as he rolled his eyes. "Let's roll him onto Judy's lawn and pick him up in the morning.

"We can't leave him passed out on the lawn all night, Richie," I said. "Not with a load of shit in his pants."

"Why not?"

"Come on Richie, cut it out! Give us a hand!"

"I hope he's through puking," Sharly said as she helped Richie, Patty, Billy and me as we tried loading his shitty ass into the back seat.

"Yeah, so do I," I said. I had just finished the Merc's interior and I didn't want asshole Paulie puking on my new mohair seat covers.

"Let's put him in the trunk," Billy suggested as he used his newly found strength as an asset.

"He's liable to die from asphyxiation," I reasoned.

"Leave the trunk open," Sharly suggested. "It's only a short ride to his house."

"Alright, let's dump him in the trunk," I said giving her an approving nod.

We finally got his drunken shitty ass into the Mercs humongous trunk then Sharly and I drove his drunken ass home. He was half awake when we helped him out of my trunk and laid him out the porch floor. I was going to have to fumigate the Merc when I got her home. Lily followed us to the O'Neil household driving Paulie's car. Paulie woke up the next morning on the front porch floor with a hangover that would kill a horse. Whiskey was good for some real beauties.

My Uncle David, Mom's brother, died young. He was a big whiskey drinker but it wasn't the whiskey that killed him. He came home loaded one night mistook the cellar door for the kitchen door, fell down the cellar stairs, fractured his skull and broke his neck on the cement floor. He didn't have a chance. His wife called the fire department an ambulance was dispatched but when the medics arrived examined his body they told my Aunt Lizzie that my Uncle David was dead. He never felt a thing.

Lily stopped by that afternoon to drop off the stiff's car. Paulie's mother explained to Lily that her son wasn't at this time entertaining visitors. Not even God if he should make an appearance. Paulie was feeling a bit under the weather. That's a nice way to say that he was still hung over.

"Yeah, he had a tough night, Mrs. Whelan," Lily said.

"How much did he have to drink, dear?" Mr. Whelan asked as he walked out onto the porch, folded his well muscled forearms across his chest and looked at her with arrows shooting from his eyes.

"Not all that much, Mr. Whelan," Lily lied. "He's just not use to drinking the hard stuff and he drank too fast."

"I'll tell him that you dropped by dear and thank you for dropping off his car," Mrs. O'Neil said as she took the keys, patted Lily's hand then turned and went back into the house. "I'll tell him to call you when he's feeling better, alright?" Mr. Whelan winked then followed Mrs. Whelan into the house.

The following evening we were all sitting in my folk's back yard, Dad was cooking hamburgers, hot dogs, Mom made up a large bowl of potato salad, a large bowl of tossed salad, there were also bags of potato chips dip and a large cooler filled with beer and soda. Mom, Dad and Aunt Louise were sipping Manhattans, Uncle Eddie and Aunt Mandy were drinking VO and ginger and my Grandfather was nipping on Jameson's Irish whiskey.

It was the graduation party following last night's graduation party. It was just for the friends in the neighborhood. Ann O'Sullivan and her gentleman friend, Mark Roberts was there too. So were Kuckie and Cookie. Sharly told me that Mr. Roberts was the only man she had been out with since her husband was lost. Mark Roberts was a tall, raw boned six foot former Marine who served in the South Pacific during World War Two. He was a friendly gentleman with a quick smile and nice easy funny sense of humor, who enjoyed a good drink and a good joke. He fit right in. He chuckled when he took the Bottle of Black Label I offered him, thanked me and when he finished his beer he switched over to VO on the rocks. Richie, Patty, Paulie and Lily finally showed up. Pauly was still feeling "under the weather".

"It looks like your friend is still getting over from last night's celebration, Stevie," Mr. Roberts smiled. "He's way too young to be drinking that much."

"You got that right, Sir," I agreed. "But Paulie enjoys taking life to the limit if it didn't cost too much."

Mark nodded his head in agreement then walked over to his love; Anne O'Sullivan and sat down beside her.

I often wondered why Mrs. O'Sullivan waited so long to begin dating. She was still a beautiful woman. Sharley said that it took her mother years to get over her husband's death. She thought that just maybe her fighter pilot husband might be still alive and held in a prison camp. But when the prisoners were sent home following the Korean War Timmy wasn't with his buddies.

"How are you feeling Paulie?" I said handing him a bottle of Black Label and a church key. "Boy was you ever sick!" I said busting his ass, "You were blowing chunks, not Chunks the dog, all over The Marsh Family's front lawn and you also shit your pants. Billy Ryan suggested that we put you in the trunk of my Mercury, and I went along with his wishes. Richie wanted to leave your drunken ass on Mr. Marsh's front lawn but I said no. Drink up, Paulie. AND I hope you took a shower and changed your fudged up under ware."

"I did so kiss my ass, shit head," Paulie whispered as pulled down about half of his beer on his first swig.

"Glad I could help, Paulie." I said placing my hand around his narrow shoulders. "Lily. Keep an eye on the lush, will you? I don't want to stuff him in the trunk of my Merc'. There's plenty of room but not a lot of room for a toilet. And I don't want you throwing up in my two door."

"Well thanks a-lot, Stevie" Paulie said throwing me a sarcastic grin.

"Think nothing of it Paulie," I said.

"I sure could go for a cigarette but I don't believe my stomach could handle it," Paulie said.

"Then why not try to give them up, old buddy," I suggested. "It could save you a little money."

"I suppose I should. Lily's been on my ass about my smoking."

"Gotta keep the ladies happy, ya know," I said. That was the day that Paulie put the Marlboros away and began smoking stogies.

The following Saturday afternoon I picked up Sharly and we drove into Boston. I wanted her to meet "The Man". I had to make my bi-weekly drop and get paid so I talked Sharly into going with me. When I first brought up the subject of meeting my boss she objected. She was sure that Fudgie would not want her going with me to meet him because of the nature of the business. "Stevie, I'm sure that Mr. Fudgie doesn't want to meet me. He's probably too busy to spend his time meeting me. I'll wait in the car."

"Come on Sharly," I said. "If Fudgie ever knew that I left you in the car by yourself while I was in here taking care of business he'd be most upset. Please?"

"Okay but I don't want to do anything that will get you in trouble."

"How in hell are you going to get me in trouble?" I said taking her hand and walking across Blackstone Street. "Come on, Fudgie's a nice guy, you're gonna love him."

I opened the large, heavy oak door, led Sharly into the Italian American Club and introduced her to Frankie Rosa. He was behind the bar wiping glasses. It was in the middle afternoon but the place was almost empty. Frankie flipped the intercom and announced to Fudgie that I and a beautiful young lady were here to see him.

"Have them come in Frankie," Fudgie said in his deep, soft, mellow voice.

I knocked on Fudgie's door then opened it and held it open for Sharly. She looked at me with fright in her eyes then walked by me and entered Fudgie's large office. He was sitting behind his large mahogany desk his hands behind his head as he leaned back in his large leather chair a smile on his face. "So you're Charlotte, Stevie's girlfriend?" He said as he got to his feet walked out from behind his desk and offered her his hand. "I'm so very happy to meet you. And Stevie was right; You are very lovely."

"Thank you," She said her cheeks turning scarlet red.

"Sit down please," He said as he led her to the large sofa that was in front of his desk. I was still standing in the middle of his office. He sat down and smiled at her like a dotting, loving father and asked if she felt a little nervous.

"I am a little Sir," She answered.

"That's because you don't know me yet," He said looking up at me. I was still standing in the middle of his office. "But you have nothing to fear does she Stevie?"

"No she doesn't," I said looking first at Sharly then at Fudgie. "Mr. Iaconio is a fine and generous gentleman and the pillar of his community," I sounded like I was kissing his ass but I meant every word I said.

"Good," He said as he walked back to his desk and sat down. "You gonna stand there all day, Stevie?"

"No," I answered as I set the bank bag that was filled with money on his desk then walked over to the sofa and sat down beside Sharly.

"Charlotte? Do you know why I have your young man as part of my family?"

"Yes I believe so," She said taking my hand. "It's because he's honest, hard working and extremely intelligent. I've known Stevie for seven years and I've been in love with him for seven years. He's the best person I know."

Fudgie looked at me then at Sharly and smiled. "Yes, that too, but he's ambitious. He knows what's it is like not to poor. Stevie's father is a fine family man who works hard to provide for his family. Eddie Shea speaks about Stevie's father with respect and admiration."

That's strange that he would say something like that. Eddie Shea doesn't know my father. I'm going to ask Eddie why he told Fudgie something like that.

I did ask Eddie and he told me that he knew my Dad and he was familiar with Dad's machine shop re-working parts for the Raytheon's production department. "Your Dad's a well respected vendor because the excellent work he does and his high standards. The production department doesn't even bother to send the parts through inspection. They'd just be wasting time."

Eddie also told me that he and my uncle Eddie were good friends and that's how he got to know my Dad.

Sharly and I visited with Fudgie for a half an hour before being excused. Fudgie had a way of telling you go to hell so you looked forward to the trip.

JUNE, 1960

Richie, Paulie, Kuckie and me, and help from Billy Ryan, Billy was and great trouble shooter and when we ran into difficulties which we occasionally did or when we couldn't quite understand what the shop manual trying say, Billy would read the instructions, and explain to us in lay man's terms what the manual was trying to explain to us and then the project became easy.

We finally did get the engine finished and dropped the flatty between the fenders. The Merc mill had to be yanked, torn down and the cylinders bored. The number eight piston was cocked in the cylinder and gouged the cylinder wall because wrist pin had snapped and the broken connecting rod had logged itself between the oil pan and the crank case. I had the eight cylinders bored out to 3 7/16 inch which increased to displacement to 296 cubic inches. That's about as big as the flatty can go if you wanted to use it for a street machine. Then we installed a new four inch crankshaft right out of the box. The original crank journal was too far gone to be able to regrind it round a new ¾ race Isky camshaft, Edlebrock high compression heads, Fenton headers and an Offenhauser dual carb intake setup and two Stromberg 97s. Frankie Ianotti used his tow truck to hoist the engine out of the Merc and helped us slide the engine down the plywood board that covered the stairs going down into my folk's cellar. Waltham Automotive did the all the intricate work. They bored out the cylinders and did the align bore. Then the engine was reassembled and with Frankie's tow truck pulled the engine out of Dad's cellar and gently lowered the flatty into the engine bay, Richie did the wiring and it fired up on the second try. This was before the exhaust pipes were screwed onto the Fenton headers. The rich blue flames blasted out of the Fenton headers, the flatty sounded real good and real strong.

The backyard mechanics had doubts that the engine would start that easily. Jimmy Grant, the owner of Waltham Automotive said that the engine would be tight to turn over but make sure that you pour a small amount of Mystery Oil into each cylinder before you put in the spark plugs and you'll probably need to give your car a push to get it fired up and be sure you have it in third gear and do not spray any ether or any type of starting fluid into the Strombergs. If the pistons hit the heads you're gonna be replacing the rods and maybe the crank. Billy Ryan told us that if I pulled the mechanical fuel pump capped off the hole in the block and mounted a Bendix electric fuel pump on the on the firewall the tight flat head should fire right up. The new Charles Atlas of Waltham's South Side nailed it. It took three tries before the engine fired up.

Babs would stop by after she got home from work, get us a beer or a soda, peanuts or potato chips and then look over Billy's shoulder pretending she was interested in what he was doing. Sharly worked right along with everybody, handing out the tools, holding the trouble light, and busting her ass right along with everybody else. She was a treasure and the project was to her a labor of love. When Babs wasn't busy handing us sodas and snacks, she would be playing suck face with Billy, and when we were finished for the night, she would bring up a couple of six packs of beer from the folks cellar. My Mom would keep an eye on everybody to make sure that we didn't have too much to drink.

We all had a lot of fun working on the three month's long project. The pearl white Mercury took center stage and everybody was in my folk's back yard, Patty Powers and Lily Shapiro, Tommy and Debbie, Kuckie and Cokie, Rosie Leonardi and Frank Ianotti. "Alright, Everybody," Babs sung out with a can of Bud in hand. She was finishing up her third. The rest of us were on our first. She started early. "Now that the project has been brought to fruition…"

"What in hell does fruition mean?" Kuckie asked Sharly.

"It means the project has been successfully completed," She replied.

"This beautiful work of art needs a name that will bring it some class and character," Babs announced as she patted the right front fender and burped. "Anyone?"

"Sharly, your sister sounds like she had a one to many," I said as I looked over at Babs.

We all looked at each other and shrugged our shoulders. "I got one," Sharly said as she put her arm around my waist and kissed my sweaty cheek. "How about Mister Machine?" She suggested looking at our family and friends.

"You guys did a great job," Frank said as he and Rosie walked around the car admiring the project. "I'm very impressed. I could use a guy like you."

"Thanks, Frank. Coming from you, a master engine builder, I take it as a compliment." I smiled wrapping my arm around Sharly's shoulder. "But you're going to have to hire all of us."

"Even Paulie, the guy that got drunk and shit his pants?" Frankie chuckled.

"Yes Frank all or none."

"Just like the Three Musketeers, right?" He said.

"Do we look like we're musketeers?" I laughed.

"The cops will love that one Sharly," Paulie said rolling his eyes as he took the can opener from Billy and opened his second Bud. "Why not paint it on the rear quarter panel in large black old English lettering."

"I like it," I said as Frank, Rosie, Sharly and I finished admiring my Monterey.

"It's a good name, I like it," Paulie said. "Now I propose a toast. May your back seat always be active, but try not to make any mistakes, I still carry a large selection of rubber goods you know; and may all your rides to the Natick Drive-in or the Ducks or The Gore Estate be safe and swift."

"Hear: Hear."

Now I was paranoid. I felt that I had created a Frankenstein. I only took the Merc out when the weather was forecasted to be sunny and mild. I was afraid that some old bat with a beat up Nash would watch me coming out of the drive way then take a bead on Merc then crash into "Mr. Machine".

Sharly said that I was being overly cautious. "You're acting silly, Honey. There's no one waiting behind the bushes waiting to crash into the car. Just drive it as you would normally drive your 40 coupe'."

"I have an idea, what you say we take the Merc into Boston the next time you visit Uncle Fudgie?" she suggested while she played with my nipples her hand under my tee shirt.

We were parked, in my 40 Coupe' in the parking lot that was beside banks of the Charles River that was referred to by the lovers parked there as the "Ducks". The "Ducks" was popular parking place where during the day Mom and Dad would bring their little kids armed with loaves of stale bread. The ducks would swim to the edge of the river bank and the little tykes would tear up the slices of bread and throw the slices into the Charles River. The ducks would eat the bread, shit in the water and smell up the already polluted Charles River. At night it was a different story. It turned into an open air, under the stars, hump, hump screw fest. The next morning the little kiddies would pick up the used condoms thrown out of the car windows show them to Mommy or Daddy and ask… "what are these for Mommy?"

"Why don't you ask me to cut out my heart and toss it in the Charles River?" I moaned in abject horror. I knew that I was being overly dramatic. My Mercury Monterey will never ride on the narrow streets of Boston. I'll take the bus or if I have to… walk before I'd ever take our Merc!"

"You mean to tell me that you would never want Fudgie to see what his money bought, Stevie?" Sharly reasoned. "Plus all the work we all did to make sure the car came out this nice? Don't you want anyone to see the "Mister Machine" name painted on the quarter panels? We all did a bang up job, you know."

"Don't say bang up, Sharly," I whined.

"Sorry, Honey. We all just want you to enjoy your ride."

"Come on, Honey," I said as I fired up the coupe'.

"Where we going?"

"Back to the folks house, we're gonna take the Merc out and cruise Moody and Main Street," I said as I backed up the 40 Ford Coupe' and drove out of the parking lot.

I left the coupe' on the street, and we walked up the driveway. There she sat in all her glory. I had to replace the rear springs to accommodate the extra torque that the engine fed to the rear wheels. The rear end sat about six inches higher than the front end which in the late fifties and early sixties look rather strange because most of the customs of that time had their rear-end lowered to about three of four inches off the pavement and had fender skirts, mine was just the opposite. She sported a rake and she didn't sport fender skirts. The original springs were too mushy and when I tacked up the engine and let out the clutch the springs begin would begin to wrap around the rear end so I had Phil Martin the owner of Waltham Auto Spring replace the springs and installed heavy duty shocks, and when the springs were installed I drove the car over to Frankie's garage and had Frankie's body man painted, in old English, "Mister Machine" in dark blue on the rear quarter panels. The paint job came out beautiful.

I opened the door for Sharly, climbed in the other side and started the ¾ race Merc flat head. She sounded sweet, as I backed out of the driveway and headed for Moody Street. Saturday night was cruise night In Waltham. All the street machines and hot rods were out in all their glory. Charly and I were stopped on Carter Street waiting for the light to turn green before we could take a left onto Moody Street when two of Waltham's finest in a Billy Mitchell's West End 1960 Chevy cruiser pulled up closer than usual beside my white Mercury. "Where you going, "Mister Machine"?" Colin

"Trigger" Vanuti grinned while chewing the shit out a piece of Juicy Fruit. Trigger and his partner, Bobby Devoe, thought he was being funny.

Colin got the name "Trigger" while practicing quick draws in front of the upstairs bathroom mirror in his mother's house, naked, with his service revolver holster strapped to his waist and before he could clear leather the weapon discharged and the asshole shot himself in the foot. Although it's a true story Trigger would never admit it and as soon as he got out of the hospital he plugged up the bullet holes in the upstairs bathroom floor and the bullet hole in floor of Mama Vanuti's kitchen.

"Nowhere in particular just cruising Moody and Main Street with my girlfriend, Officer Vanuti, and listening to Rock and roll on the radio," I replied in a patronizing, wise ass voice.

"What's the young ladies name, Stevie?" Trigger asked. I knew Trigger from working at The Sport Mart, he'd stop in from time to time looking at fishing equipment; he never bought a fucking thing, and Bobby came from the Bleachery and lived five houses down from my folk's house. We all knew most the younger cops and as a group they were a bunch of good guys. If they caught us speeding they would usually try to scare the shit out of us with threats of either going to reform school or making us join the Army or how disappointed our folks would be then let us go on our way.

There was one cop that we all knew well, Ed Tuite. We went to school with his son Jimmy who also became a police officer. Ed Tuite was a large cop who was about ready to retire. He worked the traffic detail at Saint Jude's Church. That's where I sold newspapers on Sunday mornings. I worked the Sunday's right up until my graduation from high school. I would meet with Eddie Shea right after nine o'clock Mass and he would give me my bag and from whom I was going to collect. Well there was a little fucking pervert that took a liking to me. He would park his black and white '53 Chevy Bellaire across the street from St. Jude's walk across Main Street and buy a Herald then begin a conversation asking me where

I lived, who were my friends were, you know drill. Then he would park across the street from Waltham High School and wait for me to leave with Rosie, we'd park in the Chestnut Street lot and cross Moody Street and we'd go to our respective jobs. Well this puny little asshole wore about five pounds of Brylcreem in his hair. He had to use a paint roller to apply all that shit. No "Brylcreem a little dab will do you" for this Bozo. He would come into the store check out the fishing equipment, the golf clubs and the weights. This dumb little fuck face couldn't lift up the box the weights came in. He would follow me, that was how he knew where I worked.

"Say, that's a nice looking girl I saw you with. Is she your girlfriend?" Bozo wanted to know. "She's very pretty you know and I'll bet that she has real nice tits. Do you play with them and does she play with you? Does she put your cock her mouth?" His eyes were sparkling as he flashed me with a lewd grin. "I'll bet that she does. She looks like a girl that loves to suck cock."

"Why do you want to know, huh? Why don't you just get the fuck out of here before I kick your short fat ass into the middle of Moody Street!" I said taking a nine iron off the counter. He put his head down, I thought he was going to cry, and walked out of the store.

"Is that the screwball you told me about?" Rosie asked as she handed me my Lime Ricky.

"That's him, Rosie," I answered

Well the next Sunday Brylcreem showed up at Saint Jude's and parked across the street from the church. "Sir?" I said looking at the cop who directed traffic when church let out, then nodding my head toward the black and white Chevy. Sergeant Reilly was placing a bet with Eddie Shea. For a cop as large as Sgt Reilly was he waited for the light traffic to go by and ran across Main Street grabbed Brylcreen through the open car window and shouted, "I ever see or hear you bothering any kids in the neighborhood or anywhere else including this young man I'll tear your arms off and beat you to death with the bloody stumps, now you start your car and get out of here!!!"

That was the last time anyone had seen or heard from Brylcreem.

Anyway; let me get back to my story:

"Charlotte O'Sullivan...Sharly,"
"I know you Sharly," Bobby shouted across from the passenger side of the cruiser. "You live across from the Dyers, right?"

"Yeah, you know where I live, Bobby," Sharly said. She sounded annoyed. "Mom, Babs and I have been living in the same house for ten years."
"And you work for the Bell Shops," The heavy set French man shouted.
"You know I do," she shouted back. "Your wife's in the store all the time."
"I know. My wife shops there and says it's a real classy place," He said. "We'll drop in from time to time to make sure everything's alright,"
"Thank you Bobby," She smiled back.
After cruising for an hour or so we went over to the Gore parking lot and parked beside the barn with the spot light shining down and were wrapped in each other's arms. It was easy making out in the Merc. The gear shift was on the floor so you wouldn't have the steering mounted shifting lever poking you in the ass; Beanbags complained about that all the time. She was tired of having the gear shift lever getting more ass than I was, but I wasn't getting any ass from Rosie.

The front seat of the Merc was like a living room compared to the '40's front seat and the new radio, thanks to Richie, sounded so much better than the stock Merc radio. Instead of the single speaker being mounted in the dash there were two speakers mounted under the rear window package holder. He got the radio out of a wrecked Lincoln from Bennie Katz junk yard. The Lincoln radio had a stronger signal and it had twice the amount of wattage than the

Mercury radio and Richie made a few modifications so the radio fit perfectly in the dash.

AUGUST, 1961

"Stevie?"

"Uh huh?"

"I love you, you know." She whispered looking deeply into my eyes as we broke off our embrace.

"I love you, too."

"And how long have we been going together?" Why all the questions, I ask myself looking back into her eyes.

"Let's see, it's early August, a little over a year, why?"

"And in the year you haven't made a play for my breasts, or tried to feel me up. You don't have to be timid Stevie," She asked. "I enjoy being a woman you know."

I was totally taken by surprise. Never in my wildest dreams I had never thought or tried to grab a feel. I had too much respect for her and never wanted to do anything that would have her lose my trust. I didn't know how to answer her question. We made out like two hungry pigs in a wallow, but I kept my hands away from her goodies. Charlotte O'Sullivan was no Rose Lyn Leonardi. Bean Bags was great, but she didn't have Sharly's class. "I would never want to do anything that would remind you of Bill Ryan, Sharly. I'm not that kind of guy. And I don't want you to think that you were back with Billy Ryan trying to fight me off."

Sharly looked at me smiled her deep blue sparkling and she said, "I've known you for a long time, Stevie and I know your Mom and Dad and I know how hard they worked bringing up Tommy and you and how proud they are of both of you, even though one of the twins works for a bookie."

"And give a lot of credit to your Mom, bring up two sisters without the benefit of your Dad being around," I pointed out as I as

I picked up her hand and kiss her palm. "Your Mom did a great job, and I don't work for a bookie, I'm Mr. Iaconio's trusted consultant, I work in a sporting goods store for a wonderful Jewish boss, " I bragged rendering Sharly a toothy smile. "He treats me like I was his son."

She returned my toothy smile and went on. "My mother really likes your Mom and your Aunt Louise," Sharly said and she turned onto her side and faced me running her hand over my cheek. "When my father was killed in the Korean conflict my mother was so strong, she moved us back here, went to work and carried on as if nothing had happened but a night after Babs and were in bed and she was reciting her Rosary we could hear our Mom softly weeping while she whispered Daddy's name."

"I know, Honey," I said. "My mother told me."

"I now that you know that you're mother, my mother and your Aunt Louise are very close. They discuss everything over their four o'clock in the afternoon tea and Irish bread."

"Yes I know and your mother and my mother were in a state of ecstasy when you broke up with Billy Ryan and I dropped Rosie." I said. "Mom though I was too good to be going out with a garlic eater."

We both broke out laughing when Mom referred to Rosie as a garlic eater. "You know Stevie, I always like Rosie. She was so funny and bubbly the way she would walk to made sure that all the guys and maybe some girls…"

"Like you?" I chuckled.

"Could check out her asset," She said ignoring my snide remark. "I'm glad that she's happy with Frankie. She really loves him."

"But not as much as you love me, right?"

"You got that right big time," She said then kissed my gently on the lips.

Then as it always does the summer melted in the fall and the fall into winter, than came spring and another summer. This was going to be our last summer together for a while. In October I was leaving for the military. Sharly and I spent most of our free time alone pleasing each other with love and affection. We decided against having sex and although we would be careful we didn't want to take the chance on making any life changing mistakes. We both had too much to lose, but we did spend many happy hours laying naked beside each other engaged in playful fun, holding each other and sleeping together. The folks, both Sharly's and mine, knew what we were doing but as long as they knew where we were, usually in the folks summer home in Rockport they would smile and told us to be careful. Dad put it more succinctly: Don't forget you rubbers, Steven! And he didn't mean my galoshes.

I was still working for Maxi and running a bag for Eddie, but it was time to get serious. It was October 1961 and I was going into the military I decided on the Air Force and Kuckie was taking my job at The Sport Mart, but Maxi insisted that he was not going to be referred to as Kuckie and definitely not Lou the Jew. Boogie Monahan called Kuckie "Lew the Jew" until Kuckie got sick of and Boogie's wise mouth and threatened him with a baseball bat.

"You could be right, Sharl, but if and when an investment opportunity comes up and I need some money right away, I don't want to have to explain to the folks why I need it. And I trust you, Honey and if anything worth investing presents itself I want it to be between you and me no one else, alright?"

"Okay Stevie, I'm your girl."

"I know," I said as we sat in the lobby waiting to see one of the banking officers.

"And you know what, Stevie? I have a feeling that you're going to have more money than you could possibly imagine. I have a feeling that you're going to do very, very well."

"So long as I still have you, Sharly," I said holding her hand.

MONDAY
16 OCTOBER 1961.
LOGAN INTERNATIONAL AIRPORT.

Everybody was there to see me off but Tommy and Debbie. Tommy was in his second year at Naval Academy and Debbie was away at college. Hell, I didn't want all of this attention. I was only going to Lackland Air Force Base, Texas for eight weeks of basic training then I'll come home on leave before I go to my next base, but Richie, Pauly, Patty and Lily took the morning off from work. Billy Ryan and Babs were there too, they played hooky from their classes. They were both going to Bentley College of Accounting and Finance and as soon as they had earned their degrees they were going to marry. That's another story.

Sharly and I walked around the concourse holding hands and talking in whispers. We were trying to get as much time alone as possible before the flight to Maguire Air Force Base was called.

"Charlotte; Stevie," Fudgie's soft voice came from behind us. We both turned around at the same time and looked at his sad but friendly smile. "My two children are going away, and I'm so very sad. I love both of you as I do my family: Stevie, stay safe and Sharly take care of yourself and don't ever forget your friends from Boston that love you both so very much."

He embraced me, gently embraced Sharly then reached into his Bruins Gallery Gods Jacket pocket withdrew an envelope and placed it into her hand, "For your future," then he turned and slowly walked down the concourse through the large glass doors then he turned and waved at all of us then walked away.

We watched him as he melted into the crowd and disappeared. Sharly and I both had tears in our eyes. He was a truly unforgettable Boston icon. "What do you thinks in the envelope?" She said holding it up at the ceiling lights. "Why not open it and find out?" I suggested looking at the envelope.

She ripped the side of the envelope open and shook out ten new, crispy one hundred dollar bills.

"That money belongs to you, Honey," I said to her. "It's a gift from a special person who really loves the both of us."

"Are you sure, Stevie? Are you sure that he wants us both to have the money."

"No, Honey. He wants you to have his gift. That's why he handed you the envelope, and believe me he knows I don't need it, and you don't either," I said.

"But that's a lot of money, Stevie." Sharly said.

"It's only a drop in the bucket, Honey," I said as I smiled into her violet blue eyes and kissed her gently on her warm soft lips.

While Sharly was placing the envelope in her purse the flight was called. "Alright you people!" A tall husky NCO shouted, "You have five minutes to say all your good byes, kiss your wives and girlfriends then form in a straight line in front of me. Hurry! Hurry! Hurry! I don't want any of you people missing the flight! You all got that?"

"What's a rank, Sgt?" Someone shouted out his echo bouncing off the walls of the concourse.

The Sgt stood facing the recruits his legs a part hands on his hips. "Just stand facing me, GOT IT?"

"Gotta go, Sweetheart," I said as we slowly walked back to the waiting well wishers, I kissed the ladies, shook hands with guys warmly embraced Sharly, kissing her gently then hurried with the rest of the recruits out of the door of the Northeast concourse and boarded the Northeast Airlines turbo prop Viscount. The flight to Maguire took about an hour, but we had a four hour wait before we could board a Continental Airlines Military Air Transport Service C-121 Lockheed Super Constellation for the eight hour trip to Lackland Air force Base and onto basic training.

I nailed a seat beside two WAF recruits who hailed from Bridgeport, Connecticut, Dianne McCarthy and Suzanne Williamson. They were nice looking ladies and I mean really nice looking, Dianne was a tall willowy redhead with amazingly large turquoise blue eyes and Suzanne a bit smaller than Dianne with dirty blond hair, deep blue eyes and a nice set of knockers. The girls turned an otherwise long boring eight hour flight into an extremely enjoyable adventure.

It was my guess that Dianne and Suzanne were more than just friends, but why should I care or be judge mental? They were very close and extremely funny. Dianne had managed to smuggle five vodka nips onto the aircraft in her pocket book but as she was getting out of her seat to go to the head she dropped her purse and the nips rolled out of her purse and rolled down the aisle of the "Super Constellation". The stewardess was right there watching Dianne while she was on her knees trying to scoop up the nips and trying to shove them down the front of her blouse but she wasn't fast enough. The stewardess, who was also on her knees looking Dianne in the face and explained in no uncertain terms that it is against Military regulations to bring any kind of alcoholic beverages on a military contract aircraft, ship or any other type of military means of conveyance. She then confiscated the vodka, said that she wouldn't say anything to the authorities than walked up the aisle, went into the flight deck and handed them over to the flight crew so they could have some free adult refreshments when we all landed in San Antonio.

The girls joined up on the "buddy" plan hoping of spending the next four years stationed together at the same bases. But of course the needs of the Air Force always came first.

On the eight hour flight, Dianne and Suzanne laughed and joked and told me about growing up in Stonington their family and friends. The girls had been friends since grade school and were looking forward to spending their lives together but first they wanted to travel, see the world. They couldn't afford to travel on their own and that was when they decided to join the air Force, spend four years seeing the country and hopefully some of the world, save their pay then go home and start a garden shop and nursery. Their story continues later in my book. You're going love what they had accomplished and you're going love the girls too.

"What did you do before enlisting, Steve?" Suzanne asked me as she lit a cigarette.

"I ran numbers for a bookie in Boston's North End," I replied waving Suzanne's cigarette smoke away from my face.

"The smoke bothers you, Steve, I'm sorry," Suzanne stated flatly as she was about to snuffed out her cigarette.

"No, that's alright, Suzanne, go ahead a smoke" I said. "I've been around cigarette smoke all my life."

"So explain what you did to two gambling neophytes like us," Dianne said as she stood up and had me sit between Suzanne and her. "What does running numbers mean? You worked for a bookie, right?" She asked as she sat down beside me.

"You got it, I collected betting slips and money from the losers, and an associate with whom I collaborated with, pays the winners and I took the losers money into the North End, turned the money over to the big boss man, and was generously rewarded for my efforts to make my boss richer then I climbed back into my '40 Ford Deluxe coupe and drive back home to Waltham."

"That's it? Dianne asked her eyes and her mouth wide open." No shoot outs in the streets, no broken arms or legs, brains splashed all over sidewalks by baseball bat swinging hit men, it doesn't sound all that exciting to me, Steve. Not like the Untouchables!"

"I assume that you mean wise guys getting whacked? Not in broad daylight, anyway, and my job was not, under any circumstances, supposed to be exciting. Just collect the money, make my drop, get paid and go home." I said looking at Dianne then at Suzanne. "The bookies and collectors and the Capos have a reputation to maintain. The rackets are a business like any other business. And they want to maintain a low profile and the least amount of attention that is drawn to them the better. Just keep the cops and the feds noses out of their business."

"What's a Capo?"

"It's a wise guy, a Lieutenant, the neighborhood God Father."

"Is he the Capo that puts out the order to have someone killed?"

"You mean whacked?" I replied.

"Have you ever seen anyone get, you know?" Suzanne said putting her finger to her head, closing her eyes and pretending to pull the trigger.

"You mean getting whacked? Nope, I never have."

"You mean to say that you never saw anyone get "whacked" then?" Suzanne asked.

"Look Dianne…Suzanne," I said trying to explain what my job entailed. "I was only a lowly bag man not a hit man. They have the made guys to take care of part of the business."

"Let's change the subject, alright?" Suzanne said looking first at Suzanne than at me. "Tell us Steve, now a good looking good guy like you has to have someone back home, right green eyes," Dianne said as she ground out her cigarette.

"Oh ya," I said reach into my back pocket, took out my wallet, removed Sharly's picture and handed it to Dianne. "Her name is Charlotte O'Sullivan but and our friends and I call her Sharly."

"God she's beautiful, Steve!" Dianne exclaimed as she and Suzanne gazed lovingly at Sharly's graduation picture. "What a beautiful smile, you must really love her, am I right?"

"She IS the love of my life," I smiled watching the girls drooling over her photo. I can't wait till I have time to write to Sharly and let her know that two girls that I met on the flight on down to Texas had just fell in love with you.

"Do you have any more pictures?"

"Yeah a couple of Polaroid snapshots I took of her in the nude," I said looking first at Dianne then at Suzanne with a serious look on my face.

"You're kidding us," Suzanne said looking at me. "Do you have the pictures with you?

"Do you?" Dianne asked. "I'll bet that she has a great body. Can we see the pictures?"

"No, that's alright." I chuckled. "And yes, Dianne she does have a beautiful body."

"How long have you and Sharly been together?" Dianne asked as she and Suzanne continued to drool over Sharly's photo. I do believe Dianne and Suzanne had just fallen in love with my girl friend.

"A little over two years," I replied. "How about you and Suzanne, will you be writing home to anyone?" Oh shit, maybe I should have thought before I asked such a personnel question.

"No not really. Suzanne and I have been best friends since the second grade and our folks owned houses beside each other." Dianne said. "We both dated a few of times but we never went out with anyone that impressed us, that's when Suzanne and I decided to, you know, remain friends until someone better came along

"I understand," I said.

"And so far no one has," Suzanne said as she looked over at Dianne and smiled.

"That's smart. There's nothing worse than going out with a guy for a year or two then find out that he's an incredible asshole." The girls looked at each other and broke out laughing. "They're out there you know."

"Yeah we know," Suzanne said. "That's why Dianne and I are together. We love each other's company."

"And I like your company too." I said.

"Thank you, Sweetheart," Suzanne said smiling.

"Thank you too, Stevie," Dianne smiled. "We both enjoy your company too."

"Maybe we'd better get some sleep," I said trying to get to my feet. "Basic training begins in eight hours."

"Where do you think you're going Stevie?" Dianne said as she grabbed my arm and pulled me back into the seat.

"I'll sit on the aisle seat so you and Suzanne can be together, okay?" I said.

"Not tonight Stevie," Suzanne ordered. "Tonight you get to sleep between two beautiful women and we promise you, Stevie baby that, Sharly will never find out." She said kissing me on my right cheek.

"Yeah, Stevie Baby," Dianne grinned kissing me on my other cheek. "Your secret is safe with us."

I was wondering what the other one hundred fifty odd recruits on the plane were thinking. Not one but two girls and me. Too bad the two girls I was sitting between were in love with each other not me, but I'm not saying a word.

It was after mid-night when the plane landed and the load of recruits deplaned at San Antonio International Airport, and as the new recruits were getting off the plane I hugged both Dianne McCarthy and Suzanne Williamson and I told them that I was sure that the three of us would meet again so let's try to stay in touch, then we were herded over to the pickup areas boarded four blue Air Force 29 passenger buses and delivered en masse to the "Recruit Training Depot". I still remember the greeting sign at the gate. "Welcome To Lackland Air Force Base. Gate Way Too the Air Force". The buses came to a halt in front of the Foreign Officer's Mess Hall and were herded inside, went through the chow line, fed, herded back to the blue buses and were driven to a barracks area, a red headed NCO ordered everybody to get the fuck off the buses, line up and answer up when your name is called. That done, the boots of flight 1632 were herded into the barracks and were told that under any circumstances were we to sit or lay on the bunks. If you want to sleep, use the fucking floor!

None of us had a chance to sleep or do anything else, S/Sgt Rizzo and a tall husky Airman First Class Powell crashed through the front barracks and ordered us to get the your stinking ass off of the floor and stand in front the nearest bunk. "Don't worry what bunk to stand in front of, just pick ONE! You'll be told where you'll be assigned later on!" The husky Airman explained to us in no uncertain terms and told us that his name was Airman First Class

Powell! Both he and S/Sgt Rizzo would be referred to from now until we successfully completed basic training as "SIR"! Not just us but everyone above the rank of Airman No Class Basic; E-1 would also be addressed as sir!

Flight 1632 was first marched to supply where a duffel bag was thrown at our heads, then came the white skivvies and white tee shirts, socks, fatigues, summer kakis, Class "A's" uniforms, a pair of black brogans boots and a pair of low quarter dress shoes. They then were marched into a large room, told to get out of your Goddamn "Rain Bow" clothes put on boxer shorts, tee shirts, black wool socks, fatigue trousers and fatigue shirts. I was amazed that all of my uniforms; although the cuffs had to be hemmed up a couple of inches; fit well. The next morning after morning chow we were marched to the barber shop. Some of the recruits went in with slick greasy hair and we came out of the shop skin heads. The first thing I wanted to do following the hair cut was to get into the shower and wash my slick head. I would take a shower and washed my hair every morning before leaving for school. I didn't wear my hair in the Elvis style. I wasn't like most of other guys in the neighborhood with pomade plastered in their hair. I like my hair neat and clean and medium short.

Then we were marched back to the squadron area, Squadron 3701, the number "1" Squadron, were ordered to stand on the street and the roll was called again. Our Technical Instructors, Sgt Rizzo and Airman First Class Powell, were two of the nastiest pricks that ever put on a uniform. In the eight weeks of basic training the two Bastards had volunteered flight 1632 for the every rotten detail, from unloading trucks at the commissary, scrubbing pots and pans at the mess hall, cleaning the foreign officer's barracks, picking up cigarette butts and before lights out running laps on the parade ground. For some reason Sgt Rizzo wanted all of us to be the best conditioned flight in the squadron. While the other flights were enjoying a patio break we were on the parade ground running laps.

When we finally completed basic there was not one boot in Sgt Rizzo flight that still smoked. We didn't have the time but what really impressed us boots that made us wanted us to succeed is that Sgt Rizzo and A1C Powell was running right along with us.

"Airman no Class Dyer! Front and center!" Sgt Rizzo shouted out.

"SIR! YES SIR!" I shouted back at him as I marched front and center.

"I CAN'T HEAR YOU, PUSSY!!!"

"I CAN'T SHOUT ANY LOUDER...SIR!!!"

"Get out of my face, shit head! Airman absolutely no class WILSON!!! Front and CENTER!!!" Sgt Rizzo shouted into Charles J (CJ) Wilson's face. CJ, Billy Toye and I became fast friends. If CJ can't cut the mustard, Billy would be next.

"SIR! YES SIR!!!"

"As you were shit head. Airman Shit head Toye!!!"

"SIR! YES SIR!!!" he screamed almost collapsing a lung.

"What in God's green earth was the Secretary of the Air Force thinking when he sent Airman Powell and me sixty-four fudge packing PUSSYS?" He shouted as he walked up and down our ranks.

"Milder...prove to me and the rest of flight that you're not a pussy!"

"SIR! WOULD THE TECHINAL INSTRUCTOR LIKE THE AIRMAN TO DROP HIS FATIGUE PANTS AND PROVE TO YOU AND THE REST OF THE FLIGHT THAT HE'S NOT A TWAT, SIR???" Milder replied in the third person.

"I saw you in the shower this morning, needle dick," Sgt Rizzo said looking at the front of his fatigue trousers. "So don't concern yourself!"

The flight all began to laugh. That was a BIG mistake.

"SHUT THE FUCK UP YOU TWATS!!!" Rizzo shouted as he positioned himself in front of the flight hands on his hips.

"SIR YES SIR!!!" We all screamed in unison.

"Now get your dirty stinking assholes back to the barracks, change into jock straps, not that any of you douche bags need them, shorts, tee shirts, sneakers and get your pussy's back here! You got five minutes!"

"SIR YES SIR!!!"

"DISMISSED!!!" He screamed in our faces. "GET THE FUCK OUT OF MY SIGHT BEFORE I PUKE!!!"

"YES SIR!!!" We all shouted in one voice and took one step back, did a right face and returned to the barracks.

The sixty four fudge packing assholes spent the last two hours of the afternoon drill running in place, doing pushups, sit ups and jumping jacks. Rizzo had us run two miles then he marched us back to the barracks, had all of us remove our PT clothes, shower, dress in clean fatigues and then marched us to the mess hall for evening chow. This same routine continued for the eight weeks. When we got through with basic training we all were in the best shape of our lives and that included the high school jocks.

Flight 1637 spent most of our free time spit shining our brogans, doing laundry sowing buttons that the TIs ripped of our uniforms. (If the instructors saw a button not buttoned he would tear it off and asked the offending boot if he wanted the button. If you replied in the affirmative he would throw it at you. If you replied in the negative he would throw it away.) writing letters and if the TI's felt in a generous mood they would treat their flight to a patio break where we could buy sodas from the vending machine, visit the BX for to do some shopping, have an ice cream or a milk shake or sit around the swimming pool, (We weren't allowed to go swimming) smoke a cigarette and bat the breeze. Most of the guys had girl friends, a few were married and a few joined up to get away from their wives or girlfriends and before lights out we were again in shorts and sneakers on the parade grounds running laps.

The days were filled with, classroom training in customs and courtesies, The Uniform Code of Military Justices, which in the military replaced the Constitution, and the transformation from civilian to military life. There was also two hours of physical training every day and in the afternoons we had drill, drill and more drill. What began as a terrifying part of the day, but as the flight became drilled to move in the same direction and paid attention to the TIs commands the drilling became a real heated competition with the other flights. There were thirteen flights in the 01 squadron and each would all try to out drill their sister flights. The TI's would sing out the commands and the boots would move like sixty-four marchers moving as one man. The thirteen flights all had a great time on the drill field. So did the TI's.

Each afternoon following noon chow the flights would be assembled in front of their respective barracks, we all got the order… rest and light them up. "Smoke 'em if you got 'em". When we first arrived at Lackland about half of the guys in the flight smoked. I didn't and neither did CJ or Billy and when basic training was completed the flight was about smoke free. I'm sure that some of the troops began smoking again as soon as basic training was completed.

Following our first week of basic training the flight began to get with the program and understand our training mission and our training routine took on a more serious tone. The TIs were there to turn us from a bunch or undisciplined young rabble into a tight, disciplined unit that reacted immediately to every verbal or written order or command. It was not the individual that counted, it was the mission. We boots were taught well and we responded to every order without question or hesitation. If the TI's voice didn't pull your head out of your ass, the TI's boot jammed it in a little further.

THE BEGINNING OF OUR SIXTH WEEK:

"Dyer! Front and center!"

I did as ordered and stopped two feet from Sgt Rizzo looking over his left shoulder. The boot would never look the TI in the face.

"Do you know why I ordered you front and center, Airman BASIC!!!"

"NO SIR!!!" I shouted still looking over his left shoulder.

"You'll be taking over as 1st Squad leader."

"YES SIR!!!"

"Return to ranks, Dyer and relieve Airman Toye," The Sgt ordered without screaming in my face.

"YES SIR!" I said as executed a perfect about face, relieved the former first squad leader and took his place. The former 1st squad leader Billy Toye was now a road guard.

"Hey, Stevie," Billy said as we stood on line waiting to enter the mess hall.

"Hey what?"

"Are you and Rizzo corn holing each other after lights out?"

"Now don't take your demotion so hard, Billy. I know you'll make one hell of a road guard, right CJ?"

"Hell ya, Stevie," CJ agreed. "He even looks like a road guard."

"What in hell does a road guard suppose to look like?" Billy asked looking at me than at CJ.

"A Pisan that looks like you."

10 December 1961.

DEAR DAD:

In the almost eight weeks of training we all went from a bunch of wise ass, smart aleck, mouthy kids to sixty-four well mannered disciplined and well trained troops. We marched well, were polite and learned more in eight weeks than we had in the first eighteen or so years of our lives. The TI's could only do so much but we had to feel the spirit of comrade ship, working as a team, the individual didn't matter, the only thing that mattered was the flight and being able to train as a team.

Except for the few "rednecks" from the south most of the troops had never seen a rifle let alone fire one but after a week of training we all could fire the M-1 Garand proficiently, and some of the troops entered the circle of expert. Most of the experts were southern "Red Necks" and could they shoot the nuts off a squirrel from a hundred yards. I wasn't one of them but I fired well enough to make marksman.

The small arms training was brief, less than a week but it was thorough. The small arms instructors were as tough as the TI's were but we weren't harassed by them as badly as we were by our instructors.

Each morning during our small arms training reveille was blown at 0545, but by then we were already out of bed, shaved showered dressed and sitting on our foot lockers waiting for Sgt Rizzo and Airman Powell (On our last day of basic we learned that Powell was promoted to S/Sgt; E-5)to storm into the barracks banging a GI can with the cover. "Well I'll dipped in shit!" Rizzo yelled as he switched on the lights and found his boots waiting to be called to attention. Before going to morning chow we cleaned the barracks, the latrine, made up our bunks than stood at attention on the street in front of the barracks.

"Following morning chow we were marched the three miles to the confidence course trained on the M-1's than ran fully clothed, brogans, weapons and all, five miles across the Texas prairie then marched three miles back to our squadron, went to evening chow, we went ten hours between breakfast and dinner, no lunch, then cleaned and ironed our fatigues, spit shined our brogans, showered then had a patio break in the center of the Squadron area for a smoke, enjoy a Doctor Pepper or visit the BX for an order of onion rings or French fries a chili dog: HUH! What in hell is a chili dog? When I finally did eat a chili dog I thought it was good but I wouldn't want it for a steady diet. They have some strange food in Texas, strange but good. And if you're constipated relief is on the way.

"I'm going to miss my buddies and the friends I have made in such a short period of time. They are a bunch of great guys and we had a lot of fun together. Fun at basic training you ask? Yeah that was when we began to take our military rolls seriously. That happened as soon as we arrived at Lackland. Most of the training was physically and mentally challenging, and the Technical Instructors took shit from no one. They were a crew of tough bastards, especially when we screwed up!

Well Dad, it's about lights out.

I'll see you all in five days.

Your loving Son: Stevie.

SECOND TO THE LAST DAY OF BASIC TRAINING:

"Airman Dyer, front and center," Airman Powell ordered. He was smiling. The flight was all though with basic. One more day and we were out of here.

"YES, Sir!!!" I said as approached the tall heavy set TI and came to attention looking over his right shoulder at the chapel steeple.

"I received a call from the WAF Area NCIOC, Technical Instructor; Staff Sgt Bowen. What I gathered from our brief conversation Sgt Bowen mentioned that on the flight from Maguire Air Force Base to Lackland Air Force Base you befriended two of her trainees, WAF Airman Dianne McCarthy and a WAF Airman Suzanne Williamson?"

"Yes Sir. We became friends on the flight."

"Well Dyer, Airman McCarthy and Airman Williamson, would like to meet you tonight at the Base Exchange for snacks, soft drinks and pleasant conversation and you WILL be there! Do you understand your orders Airman Dyer?"

"Sir! I will be there, Sir!" I shouted.

"You will rendezvous at the Base Exchange with Airman McCarthy and Airman Williamson at 1830 hours sharp! Airman, uniform of the day will be 505 tans, spit shined low quarters and garrison cap with the bill spit shined! YOU GOT THAT, DYER?"

"YES SIR!" I shouted in hopes that, that will be my last YES SIR to and enlisted man

"You are DISMISSED!"

"YES SIR!" I shouted, then did a perfect about face and marched back to my position in the flight.

I brushed my teeth, shaved, showered, put on my 505 summer tans and hurried across the squadron area the patio and into the BX. The girls were waiting for me at the soda fountain dressed in Air Force blue skirts, blouses, and heels. They both looked real nice. Basic training seemed to agree with them.

"Stevie!" They both shouted as the slid off their stools rushed up to me with open arms and a back breaking embrace. "How are you, Stevie, you look so good, all tanned and standing tall! Good enough to eat!" Dianne squealed kissing me on the lips.

"I couldn't be better Dianne, Suzanne and how are both of you?" I said looking at Dianne then at Suzanne. "You both look good enough to eat too!"

"Come on BAGMAN man," Suzanne said as she walked towards the soda fountain. "Why don't you and Dianne find a booth while I buy the sodas?"

"I'd rather have a beer," I said.

"So would I," Suzanne agreed.

"Let's go," I said as I took Dianne's arm and led her to the only empty booth left in the Base Exchange.

"Now that basic training is about over, where are you and Suzanne shipping out to?" I asked Dianne. "Are you and Suzanne shipping out together?"

"Yeah, we got lucky I suppose," Dianne sighed.

"Okay Dianne, you don't look happy," I said smiling looking into her sad blue eyes. "You can tell your ole Uncle Stevie."

"Let's wait 'til Suzanne gets back with the sodas, okay, Stevie? I don't want to tell the same sad story twice."

"Okay," I said smiling.

Suzanne returned with the soft drinks, sat down and said that the reason they were disappointed was because of their shitty assignment. The Air Force suspected that they were more than just friends so they were both got orders for Point Barrow, Alaska radar station.

"You gotta be kidding!" I exclaimed looking first at Dianne then at Suzanne. "What in hell are you going to be doing up in Point Barrow? If they ever give the world an enema that's where they'll will stick the tube."

"We don't know, Stevie," Suzanne moaned. "Our orders said that our duties would be explained to us as soon as we arrived."

"And where are you going?" Dianne asked as she gently took hold of Suzanne hand.

"First up to Francis E Warren Air Force Base Cheyenne, Wyoming for sixteen weeks training then on to March Air Force Base, apparently the air Force would like me be a heavy equipment operator."

"As soon as you get up to Cheyenne write us will you, Honey?" Suzanne said. "Here's a copy of our orders."

"You're being assigned to the 12th Hospital Group," I said as I looked over Dianne's orders. "I would guess that you two going to be assigned to the hospital administration section."

"Why do you say that, Steve?" Suzanne asked as she sucked on the straw.

"Because the first three numbers of your AFSC is 443, that's an Administration Code."

"Maybe we're going to medical school and the Air Force is going to train us to be doctors," Dianne chuckled.

"Yeah and in eight weeks it'll be Doctor McCarthy and Doctor Williamson and I want to be your first patient and believe a hernia check is included in the exam," I kidded.

"Doctors Williamson and McCarthy will be giving you a complete physical." Suzanne chuckled.

"Yup, from head to toe, Stevie and we're going to examine every square of your beautiful body."

"Does that include my private area?" I asked looking at Dianne then at Suzanne with a lewd grin.

"Oh yes that's where we'll begin but only because we love you, Stevie, and we will love looking at your equipment too. Won't we, Suzanne?" Dianne sighed.

"I hope Charly doesn't find out," I said sipping my soda.

"We won't say a word, Stevie," Suzanne said batting her eyes, "You're secret is safe with us."

"So what time is your flight?" I asked changing the subject before the fly on my 505 trousers explodes.

"We're both on Eastern Airlines flight 332. Our flight leaves tomorrow at 0855 hours, why?"

"I'm taking the same flight, ladies. Let's see if we can get three seats together."

"That will be great, Steve, we'll meet at the Eastern ticket counter. We'll be at the airport about an hour before we board the plane," Dianne said.

"Okay, I'll see you both at the Eastern counter."

"Thank you for being a very special friend, Honey," Dianne smiled. "We both love you, ya know."

"And I love you both almost as much as I love Charly. See you in the morning." Kissing them both and returned to my squadron.

14 DECEMBER 1961: FLIGHT 1632'S LAST MAIL CALL:

"Fugger!"

"Here Sir!" the letter was tossed at his head.

"Sanderson!"

"Here Sir!" the letter was tossed at his head.

"Dyer!" Sgt Rizzo shouted as he ran the envelope under his nose. "Well, well, well, another perfumed letter that smells like it was mailed from a New Orleans whore house, Airman, but the return address is post marked as usual from the South Boston Post Office, Boston, Massachusetts. You know all the right people don't you, Airman BAGMAN?" Sgt Rizzo said chuckling.

"Yes, Sir!" How in hell did he know that? I said to myself giving the TI a strange look.

Sgt Rizzo approached me looking me right between my eyes and said: "Because Fudgie Iaconio has long reach, but we both know that don't we, BAGMAN?" Sgt Rizzo whispered a sarcastic grin on his face.

"We do Sir?" I questioned.

"Yeah…Fudgie Iaconio is Jean and my God Father."

"You have to be…"

"No, I ain't kidding BAGMAN," He said again calling me BAGMAN. "I was born and raised on Salem Street."

"You know Jean Sagan, Sir?" I whispered.

"Yeah, but her last name isn't Sagan, BAGMAN, it's Rizzo, she's my sister; oh and she enjoyed playing around with you on the golf course," He smiled then continued mail call.

"Yes Sir," I said under my breath.

After mail call we were dismissed then we all walked slowly back to the barracks. Fudgie Iaconio certainly did have a long reach. All the way to Lackland Air Force Base!

I felt bad for the troops who had never received any mail, not even advertising flyers, but most of the guys got mail almost every day. Sharly was so loyal. A mail call never went by without a letter or a package came for me. She would send me stuff that I could buy in the Base Exchange for half the price, but the gifts she sent me made her feel like she was doing something important. Nothing was too good for her flyboy friend.

12 DECEMBER 1961:

Hi Honey:

Only two more days and I'll have you back in my arms, if only for a short time then you'll be off to Cheyenne, Wyoming for heavy equipment training then on to California. It a shame that you couldn't have been assigned somewhere closer to home like maybe Hanscom or Westover but my Dad would say; "If you lived on the East Coast the military would find a way to send you to Texas or if you came from Florida you would get orders for Alaska". That was my dear old Dad. He's been gone for almost ten years and I still miss him. He loved the Air Force.

Guess who I ran into? I know you don't know... Rosie Leonardi! She came into the store looking for a leather coat, (what's with the Italians and black leather?) and we had a nice talk. She's still going out with Frankie Ianotti and she really loves him. While we were talking it was Frankie this and Frankie that and how nice he treats her; AND she's still working for him! Ain't that great? That how she phrased it: Ain't that great? She's a real nice girl. I can see why you went out with her, God she has a huge set of tits and I can also see why you broke up with her. She's a bit of a nut, but ain't we all a little out there.

She wanted to know how you were doing and when I write you tell him that Rosie "Beanbags" sends her love.

Richie and Pauly are regulars at the store. They don't buy anything because they're not yet dressing in skirts, ladies blouses, panties or bras, they just drop by for a visit. So does Babs and Billy. We're all looking forward to seeing you.

We are all very busy with Christmas being only two weeks away. All the stores on Moody and Main Streets are open until nine-thirty every as you know when you worked for Maxi. The stores are crowed and Moody Street is a parking lot, but everybody is in the Christmas Spirit and spending lot of money.

I also enjoy visiting The Sport Mart and talking to Maxi and Kuckie and now it being two weeks before Christmas Maxi has his four brothers working in the store, each stationed at a certain area so when a customer enters the store he or she has to wend their way around Frank, Mack, Sam and Nick before they can get the hell out of the store but they usually ended up buying something that they don't need just to get out. Maxi and I would stand in the back of the store and laugh our asses off; a Paulie metaphor.

And of course Kuckie was nothing but an errand boy for the four brothers, going down to Marion's Deli for sandwiches and coffee and to Swanson's Sales for soft, gentle toilet paper to baby Sam's tender sensitive rectum. Sam could also use some mouth wash. He had a breath could knock a buzzard of a shit wagon. That was another Paulie Whelan metaphor.

Oh Stevie! I miss you so much! More than I thought I ever could. I miss the way you hold me, caress me, your large warm hands gently caressing my breasts my hands returning your favors. I can't wait to see you and I pray every night that you are safe and that basic training hasn't worn you out. When you get home I want you big and strong. Just like Jolly Ole Saint Nick.

I'll see you in two days!

I Love You So Much, Stevie.

Charly.

12 DECEMBER 1961

Hi Sharly;

How you doin? That's the way the Piasans in North End greet each other, but you already knew that.

Yeah, Honey: That's her chest although I had never made an in depth study but they are all hers. I'm glad that Rosie and Frankie are getting on so well and I know that they'll have a nice future together. He was a so good helping all of us building the Mercury engine. He's not only a fine engine builder and teacher, but a great guy.

It's ironic isn't it that I'm being assigned to the same base where you, Babs and your mother was stationed when your Dad was training on the new jet fighters. The old F-86 fighters were in there time, fantastic.

You know, Honey, basic training was a great learning experience. You grow up fast because we had two real tough but great Technical Instructors.

They had to have eyes in the back of their heads because they didn't miss a thing.

I can't get home to you fast enough to see you and holding youin my arms once again. The last two months has been the longest two months in my life but also the quickest. But I'm lucky; I made two good buddies, CJ Wilson and Billy Toye and we along with the other 64 guys helped each other get through basic training. Now we're going to be stationed together. It's nice to know that you going to a strange base with two good friends. I have a premonition about Billy and CJ. I do believe we're being stationed together for a reason.

You know something Honey? We had a few of guys that got "Dear John" letters. I felt so bad for them, but the TI's made sure that they got over their heart break real quickly and got back to their intense training. If you feel like crying you can but when reveille is blown, get your asses out of the rack! You have thirty minutes to shave brush your teeth shower and whatever else dress and be ready to begin the hot, sweaty, grueling day.

Some of the guys missed their girls so badly they that when they called their girlfriends they proposed marriage. They wanted to get married as soon as they got home. I never thought that was a good idea do you? I love you so very much Sharly, but I want to be able to support you and give you a comfortable life. I don't know how to be poor and neither do you. I want us both to be happy Honey; happy and RICH! Well happy anyway.

Two days and I'll be home, Babe; can't wait.

I love you Sharly; so very much,
Steve.

PS: When you see Maxi and his brothers again tell
them that I wish them all, including Kuckie a very,
VERY MERRY CHRISTMAS, a Happy New Year
and we'll drop into the store when I get home.

With basic training being finally completed, our re-assignment
orders had been handed out and Sgt Rizzo and Sgt Powell gave the
sixty-four one stripers (E-2) their final orders. "Now get the hell out
of here, DO NOT miss your flights and never forget the lessons
that we tried to drill into your thick heads! Good luck Gentlemen!"

"YES SIR!" We all shouted in one voice.

"You DON'T call us SIR GENTLEMEN!!! We are not officers!
We're all the same now, we all work for a living!!!" The newly
promoted Sgt Powell shouted as they both turned on their heels
and walked out of the barracks.

Before CJ, Billy and I were due to report onto Francis E. Warren
Air Force we had a fourteen day delay en route leave. That was
nice of Uncle Sammy. Our leave plus delay in route was over the
Christmas Holiday and we all wanted to get home. It might just be
the last Christmas we would be home for the next four years. Some
of the guys were held over on the base assigned to the casual barracks
and were referred to as "P.A.T.S": Personnel Awaiting Tech School.
They were waiting to begin training as soon as the current class
was graduated. Most were going to be trained into the Air Police or
Medics squadrons. We called them "Ape Shits and Pecker Checkers".

I met Suzanne and Dianne at the American Airlines counter.
They were easy to find. "Stevie!" Suzanne and Dianne sang out
as they raced across the concourse and threw their arms around

me. "God we're glad to see you!" Suzanne cried as she and Dianne kissed my cheeks. It was only two days ago that we met at the Base Exchange.

"Lovely to see you again, my two loves" I said hugging them faking an English accent. They may be in love with each other but I know in their own way they loved me too.

"Steve, you were almost right," Suzanne said as she picked up my duffel bag and Dianne grabbed my hand and led me to the ticket counter where I presented my ticket. "We're training as medics not clerks."

"That's great, but how did you find out?"

"We asked Sgt Bowen," Suzanne answered my question.

"Really? But why aren't you training here at Lackland? Lackland's where all the medics train."

"Ours is not to reason why..." They both chimed in.

And I completed the Tennyson poem, "Ours is but to do or die."

"Let's go Stevie. Their calling our flight," Dianne said as we all picked our duffel bags and hurried across the ramp and boarded the jet liner. "It's time to go home."

"It's too bad that you don't have any nips," I said as we took three seats in the rear of the new Trans World Airlines Boeing 707. "I wouldn't mind having an in-flight cocktail."

"Who says we don't," Dianne grinned as she opened her black, leather, oversized purse and displayed twelve little plastic nips filled with Smirnoff vodka.

I was shocked as I gazed into her new oversized, black purse. "How in hell did you two manage to scrounge up nine nips?" I asked.

"Dianne had her brother wrap up the little buggers, individually, in tissue paper then carefully place them in a shoe box then stuffed the box large post office insulated envelope, than sent them down here to Lackland. The package arrived three days before we completed our training."

"I don't believe this," I added laughing, "But you took one hell of a chance, you know."

"You ready for an eye opener, Stevie?" Dianne asked reaching into her black, oversized purse.

"Let's wait until we're in the air," I whispered. "That way they if we get caught they can't throw us off the plane, Okay?"

"Yeah and we have to wait for the stewardess to come around with the soft drink anyway, unless you want drink it straight," Suzanne said.

"Steve?" Dianne whispered while she and Suzanne turned and looked at me they were both smiling.

"Uh huh," I replied sipping my vodka and tonic while I returned their smile.

"Well you know we both love you, you're so handsome, smart and a real good friend but Suzanne and I are more than friends, we are lovers. We have been in love with each other since we were in junior high school but we really needed to keep our relationship a secret but we decided because we trust you to explain…"

"Dianne, Suzanne," I interrupted as I took their hands gently caressed them. "You have nothing to explain to me or anyone else. Just be happy, enjoy your gift of love and never forget this: I love you both because of your friendship, your incredible sense of humor and for your love of life."

"Thank you, Stevie…Thank you," They both whispered tears streaming down their cheeks.

When the flight landed in Providence to let the girls out the twelve little empties ended up in the bottom of Suzanne's purse but we felt no worse for the wear and tear on our brain's grey matter. And besides drinking the four nips apiece we were also plied with snacks, dinner and coffee. It was an enjoyable flight.

Sharly, my mother, my Aunt Louise and Mrs. O'Sullivan were waiting for me when my flight landed at Logan International Airport, the flight arrived in the late afternoon. When Dianne and

Suzanne got off the plane in Providence I gave them a copy of my orders and we said that we would try and stay in touch. And for most of the four years we did. I'd usually hear from them around Christmas time, a card at Easter and Halloween and on my birthday. But when I shipped out for Vietnam we lost touch only to meet again when I returned.

Dad couldn't make it. It was a busy time of the year in the shop and he had a project that had to be to completed before the New Year. Sharly drove my Dad's Lincoln because Mom would not drive into Boston and Sharly would not drive my 51 Mercury Monterey or my '40 Ford coupe' the '40 coupe' was too small for four passengers, the Merc was too fast and Sharly could never get used to shifting the floor mounted three speed. I tried to teach her to drive both cars in the Raytheon parking lot but she earned her driver's license in her step father's 60 Buick Road Master. Her step father's Buick was almost as big as my old man's Lincoln.

Charlotte looked incredibly beautiful as she rushed across the American Airlines concourse. It was at that time that I realize how much I missed her or how beautiful she was. Mom, Aunt Louise and Mrs. O'Sullivan- Fuery looked wonderful too I thought as I looked at their smiling faces. Sharly felt so warm in my arms, her large firm breasts pressed against my uniform blouse, her hips pressed against my uniform trousers and her warm breath on my neck.

"Hi Sharly," I smiled as I gazed deeply into her violet blue eyes. "God I missed you," I said taking her into my arms.

"I love you, Stevie," She grinned stepping back admiring me the love of her life. "And God," She groaned. "You do look so handsome in your Air Force Blues."

"After eight week of insults and degradation, it's nice to finally hear someone say something nice to me." I smiled.

"After eight weeks of missing you I'm going to do more than talk nice to you," she whispered. "I'm going to do nice to you too, Sweetheart."

"And we're really going to enjoy each other, Sweetheart," I whispered back. "I promise you."

"Hi Mom, Hi Aunt Louise, Hi Mrs. O'Sullivan," I laughed hugging all three of them. "I missed you all so much! Hey, where's Dad?"

"Working hard as usual and I wrote you that Tommy is home for Christmas," Mom beamed. "My sons home together, both of you in our countries service and in our countries uniform."

"That's good. I can't wait to see him. It's been over a year," I said as I reached down and retrieved my Air force blue duffel bag and we all walked out to the parking lot.

"By the way, who drove you in?" I asked looking at my mother.

"Charlotte drove us all in, and in your father's Lincoln," Sharly's mother proudly announced. "She's very brave."

"You must be, Honey, I don't like driving the Queen Mary either, how did you do?"

"It took a little getting used to, but I managed," She said rolling her eyes. "I'm just glad you're here now. I really didn't feature rowing the Queen Mary back to Waltham."

"You should have taken the Merc," I said. "It's not as big and easier to drive."

"You're nuts, Stevie! Can you see me trying to work the damn floor shift and the clutch? We'd still be in the driveway!"

"Why didn't Tommy drive you all in?" I said. "He could've driven Dad's Hot Rod Lincoln."

"Oh… he and Debbie have other plans," Sharly winked as she ran her tongue against the inside of her cheek. I winked back knowing just what she meant.

"Come you two," Aunt Louise said, "Its cold standing out here in the middle of the parking lot; come on now we all need to nip along smartly shall we?"

I really loved my Aunt Louise, so did everyone who knew her. She never married. Her family was all she wanted and her father to care for. When Pa was in his forties he was hit by a coal truck and his hip was broken. As he grew older he had trouble getting about without a cane and finally he had to resort to a walker. He was a funny Irishman with a dry sense of humor who loved the Blessed Mother. He drove an old 1919 Ford Model "T" sedan for years but he never bothered to get a driver's license. All the cops knew "Pa" and they knew he was operating without a license but so long as he didn't kill anyone and stayed right of the yellow line they never bothered stopping him. If one of Waltham's Finest ever stopped him they would have to answer to the Chief of Police. The chief was my Uncle Eddie's cousin and Uncle Eddie was my Grandfathers only son. When they saw him tooling around the streets of Waltham, they would smile and wave. Of course "Pa" never drove outside the city limits except to visit his sister Maggie who live in Watertown.

The ride back to Waltham took less than an hour. The late afternoon traffic was heavy with people driving home from work but the Lincoln sped effortlessly along Storrow Drive. My Dad's Lincoln was a beautiful car, all six thousand pounds of it. There was three tons of iron, steel, rubber and fabric cruising at seventy five miles an hour without working up a sweat. I turned the big Lincoln into the driveway, got out, opened the door for Sharly, Mom, Aunt Louise and Mrs. O'Sullivan, then opened the trunk grabbed my duffle bag, swung it over my shoulder, walked to top of the driveway and checked out my Mercury Monterey, my 40 Coupe' and Tommy's '56 Crown Victoria, my Dad's back yard resembled a classic car display. I wanted to check the cars out and make sure that all three were okay. Sharly followed me while Mom and Aunt Louise went inside. Mrs. O'Sullivan (I could never get used to calling Mrs. O'Sullivan Mrs. Fuery and I would never call her Ann anymore than Sharley would call my mother Mary) joined Sharly and me while we walked around the classic cars. Ann O'Sullivan said that all the work and effort that Sharly and the guys put into the Mercury and the '40 coupe' was a work of art.

Tommy and Debbie came outside; they both looked like they both enjoyed a roll in the hay while Sharly drove the big Lincoln into Boston; and when I approached my twin brother we both came to attention and I popped Tommy a "High Ball"; Tommy wasn't an ensign yet, he still had two years to go, but as a sign of respect for his accomplishment I saluted him. Tommy returned my salute then threw his arms around me and we gave each other a warm hug. Debbie also warmed me up with a loving hug, and then Sharly gave me a warm, moist kiss on the lips then we all walked back to the house.

Mom had made her famous meatless meat sauce and spaghetti sauce, and baked three loaves of Italian bread. It was Friday and Tommy and I being in the military we could have meat on Fridays, but we decided not to push the subject. Mom, Aunt Louise, and Sharly's mother, were all devout Catholics, so Tommy and I decided to follow the family tradition. Dad couldn't care less about meatless Friday and so could Tom Cohan, our Grandfather. Pa was sitting in the living room watching the news and sipping on a glass of Jameson's Irish whiskey. Pa loved his Jameson's but always straight. No ice or mix. That would be a sacrilege. Ireland's 11th commandment: Thou Shalt not Mix Irish whiskey or chill it with ice. EVER!!!

"How about a beer Stevie?" Tommy asked as he opened the refrigerator.

"Yeah, how about you, Sharl?" I asked taking a bottle of Budweiser from Tommy's outstretched hand.

"Or would you rather have a glass of wine served in a Waterford Chrystal goblet Dear?" Mom asked. "Bill placed a bottle of a fine Merlot in the refrigerator down stairs when he came home for lunch."

"Yes I would, how about you, Deb?" Sharly asked as she headed for the cellar door.

"Wine will be fine with me," Debbie replied as she climbed to her feet and went down stairs with Sharly. "Oh and I called Barbara and she said that she and Billy will be dropping by a little later."

I excused myself went into the bedroom removed my uniform, put on a robe then went into the bathroom to brush my teeth, shave, took a quick shower went back the bedroom, put on civvies and walked back into the kitchen. "That was fast." Sharly said sipping her wine.

"First thing we all learned in the Air Force. Get in, shower and get out. We weren't given a lot of time to toddle," I explained grinning thinking about the naked young airman trying to shower at the same time. That's when the faggots were weeded out. No worries.

Tommy and the rest were sitting at the kitchen table or leaning against the counter talking and laughing about all the Christmas' we enjoyed in while living in the Bleachery and all the fun the that we all had. The only family in the Bleachery that didn't celebrate Christmas was Kuckie's folks. But Mr. and Mrs. Cohen always wished us a Merry Christmas when they passed us in the street or when we went to Kuckie's house. Kuckie's folks, unlike their son, were fine people. Kuckie Cohen has a long way to go.

"Stevie, remember when we had the school play when we were in the fourth grade and the only kid in class that didn't have a speaking part was you?" Tommy laughed as he took a swig out of is bottle of Bud.

"You had to bring that up didn't you, Ensign?…thanks a bunch," I said almost flipping him the bird.

"Well you know me, Stevie. Always glad to help."

"Yeah I do," I said as I gave him a sarcastic smile.

"Why was that, Stevie?" Sharly said.

"Because Miss Hurley didn't want to take a chance on my stuttering and screwing up the play she wrote," I answered. "I really couldn't blame her. My stuttering really sucked." I blurted out without thinking. In my mind I was still back in basic training.

"Stevie! For crying out loud!" Sharly groaned shooting me daggers. "Watch your mouth!"

"Oops…sorry," I said as everyone chuckled.

"So did the play," Tommy said. He was right, Miss Hurley wrote the play and it really fuckin' sucked. Sucked... a new word I had learned in basic.

While we all were talking, drinking and joking, the old man came home from work, smiled at all of us and with a firm grip shook Tommy's hand then mine slapped our backs and welcomed us home, than spied Sharly and gave her a warm hug and a kiss then went to the stove pick up the cover of Mom's sauce pan, took a whiff, closed his eyes grinned replaced the cover then walked over his pride and joy, his portable bar, made a drink for Mom, Aunt Louise, Mrs. O'Sullivan- Fuery, her husband, everybody except Tommy and I were either having a cocktail or drinking wine, then he raised his glass and proposed a toast. "Now to my sons a toast to Tommy and Stevie, both in America's service and in our country's uniform. Now I feel safe. We won't have another Pearl Harbor now that my son's are defending our country... well here's looking up your old address."

We all had to laugh, Dad was so dry but so funny. No matter how bad things were, you could always count on Dad to make with the jokes and have everyone laughing. When I had trouble trying to put two words together without tripping all over my tongue Dad would suggest that I should think of something pleasant such as focusing my mind on a happy thought such as a beautiful woman, maybe a tall blond woman with a large chest that trod the boards at The Old Howard. "Bill Dyer! Stop putting filthy thoughts and pictures into OUR SON'S head! I don't want him confessing such sins to our Pastor, the Saintly Father McCabe!"

"Then go to the Guinea Church, Stevie, you can confess your sins there and you're out real fast. Just say an act of contrition three Our Father's and you're back on the street ready to sin again." Dad said as he attempted to soothe my worried mind. "Those Dago priests don't understand you if you talk fast enough. Or you could go to French Church and while you're confessing your sins the good Frog Fathers are taking notes such as what's her name? What's her phone number? Where does she live? Does she put out, you know, things like that."

"Jesus, Mary and Joseph," Mom cried looking at her husband then over to me. "Steven, your father's trying to corrupt your very soul…"

"Come on Mary, I'm only trying to stimulate our boy's imagination and help him to get over his stutter, that's all. You know, Mary, the successful end always justifies the means," Dad reasoned.

I tried taking Dad's advice. Those beautiful women thoughts, while lying in bed trying bring beautiful women to my bed. Of course none of my erotic thoughts came to fruition. As soon as I opened my mouth to speak to the strippers my saintly mother's face would appear and the dreams would turn into a mist and disappear. It was a bitch for me trying to talk and nothing came out of my mouth that anyone could understand, so I kept his mouth shut and listened. I was amazed at how much I learned by just listening. What I learned was mostly jokes from my brother, Kuckie Cohen and Paulie.

Kuckie was a hot shit and so was Paulie. Between them and my brother they knew every joke in the world. But the funniest of all of them was Tommy. He not only knew every joke and he knew how to tell them. He put his heart and soul into every one of his jokes just like Al Jolson in black face his white gloves on and on one knee singing "Mammy".

The funniest joke that Tommy ever regaled all of us with was about a guy that takes his Bassett Hound into a talent agent's office in Scollay Square and explain to the agent that his dog can sing, "The Star Spangled Banner."

"So? Who gives a shit? I get to see a hundred of these dog pound queens a week. Who cares? Take your pooch and screw. You're wasting my time!"

"Will ya wait for Christ sake? Look will ya," He begged hugging his dog pound queen. "Rover can not only sing, "The National Anthem" but he can sing it out of his asshole!"

"Are you serious?" the talent agent questioned. "Rover can sing out of his asshole?"

"Yup, right from the depths of his bowels," He added smugly puffing out his chest. "Yes sir, Rover's got a lot of real natural talent."

"Well let's see what he can do. Put him on my desk."

So the guy places the dog on the desk and the dog squats down and covers the talent agents with a blast of runny, rotten smelling, shit that Rover fired out of his asshole!

"Hey! What the fucks going on! You tell me that your dog can sing out of his asshole and all he does is squat down and shits all over my desk! What's your story?"

"He was just clearing his throat!"

When I first heard Tommy tell that joke I totally fell apart. So did everybody else. It's still one of the funniest jokes I had ever heard.

"Hey! What has yellow balls and catches flies?" Kuckie chimed in.

No one spoke up. We all knew the punch line but we didn't want to screw up the joke and make Kuckie look bad. I heard Eddie Shea tell that joke years ago.

"You all give up?" Kuckie asked folding a Herald and placing it into his bag.

"Yeah, Kuckie," Richie said. "We all give up. What has yellow balls and catches flies?"

"A Japanese outfielder!"

Good one Kuckster.

"Hey! Did you hear about the nervous coon that walks into a bank, pulls out a gun and yelled," 'Alright you mother stickers…this is a fuck-up!'" That was a Paulie Whelan effort.

"Did you hear about the absent minded cop that jumped on his whistle and blew his horse?" Elaine "Lainie" Hartley chimed in. It had to have taken a lot of courage for "Lainie to join in. She came from Rangley Acres. Rangely Acres was a snob neighborhood that bordered on the northern part of the Bleachery and the fact that she even bothered to venture from the acres and associated with blue collar workers from the Bleachery stood her in good stead with the crowd. Kuckie began calling her mouse because she stood less than five feet tall and weighed in at ninety pounds. And without her folk's knowledge or permission, Lainie had been seeing Jimmy Falzone on the sly. Mr. and Mrs. Hartley would never allow their blue blooded Yankee, virgin daughter to go out with an Italian, but Lainie Hartley wasn't a snob she was a funny, down to earth pretty sandy blond hair blue eyed lovely young lady. Jimmy was tall for an Italian, a tough as nails Italian from Watertown who played football for Watertown High. He was one of the nicest guys we had ever met, except when he was on the gridiron. He was a quick running back that would score a ton of points playing for Watertown High.

He was awarded an appointment to the United States Air Force Academy on a football scholar-ship and upon graduation went on to flight school at Hurlbet Field where he was taught to fly "choppers", then was assign to an Air Force Rescue and Recovery Squadron, out of Pleiku, Vietnam. He served the year plus another six months at Na Trang, and when his tours of duty was over he was promoted to Captain, then returned to Watertown on leave to marry Elaine Hartley then Jimmy and Lainie returned to Hurlbert Field. The new Captain was assigned to the 43rd Special Forces as a flight instructor.

Following thirty years of a distinguished service career with the Air Force, Jimmy Falzone retired holding the rank of Brigadier General and for more than thirty years with Lainie and their three boys.

15 OCTOBER 1965.

MARCH AIR FORCE BASE CALIFORNIA

That morning I was dressed in my tailored class "A" blues, spit shined shoes, hair trimmed I re-enlisted in Lt. Col Jacobs office. Col

Jacobs was the 22nd Transportation Squadron Commanding Officer. The Colonial was heavily invested in Black Gold Investments. Thanks to Charlie and Billy we all had made a bundle in the stock market. He had made Black Gold a bundle too. Charlie and Billy dressed, in civvies, were there to watch me their fellow millionaire take the oath to faithfully uphold the constitution of the United States, and protect the USA from all enemies foreign and domestic, than the three of us drove to headquarters so CJ and Billy could pick-up their discharge papers. I went with them, than we took CJ's GTO into Riverside, closed the office, the building we owned had already been sold and all the files and investment portfolios were removed and flown to the new office in New York City. Black Gold Investments occupied the fourth floor in the Chase Manhattan Bank building on Madison Avenue. CJ, Billy and I had come a long way in four years. Billy was pissed because I decided to re-enlist. "What! Are you fucking crazy!" he shouted as he came nose to nose with me his black Italian eyes ablaze. "Maybe you don't know this but your next stops gonna be Viet" fucking "Nam, Stevie!"

"So what, Billy you and Charlie can run our little store until I get back."

"Our little store as you so succinctly put it is worth well over one hundred million dollars in investments plus the money in our own personnel accounts! How much you got in the bank?"

"The same as you and CJ, about five million dollars."

"Is Sharly's name still on your account?"

"Yeah, why?"

"She'll live like a queen," Billy said as he turned on his heel and walked down the section hall way and out the door. That was not to be.

I signed up for Vietnam then talked to the retention NCO. Master Sgt Phil Norris. Phil along with Billy and Charlie were good friends and with some of the officers and some of the super stripes, Phil was a short money investor. He invested the minimum, went with an aggressive high risk investment, made a few buck then bailed out. He made about a hundred grand after taxes.

Col Jacobs did well. We were all happy. Col Jacobs was better than the best and when he found out that I had volunteered for 'Nam he called me the newly re-enlisted Airman First Class into his office and wanted to know why. "Steven, you're going to a dangerous part of the world. If you want to change your mind I can have your orders red-lined. Thailand isn't all that bad."

"Thank you Sir. I want to see what it's like to live on the edge of the world. To feel what it's to be really like to be involved. I just want to go, Sir."

He looked at me as though I had grown a third eye. "Alright Airman, just be careful. OK? When it comes to my boys I don't like hearing bad news."

"Yes Sir. I understand."

"That will be all, Airman Dyer," the Col said as he stood up and shook my hand. "Good luck."

I popped Col. Jacobs a perfect high ball, Col Jacobs deserved nothing but the best when it came to respect, then I did an about face and marched out of his office. Charlie and Billy were waiting in the day room to drive me to L.A. International for his flight to Boston. Most of the troop from all of the branches of the service flew TWA because the airline treated all the GI's with respect. If there were any open seats in the first class section the stewardesses would make sure that we seated right up front. And the drinks and the cigarette were on TWA's tab.

23 JANUARY 1966

I had arrived at Logan in the early evening and Sharly was there to pick me up. I was glad that the whole world didn't show up.

Sharly looked beautiful dressed in a knee length charcoal grey skirt, a light brown turtle neck sweater, black flats, her long blond hair tied up in a pony tail her violet blue eyes glistening and a gorgeous smile that lit up the airport. I was dressed in my class A blues, spit shined black low quarters, and my garrison cap with the spit shined bill. I usually didn't travel in uniform but I had just reenlisted, and had a few ribbons on my chest and three stripes on my sleeve. I thought that it would be nice for Sharly to see me in uniform. Except for when I got out of basic training and came home, I had never worn my uniform while home on leave or when she visited me while I was at March.

"Hi Honey," she squealed as she ran into my opened arms and held my chest tightly against her breasts. "God you look good."

"So do you, Sweetheart," I groaned feeling her warm breath on my neck and her arms around my waist. "God, I've missed you."

"Still love me?" She giggled giving me a warm, passionate kiss.

"Oh yeah, Honey," I replied as we broke off our warm, passionate embrace feeling a class A feeling in my class A uniform trousers.

"I love you too, Stevie so very, very much."

"When I get home from 'Nam, Sharl, I want to marry you. Seeing you only a few times a year really doesn't make it for me. Living in the barracks, sleeping alone..."

"Is this a proposal?" She asked. "If it is than I accept, I'm tired of sleeping alone too.

Yes it was. I loved her and nothing would make me happier than marrying the woman that I loved, but the marriage would have to wait until I returned from Vietnam. I wasn't going to marry her, go to 'Nam and get killed. I wasn't going to leave her a twenty-three year old widow millionaire. Was I in for a kick in the head!

"What do you want to do, Honey?" She said as she massaged my leg about one half inch south of my balls. Billy Flynn let Sharly drive his new jet black 1966 Mustang fastback. Under the hood was a 289 cubic V-8; 271 horse powered Hi-Performance with a console mounted three speed C-4 automatic transmission shifter. I've always been a Ford fan from the ancient venerable flatheads to the boss 429 cubic inch engine but Billy's Mustang was a real nice car that took off like a raped ape!

"I was thinking that as soon as I return from 'Nam let's get married. I'll have a thirty day leave so that will give us plenty of time for a honeymoon and for me to get you pregnant." I said giving Sharly a stupid grin.

"Yeah know, Stevie," Sharly said snapped my nose with her thumb and fore finger. "You've been hanging around the wrong people. Do CJ and Billy talk like THAT?" Putting the emphasis on the word THAT then she snapped my nose again. "I'll just bet they don't!"

"You do that to my nose again you're apt to break it."

"I'm sorry Honey," Sharly said as she place a gentle kiss on my throbbing proboscis. "I know you were only kidding but it just sounded strange hearing you talk like that."

"I know Honey," I said. "But you have thirty days to clean up my act."

"Where should I begin?"

It took us about an hour to reach my folks house, I went into the bedroom and change out of my uniform and into a sweat shirt, Levis and tennis sneakers. Sharly told me that my Dad invited a few friends over to help him break in his new family room and wet bar that he had built in the cellar. A few friends? Everybody was there but the Pope. I had hoped that Sharly and I could have had some time together alone but when we arrived home the booze was flowing, the catered finger food from The Three Sons was being devoured and Kuckie had the old man's playroom rocking tunes with two turntables spinning out all the latest hits. Kuckie was on his way to becoming one of Toronto's premier disc jockeys. He finally found something to take the place of his nudie magazines. He and Cokie split up when he got his DJ gig in Canada and against his folk's objections, married a beautiful French Canadian Catholic girl from Quebec.

"Hi Kuck, how are you doing?" I said as I shook his hand slapped him on the shoulder. "When are you moving up to Toronto?"

"My gig starts the first of March so I'll go up there a couple of weeks before my job begins, find an apartment, get settled in then go to work."

"You must be excited."

"It's gonna be fun, Stevie, telling all those Hebe jokes I learned from Paulie and your brother."

"Is Cokie going with you?"

"No, Stevie, she broke up with me as soon as I told her about my gig."

"I'm sorry, Kuckie," I said.

"Don't be, Stevie. I'm not," He said while he cued up a Beach Boys surfing tune. "I liked Cokie, she was really nice to me but I really didn't want to marry her. Jewish wives can be a real pain in the ass. It would be like being married to my mother."

Tommy and Debbie were in from San Diego, Tommy had made Full Lieutenant and Debbie was pregnant with number one son. Frankie, Rosie and the Coyle Brothers were up from Florida, they were entered in the Winter Nationals in Gainsville. They had a million dollars worth of racing equipment ready to blow the doors off anything that went up against the Coyle and Ianotti racing team burning up the quarter mile.

Richie and Patty Brady showed up along with Paulie and Lily Whelan. They both were married. Richie and Patty had a boy and a girl, Paulie and Lily had a boy that will probably turn out just like his father.

It was good to see all the old gang. We all danced, drank, ate and laughed while we reminisced about all the fun we had growing up in Waltham. "You know, Waltham's a great place to live. There was everything we would need to have a wonderful time," I said while I looked around at my friends and my folks. "The Embassy Theater, The Wal-Lex rollaway…"

"The Ducks, Prospect Hill, the Natick Drive In," Paulie cut in. "All the pleasure pits."

At mid-night the party broke up, I was really knocked out still being on California time. Sharly and I said our good night sitting in the front seat of my 1951 Mercury Monterey the motor running and the heater humming, the radio on and were wrapped in each other's arms trying to wear the skin off of our lips.

But the folks were cool: They left us alone.

The next morning I climbed out of bed, brushed my teeth, shaved and took a long leisurely shower, dressed. I was the only one except for Mom and Tommy that didn't have to go to work. Tommy was on a fifteen day leave and I was home for a month. Sharly still had to work, and so did most of my friends. Tommy and Debbie spent some of his leave in Florida with Debbie's folks.

At five thirty I would pick her up and either drive into Boston for dinner weather permitting, it was February and the weather could be unpredictable, or have dinner with my Mom and Dad or Sharly's family. Then Saturday night I would take my '51 Mercury out of moth balls, I always kept the old girl registered and insured, then fill up the tank with SUNOCO high test then drive up to Rockport and spend the night. Dad would hand me the keys to the summer house, Mom would say drive carefully and don't forget your rubbers, I wouldn't want you to get your feet wet or come down with a cold, but we both knew what Mom was saying.

The week-end before Tommy was due back in San Diego he and Debbie drove up with us and we had a wonderful evening together. Debbie wasn't feeling all that well being pregnant but after a glass or two of VSQ she began to come alive.

Thirty days later my leave was over, I said good bye at the airport to my Mom and Dad, Mrs. O'Sullivan-Fuery, Sharly and boarded the big TWA 707 for California, spent a week at Hamilton Air Force Base, just north of San Fransisco training on M-16 rifles, 20 millimeter machine guns, and the proper way to toss a grenade and a quick release so you wouldn't have your head blown off; then I stepped aboard a C-141 Air Force cargo AC and flew seated back ward to 'Nam by way of Wake Island, Clark AFB Philippines where we picked up a real dumb seaweed. He had to show us pictures of his wife. She was gorgeous tall slim blond with a slim waist, small breasts with huge nipples and long shapely legs. The ten or so photos the petty officer showed everybody within arm's reach were posed in the nude. Typical navy asshole; then we finally blew into Saigon. I spent my first night in Vietnam bunked in a tent near the Tan Son Nhut flight line then in the morning boarded an Air Force bus with chicken wire on the windows for the twenty mile ride to Bien Hoa Air Base. It was the end of February and hot as hell. When I departed Boston it was snowing, the wind was blowing snow across the flight line and the temperature was twenty-two degrees. Let's go get the bus going and get the year over!

In the seven days since flying out of Boston I went from below freezing to a hot ninety degrees with the humidity that hit you in the face like a wet, hot face cloth. "What unit, buddy?" The three striper bus driver asked me as he stopped at the front gate waiting to be waved onto the base. I was sitting behind him.

"Motor pool," I said looking at the AP as he walked up and down the aisle checking the IDs and orders of the ten or so passengers.

"What's your name?" The driver asked as he looked at me in the rear view mirror.

"Dyer, Steven W." I said looking back at him. "Who are you?"

"Polly, Benny D."

"Charmed,"

"You're gonna love being stationed here a Bien Hoa, Dyer, bunking in a small, hot, smelly, twenty-nine man tent."

"Tents?" I said as I looking at the wooden hootches in the cantonment area. "Who's living here?"

"Hold on, Dyer," he said. "We'll be there as soon as I drop off the rest of the troops in front headquarters."

"Right," I said while I looked around the base. There was a definite French influence here in Vietnam. The large French built homes were quarters for the high ranking Vietnamese officers and their families and their concubines. The married Vietnamese enlisted men live with their families in rundown shacks near the west end of the flight line. The F-100 fighters would take off at 0500 sharp with one hundred thousand percent power with raw JP-4 injected into the afterburners and blast right over their quarters. I don't know how their hovels remained standing.

The bus driver swung opened the door doors, let out the FNGs, (fucking new guys), then drove the two miles down the flight line and headed over to the tent area that ran parallel to the east end of the bases only flight line. There was F-100 Super Sabers, F-5 Freedom Fighters, F-4C Phantoms that were assigned to the three different fighter squadrons, C-130's Hercules assigned to the 8th Ariel Port Squadron and C-123's Providers assigned to Ranch Hand. Ranch Hand sprayed "Agent Orange" all over the three corps area of operation. Agent Orange was some nasty shit. It not only killed the jungle foliage but over a period of time killed a lot of the American and Vietnamese troops and Vietnamese population.

A1C Polly, Benny D. dropped me off in front of the Squadron Headquarters tent I opened the door and walked into the office, placed my duffel bag on the floor and reported' as ordered, to the Commanding Officer with my orders. "Welcome to the 3rd Transportation Squadron. I'm First Sgt Walker and this is Sgt Dale Ripple, the orderly room clerk. I shook hands with both and took a seat beside Ripple's desk. "As soon as Polly parks the shuttle bus he'll show you where you'll living for the next year or so." Rip said filling me in.

"Where do I go to clear the base?"

"Right here and you just did," He chuckled as he handed me a locater and showed me how to fill it out. "This isn't stateside, Dyer. It's a war zone and we pretty much run our own show here, and we're very informal okay? You'll be assigned to Sgt Henderson's section. He'll show you what truck you'll be operating. We're short of heavy equipment people and semi drivers so I'm sure he'll find you something interesting to do, and when you get to the post office hand the card to one of the clerks and he'll assign you a post office box, all right?"

"You know I have a lot of miles accrued driving eighteen wheelers, between March, Edwards and 29 Palms Marine Base," I said trying to impress him with my five years of experience. It didn't work. I was an FNG. (fucking new guy). And you were a "new guy" until you were in country for ninety days. It took that long before you were no longer an FNG and began earning some respect.

"It's a lot different here, Dyer. You're trips will be between Long Binh, Zion then down to Tan San Nhut, East to the Saigon Docks and back here. For the first week or so you'll be riding with one of the drivers. It'll more than likely be Benny Polly the bus driver. He's been here for a while. Sgt Henderson can fill you in a lot better than I'm able to do. I'm only a lowly clerk." He lamented then smiled and handed me some forms and showed me where to sign my name. Then he gathered up the forms, inserted the forms into a manila folder with my name on it, climbed to his feet, walked over the file cabinet, opened the draw and dropped in the folder.

While we were talking, Benny Polly stumbled into the tent, came over to me and shook my hand. He was always grinning, a Salem cigarette hanging from his lips or clinched between his teeth. "You gonna be staying in my tent…"

"You own your own tent in a war zone, Ahab?" I joked.

"Cut the shit, Dyer," he laughed. "It's the heavy equipment operators QUARTERS." He put the emphasis on the quarters. "We're all NCOs and you're gonna love it here."

"You already told me that," I said.

"I guess it's true then," He grinned.

"Get him squared away, Ahab." Ripple said as Polly reached down, picked-up my B-4 bag while I picked up my duffel bag and led me to the tent area. There were no sheets, blankets, or pillows. All we had to sleep on were smelly sleeping bags mounted on a spring and a thin mattress. The sleeping bags were turned in every month for clean ones but they still smelled moldy. The sleeping bag that I was issued looked like it came from the Korea "POLICE ACTION". It was. "There's an empty bunk over mine. Why don't you grab it?"

"Ripple said that I'll probably we riding with you for a while."

"Yeah, until you learn the route. It's easy and it won't take any more than a day or two."

"Where you from, Polly, Benny D.?"

"Outside New Orleans." He proudly answered. "How about you Dyer, Steven D.?"

"I'm from Boston. That's in Massachusetts."

"No shit?" he grinned. "I thought from the way you talked that you were maybe from London."

"London's in England."

"Yeah I know where London's from."

I grabbed the bunk over Polly's bunk, emptied out my duffel bag and my B-4 bag on my bunk and hung up my clothes into one of empty steel lockers. All the empty bunks were on the top. Later that morning I reported to the Squadron Commanding Officer Lt. Col. Burns. He welcomed me to the section shook my hand gave me a half hearted pep talk; he didn't give a shit, in ten days he was going back to the world. "That will be all, Airman," I saluted the CO, walked out of the orderly room tent walked onto the wooden catwalk back to the tent, met Polly there, went to chow in the Red Horse Tent then to base supply where I was issued three sets of jungle fatigues, boots, an M-16 with one hundred rounds of ammo, a 38 caliber Navy revolver with ammo belt and holster then a quick trip into the city of Bien Hoa for the ten cent tour. What a shit hole! I can't believe that were sacrificing American lives to save a people that would kill us for the change in our pockets. Then we drove back to the tent area where I dropped off my equipment and on to the motor pool where I was introduced Sgt Henderson. Henderson was due to rotate next month. He was heading for Lowery AFB, Denver, Colorado.

"How about a beer, Dyer," he asked as he stood up, shook my hand then led me to a small drivers lounge that was connected to the rear of the vehicle maintenance hangar. "The other drivers should be returning soon. They're a good bunch of guys. A couple of them are a bit strange but you'll really like them."

"I'm really not a beer drinker, Sgt."

"That's Okay, Dyer, this shit isn't really beer," he said as he opened the refrigerator, "Came here from a World War Two warehouse on wake Island," he said as he handed me a rusty bottom can of Pabst Blue Ribbon and a church key. "First thing tomorrow morning Benny's gonna drive you over to supply. You'll need jungle fatigues, jungle boots, and an M-16. You don't wanna drive off the base without carrying some kind of heat, Dy. Maybe he can get you a 38 and a holster too. Benny's good at scrounging."

"We went to supply already, Chaz," he said as he reached into the fridge and grabbed a PBR. "And you gotcha self a handle Dy."

"I hope the hell my handle doesn't determine my future."

Nobody here in the heavy equipment section was called by rank except of the officers. They all had odd nick names. It made it easier than trying to remember each other's names and most of the troops didn't really care what your name was anyway. So long as you weren't a screw off, did your job, sweated along with everybody else and covered your buddies ass you were golden. Vietnam duty was a lot different from stateside duty. Nobody gave as shit whether you were an E-4 or an E-9. They were all NCOs and that's all that really mattered. There was no lower ranking airman in the section. They were all career NCO's. They didn't want to have to rely on inexperienced, untrained FNGs. Everybody wanted get back to the world standing upright!

As the weeks turned into months the trips to TSN, Long Binh and Zion was now routine but never boring. You kept your eyes and your ears wide open. There's was always some little slope head ready and waiting to blow out your brains.

Sgt Henderson and Major Burns had gone home and now Tech Sgt Jefferson, an African American, was the new motor pool NCO. He was a bit more abrasive than Henderson and a lot harder. He missed nothing. You fucked up and he was down your throat. Don't ever think about leaving the base with a full load and flat tire. He would check out each rig personally. He had a hug tire iron and he would beat the shit out of each tire to make sure it was aired up. He really cared for his drivers and he made it a point that when each rig left the base it was fit for the trip. "You drive off the base with a flat tire and you have two more shot out, your ass is in trouble like you can't believe! And when I get a hold of you your ass is grass and I'm the lawn mower! Fifteen tons of cargo and supplies and you have two flat trailer tire, you Momma and Daddy's gonna get a sad letter from the DOD!"

FRIDAY
30 AUGUST, 1966
Two days following my 24th Birthday
1730 hours.

"Hey Stevie," Benny said as I walked into the tent. He looked disturbed. He wasn't wearing his usual shit eating grin.

"Hey Benny, what's going on?" I said as I walked to the refrigerator and grabbed a Falstaff. I had just returned from Zion after dropping off a load of ply wood for the AMERICAL Division. The Zion troops were putting up a new day room. "Is everything alright?"

"Rip wants to see you ASAP, Stevie," He said looking out of the tent door. Tech Sgt Ripple was the squadron's new 1st Sgt.

"What's going on? What's wrong?" I said grabbing him on his shoulder and spun him around.

"He wants to see you, now go, go, go," He said slapping me on the ass.

I entered the headquarters tent and walked over to Rip's desk. "Benny said ASAP. What's going on Rip?"

"Col "T" wants to see you, Di," Rip said as he walked me into the CO's office. "You don't need to report in."

I walked into his office, removed my "Go to Hell hat" and saluted Col "T", "You wanted to see me Sir?"

"Yes, Di, please take a seat," he said returning my uneasy salute.

"Yes, Sir," I said sitting down my hat in my lap. Why was he calling me by my nickname I thought to myself. Col "T" always addressed his men by their rank.

"An hour or so ago I received some bad news from the Red Cross,"

"Yes, Sir?" I could feel myself beginning to shake. Was it Mom? Was it Dad? Was it Tommy?

"It concerns your lady friend, Charlotte?" He said looking down at the Western Union Telegram.

"Yes, Sir," I answered. I could feel an incredible sadness creeping through my body.

"She was killed in an unfortunate accident. She was struck by an automobile while she was crossing the street on her way to work. I'm sorry, Di. I truly am. Anytime something such as this happens to one of my boys I feel a profound sadness for my troops and their families," He said handing me the telegram and the envelope.

I sat there numb. I couldn't stand up, I couldn't move. Sharly was dead and I'm here in a combat zone and I couldn't do a damn thing. I had to go someplace, he needed to be alone.

I don't know how long I sat there before Rip came into the CO's office, helped me to my feet and walked me back to the tent. Benny was standing beside the tent flap with tears running down his cheeks. In the six months I was here at Bien Hoa, Benny Polly and I had become closer than brothers. I was told before leaving March AFB, DO NOT make any close friends! But Benny and I hit it off right away. That's the reason why Benny looked so sad. Rip and the 1st Sgt knew we were close, that's why before I drove back onto the base they told Benny about Sharly death and to keep an eye on me. I was glad that they did. Because right now I need a buddies shoulder to cry on. "Come on Di, let's go to the bomb shelter, you chase away the rats and I'll bring a bottle of the good the stuff," he said slapping me on the back. "And there ain't no one there that's' gonna bother us."

We sat in the bomb shelter among the sand bags, taking swigs from the bottle of Jim Beam and washing the bourbon down with cans of warm Falstaff beer. Sgt Jefferson gave me a couple of days to get my head on straight my shit together then I was back on the road. I was glad that Jeff didn't let me hang around the tent drinking and brooding. I needed something to do so I could keep my mind off Sharly's death and stay focused on the mission. "Hey Di," Jeff said as I walked from the tent area to the motor pool. "I'm really sorry about what happened to your lady, but the sooner you get back on the road the sooner you'll get your edge back. I need you Di. I need all my guys, okay?"

"Okay Jeff. I'm alright. Just show me my rig and I'm on the road again. I'm cool."

"Fuckin' "A"!" he smiled slapping me on the shoulder. "Oh and by the way there's a new E-5 here in the outfit, here's your orders. You got twenty four hours to pick up the four stripes head on down to the Bomb De Bomb stands and have Mama-San Betsy Ross sew them on. Congrats."

He had me back driving cargo and whatever else the Supply Squadron loaded onto my 40 foot Fontaine trailer then driving south to Tan Son Nhut. And if there was a little more sun left I would drop my empty trailer, pick up a loaded 40 foot and drive north on Highway 1 and drop off a load of wood, or plywood, shingles, plumbing or electrical supplies up to Long Binh. Most of the building supplies and construction equipment was flown into Bien Hoa's 8th Ariel Port and we delivered the supplies, booze, beer and equipment and whatever else that was needed, but we had no problems with the dog faces. The army let us eat chow at their mess hall. The army ate well, almost as good as the chow that the Red Horse mess tent served. Red Horse was a construction outfit out of Florida and these guys were the best construction outfit in the military. Sorry Sea Bees, you are good, but the Red Horse construction guys could lay out a flight line while you guys were still eating breakfast.

Three months following my tragic news Benny got orders sending him to Bolling AFB and in January 1967 I got my orders sending me to Bolling too. Now I finally had something to smile about.

A week following the news of Sharly's death I received a beautiful letter from Charlotte's mother and a copy of Sharly's obituary from the Waltham News Tribune. The obituary mentioned that Miss O'Sullivan was engaged to U.S. Air Force Airman 1st Class Steven W. Dyer. Airman Dyer was from Waltham and is currently serving with the 3rd Transportation Squadron, Bien Hoa Air Base, South Vietnam and at the end of February Sergeant Dyer was due to come back to the "States" and assigned to Bolling Air Force, Washing D.C. That's how it was written.

The gear jammers (drivers) the gear heads (mechanics) and the dispatchers when they heard news of my lady's death were fantastic. I received sympathy cards and letters from the wives and girlfriends of the transportation troops expressing their profound sadness at my loss. These were the woman at home praying for their troop's safe return and they were also praying for me. I had to have received a hundred card and letters and when I found time answered, every one of them.

When I received Mrs. O'Sullivan's letter she told me that Benny's wife who was a Cajon Catholic, sent her a Mass card and a beautifully written letter expressing her and Benny's sorrow. Leave it up to the gear heads, truckers, heavy equipment operators and the support guys to stick together and I had never in my life ran into anyone who could come up to them in support, comrade ship and testicular fortitude… "BALLS!"

Benny was given a proper Air Force send off, on the grill there was steaks, chicken and water buffalo expertly grilled by Col T and Danny MacHale. The picnic table was arrayed with Jack Daniels, Jim Beam, Barcardi Rum, Beefeater Gin, Smirnoff vodka and a fifty gallon barrel loaded with ice and beer. Danny had already gotten his orders for Tindal Air Force Base, Panama City, Florida. In thirty days he would be gone and Col T was leaving too. He was going back to San Antonio. After twenty six years and three wars he was retiring; getting out.

We all had our fill of water buffalo steak, good booze but nobody, not even Tommy Stilly got shitfaced. It was another duty day for the truck drivers of the 3rd Motor Pool.

And because of our close friendship, Jeff let me drive Benny down to TSN, to see him off and we promised to stay touch; we did and when I wrote Benny telling him the good news of my orders sending me to DC Benny wrote back to let me know that he wanted to be my sponsor. Benny took me over the rough spots, kept me sober and focused. Benny was the only GI in Vietnam who knew about my business and my connections and how well I was doing. I didn't really think that Benny gave a fat rat's ass. All that he cared about was our friendship. What Benny didn't know that he was going to be the richest man that ever came out of Bogulsa, Louisiana.

Thursday 24 February 1967 was my final day in Vietnam and I was anxiously waiting in the long line of two hundred or more G.I.s finally waiting for the announcement that meant their "Freedom Bird" was ready to board. Pappy Scott and Tommy Stilly drove me to TSN in a blue Air Force staff car. It was the only staff car in the motor pool. Tommy was the motor pool dispatcher and the Squadron lush. He was sober during duty hours but when he was off duty he really hit the bottle. I don't know how many times we had to pick him off the picnic table, throw him in the shower clothes and all then wet clothes and all except his boots, dropped him on his bunk and covered him with a blanket. But the next morning he was cleaned up, shaved and shined ready for duty. That's why the CO never came down on him. On the ride to TSN he had a half empty bottle of VAT 69. When three arrived at Ton Son Nhut the bottle was empty. He was the only one drinking. I didn't drink any of Tommy's scotch and neither did Pappy. I wasn't about to screw up my flight home and neither did Pappy. Pappy had a month to go before going home to Texas.

We swapped addresses, promised to stay in touch, shook hands, said good bye and I hurried along with the two hundred odd troops out on the ramp boarded the big Pan Am Boeing 707 and flew home. This was the first time I really had a chance to think about Sharly and how much I missed her. She was the best person I had ever met. She was bright, witty, and beautiful. I thought that if I had married her before he left for 'Nam or if hadn't re-enlisted would Sharly still be alive? Yeah probably. When I mention to Benny what was on my mind, he told me not to put the blame on myself. You cannot change what's already happened, Di. Just live your life the best that you can and keep Charly's memory alive and never forget how much you loved each other. He writes more eloquently than he talks.

Thanks Benny. I can't wait to see you again my friend.

On my trip down to Bolling I stopped by to see CJ in the Black Gold's downtown Manhattan office. He and Karen were married and on their way to parenthood. Karen was about ready to drop their first girl, and when I was settled in at Bolling I flew out to Chicago to see Billy. Billy managed the Chicago office and as soon as Billy could hire and train the new office manager he was going to open our third office back in California. CJ Wilson and Billy Toye were incredible when it came to finance. While I was away in Vietnam they made more money in that short time than the first three years of Black Gold Investments existence. Now they wanted to start a large charter airline company to chauffeur corporate executives and anyone else that could afford to charter his or her trip. Why fly commercial when you can reserve a corporate jet to fly passengers anywhere in the country in half the time. "That sounds like a good idea guys but we're going to need to hire someone qualified to run this venture anyone in mind?"

"Hell, Stevie, you're in D.C. now and we hire from the inside. Want the job?" Billy asked as the three of us sat at the bar in the Bolling Air Force Base Club NCO Club having lunch. I had been at Bolling for a couple of months and had the base and Washington DC pretty much down pat. I was also dating a real nice looking WAF who worked at the base locater section, but I'll cover that later.

"You're telling me that you want to rent hanger space here on the base? I don't think the base commander is authorized to rent space or have private aircraft landing on his base," I joked as I finished my drink and signaled the bar tender. "You guys want another round?"

"Yeah, I will," CJ said.

"How about you, Billy? You can't fly on one wing."

"Yeah, please" He said then broke out in a grin.

"Okay, now let's say we rent hanger space over at Washington National. I know for a fact that there are three empty World War Two hangers down the far end of the runway. And I'll bet we can rent them on the cheap."

"How about planes and pilots, Billy? Can you get them on the cheap too?"

"The Air Force has a shit load of C-140 Saber Liners that they want to salvage out."

"Where would that be?" I asked.

"Arizona. Davis Monthan Air Force Base," CJ spoke up. "Most of the C-140's had the engines yanked but we can get rebuilt fanjets from General Electric for around $25,000 per unit. And Lear's coming out with a new fourteen seat air craft with dual J-2500s."

"How much?" I asked feeling my blood pressure beginning to sore. Now I was ready to get back in business.

"I couldn't get a figure right away," Billy said. "But when I can find the time, hopefully next week, I'll take Lee Ann and fly out to Denver and talk with Mr. Lear."

"Any idea of the startup cost?" I asked as the bar tender took our drink orders.

Billy leaned back in his seat and fiddled with his tie, "Oh about ten million dollars I would imagine."

I looked first at CJ and then Billy then down at my glass. About ten million dollars I thought to myself. And they wanted me to run the operation. "Look guys, the moneys alright but the only business experience I've ever had was running a bag for a high roller from Boston."

"That's right and you made us all multi-millionaires," CJ said. "Hell if it wasn't for you and a large set of balls Billy and I would be counting beans in some corporate head quarters office building in downtown Manhattan!"

While we were sorting out the details and trying how to figure out how much we could write out off in taxes just in case the project bombed, Donna walked into the bar. I waved at her she caught my signal, and glided up the table. I stood up pulled out a bar stool and introduced her to CJ and Billy.

"Donna, this is Charles CJ Wilson and Billy Toye, my two best friends and business partners," I said as I helped Donna into her seat than sat down.

With the introductions over Donna ordered a dry vodka martini and chicken Cesar salad.

I was quiet for a while trying to absorb all the information. Billy and CJ were brilliant investers and they wouldn't piss away millions on some scatter brain idea. "You guys said the start up cost is...?"

"In the neighborhood of ten million dollars," CJ replied as he sipped on his scotch and soda.

"Is that something the company can absorb if this venture doesn't fly?"

"Oh yeah, that won't be a problem, but Stevie, If we don't start spending a lot of money Uncle Sammy is going to tax Black Gold Investments Inc back to the stone age." Billy said

I was skeptical at first but the more we discuss our new venture the more the project became a reality. "What say we do our research and if it's something doable? Good. And if we lose our ass we can always charge the company's losses back to Uncle Sammy, right?"

"I wouldn't mind taking the IRS downtown," CJ said.

"Anyone come up with a catchy moniker?"

"Yeah," CJ said. "We came up with Executive Airlines. How does that sound to you, Stevie?"

"Good and here's to Executive Airlines," I said as I raised my glass.

"To Executive Airlines," Billy and CJ chimed in raising their glasses.

BOOK THREE

BOOK THREE

BOLLING AIR FORCE WASHINGTON D.C.

The following Monday, 23 March 1967. I reported to the 1100th Material Squadron with my orders, spit shined low quarters, and brand new class A's. The uniforms that I brought to 'Nam were packed in my duffel bag and sat on top of my locker for a year and became moldy. I suppose I could have had them cleaned when I returned stateside but I tossed them out, went to the Hanscom Air Force base clothing sales and bought five sets of blues, five sets of summer tans socks two pairs of low quarters. My fatigues and jungle boots I brought back with me from 'Nam. The sales clerk looked as I peeled off two one hundred dollar bills. Then I took the uniforms to the cleaners and had them tailored. I'm not going to wear a uniform that didn't fit right.

1st Sgt Williamson took my orders, glanced them over without much interest than told me to take a seat the C.O. Col. Rosa should be in shortly. Ten minutes later Col. Americo "Ricco" Rosa walked through the door and 1st Sgt called us to attention. The CO gave us an as you were. "You Sgt Dyer?" he asked looking at me.

"Yes Sir." I said, that's how my name tag over my right blouse pocket lets know, I said to myself.

"Follow me," he said cocking his head toward his office, opened the door held it for me and let me in, closed the door and I approached his desk his desk.

I came to attention and began to report in. I raised my hand to render him a salute "Sir! Sgt Dyer…"

"Sit down Steve, leave the reporting shit for the ass kissers," He said as went over to the coat rack and hung up his hat.

"I'm glad to have a chance to talk with you Steve. Fudgie knew that you were in Vietnam and he called me and wanted to know if I could pull some strings and get you back on the east coast."

Col. Rosa looked and talked like an Italian right from the North end. He was fairly tall for an Italian, well built with a thick neck dark eyes short dark hair, fist like hams and a thick Boston accent. He looked like Rocky Marciano

"You know Fudgie...ah, Mr. Iaconio Sir?" I was flabbergasted.

"Yeah I know Mr. Iaconio...Fudgie. We grew up together hanging out in the North End, Fudgie and I go way back and when the Square was torn down by the Boston Redevelopment Authority Assholes Fudgie and Frankie moved their shit down to Florida."

While he was talking to me I glanced at his medals and ribbons and the Command Pilot Wings. He had the Air Medal, Silver Star, Purple Heart, World War Two and Korean War Service Medal.

"How's he doing Sir?" I was still dumbfounded. I couldn't believe Fudgie had that long of a reach.

"Great. He has a great deal going on in Miami. He has interests in three hotels, a race track and two dog tracks."

"Is he still a running book, Sir?" I asked.

"Na he got away from that shit when he moved to Florida. He also wants to express his sadness for you loss. You know he really didn't care for the nickname Sharly but he love the name Charlotte. He said her name made her look regal and she was the only woman besides his mother that he ever loved. Did you know that Fudgie went to her wake and funeral?"

"Yes, Sir. My Mother wrote and told me but I haven't heard from Fudgie since I left for basic training. God that was six years ago, Sir."

"He also had a flower car filled with roses sent to the funeral home and a check for her funeral sent to Joyce's Funeral Home."

"Yes Sir, I know, I really should call and thank him, Sir," I said as I thought of how generous he was with his time and money.

"Ya know, Fudgie told me you're the only person he knows that has more money than he has," The Col chuckled. "Here's his phone number, Stevie."

"Thank you, Sir," I said as I took the slip of paper from Squadron Commander. "Would you be any relation to Frankie Rosa, Sir."

"Yeah, the old "canvass back" is a cousin. He's down in Florida with Fudgie, still tending bar and running one of Fudgie's restaurant and watching his back. You know Steve, Frankie told me that you were the only non-Italian Fudgie ever trusted. He really didn't trust Eddie Shea. He liked Eddie he knew Eddie would never try to screw with him but there was something sinister about him. He also didn't trust Billy Harrigan all that much either but he did love Rosie Leonardi. He told me that you spent more time with your head between her tits than you did working for him."

"Yes Sir," I grinned looking down at my spit shined low quarters. "She was and still is a national treasure, but Sir, I liked Billy Harrigan and I'm still good friends with his son Emmy, Emmy joined the Navy about the same time I joined the Air Force, but it was like Billy and Eddie were cut from the same bolt of cloth."

"You nailed it, Steve, right on the head," He laughed. "By the way, where are you staying?"

"I'm staying at the Park Plaza but on Monday morning I'll be relocating into the barracks. I'm also in the process of buying a two hundred year old salt box colonial a couple of miles south of Arlington, Virginia," I said trying not to sound like I was bragging.

"That's a real nice neighborhood," He said whistling through his teeth.

"Now for a little fatherly advice, Stevie: Bolling has some of the best looking WAFs in the Air Force. They're pretty much handpicked as soon as they get out of basic training. Most of the girls are very nice but you're apt to run into a gold digger or two and they all know who you are. Bolling is a small base and news, good or bad, true or false goes flying around Bolling like shit through a goose. You're a nice looking guy with a ten million dollar smile and some of our lady Airmen know how to work on you and before you know it, well you know what I mean. Just stay loose and keep you bank book in your jock strap, capice?"

"Yes Sir, I capice."

"Now get out of here, I got work to do," He said as he got to his feet and shook my hand. "And Sgt, when you talk to Fudgie tell him Angie's doing fine. He'll know what you're talking about."

"Yes Sir," I saluted him did a perfect about face and was about to walked out of his office called out, "Hey Stevie," Col. Rosa called out as I opened his office door, "Welcome home!"

"Thank you, Sir."

When I arrived on the base a week before I was due to report into the squadron, I drove over to the motor pool and looked up Ben Polly. He hadn't changed on bit. He still had the shit eating grin on his face and a Salem cigarette hanging out of his mouth. "Hey Di," He shouted as he hurried across the parking lot toward me. I phoned him to let him know that I would be arriving on the base on the 20th of March. It was good seeing him again.

"Hey Benny!" I shouted out as we approached each other, and warmly hugged. I don't care what anyone thought. He was my best and friends and closer than brothers. I needed someone like him while I was going through a shit time in my life. "How ya doing old buddy, buddy? You look great!" He laughed, slapping me on my back

"Good Benny! Real good, how are you doing?"

"Can't complain, Stevie, this is real good duty and they have Air Force ladies on the base and most of them are God-damn knock outs. It looks like you dun cum to de right place where ya'll stayin?"

"At the Park Plaza," I said looking at him grinning.

"That's a bit pricey, even for a rich bastard like you," he chuckled giving me a gentle punch in the stomach as he bit down on his tongue.

"Rich? What gave you the idea that I was rich?"

"The brand new Corvette," he mentioned looking over my shoulder at the car. "The new threads," he said as he turned me around, "Lookin' good old buddy. Come on, Stevie, I want you to meet Sgt Blakely; he's gonna be your sponsor."

"I thought you were going to be my sponsor."

"Not since you made staff E-5, ole buddy. If you were still an Air One, I'd be clearing you in, but anyway, he's a good guy and funny as hell, and somewhat off the wall, but he made it clear to all who gave a shit that a millionaire Staff Sgt from Boston would be leaving Vietnam and would be arriving shortly," Ben grinned as he lit a cigarette. "And I know that you be that rich New Englander, is I right?"

"Cut the shit, Ben, Vietnam: Remember?" I said. "Let's maintain a low profile, shall we?"

"Way too late for that Stevie, everybody knows who is," He said. "And by the way, how are you holding up?"

"Just fine, Ben," I said. "And I have you to thank you and the rest of the gear jammers, gear heads and office guys for keeping me from going insane.

"I appreciate that, Stevie," Benny said slapping me on the back. "Come on into the section, I'll introduce you to the troops and show you around."

"Not just yet, Benny, I'm still on leave." I said. "I'll see you Friday."

"Okay, I'll see you Friday, Stevie."

Following my welcome to Bolling's Transportation CO, I walked out of Col Rosa's office went back into the 1ˢᵗ Sgt's office and was introduced to Staff Sgt Curtis James Blakely. "The Blake" was a tall handsome African American who dressed almost as sharp as I did. He looked like he was in the Honor Guard instead of being a motor pool vehicle dispatcher. "You spent more time in the Col's office than the Base Commander ever did, Dyer," 1ˢᵗ Sgt chided me. "What in hell were you two talking about if you don't mind my asking?"

"No not at all, Top. We have mutual friends from Boston's North end we just discussing ole friends."

"Yeah, that's right the Col's from Boston, but how did you get to know him? He's been in the Air Force since the Pearl Harbor. He went in as an enlisted man, became a flying Sgt earned a commission and came up through the ranks"

"Oh, I didn't know Col Rosa, I worked for one of his boyhood friends and I was friends with his cousin Frankie."

"I do believe he likes you, Stevie," The 1ˢᵗ Sgt chided me again.

Sgt Blakely was waiting patiently for the 1ˢᵗ Sgt and me to wrap up our bullshit session when he stuck out his hand and introduced himself, "I'm Sgt Blakely. I'll be your sponsor."

"I'm pleased to meet you Sgt," I said taking his hand smiling. "I'm Sgt Dyer, Steven."

"Nice teeth Sgt Dyer, Steven," he said smiling back handing me my in processing papers then we walked out the door and onto the parking lot. Blakely had a real nice brand new Marina Blue 1967 Camaro RS, but he insisted that we go in my 1967 Marina Blue Corvette. "I don't know my way around the base yet," I said

"Of course you don't, even though you arrived here a week ago and couldn't find the time to come into dispatch office and have Benny Polly introduce you around the but that's no problem," he smiled, "I don't and I've never as yet had the opportunity to drive a brand new Corvette or an old one for that matter," He said as he ripped the keys from my hand, walked to the driver's side of the car and jumped in then reached across the seat and opened my door. "You know Dyer," He said as he started my car then put it into first gear. "It's gonna be fun having a rich Sgt under me," He said as he laughed then drove off.

"Why in hell don't you get off the subject of money, Blakely," I said. "You're beginning to annoy me. It's not my fault I got lucky,

I just happened to be in right place at the right time. I have two partners and they do most of the work."

"You know, Stevie? I really love your car." The Blake said mimicking the 1ˢᵗ Sgt.

"I'm glad. Why don't you keep it and I'll go out and by another one for myself. I've read that General Motors is coming out with a brand new "Vette next year called the String Ray, a total new sports car concept. That way we won't be tripping all over each other in a foot race trying to beat each other to see which one of us is going to drive MY car today."

"You'd do that for me?" He asked as he put the four speed into first then let out the clutch and peeled out of the parking lot.

"Be careful Blake, She's fast, real quick. Don't let my car get away from you or you're gonna owe me big time!"

Clearing onto Bolling was fast and simple. When CJ, Billy and I cleared onto March it took the better part of two days because the base was spread out all over Southern California, but here at Bolling all the sections were in three buildings and they were all on the same street. Finance, supply, bas locator, Air Police, NCO Club; I didn't need anything from supply, but I still had to have my clearance sheet signed, then the post office, vehicle registration, NCO Club, dispensary with my shots record, Bolling only had a dispensary. If you felt the need to go to the hospital, Andrews Air Force Base was a twenty minute drive on the Capitol Beltway, then the dental clinic and last but not least, the base locater's office. The base locater's office was in the same building as the Base Exchange, commissary, barber shop, cleaners, bank and the cafeteria. Sgt Blakely introduced me to A1C Donna Hutchinson. She reminded me somewhat of Sharly, deep violet blue eyes, long sandy blond hair, oval face, up turned nose and full ruby red lips. Her dress blue uniform fit her like it was tailored to her tall shapely frame "Donna, meet Sgt Dyer, Sgt Dyer, say hello to Donna Hutchinson."

"I'm pleased to meet you, Donna," I said giving her a warm smile; don't come back stutter...please!

"I am too Sgt Dyer," She smiled as she reached out and took my hand that was hanging beside the seam of my right leg a shook it. What in hell is the matter with me? "Do you have your clearance sheet handy?"

"Huh?" I said as I gazed into her eyes.

"Sgt Dyer," Blake said looking at the clearance sheet that I held in my hand. "She wants your clearance sheet. The one you were handed this morning? I believe it's in your left hand. You'll have to forgive the young Sgt. He's just back from Vietnam."

"Oh these?" I said feeling my face turn crimson. "Excuse me, Donna for being rude. You just reminded me of someone... I apologize."

"That's alright," she said in a soft soothing voice. "You're on a new base you're just back from Vietnam. There's no need to apologize, Sgt."

"My friends call me Steve," I smiled my senses returning.

"Well you know something Donna, even Col Rosa calls Sgt Dyer, not Steve but Stevie," Blake remarked with a small smirk on his face. "Isn't that right Stevie?"

"Col Rosa and I have mutual friends from Boston," I replied returning his smirk.

"Alright, it's Stevie," She said as she gave me a warm, beautiful smile. Her teeth were white bright and even.

Then she handed me a form and pen. "Fill form out, and when you have it completed give it back to me please," She said looking at me as if I had to have every small detail spell out to the letter.

"Okay," I grinned as I did as instructed and handed it back to her. The Air Force wanted to know how to get in touch with you in case of emergency. Right now I'm living in the barracks and sharing a room with another returnee from 'Nam. He was a nut case semi-pro boxer from Alabama. He was a real canvas back. Sort of like

Frankie Rosa. Freddy Gray had taken to many shots to the head so may bwe moving out soon. He lived in the barracks for less than a month then discharged and sent to a Veteran's hospital in San Antonio, Texas. My new bunkie was a radical that hated anyone that wasn't black or poor.

I detested the word "poor". Poor was a state of mind, something that controlled your life and your future. I'd rather be broke than poor. Being broke was a temporary situation; being poor was a way of life and as Mike Todd so glibly put it: "I have been broke but I have never been poor!"

Blakely drove us back to the motor pool area, parked my 'Vette across from the driver's school building, handed me my keys and I followed him into the operations office where he introduced me to

Master Sgt Ned Cushing, a Mick from "Frisco and the NCOIC of the section. He had just received his orders sending him once again back to Vietnam; his wife had recently passed away so the Air Force in their infinite wisdom believed another trip to Vietnam would help him get his mind off his wife's death so off he went. Then there was TSgt Bob Shadley the operations NCO. Shad, a large well built blond haired, blue eyed NCO from International Falls, Minnesota; he had arrived from 'Nam about three months ago. Then there was Staff Sgt Billy Jacobs a tall slim black NCO from Austin, Texas. Billy Jacobs ran the drivers school.

Billy was a heavy equipment operator stationed down in the Delta area. He got back from Vietnam a year ago and was a bit strange, most of us returning vets were a bit out in the trees, and there was A1C Roger Hicks. Hicks and Polly had become good friends in their three month stationed here at Bolling. Roger had just returned from Korea, he was as dopey as the rest of us. It appeared that almost everybody I had met except for Donna Hutchinson were a little strange.

"Hey, Dyer," Blake said tapping me on the shoulder; I was talking to Roger Hicks and Benny Polly. "The Chief wants to see you."

"Now?"

"Yeah, right now: Go."

That would be Chief Warrant Officer Mason "Robby" Robertson. Blakely gave me the word about the CWO on the drive back to the motor pool. Mr. Robertson joined the Army Air Corps following Pearl Harbor flew twenty five missions over Germany was sent to Wendover Field, Utah to learn how to drop an atom bomb then was shipped to Tinian Island. He didn't go up with guys that dropped the bomb. He was a stand by, you know, just in case the first two B-29's didn't make it to Japan. I don't know what he or the other flight crews was going to do. They only brought two bombs with them.

Well we all know, as history bares us out, both bombs worked, we blasted the shit out of Hiro Shima and Nagasakei, and ten days later Hirohito threw in the towel and that finished Japan. Following the war Mr. Richardson re-enlisted and made the Air Force his career and before the Air Force became a separate branch of the military Mr. Richardson was commissioned a warrant officer.

I reported in, rendered him a perfect salute, talked for about ten minutes, he really wasn't interested in what I had to say, didn't asked me about Vietnam, I don't think he even gave a shit, shook my hand and I was dismissed. I went back to the dispatch office where Blakely was waiting for me and asked what I thought about the "Chief".

"I know he's just putting in his time, and he looked tired and bored."

"He has less than a year. That'll give him twenty eight years."

"That puts him around forty seven, forty eight years old." I mused. "I hope I look better than he does when I reach that age."

"Yeah so do I," he agreed. "What did you think of Donna Hutchinson?"

"Yeah, she's pretty. She reminded me of a girl I went out with," I answered my mind going back to Charlotte and the great times we had together. Maybe I'll feel the same way about Donna if we it off. A little voice inside of me is saying it will. I heard the same soothing voice when I was visiting Sharly's grave.

"Yeah, Polly told me about Vietnam and losing your lady. I'm sorry, Di, but if you're interested, Donna is not seeing anyone."

"Really?" I was amazed. "You'd think half the guys on the base would be running after her with their tongues dragging on the ground."

"That's not her style," Curtis explained. "Donna has way too much class. She's been here on base for about three years now and nobody has ever seen her out with anyone. She'll stop by the club with some of her girl friends for a drink but that's about all."

"You don't say," I mused. "I wonder why."

"Bolling's a small base and news, good or bad goes around this place in no time at all. Your arrival here for instance was anticipated. Everybody knew that an extremely wealthy E-5 named Dyer, Steven Dyer from blue blood Boston would be arriving shortly."

"Col Rosa said the same thing. He told me to play it cool."

"That's good advice, keep an eye on your wallet and watch out for free loaders. Some will try to steal the silver out of your teeth."

"Does that include gold caps?" I said admiring his gold capped two front teeth.

"I'd like to see any of these clowns around here try it," He chuckled as he climbed to his feet and went into the head.

"So would I," I said under my breath.

When Curtis came back from the head he pointed to the chair and told me to take a seat. I sat back in the chair, crossed my legs and began the conversation "You know Blake, I just want to be like the rest of the guys in the outfit, just like out at March or 'Nam, show up for duty, do the best job I can, get off duty, drive to the mess hall, have something to eat then drive over to the NCO Club for a drink play some golf. You know, mind my own business be cool and maintain a low profile?"

Curtis looked at me then leaned back in his chair and rested his head against the wall. "You know Steve, Donna's a real lady and just because she particular when it comes to her personnel choices doesn't mean she's stuck up or looks down her nose at anyone waiting for the right white guy to come along."

"Do you think that I'm white enough?"

"Well let me check," he said picking up the phone.

"Come on Blake…" I said climbing to my feet. He had already dialed the four digits.

"Hi Donna, the Blake," he grinned looking up at me and grinned displaying his two gold capped front teeth. "What are you doing for lunch?"

He waited a second or two for her to answer. "That's good, good. Sgt Dyer will be picking you up at noon. He has a brand new Marina blue Corvette. You can't miss it. It's the only one on the base." He waited for her reply then said, "He'll see you then. Good bye, Donna."

I looked down at his handsome black face in utter surprise. My mouth and eyes were wide open. "The Blake?" I said with a puzzled look on my face. "You must know her very well."

"Yeah I do and you can thank me later."

"May I have your permission so I may use my new 1967 Marina Blue Chevrolet, Corvette Sergeant?" I asked as I reach across his desk and retrieved my car keys.

"Of course, young Sgt, just be sure the gas tank is full when you bring her back,"

I left the dispatch office a little before noon and drove over to Base Exchange building hurried up the steps that led into the building and walked down the hall to Donna's office. I was excited but apprehensive too. The only girls that I had dated over the past nine years were Rose Lyn Leornardi and Charlotte O'Sullivan. They were both beautiful woman in their own right. Beanbags with her love of life and Charly with her love for me. Let see what develops between Donna and me. I'm sure that it will be interesting.

"Hello Donna?" I sung out knocking on the bottom of the Dutch door with a sign that read, Authorized Personnel Only!

"Oh hi, Steve. I'll be with you as soon as Airman Carter gets back from the post office."

"Ah, Donna, I just want you to know that I didn't put "The Blake" up to making a lunch date for us. He did it on his own. I hope he didn't embarrass you. I would never want anything like that to happen."

"Curtis can be a little off the wall but there's no better NCO on the base, Steve," she said as she opened the bottom of the Dutch door. "Come in and have a seat."

"Is it alright?" Pointing to the yellow sign thumb tacked to the door.

"Yeah, it's alright, come on in," she replied smiling.

"Thank you," I said as I walked into her office and placed my hat on her desk.

"Sure," She said smiling at me.

"So, where would you like to have lunch? Some place close, alright? I'm not all that familiar with the base yet."

"How about the NCO Club?" She asked. "It's only a short distance."

"Okay, the NCO Club. That's a nice club. I was there this morning while I was processing in," I said as A1C Suzanne Carter and A1C Dianne McCarthy walked into the office. "Suzanne, Dianne, remember me?" I said jumping to my feet. You could have knocked me over with a feather. Who would have thought that Dianne, Suzanne and I would have ever end up here at Bolling. "We met on the plane going to basic training, remember? Dianne, you dropped six vodka nips out of your purse and they rolled down the aisle!" I said laughing. "And you tried grab them and stuff them down your blouse!"

"Stevie Dyer!" They sang out said in unison giggled and I snuggled them into my arms. "God you look good and as handsome as ever," Suzanne exclaimed. "How long have you been on base?"

"I just got here. Donna and I are going to lunch."

"You just arrived on base and you and Donna are going to lunch?" Suzanne remarked as she hugged me again. "You work fast Sergeant Stevie."

"Not really, Sgt Blakely was the perpetrator. He called Donna and asked what she was doing for lunch etc...etc."

"That's wonderful I'm happy for you both," Suzanne said then took my arm and walked me out of the office and onto the hallway.

"What happened to you and Charlotte?" Suzanne asked looking at me while she adjusted my tie that didn't need to be adjusted.

"She was killed, Suzanne: I was half way through my tour of duty in 'Nam when I got the news that she was killed by a drunk while she and one of her friends were returning to work, they had just finished dinner," I said looking into her deep blue eyes. I still can't believe that she and Dianne are gay. They are two beautiful ladies but I really do love them.

"Welcome home, Stevie," Suzanne whispered then kissed me gently on the cheek. "And I'm so sorry. I'll let Dianne know."

"Thanks Sweetheart," I whispered back. "I love you both."

"And we love you too, Stevie," She said giving me a sad smiled a slight tear in her eyes. "And that's forever."

We took the short walked over to the NCO Club it was quicker than driving and trying to find a parking space. While I was clearing the base I join the NCO Club but I didn't have a chance to look around. Most Officer's Clubs weren't as nice and the Bolling NCO Club. The interior resembled an old New England sea side restaurant, oak panels, oak floors, high ceilings and floor to ceiling windows with window seats. I was impressed. Breakfast and Lunch was served buffet style and dinner was sit down served by uniform waiters wearing white shirts and ties and black tuxedo styled trousers with black pattern leather shoes.

While we had our lunch we talked about our friends and home, Donna came from Harrisburg Pennsylvania, our jobs, our families and why we joined up. In the blink of an eye the lunch hour was over and we were on our way back to her duty stationed. I walked her to her office, asked when she would free again. "How about when we get off duty we have drink at the NCO Club Rathskeller?

"How would one find the Rathskeller?" I inquired.

"One would meet the other in front of the NCO Club and could be shown where the Rathskeller is located, but why don't you pick me up in the parking lot across from the Base Exchange?" She said giving me funny face smile as she wrinkled her nose while we walked back to her office.

"Say around 5 o'clock?"

"Yeah. I'll see you then Stevie."

"I haven't been called Stevie since I was a kid," I chuckled.

"You don't mind do you?"

"It depends on who you are."

"See you after work, Stevie."

"Perfect," I smiled. "Say bye to Dianne and Suzanne for me will you and tell them I'll drop by and see them again, Okay?"

"You know they're both so nice and real funny and really in love with each other but who cares, I don't."

"Neither do I, I just hope that they don't try to move in on me," I joked.

"Put it out of your mind, Stevie, and besides they ain't my type." Donna said as she placed a gently kiss on my check.

My first afternoon on my first day in my duty section was spent with Benny Polly. He introduced me to the drivers, civilian and military, the vehicle maintenance area, and the driver's school but no matter how interested I try to appear, the clock had stopped. "Why you keep on looking at the clock, Stevie. "Ain't gonna make the time go by no quicker."

He was right. I tried to avoid looking at the clock or my watch but once Benny's tour of the section ended and we returned to the office there wasn't a hell of a lot to do. There were four of us assigned to the dispatch office with only three desks and three phones. Blake told me to take a ride around the base and familiarize myself with the layout. I did. I drove my corvette up and down every street all the way to Anacostia Naval Air Station, then over to the golf driving range, the picnic area then back to the motor pool. The trip with the stops took less than half an hour. If I walked the base on foot it would have taken me less than an hour.

Now what? I wasn't about to drive off the base. I still didn't know my way around DC at all. When I drove down from Boston to the Capitol Beltway I had no problem, until I became hopefully lost in the Northwest section of the city and had to ask a black cab driver how to get to Bolling. "You drop me a sawbuck in my hand "boy" just stay behind me and I will take you right to the main gate. Just follow me. Only take us 'bout ten, maybe fifteen minutes." He said as he held out his hand and gave me a yellow toothed grin. It was an easy ride he took me to the main gate and left me there. I showed the Air Police my ID, orders, vehicle registration and insurance papers. He directed me to the Visiting NCO Quarters, I checked in for the night then the next morning I check out of the NCO Quarters asked for directions to the Park Sheraton then drove down town and checked in. If I was going to wait the week before signing onto the base I was going to live in comfort and luxury.

I drove back to the motor pool, walked into the dispatch office and sat down on the radio consol. There was nothing going on. "Hey Ben, is it always this busy?"

"Naw. They ain't much going on around here right now, but once in a while we have to drive a general to the pentagon or Andrews or National. You're gonna find duty here a sometimes boring and sometimes not so boring. Right now it's a little slow."

"So why are there so many people just sitting around drinking coffee, playing cards, watching television, reading news papers?"

"Look Stevie," Benny said. "This ain't Viet fuckin Nam this is Headquarters Command, USAF. There's thirty three general officers assigned here at Bolling and all they's ass waiting to be suck. Plus congressmen, senators and reps that need to have their asses kissed too and we also gotta supply transportation for the honor guard, the Air Force Band and whatever else comes up. It can get a bit hairy here at times."

"Since you've been here have you been doing any driving?" I asked.

"Oh ya," he said. "And so will you. Still got your 246? Or did you leave it behind when you left 'Nam?"

The DD form 246 was you military drivers license listing all the vehicles that you were authorized to operate.

"No, I have it in my wallet."

"Well for you to get over to Fort Meyer, old buddy, you're gonna need to drive through part of DC."

"Why would I need to drive a tractor trailer over to Fort Meyers? Fort Meyer's an Army Base."

"When the Army wants their heavy equipment moved they call us. They ain't got the wheels." Ben explained. "You gonna be one of the go to guys same as me."

"I certainly hope someone shows me the way to Fort Meyers and not just hand me the keys and send me on my way." Benny could see the panic in my eyes.

"Naw, that won't happen," He said in an attempt to console me. "I'll take you over there myself and show you the lay out. It's really easy 'cept tryna get that big assed forty foot Fontaine flatbed 'round the Lincoln Memorial. That can be a real bitch 'specially 'round rush hour."

"Ben's right Di, so I suggest that you have a change of fatigues and boots in the driver's lounge," Curtis advised. "One of our former drivers, Sgt Hall is on his way to Viet fuckin Nam so you get his truck."

"All I have to wear is jungle fatigues a floppy boonie hat and jungle boots. Is that authorized here on the base

"That will not be a problem even if you do scare the shit out of the locals."

"How about blousing my boots?"

"Not unless you're wearing an Air Police dark blue band on your arm. Don't blouse them, Di."

"Hey Benny," I caught him outside the driver's lunge. The driver's lounge was located between the vehicle maintenance area and the motor pool. "Why does Blake call me Di? I haven't been called Di since 'Nam."

"When I got here I told Blake that you were on your way and you'd be here around the end of March and when I referred to you about something or another I called you Di."

"Oh."

"You remember Billy Simpson?" He asked

"Yeah, Simple Simpson; from vehicle maintenance," I said. Billy wasn't simple and it was Tommy Stilly that tagged him with the nick name when he arrived on the base. The fact of the matter was that Simple was quite intelligent. He had two years at Arizona State as a history major before he enlisted. It was a shame that he ran out of money before he could complete his studies.

"Yup, well he's still in vehicle maintenance right here on the base."

"You don't say? Since when?"

"He got here around the middle of January. Ya know he and Blake were stationed together in Greenland? "No I didn't."

"Yup they were stationed at Thule."

"How come we didn't see him in the vehicle maintenance shop when you showed me around?"

"He's down town taking computer classes."

"Well I'll be go to hell." I smiled at Benny.

"Oh, and he made Staff,"

"It's about time," I said. "He's been in almost as long as Blake."

"Yeah, shame he got busted when he was in Tech school."

"You're next Old Buddy," I said slapping Benny on his shoulder. "By June you'll be sporting four stripes."

"Ya think?

"Yup, I can feel it in my bones."

"You sure 'bout them bones?" He asked lighting a cigarette.

"Yeah, if the butts don't kill you first," I grinned slapping him on his shoulder again.

"They ain't no proof that cigarettes is gonna do no harm, aint no proof a tall." Nobody could butcher the English Language better than Benny Dean Polly. We've been friends for over a year and the one thing I learned about him, he ain't dumb.

"You say what you want?" I said shielding my eyes from the sun. "But I do believe that smoking cigarettes is about the worst thing that you can do to your body."

Donna was standing in the parking lot waiting for me to arrive. I started to get out of the car so I could get the door for her but she waved me off opened the door and climbed in. "Hi Stevie," she said as she smiled at me. "Nice car. I love Corvettes and the new Camaros too? What do you think of them?"

"The '67s are going to be a classic. Mark my words, Donna. In thirty years the three thousand you paid for the car today in show room condition will be worth at least forty grand."

"How do you know?"

"Because I know how people think when it comes making investments. This car that we are sitting in now will be worth at least a fifty grand thirty years from now," I said as I put the 'Vette into reverse and backed out of the parking space.

"And that's how you make your living?"

"I find that it works well for my partners and me," I smiled.

"I have an idea, Steve. Instead of going to the NCO Club, there's a nice restaurant right outside of the base; Dino's Café'. We can get a drink and have dinner. It's easy to get to. I'll show you."

"OK, now how do I get off the base?"

"The same way you got on. Only do it backward."

"I can see right now that we are going get along real well."

Apparently we weren't the only GIs in the place. Dino's Café' was half filled with men and woman in uniform sitting at the bar or in the booths that lined the walls. "This place reminds of the bistros in Boston's North End." I noticed as we waited to be seated. "And I love Italian food."

"Glad I thought of it?"

"Yeah, this place is nice and I feel real comfortable here; I feel like I'm back in Boston."

We were seated, handed menus, then we ordered our drinks. Donna ordered a Beefeater and tonic I opted for an Absolut and tonic. Our waiter was a short, stocky, bubbly Paisan with curly black hair, deep set black eyes and a smile that would light up any room. He looked like the Italian waiter in the movie "The Lady and the Tramp". I had to ask him if he was familiar with Boston's North end. He said he was, he was born and raised in East Boston. I then had to ask if he Knew Fudgie Iaconio. "Oh yes Sgt. Fudgie was a very important man and a very beloved man too. He lives now in Florida.

"Before I joined the military, I worked for Fudgie." I said.

"NO! You kidding! What did you do, if you don't mind my asking?"

"I was a bagman for a bookie from Waltham..."

"Ah, Waltham, and the Three Sons. They have the best Italian food outside of Boston."

"I lived right down the street from the Three Sons. Anyway I picked up the money, Eddie Shea paid off the winners and I dropped off the money at Fudgie's office on Hanover Street," I said looking at Donna.

"OH, forgive me for being rude Sir, my name is Steve Dyer and this lovely lady, Donna Hutchinson, my dinner guest."

"No, no. You and you," He said shaking his finger between Donna and me. "You two call me Angelo. I'm one of the owners. We're friends now. Now, what would you two nice people like for dinner?"

"What do suggest, Angelo?" Donna asked.

"You asking me? Everything on the menu," he said giggling. "I'm only being silly, but try the Chicken Marsalla. It's the best in the world. The recipe is right from the old country."

"I didn't know Chicken Marsalla originated in Ireland. It doesn't sound like an Irish dish to me." I joked.

"Now you're being a wise guy, Stevie," Angelo said shaking a finger in my direction.

"Donna? What do you think?"

"Two please, Angelo," She smiled.

"She's very lovely, Stevie," Angelo said as he picked up the menus and held them to his chest. "You're a very lucky Paisan," he said then hurried off.

"You know Angelo's right," I said sipping my drink. "You are lovely and I'm a real lucky Piesan."

"Oh yes you are, Stevie… if I have anything to do with it," She said looking over the rim of her cocktail glass smiling.

We finished our dinner enjoyed an after dinner brandy then Angelo introduced us to the two other owners, his brother Bruno and Bruno's wife Rosie. They were all from East Boston and they all knew Fudgie, Fudgie's brother-in-law Frankie Rosa the boxer who had seen more canvas than a sail maker, Col Rocco Rosa and with Fudgie's generosity helped them open their restaurant. No check, the food and the drinks were on the house. I dropped a "C" note on the table, shook hand with the owners, promised that we would be back: And Bruno let us know in no uncertain terms that if didn't eat at their restaurant once a week he would send his friend from East Boston to look us up and show us where the restaurant could still be found. Donna and I both laughed and I took her hand and we walked out to the parking lot.

"You're incredible, Stevie," Donna said as we climbed into the 'Vette. "One day in DC and you made more friends than I've made in three years. How do you do it?"

"By carrying a bag for bookies, running a business with my partners C.J. Wilson and Billy Toye and the Irish gift of gab that I inherited from my mother, she's born and raised Ireland."

"Do you have any brothers or sisters?" Donna asked as she headed me in the right directions back to the base.

"Yeah I have a twin brother, Tommy," I replied. "He's a Navy Lieutenant."

"You don't say."

"Yeah, he graduated from Annapolis class of '65."

"I'm impressed," She said.

"So am I Donna." I said.

"Now let me ask you this, Stevie, and please be honest," Donna said as she turned and looked my profile as we approached the main gate. "If Blake hadn't called me would you have?"

"No I wouldn't have. I would have asked you out in person. Except for business, I don't like using the phone when I can talk to somebody face to face. Phones are for conducting business not for asking lovely ladies such as you to have lunch or dinner with me. And I know class when I see it."

"And I know that you're successful, I can tell by the way you dress, how you speak, you are well educated, aren't you?"

"Only high school, Donna, and street smart," I said as the Air Policeman waved us onto the base. "And when Blake introduced us I acted dopey because you reminded me of someone."

"You don't have to be a college graduate to be well educated, Stevie. My Dad is a pilot, and a captain for Eastern Airlines. He's only high school educated, but during the war he was a cargo pilot for the Army Air Corps and when he was discharged he went to work for Eastern but when he speaks you'd think he was a Rhodes Scholar."

"The same as my Dad he had only a high school education AND when he came down from Canada in 1928 he had exactly ten dollars in his pocket but he believed in the American dream, got a job with a machine shop in Cambridge, he assembled automobile starters and during the war he worked for a defense plant invested part his salary in defense bonds, and following the Korean he cashed in the bonds and opened his own business."

"And I'll wager he's very successful."

"Yeah he's doing well. New England Tool and Die is one of the more successful small business' in the Boston area."

"Now I can see where you get all your investment expertise,"

We stopped off at the NCO Club for a night cap. The Rathskeller was crowed and foggy with cigarette smoke, the juke box was playing "She'd Rather Be With Me" by the Turtles and there was a basketball game on the television, the Boston Celtic were taking on the New York Nicks. Donna and I found an empty booth then I went to the bar and ordered two glasses of Hennessey Cognac. The bartender had to brush of the dust off the bottle. "Not much call for cognac down here," the tall, skinny, Negro bartender said looking at the bottle. "I hope I can get the cork out of the thing."

Donna and I sat in the booth and talked about me growing up in Massachusetts and Donna in Pennsylvania. Donna had a younger brother, Kevin who was in the Army, stationed in Korea. He was sweating out being shipped out to 'Nam and he still had three years to go on his enlistment. Donnie enlisted, went to Fort Rucker for training then was assigned to an air cavalry unit. The Army waited until Donnie had a year to go before his enlistment was up and they shipped him off to the 173rd Airborne Brigade, Bien Hoa Air Base Republic of Vietnam. He came home without a scratch.

We didn't want to close up the place we both had be on duty in the morning. I dropped her off at the WAF Barracks that was across the street from the NCO Club, and I insisted on being a gentleman and opened the door helped her out of the cramped bucket seat and walked her to the barracks door, held her hand, gently kissed her on the cheek, asked her what she wanted to do tomorrow night if she was still interested. "Of course I'm still interested, silly, and tomorrow being Friday, there's usually a real good rock band upstairs, and I could use some good ole rock and roll, you know? Get out on the dance floor and get down?"

"Yeah, nothing like some good ole rock and roll, I just hope I still remember. It's been a long time, and I haven't danced a lick since high school."

"It's like riding..."

"I know," I smiled interrupting her. "A bike,"

"You'll do fine."

"Anyway... would you like to meet for lunch tomorrow?"

"Yeah I would. I'll be waiting in front of the NCO Club. It will be easier for us meeting there than coming all the way to my office."

"I'll be there. Good night, Donna."

"Good night, Stevie. And thank you for a wonderful evening," She said as she kissed me softly on the lips.

"It's been all my pleasure." I said returning her kiss. "Thank you, Donna. Goodnight."

AUGUST 1967

"Hold on a minute please, sir," Curtis said as he punched the hold button. "Benny! Where in hell is Dyer?" Curtis shouted.

"He's in Shad's office," Benny answered as he poured himself a cup of coffee. "Kissing his ass."

"Would you please tell him he has a phone call, will ya and tell him that it's important, please!"

Benny hurried down the hallway stuck his head into Shad's office and told me I had an important call.

I hurried into the dispatch and asked Blake who it was. "Why don't you pick up the phone press the button that's blinking and let him know it's you. Tell him it's Sgt Dyer," He said as he filled out the transportation for the next day. That was usually my job.

I answered the phone it was the receiving office at Union Station. My 1940 Lincoln Continental Cabriolet Convertible had arrived from Riverside, California. I bought it when I was stationed at March Air force Base and while I was stationed in Vietnam I had it stored in the Coyle and Iaconio Racing Facility. When I got back from 'Nam I had Rosie make arrangements to ship the car too D.C. The Lincoln was currently registered and insured in California so I would have no trouble driving it from Union Station to Bolling Air Force Base.

Rosie called me a week ago to let me know that my Lincoln was on the train and it will be in D.C. in about seven to ten days. It was nice talking to her. She would phone me from time to time and tell me what was going on with her husband Frank their daughter Anne the Coyle brothers and Iaconio and Coyle Brothers Racing. And then we would talk about the neighbor hood, all the fun we had and how much we miss the old place and all our friends.

"When's the last time you were home, Rosie?" I asked without thinking.

"Sharly's wake and funeral," She answered in a low voice. "Oh God, Stevie it was so sad." She lamented.

"The year went by so quickly, Rosie. It was a little over a year that…well you know."

"Are you seeing anyone?"

"Yeah I am," I said no sense in lying. "She stationed here at the base. Her name is Donna Hutchinson."

"Well knowing you as well I do I'll bet that she has a nice set of vaa vaa voom's, I'll bet she's really stacked!" She chuckled.

"Yeah but not as nice as yours, Rosie," I said. "Nobody but nobody has a nicer set of knockers then you Rosie Beans."

"Not even Virginia Bell?" Rosie asked.

"Nope, not even Virginia Bell."

"Good bye, Stevie, love you Honey."

"Good bye Rosie, love you too and thank you and Frankie for everything."

I hung up the phone looked across the desk at Blake and said: "Curtis. How about driving me to Union Station?"

"Why? Are you planning on buying it?" He said while he kept filling out the transportation requests.

"Na, there's no money in railroads, but listen, my antique '40 Lincoln Continental Cabriolet Convertible just arrived and I could use a ride from someone who knows the city, ole buddy," I said throwing my Corvette keys on his desk. Curtis grew up in the city and knew every section and every one way street in the city. Union Station was located in the North East section of D.C.

"Let's go but let's take my Camaro. I'm a little uncomfortable taking our 'Vette downtown," He said grabbing his cap from his desk. What's this, "our Corvette" shit"? I asked myself.

While Curtis went to fetch his Camaro, I went into Bob Shadley's's office let him know where we were going said that we'd back in about an hour then I met Curtis at the side door and we drove off.

In no time we were pulling into the parking area behind the station and Curtis was asking for direction to the receiving area. It was easy, just drive down to the lower floor of the parking garage, go left and it'll bring to the loading and unloading docks. And there she sat my 1940 black lacquered Lincoln Continental Cabriolet Convertible.

And she was a beauty. Almost everything on or in the car was original, except the leather upholstery, the convertible top and the ignition. While Frankie was rebuilding the V-12 engine the transmission and the rear-end he converted the electrical system over to 12 volt, replaced the 6 volt generator with an alternator, and did something with the dual point distributor so it could handle the 12 volts. The tires were a copy of the original 16 inchers vulcanized by Firestone, inner tubes and all and the stainless steel exhaust system was custom fabricated by "All Stainless Fabrication" out of Fresno. When you have the money you can have anything built. Money talks real laud.

I found the shipping and receiving office paid the bill picked up the keys and the paper work and walked out into the parking lot, found the black beauty, unlocked the door, started the big, but underpowered V-12, and dropped the top.

"Curtis, take it easy going back to the base," I said pulling beside his Camaro. "Oh and don't say anything to Donna, I want to surprise her."

"Hey Stevie," He shouted.

"Hey what? What do you want?"

"You look like a pimp!"

"You think so?" I said as I looked at my reflection in the small rear view mirror.

We pulled up at the main gate, Curtis kept the speed down to thirty miles per hour going thru town and we arrived on base without any problems. Sgt Patrick Sullivan, "Sully", a large blond Mick from Queens, New York City was at the main gate. He and Curtis exchanged a few words then Sully waved him thru then signaled for me to stop. "What's happening Sully," I said as I looked up at the blue eyed Irishman.

"Well, let us see Sgt Pimp," He said as he walked around the 1940 classic. "When you first arrived on base you were driving a new Corvette, right Sgt Pimp?"

"What's this PIMP shit, Sully the Mick?"

"Just answer my question, pimp."

"That's right."

"Okay, Stevie," He said as I handed him the California registration, the title and the insurance papers. "What is it?" He said looking at the folder holding all the documents.

"It is a 1940 Lincoln Continental Convertible." I smile looking up at him.

"Yeah, that's what Blake said it was," Sully said as he walked around the classic tapping the folder against his thigh.

"What did "The Blake" tell you?"

"Oh he said that you made all your money pimping so you could buy a collection of classic cars, and let's see now, you have a '58 and a '63 Corvette a 65 Hemi-Charger and a '64 Ford 427 Thunderbolt stored down at your folks summer place in Florida." He said handing me back my folder without looking at the papers. "Then he also told that you also own a 1940 Ford Coupe and a 1951 Mercury Monterey stored in a warehouse outside of Boston."

"He's right about the cars, but he missed one, I also have a 1956 Ford Victoria," I said. "But do I look like a pimp, Sully? Come on."

"No, Steve, you da wrong color," He grinned as he waved me thru.

Curtis was right on about my classic automobile collection, while I was stationed in California, Frank Ianotti would buy blown out cars from the drags then he and the Coyle brothers would rebuild the engines and whatever else that had to be rebuilt then park them on company parking and put them up for sale. That's where I picked up my two 'Vettes and my Charger.

When I got back to the duty station I call Donna to let her know that I'll pick her up when she got off duty and I had something that I wanted to show her but fucking Blakely beat me to it. While Sully had me tied up at the main gate Curtis hurried back to the dispatch office phoned Donna and spoiled my surprise. When I pulled into the parking lot across from her office with the top down the classic naturally drew a crowd. You don't get to see many 1940 Lincoln Continental convertibles on a military base or any place for that matter.

Donna was waiting on the steps when she spied me pulling into the parking lot driving the Queen Mary and she hurried across the street and approached me. I was standing in front of the car. "What a beautiful Lincoln, Stevie," She exclaimed as I walked her around the car. "I had no idea that a Lincoln from 1940 would be in such pristine condition."

"How did you know the car was a '40Lincoln, did Blakely call you?" Fuck head Blakely I whispered under my breath.

"Yeah, he phoned me and said that you were on your way over and you had a surprise for me," She said. "I asked him what it was and he told me, sorry Stevie."

"He can be such an incredible asshole," I said. "He knew I wanted to surprise you."

"Now, now, Stevie," She said patronizing me. "Let's not whine, shall we?"

I look at her and began to laugh. I rarely got upset but when I showed a little anger and it was usually aimed at "The Blake", she would say: Let's not whine shall we.

"Care to go for a ride?" I said opening the door for her.

"Love to," she said as she climbed into the front seat and I closed her door walked around to my side opened my door got in fired up the 292 cubic inch V-12 and we pulled out of the parking lot, drove down to the Air Police and register my gem.

"I gotta see this, Stevie," Sgt Theo Owens said looking over the registration and insurance form.

"She's right outside Theo," I said holding the door for the tall well built E-6. Donna was posing leaning against the Continental's huge right front fender a sexy grin her hands behind her back.

Theo greeted Donna with a bright white toothy smile then he had to have walked around the car three times before he said anything. "You know Stevie," He finally began speaking. "I've seen pictures of cars like this but the pictures do not do this car justice. What a gorgeous piece of work you have here. Mind showing me what's under the hood?"

"No not at all," I said popping the hood and let him gaze at the twelve cylinder engine.

Now we were beginning to draw a crowd. Half of the Bolling Air Police flight was there in the parking lot, so was the curious that were walking past the Air Police building.

"I do believe your car has made an impression on the folks, Honey" Donna said taking my hand.

"I think it is too, Honey," Theo grinned. "Come on inside and I'll get you registered."

I dropped Donna back at her section the tooled the Lincoln back to the motor pool. To get from the main part of the base to my duty section you had cross a wide part of the flight line. I was tempted to open her up and see what she could but I thought better of it. The speed limit was thirty miles an hour and the big classic stuck out like a black eye. I would have been nabbed before I drove half way across the large cement slab.

I kept the Lincoln on base for a year or so then had the car shipped down to Florida. There really wasn't any place to drive the classic Lincoln, the base was too small unless I wanted to spend my off duty time driving up and down the inactive flight line from Bolling to Anacostia and then back to Bolling and I didn't want to take her into the city. Too many crazy drivers that loved to drive about a foot from your rear bumper. But on Sunday afternoons Donna and I would drive the Lincoln over to the Andrews Air Force Base NCO club for Lunch and a drink beside the pool.

The first time that I had driven the Lincoln over to Andrews, as I approached the main gate the Air Policeman asked me to stop and wanted for some ID. Donna and I both showed him our ID's he looked closely at our picture and rank then returned them to us. "Any problem?"

"I thought with a car like that, well...I thought that you were VIPs or something."

"Na...this was a gift from my Daddy for not getting wasted in 'Nam."

I was going to pick-up Donna for lunch but I had to catch a ride from Benny because "The Blake" had what he considers "our" Corvette. The son of a bitch always had "our" car. Christ he even had his own set of keys made! That's when I decided to buy a Lincoln Mark III. The Mark III Sports Coupe' was more practical than the 'Vette and the winter was on the way and anyone with an ounce of sense would not drive a 'Vette in the snow and though it was in the middle of September and the new '68 Lincolns Mark III's weren't due out for another month Donna and I flew out to Detroit and picked up a brand new right 1968 Lincoln Mark III right off the assembly line. It was the first year for the two door hardtop Luxury Sports Car. The big Lincoln was powered by a 430 cubic V8 turning out 365 horsepower. When I first had seen the car advertised in Motor Trend Magazine I went to an Arlington, Virginia Lincoln Mercury dealer. I wouldn't be happy until I owned one. I loved the Corvette but not in the winter. Let Curtis kill himself. The owner of the dealership explained that the new cars weren't ready for delivery but if I wanted to he would call Ford and see what he could do. Maybe if I went out to the factory and the price was right it could be possible that I could be driving a new Mark III as soon as Friday. He said that he would call me back. It was lunch time when I dropped by Donna's office and explained to her what I had in mind. "How would you like to go too Detroit, Honey," I asked as gently kissed her.

"I'd rather go to Florida," she smiled while I helped her on with her uniform blouse.

"I know you would, and I would too, but this is important, and I would really like you to go with me."

"I've never been to Detroit, Honey. Is it nice in Detroit?"

"No, it's a dump, but we're not going there to see the ghetto sights. We're picking up a new Lincoln Mark III."

"When are we leaving?"

"Tomorrow morning. I got OK from the chief, than I called Executive and booked a flight. We can get out of National around eight, fly into Detroit, the flight takes about an hour, take a cab to the factory, pick up the car and drive on back to DC. We should be back on base Sunday afternoon. What do you think? Wanna go?"

"God, Honey. You're really excited! You said all that without taking a breath."

"I get that way whenever I'm with you." I laughed looking into her eyes.

"I'll ask Captain Holmes when we get back from lunch, and I'll get back to you, Okay? Keep your fingers crossed, Sweetheart."

Donna phoned me that afternoon said it she had the okay and she was going back to the barracks to pack an overnight bag

We boarded an Exec Airline, fourteen passenger Sabre Liner jet, a rebuilt copy of an Air Force C-140 VIP passenger carrier and set off for Detroit. The flight into Detroit Metropolitan Airport took less than two hours then we got a cab from the airport to the Dearborn assembly plant, explained to the plant manager who I was, he knew, I put sixty seven hundred cash on the his desk and he handed me the keys. The Mark III, just as I had ordered was driven out of the assembly plant side overhead door and was parked in front of the factory show room. The car was gorgeous. It was cranberry red with a black interior, thin striped red wall tires that matched the car exterior, a stereo with four speakers, air conditioned, with power brakes and power steering. I bolted on the black Virginia tags; I got the bill of sale and a temporary title mailed to me from the factory and registered the car before we left Virginia; filled the gas tank with ESSO high test and drove south east. We spent the night in Harrisburg, Pennsylvania, got up early the next morning and left for DC. It was early Sunday afternoon when we arrived back on Bolling. I stopped at the main gate. It seemed as though every time I show up at the main gate with a different car Sgt Patrick "Sully" Sullivan was on duty and he asks me the same question.

"Alright Steve, what is it?" He asked as I handed him the bill of sale, the registration and the insurance papers. He looked at them with little interest then handed them back to me.

"It's the car of the future, Sully." I said looking up at the tall, newly promoted Staff Sgt.

"OK, I'll ask Donna," he said as he slowly walked around to the other side of the car and kneeled down beside the side of the car and looking in at Donna. "Donna, what is it?"

"Just what Stevie was trying to explain to you, Sully," she said. "It's a new, right out of the Dearborn, Michigan Ford factory, 1967 Lincoln Continental Mark III."

"You're saying that you both went up to Detroit and bought it right out of the factory?"

"Yup. I couldn't get one of these around here and you know me Sully. When I want something bad enough and I know where to get it, well that's what I did. Check out the serial number on the registration." I said as I handed it back to him.

"Well I'll be go to hell; 1000000023."

"Yeah. It's only the twenty third copy built."

Sully handed me a visitor's pass and waved us through, we went to headquarters signed the morning report then went to the NCO Club rathskeller for a drink and a couple of steamed hot dogs, a couple of Kosher pickles a bag of potato chips and sailed for a booth. The early Sunday afternoon crowd was sparse. Most of the drinkers were home sleeping off the previous evening.

"Steve?" Donna said as she put down her hot dog and smiled.

"Uh huh?" I answered as I smeared mustard on my hot dog.

"You know you didn't have to get separate rooms last night. We could have shared the same bed. I do love you, you know."

"And I love you too," I said as I looked into her violet blue eyes and smiled. "When I was in Vietnam I was going out with girl that I loved so very much, her name was Charlotte O'Sullivan. We had known each other since the seventh grade. I had six months left in my tour of duty and I couldn't get home soon enough. Anyway

Donna, Sharly was killed crossing the street by a drunk driver and you know Benny Polly?"

"Yeah, I know Benny," She said looking at me then closed her eyes and nodded her head.

"He got me through my heartbreak. He was my best friend there and when my orders came through for DC, Benny was already here, I couldn't believe my good fortune."

"Oh Steve, I'm so sorry, Honey," she said taking my hand. "Why didn't you say something sooner?"

"It wasn't the right time, Honey. I wanted to make sure my head was on straight."

"I love you so much Stevie," Donna said as she gripped my hand.

"I love you, Donna, and that's forever. I fell in love with you as soon as I walked into your office and the Blake introduced us. You took my breath away."

"You know not just me but everybody on the base knew that there was a rich you Sgt arriving…"

"Col Rosa told me the same thing," I smiled.

"But you didn't look rich. Except for you tailored uniform, your spit shined shoes, and your incredible good looks you looked like a regular G.I. reporting in."

"I'm just a regular guy like all the rest of the GI's. I was brought up in a middle class hard working neighborhood, and as I said my Dad owned a machine shop Mom was a stay at home Mom and Tommy and I were brought up no better and no worse than the rest of the guys and girls in the neighborhood."

"Are you OK with me? Are the nightmares gone? That's means a lot to me you know?"

I looked at her, thought about what I had been through while I was overseas, the painful leave when I got home and how glad I was when I finally arrived at Bolling and the great people I had met since I had arrived. "There are no nightmares, Honey. There never was," I said reassuring her. "Donna, what say we move off base? It's about time for me and I really want to make a life together with nyou, you think?"

"Do you think that we can we afford it?"

"Well at last count I'm worth in the neighborhood of, oh I don't know, ten… twelve million dollars, yeah I think we can handle it,"

"As long as you're being honest with me I suppose I should be honest with you," She said looking down at her clasped hands.

"OK," I said.

"All right, here goes," She said looking at me then taking a deep breath. "I was working in a department store in Harrisburg and I ended up having an affair with one of the salesman," She said looking down at her hands again. "I didn't know that he was married but his wife found out and followed us to a motel in Carlisle. That's outside of Harrisburg."

I leaned back in the booth, folded my hands across my chest and grinned. "Go on, please."

She looked up and noticed that I was chuckling. "You're enjoying this, aren't you, you shit head," she said than she began to laugh.

"I love to see people squirm," I joked. "Please continue."

"Well we were caught. The inn keeper let the salesman's wife into the room while we were making love, I jumped out of bed ran into the bathroom and locked the door."

"How long did you stay until the coast was clear?"

"Oh, there was a lot of yelling, many unkind words were spoken, and threats of castration but I stayed in the bathroom until everybody left the room. Unfortunately I had to call Mom to come and pick me up."

"You should have taken separate cars," I mentioned as I slid out of the booth still smiling. "Want another drink, Honey? This is getting good."

"Yeah, I need one and Stevie… and try not to take my sad sorry too hard, will you?" She said giving me a sarcastic smile.

I brought the refills back to the booth and sat down and placed her drink in front of her. "Donna, I really don't care about your past.

That was before we met and it doesn't concern me and it doesn't change my feeling toward you. Just don't let it happen again."

"How about you, Sunshine?" she grinned staring at me. "Why don't you regale me with some of your more amorous adventures?"

"Well there were two girls I went out with before I signed up. Before I went out with Sharly O'Sullivan I was going out with Rosie Beanbags Leonardi..."

"You were going with a girl you called Beanbags?" She squealed clapping her hands. "Beanbags couldn't be her real name could it?" She said sipping her drink looking at me over the rim of her glass.

"No. There was a guy in our crowd, kuckie Cohen. He read a book called "The Amboy Dukes"..."

"Yeah. I read that book in high school. There was another character in the book named Larry Tuna Fish I believe."

"You're right," I chuckled. "Well anyway, I went out with Rosie for about six months. She was fun to be with but I wanted to go out with someone that wasn't as out there as she was. My mother would drive me crazy, she said 'how could you go out with a girl, oh I'm sure she's a fine young lady, but being referred to as Beanbags?' Mom came from Ireland but I would tell her not to worry. We had no plans to marry."

"Were you and her, ah, how can I say this, lovers?" she asked setting down her drink.

"No not really, we were only sixteen. We had a lot of fun but that was all," I wasn't about to tell Donna about me wallowing in Rosie's 44 double D's.

"Did you see her when you got back from Vietnam?"

"Yeah I did. When I flew in from Hawaii and landed in LA. We went out to dinner; oh and I might add her husband who is an old friend and business owner Frankie Ianotti picked up the check."

"And after breaking up with Rosie Beanbags then you began going out with Sharly?"

"Yup, but we never really fooled around. We would go parking or go to the drive-in make out, but that was about as far as we went. We didn't want to do anything stupid. We both had plans for our future and being teen-age parents didn't enter into the equation."

"What about Vietnam? There were a lot of hookers over there or so I've been told."

"And you've been told right, Donna, the City of Bien Hoa was one big stinking whore house, but I was in love with Sharly and even if I wasn't going out with her I wasn't about to compromise my health with a whore. I have too much self respect and an incredibly large bank account," I chuckled.

"So basically you're still pretty much a virgin?" she grinned gazing at me over the top of her cocktail glass.

I looked into her violet blue eyes, smiled and said, "Yeah, pretty much so, but I'm looking forward to loosing it to a beautiful lady from Pennsylvania."

"Well if it wasn't for snake oil, Honey, I'd still be a virgin too," She said giving me a warm smile. "Now, when and where would you like to move so I can take away your virginity?"

"We can move tonight if you'd like."

"All right," she gazed at me with a delightful look in her eyes. "But tell me, where are you planning on relocating us?"

"The back seat of my Mark 111," I said.

"Will you cut the shit, Stevie," She said handing me her empty glass. I went to the bar for two refills then walked back to our booth.

"I bought a two hundred year old colonial farm house outside of Arlington, Virginia. It's all furnished. All we need to take with us is our clothes and personnel stuff."

"You're kidding! When did you by a house?" She said her eyes gleaming.

"A week before I was due to report into my section, I really like this part of the country and I thought I might as well own part of the history so I went to an Arlington, Virginia realty office, explained to the real estate lady what I had in mind, she asked me how much

I could afford, I said the price wasn't a problem, I would be paying cash, Lyn Murphy showed me three homes and I bought the last one and depending on the traffic and if we catch it right we can be home in less than half an hour."

"How about say we move in next week-end, Honey?" Now she was excited. "Is that too soon?"

"No but here's what we're going do. When we get off duty tomorrow, we'll drive out to the house. I'll show you around than you can see if you like the place. I believe you're going to like the old Colonial."

"How do you know that you're going want to live with me?"

"Well we're been together for eight months and I've loved every minute of it. You've been my constant companions. I really love you Donna."

"Do you love me enough to maybe marry me?" she asked

"Yeah. Do you love me enough to marry me?" I asked back.

"What do you think?"

"I don't think, I know, come on let's get outta here, Honey."

We finished our drinks, left the NCO Club, drove down the flight line and parked in the parking lot across from the Bolling AFB marina. The light from Washington National Airport made the Potomac River shine like a jewel, not the filthy, polluted sewer that it really was. In the summer when the humidity hung low over the city the smell that came off the river, especially from high noon until twilight was over powering. Hell the Potomac was DC's sewer system. It had since then been was cleaned up.

I shut off the big Lincoln's engine but left the radio on. FM stereo radio was just coming onto the airwaves and Ford Motor Company's Lincoln division wasn't going to be left out. The sound system was incredible. The Rolling Stones, The Beatles, The Human Beans, Bobby Fuller Four and all of the other late 60's bands had never sounded so good. That was the new age of rock and roll.

Donna and I were lipped locked in an embrace her breasts crushed against my chest my hands caressing her back. In the eight months we had been dating we never got our bodies closer than slow dancing at the NCO Club. I didn't know how to approach her when it came to parking and sharing a kiss. I had never tried to grab a feel on her ample breasts. She was smaller than Beanbags, but was a bit larger than Sharly. No girl that I had ever met, or stripper I had ever ogled at the Casino, except for "Ding Dong" Bell could have match Rose Lyn Leonardi's knocker's. They're tits went on forever, but at the Bolling Marina, I took my liberties. I didn't really know how far I could go before I had my face slapped but nothing ventured, nothing gained. I didn't have to wait that long. She lifted her blouse then reached behind her back, undid her bra then gently grasped my hand and placed it on her breast. Her breasts felt warm, full and soft. Now what? Do I approach her advances aggressively or do I lay back and let her take control.

"Oh Stevie, I love you so much," she moaned as she placed her hand on my crotch and began to fondle my erection through my tight fitting continental cuff less slacks.

"I love you too, Donna." I said. She stopped what she was doing to my erection, lifted her backside up from the seat, hiked her skirt up to her waist and moaned as she guided my hand down the front of her panties.

The next day after Donna and I got off duty I was picking her up in the parking lot across the street from the BX; my new cranberry red Mark III caused a small crowd to gather around the Lincoln. Most of the curious on lookers didn't know what the hell it was,

"Does this boat come with oars, Sgt Dyer?" The Base Commander, Col. Knutson asked as he approached the Lincoln Continental.

"Ten hut!" Someone in the gathering crowed shouted.

"Come on guys, at ease," The Col. Said as he returned the gathering's salute. "This is an informal gathering, alright?"

"It should come with oars, Sir." I smiled as I came to at ease and showed him around my Mark 111.

"What a beautiful car, Sgt Dyer," he said looking in the window. "May I ask what it is besides being a Lincoln that doesn't appear to come with headlights?"

"It's a 1968 Lincoln Continental Mark III, Sir," I said beaming while the Base Commander strolled around the car. Now the gathering was increasing in size. Col. Knutson was very popular was well liked and respected by everyone on the base and the pentagon. "Yes Sir; when the head lights are turned on the two small doors opened showing the four headlights."

"You don't say, Sgt, well, that's unique."

"Yes Sir."

"Now explain to me Sgt Dyer, how did you manage to purchase a 1968 Lincoln?" The Base Commander wanted to know. "According to my Air Force calendar mounted on the wall in my office this is still 1967. How did you go about purchasing a car that hasn't yet been built?"

"Actually this is the twenty third copy that had been built, Sir, but right now if you would want to buy a Mark 111 you will need to go to Detroit and pick it up at the factory."

"Without getting to personnel, may I ask how much it cost you?"

"A little under six grand, Sir."

"Well if anyone can make the difficult look easy it's you Sergeant, carry on."

"Yes Sir," I said, saluted him and watched him melt through his admirers and walk back to his office in the Headquarters building.

Donna arrived just as Col. Knutson left. I opened the door for her and we drove the short ride across the Wilson Bridge, went south on Route 1 for ten miles turned west on Route 66 then drove onto newly paved drive-way and parked in front of the large red barn that was attached to the side of the red two hundred year old colonial with a door in the kitchen connecting both the house and barn. I opened the sliding glass door that went from the deck into large pantry that was adjacent to the period dated kitchen. The house had been brought up to code, new heating and air conditioning system, pluming and electricity, but the windows and the doors were original along with the rest of the house.

"What a beautiful home you have," she said as we walked from room to room then up the spiral stair case to the second floor. That was where all the bedrooms were located. There was a large master bedroom and three smaller bedrooms. In the master bedroom was a full bathroom with a huge walk in shower and a hot tub. There was also another half bathroom at the end of the hall and another full bath down stairs off the kitchen. "It had to have cost you a bundle to remodel this treasure," she said as she looked at all the rooms and the walk in fire places.

"Yeah it was a little expensive, Honey," I said as we walked into the master bedroom. "But it was worth it. The house ran me a quarter of a million and the restoration ran me another quarter of a million."

"But most of the house is original?" she asked.

"Yeah, from the field stone and granite foundation to the cedar shingled roof, the wide oaken wooden floors to the red clay brick fire places."

"When was the house built, Steve?" Donna asked as she sat on the two hundred year old bed.

"The deed says that it was completed in June 1770. It probably took about three years to build."

"That's a long time to build a house," She remarked as she bounced up and down on the hard mattress.

"Yeah, now it is, but not two hundred ago when everything was pretty much by hand," I said sitting down beside her. "All the wood was cut in a lumber mill and Lyn the reality broker said that all the oak and hard pine came from central Maine and Bogalusa, Louisiana, shipped here by boat and delivered by wagon."

"You have a nice house, Stevie and I do believe I'm going to really love living here with you."

"This is not my house, Sweetheart. It belongs to the both of us, alright?" I said as I put my arms around her shoulders and pulled her close to me.

"How about we try out the bed and see if it works," She said as she stood up and began removing her uniform.

"What say we take a shower? You wanna go first?"

"Let's say we both go first," She smiled as stood before me in all her naked glory. God she was gorgeous I said to myself while I dropped my laundry and took her into my arms.

We were both standing in the bathroom naked trying to figure out how to get the shower to work. I suppose I should have checked out the house before I bought it.

"Think we can get the shower going before we have to report for duty in the morning?" Donna asked.

"I'll tell you what, Stevie. You screw around with the shower while I pour us a couple of glass of VSQ." She said as she walked out of the bathroom and went into the bedroom. We stopped off at the NCO Club Class Six store before leaving the base and picked up a bottle of VSQ brandy, a bottle of Beefeater gin and a bottle of Smirnoff vodka and to the four seasons convenience store that was near the main gate for tonic water and limes.

It finally occurred to me that since no one was living here maybe the water had been shut off. I went down to the cellar, turned on the water main and hurried upstairs. The furnace came on and began heating up the water and In a few minutes we were in the shower luxuriating in the in the soothing water and the comforting feel of each other's hands.

The next week-end we loaded up the trunk of my Mark III the back seat and whatever we could fit into the Corvette and moved out of the barracks. Benny his wife Linda, Curtis, Barbara, Dianne and

Suzanne lent us a hand and in one trip we were moved in. Curtis and Benny fell in love the huge barn housing some my cars and my machine shop but Linda and Barbara fell in loved the house. Donna was in her glory showing Linda, Barbara, Dianne and Suzanne each and every room and explaining in detail the history of the house, the outside gardens and the fields behind our propriety.

I thought that Dianne and Suzanne were going to have an orgasm as they walked through the beautifully laid out gardens. "How do you find the time to cultivate a garden this extravagant, Steve?" Suzanne asked while Dianne began snapping pictures.

"I have a landscaping company that takes care or the gardens," I replied.

"Any chance Dianne and I could look after your gardens?" Suzanne asked. "We'll do it for nothing just pay us gas money. What do you say?"

"I'll pay you the same as I pay the landscapers, plus gas money, okay?" I said. "I have all gardening tool that you'll need in the barn. If you need anything else let me know and I'll give you the money and don't be shy. If you need it you got it, alright?"

"When can we start?"

"Whenever you want, and if you would like to move in there is a large furnished three room apartment over the barn."

"Do you think Donna would mind?" Dianne asked as both she and Suzanne look at me in total awe.

"No she's won't mind but let me ask her anyway, Okay?" I said as I walked into house and found Barbara and Linda in the living room Barbara sitting at the piano playing a Duke Ellington compositions. Curtis told some time ago that Barbara played the piano the organ and the guitar, she was very talented. Benny and Curtis were in the kitchen mixing drinks.

"Donna, may I see you a minute?" She excused herself and followed me into the dining room. I explained to her about hiring the girls to take care of the grounds and letting them take the apartment over the barn.

"It's fine with me, Honey," She said. "You're not going to charge them rent, are you?"

"I wouldn't think of it."

I went back out into the gardens and gave the two love birds the good news. I told them that they could have the place rent free and for their services I'll pay them each a hundred dollar fifty a week and they can park their Volkswagon Beetle in the barn. "Just try not to hit any of my classic Okay?"

"Oh Steve," They cried as they both hugged me Dianne smothering my face with kisses. "I don't know how we can ever thank you enough!"

Good Christ, I said to myself as I peeled them off my body. You thought I had given them a million dollars, but when I look back on what the girls had accomplished in a short time. All I did was to give them the opportunity and the resources to create a flower and a greenhouse business that became one of the largest Landscaping and floral business in Rhode Island.

Upon their discharge from the Air Force Dianne and Suzanne lived with us for another year to hone the gardening expertise, and they were there, thank God, when I returned from my second tour from 'Nam, the girls were there to help Donna; but their accomplishment working in the gardens for the past three years were incredible. I had over three acres of land but the gardens and the lawn covered a small part of the overall property. When the ladies moved to Rhode Island and opened their business there was almost an acre of beautiful lawns, gardens and a waterfall and a small pool that they built by damming one of the small streams that ran from the conservation land and through my back yard. Then they hired an electrical contractor and had him install different colored lights around the pool and the stream.

After Donna and I got off duty we'd drive into D.C. shopping for things we would need to make the Colonial house comfortable.

New towels, sheets, pillows and pillow cases and all the other shit that came in handy and conducive for our style of living. Donna picked it out and I paid for it. I didn't care. I could have if I felt like it, bought the whole store. Dianne and Suzanne would come along with us and help Donna with her shopping while they bought things they needed for their cozy "Love Nest". When they had their apartment finished they invited Donna and me up for cocktails and dinner. The bottle of Absolut and the bottle of Hennessy Cognac looked vaguely familiar. It looked like it was bought at the base class 6 store and now that the girls were out of the service and their base privileges had ended I now assume that their booze once belong to me but I could care less. Take what you need my friends and don't give it a thought.

When I bought the colonial it needed a lot of work and I spent a bundle getting the old manse up to code but I let the barn go because all I wanted was the space for my cars so the apartment over the barn was put on the back burner but when I offer the place to Dianne and Suzanne the apartment needed some improvements but their three room digs was in nice shape and up to code. I'm sure that the last owner used the barn for a work shop and the three room upstairs apartment was the former owner's home.

It was the night before Halloween when we had finally finished moving in, Donna, Dianne and Suzanne cooked a gourmet dinner, the fire place in the living room was burning romantically and the Hennessy cognac was going down real smooth. And when the dishes were finished, the kitchen tidied up Suzanne and Dianne bit us a good night, lifted an expensive bottle of wine from behind the bar and retired to their apartment, Donna and I had a large quilt over us while we were stretched out on a huge real bear skin rug. I felt a bit strange laying on an animal that was shot two hundred years ago but I was a city kid and didn't know what our forefathers did to make a dead bear's skin from rotting away. Of course Donna being a country girl brought up outside of Harrisburg knew all about how to cure dead animal's skin. Donna enjoyed being in her own home making both of us happy.

"Are you comfortable Steve?" Donna said as we were cuddled up in front of the fire place sipping brandy and enjoying the warm friendly fire. We were both au natural.

"Oh yeah," I said. I wished in hell we were off duty tomorrow, I said to myself. I'd love to sleep in.

"Tomorrow is Halloween, Honey and Dianne and Suzanne picked up some Halloween goodies," Donna said as she threw back the quilt, climbed to her feet and placed a couple of logs on the fire. Donna found the oaken logs down in the barn cellar looked like it was as old as the house so the wood h was well cured. There was, Donna said that there was about three cords of wood stacked up against the far wall in the basement. I had no idea of what in hell a cord of anything was but Donna explained it all to me a total woodsy neophyte that cured oak logs that were split burned hot but slowly. I watched her as she moved gracefully across the living room floor aware that she was nude and driving me nuts, her large soft breasts swayed as she moved about the room, picked up an arm full of wood and placed the logs in the fire place then walked slowly back to our bear skin rug bed, she smiled and me while I hungrily gazed at her Playboy center fold figure then she climbed beneath the quilt. We both drank from two hundred year old crystal glasses half filled with cognac. I'm not a glass blower or do I know how glass is made but whoever fired these crystal goblets were a master craftsman. Snap your fingernail on the side and the glass rang like a "Ping" putter.

There were many parts of Americana that came with the beautiful historical southern Colonial house. When I showed around Donna the house this was the first time I really had a chance to explore our home. After I bought the house, I took a walk through the eleven rooms, was impressed with the workmanship, loved the antique glasses, plates, china ware and silver ware, locked it up and drove back to the base. One of these days I was going to move in, but until Donna came along I really didn't give the old manse a lot of thought, except when I got the tax bill in the mail.

"How are you doing, Stevie?" Donna said as she puffed up her pillow and lay her head down. "You look so good laying there bare on a bear skin looking handsome and enjoying your brandy and all."

"I have something for you, Honey," I said handing her a small velvet box.

"The answer is yes, Honey," she giggled as she sat up and opened the box. Inside was a two karat pear shaped diamond ring in a platinum setting.

"You mean you're gonna re-up?" I joked as I raised the quilt and gazed at her gorgeous naked body.

"I don't know if I will, but I know I want to marry you." She said as she handed me the ring and I placed it on her finger. It was a perfect fit.

"I still can't believe that eight months ago you, a shy handsome Sergeant with more money than God walked into my office and stood there looking like a deer with its eyes caught in the headlights."

"It was you, Honey," I said as I ran my fingers through her soft auburn hair that covered her crotch. "You knocked me out."

"Am I really that pretty?" She asked looking at her ring while she stroked me.

"You gotta be joking, Donna," I replied as I turned onto my side a gazed at her. "You're beautiful Love."

"Thank you, Stevie, and you're nice looking guy," She returned compliment then turned into the passionate woman that I love so much. She knew what I wanted and I knew what she loved and that's what really matters.

I wasn't kidding her. Donna was a beautiful creature.

The following morning before leaving for the base we met Dianne and Suzanne coming down the stairs from their apartment. Donna couldn't wait to show them her ring, but the ladies played it cool, hugged Donna and didn't let on that they had a hand in helping me to pick out the gem.

"Thank you so much." I whispered winking.

The minute I walked into Donna's office with Curtis and set my sea green eyes on Donnas' warm velvet blue eyes and beautiful face I knew that I was in love. And now we are together in our new old home laying there in front of the fire place sipping brandy and planning our marriage. I thought with the death of Sharly I was never going to fall in love with another woman the way I loved her. I was just kidding myself. Sharly had been dead for over a year and a half and now we were lying on a bearskin rug on the wide oak living room floor with a large, wool quilt covering us. I was totally absorbed in thought. "What are you thinking about, Honey?" Donna asked as she caressed my cheek with the back of her long slim fingers. "Sharly maybe?"

"No not Sharly, Honey, I don't think about Sharly that much anymore. My memory of her is fading as it should; no I was thinking of the skilled workers who built this house and the folks that lived here. This house is American history. We're only passing through history. And when we're finished living here and a hundred years from now? Will our home still be here? Or maybe it will be a shopping mall or a parking lot. I think about shit like that."

"Steve? May I ask you a personnel question?" Donna asked as she reached across me and retrieved her glass of brandy from the night table.

"Ask me anything," I answered as I caressed her warm soft breasts.

"With your outside investments and your extremely (the emphasis was on extremely) successful charter airline, why are you staying in the military?"

"I don't know, maybe it's because I love the Air Force almost as much as I love you. I like the guys, Benny, Roger, Simple Simpson, Curtis, Bobby Shad, The Chief and the responsibilities, and I love everything that goes along with it. Charley Wilson and Billy Toye are the heart and soul of Black Gold Investments and Executive

Airlines. I just happened to have had the upfront cash to make it happen."

"But you all split everything equally," She reasoned. "Has CJ and Billy ever said that they wanted to go out on their own?"

"I gave them both the opportunity and they both said, 'what are you crazy? If it wasn't for you we would probably be working in some boring office job pulling down two bills a week instead of making a million dollars a year, I can't believe that you're for real!'"

"And I can't believe that you're for real either, Baby!" Donna said as she place her brandy glass on the end table and rolled on top of me, kissed me hard on the lips than squirmed down my nude body and made mad passionate love to me with her lips tongue and mouth and of course me being the kind of guy that likes to return a favor I paid her back in kind.

OCTOBER 1967.

"Donna?" I said while we were sitting in the Park Sheridan Hotel bar having an after dinner brandy. "Next Friday evening I'm meeting Billy and CJ at Washington National. Le Anne and Karen will be there, come with me?"

"Are you sure? I'd like too, but I don't know them and I may be in the way."

"In the way? In the way of what, Donna? We're all not just business partners but we're close friends and I want you to meet them and if you turn chicken they're gonna really upset."

"Why Stevie? They don't know me," She said as she stirred her brandy with her finger.

"Oh yeah, Honey. They know you..."

"Did they know Sharly?" She asked.

"Yeah, we were all very close and they were happy to see that I put that part of my life behind me and met a woman and fell in love with her, and Donna...I love you, I love you like you could never believe."

"Do you believe in fate, Honey?"

'Yeah, and I believe in you too." I said. I could almost feel Sharly hands gently caressing my shoulders as she pushed me toward Donna.

"What should I wear?" she smiled as she handed me her empty glass.

"Wear something casual. We're just having a couple of drinks and dinner."

"Ah… Stevie Honey? Washington National is in Virginia and Virginia is a dry state," She said looking up at me.

"Well I'll be go to hell!" I was amazed. "How can a major airport like Washington National not sell booze?"

"You have the money, Love. Hire a lobbyist and get the rules changed."

"I suppose I could buy the airport but keep the flight lines in Virginia and have the terminal relocated at Bolling. There are empty buildings on base around the hanger area and we could have a ferry service crossing The Potomac. What ya think Donna?"

"Instead of a ferry service, just build a bridge. That way your customers wouldn't need to worry about the river freezing over in the winter months and with a bridge you could handle a lot more paying passengers."

"I suppose that would make more sense than a ferry boat and we could charge a toll to help defer the cost of building the bridge. I'll get on it right away."

"The DOD would have you placed in a strait jacket and shipped off to Belvoir."

"They'd do that to me?" I said with a deadpan look on my face.

"Just beer and wine, Honey," She replied ignoring my rhetorical question.

"Well that blows. Wait 'till I call the guys and tell that it's gonna be a dry night."

"Why don't we meet them downtown?"

"It won't work Donna, we're renting an empty World War Two hanger and the airport is where we had planned to meet.

"I have an idea, Stevie," she said looking at me while she stirred her drink. "Why don't we pick up some booze, ice and glasses, some take out Chinese food, grab a wagon from the motor pool, because we'll never get all that shit in you Corvette, then meet them in front of the airport and drive down to the hanger."

"That's a great idea Honey except for one little problem."

"Yeah I know, you're not allowed to bring alcohol into a hanger, hanger office, control tower or the maintenance area. The FAA takes a dim view on that crap but maybe we could hide the shit in the rear of the wagon," She said.

"Honey, if we get caught we'll never be able not only rent the hangers but we'd never be able to start the airline."

"That was a dumb question," She said.

"No it wasn't, Donna. I thought about doing what you just suggested."

We had another brandy then we drove back her barracks and parked in the parking lot. I asked her the way to Washington National, she told me that it was easy. "You know the way to Fort Meyer, right?"

"Yeah, Benny and I drive our "hounds" and semis over there once or twice a week." We referred to our 45 passenger coaches as "hounds" because they resemble Greyhounds buses.

"Well don't go that way. We'll take the belt way across the Woodrow Wilson Bridge then follow the signs to National. It's easy."

"Well thank you Honey," I said kissing the back of her hand.

"How about you kissing me where it counts?" She said.

Alright, I thought to myself: How about you dropping you laundry, Honey, but I'd never say anything as filthy like that; it's too difficult trying to make love in a Corvette and besides Donna had way to much class for me to ever suggest anything nasty like that.

We kissed good night and I drove the two minute trip back to the barracks. I parked the 'Vette in the parking lot beside barracks and walked into the NCO barracks day room looking for a card game. There usually was a Friday night poker going on.

And there was. It wasn't a penny anti game, nor a high stakes one hundred dollar buy in poker game. It'll cost you ten buck to sit down. I wasn't a poker player and the fact of the matter was I sucked when it came to table games. Horses, greyhounds, no problem but I tried playing poker in 'Nam and I sucked. If you can read and understand the racing form you have a pretty good chance of winning maybe half of your wagers, but poker's different. Good poker players always win because bad poker players like me get suckered and I'm not good at reading faces. Not like CJ and Billy. If my partners were here they would clean out these hi-rollers in a New York minute.

"Hey money bags, your money's good here. Care to take a seat?" The tall heavy set Master Sergeant asked a cigarette hanging out of the side of his mouth. I had been living in the barracks for four months now and still didn't know most of their names. Just my roommate and I only saw him a couple of days during the week. He was black with a hate the whitey attitude. I wanted to go to the 1st Sergeant and see if I could move, but I thought better of it. I can hear the 1st Sgt now: "If you don't like your room mate Dyer then why not move your rich ass downtown and buy a hotel? You can afford it."

"Yeah I'll sit in if you guys can afford losing all of your money." I smiled.

"We've seen you play cards, before Dyer. You really suck you know."

"Yeah but I don't suck I'm just not all that lucky," I said taking a seat that had been left vacant by a looser.

"Just horses and dogs," The Sgt laughed.

"That's right Sgt, puppies and ponies," I smiled.

"Oh, by the way, big time," Sgt Fredrick chimed in. "It looks like your room mate won't be coming down for breakfast."

"He's dead right?" I asked. I was really only joking around.

"You got it deep pockets. He was killed trying to knock over a 7-11 store."

"Well God rest his Saintly Soul, and just when we were just beginning to get along. We were going to go out for Chinese," I said taking the deck of cards. I should feel some sort of sadness but I don't. "Where did he get it, Fred?"

"Right between the eyes, Ace" Sgt Fredrick said. Fred had the room across the hall from me and became pretty good friends. He was in 'Nam a year before me.

"No, no," I said looking at Fred. "What 7-11?"

"He walked into the store down at Bailey's Crossroads, pointed a 38 Navy special at the clerk but the clerk had a 9 millimeter in one of the drawers under the counter pulled it out and place a slug right between his eyes. He was dead before he hit the floor."

No great lose I thought to myself. I have no prejudices. I treat everybody the same way they treat me. If I don't like someone I to stay away from them but my roommate, especially when he had a few drinks would go on about how whitey kept the Negro people down, made them slaves, how the KKK would round up the negro men and kill them. "I hate whitey for what they did to my people. People like you, worth millions, making millions from the black man's sweat! And what about the WAF you're seeing? Think she would wanna be seen with a black man?"

"I don't really know, but what you refer to as sweat jobs Black Gold refers to those jobs as positions and the people that work for the companies that Black Gold have an interest in. These men and woman both black and white make good money! Even the laborers, tradesmen, sales people! Black Gold has made millionaires out of thousands of our investors."

"I know why ya'll call your company Black Gold, Dyer, 'cause ya'll use the brothers to do all your slave work, and their sweat is ya'alls black gold!"

"No Bryant. It was the oil fields out west that helped my associates and me turn a ten thousand dollar investment into a multi-million dollar enterprise. You know as soon as you get that chip off your shoulder you just may amount to something! I may even give you a job but never a position." I said painting the racist jerk a sarcastic grin.

"Fuck you mother fucker!"

"From you, I expect nothing less," I said then I walk out of my room down the hall into the latrine shaved, took a shower, dressed, Bryant had left for the night. I walked out of the barracks and I drove over to the NCO Club met Donna in the lobby and we walked into the dining room for dinner. I was still upset

"What's wrong Honey?" Donna asked. She had never seen me really pissed but I was still mad. "Is everything OK?"

"Ah, it's my fucking coon roommate; sorry Honey, my fucking nigger roommate. He had a few drinks and was bad mouthing me because I'm successful and you're dating a white guy. He wanted to know why you're going out with whitey instead of a Black man. I don't really know how the black bastard is still wearing a uniform. Nobody not even his black brothers like the guy. Blake says he's a real fucking asshole!"

"I know, Stevie," she soothed me with her silky voice. "But just try to tough it out and clean up your mouth okay?"

"Yeah…" I sighed. "I'm sorry. I'm just upset that a black man could be so stupid!"

"Come on, Honey. Today is pay day. I'll spring for the first round."

"Love you, Donna."

"Love you back, Stevie."

The next morning as I was leaving the barracks and on my way to the parking lot 1st Sgt Bucky Glenn grabbed me and said to take hang around the orderly room. Col Rosa wanted to talk to you. Bucky told me that he would phone my section and let Sgt Blakely know that I was with the CO and I would be back in the duty section as soon as I was finished with Col Rosa.

A few minutes Col Rosa walked in with two men in civvies walked into his office and closed the door. I waited for another ten minutes then one of the guys in civvies open the door and invited me into the CO's office. I reported in then saluted Col Rosa and then was introduced to two men in civilian clothes. Mr. Johnson and Mr. Sanderson were investigators from The Office of Special Investigation and both were tall and well built and both were packing heat under their suit jackets. They were investigating Airman Bryant's murder.

"Okay Steven sit down and relax, the interview won't take that long. We have a few questions we want to ask you OK? Now, how long were Airman Bryant and you roommates?" Mr. Johnson asked me as though he was talking about the weather. "About two months, Sir." I answered looking into the OSI agent's eyes.

"How well did you and Bryant get along?" Mr. Johnson asked.

"We didn't, Sir. We didn't like each other."

"Was it anything personnel, Steven?"

"With Airman Bryant it was, Sir. He didn't like white people and as you can see, I'm white."

It was now Mr. Sanderson's turn to ask a question. "How did you know that he didn't like whites, did he tell you that, Steven?"

"In no uncertain terms Sir, he resented the fact that the whites were shown favoritism over the Negro. In the work force, whites only hired whites for the good jobs and his black brothers were relegated to be lowly paid field hands. Or as he referred to them as; and I quote… "Field niggers"."

"Did he resent the fact that you were, how can I put this…" He said pursing his lips.

"Successful, Sir?" I filled him in. "Yes sir, he did. I along with two partners own an investment company in four major cities and a new charter airline here in the Capital and he resented the fact that we haven't as yet hired any Negros."

"Is there any reason why he felt that way, Steven? And if that's a fact, then why don't you hire Negros?"

"If we are hiring and a qualified Black man or woman with the proper education and credentials or experience applied for a position those individual will be offered employment at the same salary as a white employee with our firm."

"How many Blacks do you have working for Black Gold Investments?"

"About thirty-five or forty Sir."

"And how many whites?"

"Around a hundred and fifty, Sir."

"And how many Blacks work for Executive Airlines, Steven?" Mr. Johnson asked.

"There are none, Sir because there haven't had any Blacks applying for any of the open positions."

Mr. Sanderson was next to question me. "You hire mostly pilots and aircraft mechanics, right?"

"Yes Sir, we also have an administration department for scheduling and a finance department, but right now we have no openings but when we do we advertise in the trade papers the news papers and on the company bulletin boards. We are an equal opportunity employer. You walk through the door, fill out an application and if we have a position open and if you're qualified, we hire you on a forty five day probation period and if you prove your worth you will be hired permanently."

"Is your company union?"

"Not a chance," I answered.

Mr. Sanderson chuckled than asked me, "How did the other men feel about him?"

"Without mentioning any names, both Blacks and Whites thought he had a bad attitude and a chip on his shoulder. The white guys in my section tried to be friendly with him but he would say something off color or degrading and they would walk away."

"What did he say that was off color or degrading, Steven? You can be open with us."

"He referred to the white guys as, excuse my language, Sir, fucking honkies."

"Did he threaten you or anyone else in any way?" Mr. Johnson asked as he looked at Col. Rosa and shook his head

"No Sir. I don't believe so. He never threatened me."

The two OSI officers looked at each other then at Col Rosa. "We have no further questions, Colonial. Thank you Sgt Dyer."

"Sgt Dyer, please wait in the orderly room. I want to talk to you," Col Rosa said. I saluted him did an about face and left his office. I waited for the OSI to leave then Col Rosa called me back into his office.

"Sit down Steven," Col Rosa said.

I sat down and glanced out the window at my Corvette.

"Now tell me Steven, you knew Bryant, did you tell the OSI all you knew? I'm having lunch with Col. Knutson and he's gonna grill the shit out of me!"

"Yes Sir, I realize that, but what I told to the OSI Officers was the absolute truth, Sir. Why don't you take me along with you, Sir? Col Knutson is heavily invested into Black Gold Investments."

"What officer on Bolling isn't invested with you and your cohorts, Steven?" He asked climbing to his feet.

"Sir, with all due respect... ah...so you are, Sir."

I know...I know..., I'll phone Col Knutson and set up lunch. You know Steven? I just found out that I'm getting my star," He smiled.

"Then it's imperative that we have lunch with the Base Commander, Sir, and congratulations on your promotion."

"I'll make the call."

I was not allowed in the Officer's Club under any circumstances, not if I owned it, not as the guest of the base commander, so I borrowed Blakely's Camero, Col. Knutson asked if he could take the wheel, he said that he was going buy a Camero as soon as his wife went home to visit her mother. I handed him the keys and I climbed into the back seat. We had lunch at Fong Lee's China Garden on South Capitol Street. It was a popular restaurant and it was only a few minutes from the base. Col Knutson asked me pretty much the same questions the OSI did but what confused him was why didn't I go to Col Rosa and let him know what was going on between the Bryant and me.

"With all due respect, Sir we en-listed guys usually try to work out our problems without going to our superiors. But you know Sir? If I went to Col Rosa or the 1st Sgt, maybe Airman Bryant would still be alive today, Sir."

"Now don't go blaming yourself Steven," Col Knutson gently smiled. "What has happened, has happened and a far as Col Rosa and I are concerned the subject is closed, alright?"

"Thank you Sir," I said as Col Knutson slid the bill my way.

Following lunch with the two colonels I drove back to my duty section walked into the dispatch office and flipped Curtis his car keys. Blake was sitting at his desk reading the news paper and Ben Polly was looking over Blake's shoulder. "When in hell are you gonna start buying your own fucking newspapers Pelly?"

"You know my name and it's not Pelly and I only want to be close you to Curtis, the newspaper is just a ploy," he grinned.

"Go lope your mule Benny," Curtis said as he folded the newspaper and handed it to Benny. "What in hell did OSI want with you, Steve? Question you about Bryant's killing?"

"Yeah," I replied taking off my blouse and hanging it up. "I had lunch with Col Rosa and Col Knutson."

"I know, hot shit! Donna called."

"Yeah," I said. "They wanted to know if any of the guys in the section liked him."

"And?"

"I told them that you hated him almost as much as you hated us white poor white trailer trash."

"Will you cut the shit," Blake grinned. "What did they ask you?"

I waited until Tech Sgt Shadley, CWO Richardson and Sgt Hicks and Sgt Polly were all in the dispatch office I began filling them in; they were hanging on my every word. Next were the questions and answers. I really couldn't tell them much more than what they already knew. No one really knew Bryant except that he was angry at the world hated everyone who was white and perhaps he didn't want to live any longer. Mr. Richardson came up with that theory. "Do you think the young airman wanted to rob the store in hopes that the owner would kill him and put him out of his misery?"

"You think that's what his motive was, Sir?" Bob Shadley asked.

"Are there any other thoughts gentlemen?" Mr. Richardson inquired as we all looked around at each other

"It could have been drugs, Sir," Roger said. "A lot of guys coming back from 'Nam got hooked on drugs, pot, some tried heroin, coke, there was a lot of shit over there and Bryant did a tour of duty in Vietnam."

"You may be right Sgt Hicks," Mr. Richardson said. "Sgt Dyer, did you ever observe Airman Bryant under the influence of drugs?"

"No Sir. I had never seen him in that condition but I know that he did like take a drink but he was hardly ever at the barracks."

"His girlfriend has an apartment on South Capitol Street, Sir," Curtis chimed in. "That's where he spent most of his off duty hours."

"How do you know that, Curtis?" I asked. So did everyone else, not with a question but by staring at him.

"Barbara and his girlfriend work together at Union Station" Curtis explained but Dolly Simms, Bryant's girlfriend never said that he had ever used drugs or anything else narcotic but he really did hate whites."

"Yeah, he let me know that in no uncertain terms and he had no use for the Spanish either."

"The store owner that allegedly killed him is name is Julio "Jimmy" Nunez." Captain Josh Kaplan an investigator from the Judge Advocate's Office announced as he walked into the office.

"But the motive wasn't out of hate for the Spanish; Bryant's motive was robbery. And you were right Sgt Hicks," He said looking over at Roger. "He was drug user and his drug of choice was crack cocaine."

"Is that something new, Captain?" Mr. Richardson asked.

"Well it's new to us Mr. Richardson. It's cocaine that's somehow freebased and smoked in a pipe. It's cheaper to buy than cocaine but highly addictive. Airman Bryant was a good customer to one of the top downtown drug dealers

"But his girlfriend never mentioned it to my wife, Sir," Curtis said as he looked at the medium built Air Force Captain with the coal back eyes and close cropped curly black hair.

"Know why, Blake?" The captain asked.

"Because she was buying for him," Curtis answered like he knew something that none of us knew.

"Give the Sgt a cigar. You're right Blake. But she wasn't home. Bryant was broke so he drove down to Jimmy's store, walked in, pulled out a Navy Colt 38 but Jimmy was a bit quicker, grabbed a 9 millimeter semi automatic and blew the unfortunate Airman's brains out. It wasn't pretty: Case closed."

"Why drive all the way to Virginia, Sir?" Ben asked. "There are enough convenience stores between South Capitol Street and North West DC."

"I don't know Polly, anyone have any thoughts that could shine a light on the reason why the late airman decided to drive to Virginia?"

"Could be he was too well known around here, Sir," I said. "If he ever tried to pull a robbery down town he would have been blown away. I'd say that's probably why he went to Virginia."

"You could be right, Dy. Let's just wait and see what develops. The DC cops have been questioning his girlfriend," the Captain told us as he put on his cap. "Sgt Dyer, may I see you outside for a minute?"

"Yes sir," I said as I grabbed my hat and followed him out the side door and onto the motor pool parking lot.

"What's up, Captain?" I asked as he stood facing me and smiled. His family was a big investor in Black Gold. Captain Kaplan was from South Hampton, Long Island and his family were extremely wealthy. He graduated from Harvard Law with a doctorate in jurisprudence. He passed the New York bar exam I his first try. He was very intelligent.

"What's hot, Stevie? My Jewish nuts feel incredibly lucky."

"Black Gold has an incredible deal coming down the pike, Cap," I said. "It's the hottest thing since AT&T."

"My Jewish gonads are starting tingle, Steve," He said jamming his hands into his pockets.

"You know why you can't win at pocket pool, Cap?"

"Yeah, because the umpire's a prick," He replied looking at me with his dark eyes squinting. "Now talk to me, Stevie"

"Know anything about a computer company called Digital Equipment?"

"No but I'm sure you're gonna fill me in."

"It's a computer manufacturing company located in Maynard and Cambridge, Massachusetts. You can buy in on the cheap but the buy in is ten thousand shares."

"How much we looking at?"

"A hundred grand, Cap, minimum," I said.

"How long has the company been in business?"

"Since 1957 but the company has a new computer line that's about to come out. And it's going to go into orbit and that's a fact. The unit is called a Personnel computer or PC desk top. You can use it at home."

"How much are you, CJ and Billy in for?"

"We're in for six million dollars, Cap, a million out of our personnel accounts and three million that Black Gold and Executive Airlines has anted up," I said.

He looked at me as though I had lost my mind. "That's a fucking bundle, old buddy! Have you lost your minds? And how do you know that Executive's gonna pan out?"

I had to chuckle looking at the Captain "Executive's going to be your next money maker, Cap and I'm even going to make your Yiddish Mother proud of you."

"Oy Vay," He said rolling his eyes.

"Look Cap this is going to be one of the biggest investments Black Gold has ever made. CJ said that in two years, Digital Equipment will be worth in excess of a billion dollars."

"Will be?"

"CJ never misses, Cap, neither does Billy," I assured him. "You're gonna do very, very well."

"OK, Stevie, I'm in for a half a mille. Let's meet tomorrow morning say around ten in Donna's office. I'll have a check for you."

"I don't want to walk into Donna's office and find you grabbing her shiksa ass, Cap."

"She's a beautiful girl, Stevie. You're a lucky guy."

"See you around ten Cap."

"Yeah see yah, Stevie," he said as I saluted him then walked back into the transportation office.

"What's the good captain buying now, Steve?" Bob Shadly asked lighting a Winston.

"I just sold him the motor pool. Now we're all now working for Captain Kangaroo Kaplan," I grinned.

"I believe that it's time for me to retire to bedlam," Mr. Robertson chuckled quoting Ebeneser Scrooge, he said walking back to his office.

When I got off duty I drove over to Donna's office picked her up and we drove up Merrill's Hill to Dino's for some Guinea food. I wasn't all that hungry considering what had evolved since the evening before. Bryant was a bigoted son-of-a-bitch, but if he came and asked me for some money I would have given it him but that's twenty-twenty hind sight but he would never asked me for anything. He hated my guts.

I parked the "Vette behind the restaurant and we began to walk around the building. Angelo had to be looking out of the window because he spied us then opened the back door that led into the kitchen and let us in. "Where you to been?" Angelo asked as he shook my hand and gave Donna a fatherly hug. "We were worried, a month and no Stevie; no Donna. Bruno thought that maybe you guys found another Italian restaurant."

"That will never happen, Angelo."

"Good…good," He giggled.

"We've been busy Angelo," I said. "Between the military and my business interests, then last night my roommate was shot and killed…"

"You gotta be kidding me Stevie," Angelo said blessing himself. "How did it happen?"

"He tried to knock over a 7-11." I said shaking my head. "And one of the clerks put a 38 cal between his eyes."

"Holy shit!" Angelo exclaimed.

"You're right, Angelo" Donna said. "Holy shit!"

"Come you two," Angelo said leading us into the restaurant. "I have you table all ready. I get your drinks and take your order. You have a nice dinner and you feel much better, capice?"

"Thank you, Angelo," Donna said smiling into Angelo dark eyes.

"I was only worried for my friends," Angelo smiled back and hurried off.

"Are you alright, Steve?" She asked as I swirled played with my plate of spaghetti.

"Yeah, Honey, I'm fine. It's just had been a hectic day. I was interviewed by the OSI…"

"Yeah I know Blake called me after Sgt Glenn called him." She said. "How was lunch with the brass?"

"I picked up the tab."

"Well that was nice of you, Honey," She said as I ordered another round of drinks.

"Yup, then Josh Kaplan dropped by the dispatch office and we all kicked around why Bryant tried to knock over convenience store in Virginia."

"What did you guys come up with?" she asked as she sipped her chicken noodle soup from her spoon.

"Roger nailed it, Honey; drugs. He was a crack head."

While we had dinner I brought her up to date on this morning's events. She sat there hanging onto every word I was saying. She said 'I don't believe it!' all the while I filled her in. I finally finished my Spaghetti and meat balls and as usual it was very good, I paid the tab said good bye to Angelo, Bruno and Rosie, then drove to Fort Meyer NCO Club for a drink. The bands were better at Meyer than at Bolling. Bolling was more the classical music NCO club, where Fort Meyer had a loud Army NCO Club. Jimmy Eller and the Little People were playing Rock and Roll and we both were in the mood for some good rock music and Jimmy had his guys rocking the place down.

On the ride back to Bolling I let Donna know that the meeting was all set up and we would all meet at National next Friday around six o'clock check out the hanger than go to their hotel for dinner.

"Where are they staying?"

"The Willard."

"Wow, that's expensive... nothing cheap for you and your friends."

"Well it's a business expense and if we don't spend money the IRS is going to take it away from us."

"Hey Stevie," Ben said as I walked into the dispatch office.

"Hey what," I said back as I sat down on the radio console and looked at Ben. "What's up?"

"Say I want to invest in your fly by night money making company, how much do I need to come up with?"

"Well to begin with I'll have either CJ or Billy set you up with a portfolio. You'll need a minimum initial investment of ten thousand dollars for a buy in."

"That leaves me out," he sighed. "If it cost a nickel to go around the world I couldn't get out of my fucking driveway."

"Don't worry about the buy in. Black gold can take care of that but I believe everyone that would want to invest should be able to. Just because you don't have up front capital, so what! What I'm going do is make up an investment plan that you all can get involved in."

"What do you have in mind, Stevie?" Bobby Shad asked.

"I want to make up an investment portfolio for you, Curtis, Ben and Roger."

"Look Stevie," Bob said. "We don't have any money to invest. We can barely make it from paycheck to paycheck."

"I know that, Bob, but this is what Black Gold will do and we've done it many times to get people to learn the investment business; we'll put up the money to get you guys going and show to you how to make intelligent investments. Actually it's a lot of fun."

"What kind of investment capitol are you talking about?" Ben asked.

"Investment capitol, I like that Ben," I smiled. "Each of your portfolios will be worth fifty thousand dollars. This is investment capitol, not spending money. It's not for rent but I will work with each of you and so will my partners CJ Wilson and Billy Toye, but do me a favor guys. We keep this to ourselves. Wives are alright but that's as far as it goes."

"Is what we're doing kosher? Bob asked. "I wouldn't want to see any of us get in trouble."

"Yeah, everything is on the up and up, I'm using private funds not investors money. It's referred to as expanding the company's worth. It's done all the time and it's a good way to introduce new faces into the world of stocks and bonds."

"So when do we get started?" Roger said.

"Any chance an old Warrant Officer getting into the action, Steven?" Mr. Richardson asked as he walked back into the dispatch office. "I could use something besides my retirement."

"You're in Sir," I said. "Do you have any investing experience?"

"I think that I could be of some help," he said taking a seat. "My brother is an accounting and he introduced me to the world of private investing.

"It looks like we are having our first meeting of the Motor Pool Dispatchers and truck driver's Investment Group." I grinned. It had a nice ring.

I walked into Donna's office at ten o'clock the next morning. Captain Kaplan was already there sitting on Donna's desk talking to her. She was leaning against one of the five file cabinets her arms folded over ample breasts. They were talking about Vietnam.

"Good morning Donna, good morning, Sir," I said as I nodded toward the officer who was still sitting on Donna's desk.

"Good morning Sweetheart," Donna smiled as she came over and kissed me gently on the cheek.

"Good morning Bubbie," The Captain giving me a lewd grin. "But don't expect a kiss. I'd rather be kissing…"

"Your girlfriend?" I cut in.

"Ahhhh… yeah," he smiled. "Come on let's make some money." He handed me a check for five hundred grand, I handed the check to Donna she looked at the check to make sure it was made out correctly then place the check into her briefcase. Donna made all the deposits that went into the DC Black Gold account and the receipts that came into the Executive Airlines account. I gave her power of attorney to handle the money, pay the airline's bills and to write checks.

"I'll call CJ and have him credited the half mille to you account and let him know you're buying fifty thousand shares of Digital Equipment Company stock.

"How long will it take for the transaction to be completed?"

"As soon as I phone CJ he'll take care of the details. What I'll have him do is to credit you account as of yesterday."

"Is that kosher?" he said getting to his feet.

"Yeah it's Kosher, Cap." I said. "I would never do anything that would compromise the company's integrity. And beside that… the IRS is watching."

"Maybe I should have post-dated the check?"

"You're in, Captain Kaplan. Everything's cool. Black Gold will deposit the half million into your account. Now all we have to do is to wait for your check to clear."

A week later the check cleared and six months later Josh Kaplan's portfolio increased by two million dollars.

MAY 12, 1968:

It was Friday early evening we were all off duty sitting beside the swimming pool at our two hundred year old colonial feasting on "T" bone steaks sucking down adult beverages. I had to spend some time and money greasing the local politician's palms trying to secure the permits to have the pool installed. The small Virginia town didn't want the property disturbed by a swimming pool in the back yard, but money talks and bull shit walks so I got the variances, the contractor pulled the permits and the pool was installed. I even had the fire department, with a generous donation to their "emergency fund" filled the pool.

Early the next morning Donna and I were flying Harrisburg, Pennsylvania, and on Sunday afternoon we were to be married, but this evening it was all the guys from the section including now Major Josh Kaplan and their wives enjoying good drinks, good food and a good time. I wish that we could invite them all but it would be extremely difficult for CWO Robinson to grant ten of my friends leave to attend our wedding. Curtis and Barbara were going and so were Bobby Shad and Marge. Suzanne and Dianne were going to be bride's maids and if the law ever changes and gays can get married Donna was going to be Suzanne and Dianne's Maid of honor.

Most everyone on Bolling had an idea that Suzanne and Dianne were more than friends but so long as they performed their duty and stayed cool nobody really minded. Dianne and Suzanne were two of the nicest girls that I had ever met and they were Donna and my best friends. Even Curtis Blakely, who was very vocal when it came to men going with men and women going with women thought Dianne and Suzanne were "cool". If Curtis thought you were "cool" that meant he liked you.

Executive Charter Air Services picked up Mom, Dad and Aunt Louise at Bedford Airport which was a civilian air terminal at the end of Hanscom Air Force Base and flew them all into Harrisburg. Tommy and Joan flew in from San Diago, and Billy and CJ with Karen and Lee Ann arrived in from Hawaii. They were on vacation and when the wedding and the reception was over Donna and I were flying back to Hawaii with them and then Donna and I are on to French Polynesia and Tahiti.

The wedding went on without a hitch and the reception was held at the William Penn Centre for Performing Arts. "Why in hell would we want our reception there?" I asked Donna. "Are we going to be dancing to chamber music?"

She looked at me as though I had absolutely no experience in the performing arts. "No Stevie. My Dad knows the curator of the "Penn" and the band is from Southern California. CJ and Billy hired them and flew them in."

"Who's the band?"

"Tell me Stevie, whose is your favorite band of all time?" Donna asked me.

"The Beach Boys," I answered as I furled my brow. "Why?"
"It's our wedding present from CJ, Karen, Billy and lee Ann."

The hardest part was going to confession. "Bless me Father for I have sinned it's been twelve years since my last confession I accuse myself; just to be on the safe side; of systematically breaking all of the Ten Commandments."
"Including murder my son?" The priest asked.
"Yes Father, I spent a year in Vietnam and I accidently ran over a Vietnamese Soldier with a ten ton tractor trailer."
"Not a pretty sight I'm sure," He said.
"No it wasn't Father. He walked right out in front of me."
"How fast were you going when you ran him over?"
"About forty miles an hour, Father."
"Not much chance of avoiding him I suppose."
"No Father," I said. "I never saw him until it was too late."
"An accident isn't a sin, my Son."

I was sure that by the time I finished my penance I'd be too old to consummate my marriage, but Father Dave was a light inquisitor and I got off with quick Rosary and had I to promise that I would be a good boy. Good Boy? Christ Father Dave I was twenty-six!
My Dad and Donnas Dad became fast friends. They both love to play golf and with Dad owning two golf courses and with Captain Lowery flying into Boston and into Tampa it looked like Dad had a new best friend. Jack Lowery who had years of seniority had his route changed to flying exclusively into Tampa-Saint Pete. Jack and Beth Lowery were Mom and Dad's constant and welcomed guests.

15 OCTOBER 1969:

I had just re-enlisted for the third time Donna got out after eight years and was working for Executive Airlines in the finance department. Barbara Blakely was also with the airline working in reservations while Curtis was sweating it out in Vietnam, Bob Shadly had retired and moved back home to International Falls, Minnesota and the rest of my buddies, Roger Hicks, Benny Polly were still at Bolling and Mr. Robinson who had also retired and they all were making a bundle with their investments in Black Gold, Executive Airlines and Digital Equipment.

The airline was expanding to a nationwide operation. I should have gotten out of the Air Force along with Donna, but over the objections of Billy and now Charley I elected to stay in. Even now General Rosa thought maybe eight years was enough and I should begin running the airline. "Steven," The general said while was sitting in his office. He did get his star and was going to the pentagon. "If I can arrange it, why not get out of the regulars and go into the reserves and if the shit hits the fan you could always be called back. You have a huge conglomeration to run and I have it on good authority that if you stay in the regulars you will be running into Curtis Blakely, capice?"

"Yes, Sir."

"Well?"

"You're right Sir."

"I'll pull some strings and this time tomorrow you'll be Tech Sgt Steven W. Dyer Air Force Reserves, Okay?"

"Yes Sir," I said grinning.

"Alright, get out of here, I gotta go to over to Headquarters and brew some coffee. I'll talk to you later."

"Yes Sir," I said as I got to my feet saluted executed a perfect about face and exited his office.

"You and the General got something going, Steve?" The 1st Sgt laughed as he looked over his newspaper. "You spend more time In the General's office than I do."

"Were pisans, Brian; you know friends?" I smiled and walked out of the orderly and drove back to the section.

"What's happening, Sgt Dyer?" It was Major White the new Squadron Commander and great officer. He was black but didn't hold it against anyone. He was a giant of a man with a wonderful sense of humor. Good thing. He could pick up the building and heave it into the Potomac River.

"May I see you in your office, Sir?"

"Yeah, come on in don't bother reporting in. Let's keep it casual."

I followed him into his sparsely furnished office just a desk, two chairs and a shelf behind his desk that held pictures of his wife and his two sons.

"Sit down," He said pointing to the chair beside his desk. "What's on your mind, Dyer?"

"I was in General Rosa office this morning, Sir and..."

"How unusual Sgt," He grinned. "Are you on a first name basis with the general yet?"

"No sir, not yet, but General Rosa is having me transferred out of the regulars and I'll be going into the reserves, Sir."

"I'm not surprised Dyer and it's a good move. You were scheduled for another tour in Vietnam."

"Yes Sir. General Rosa mentioned that to me."

"Ok, Sgt. As soon as your orders come down, probable later this afternoon or tomorrow morning report to the orderly room and pick-up your clearance sheet, alright? Good luck Sgt Dyer," Major White said as he stood, smiled and up and extended his hand.

"Thank you Sir," I said taking his hand, then saluted did an about face and walked out of his office.

ANOTHER TOUR IN VIETNAM

JULY 4 1970:
Binh Thuy AIR BASE, SOC TRANG PROVINCE,
VIETNAM:

So I got out of the regulars and re-enlist into the reserves. Donna was happy Billy Toye was, in his own words: "Fucking Ecstatic!" CJ Wilson thought that it was a smart decision, Curtis Blakely, newly returned from Da Nang and now stationed at Andrews driving his own Corvette also told me it was a good thing I left the regulars, because I was on my way back to 'Nam if I did stay in, so what in hell am I doing back in Viet-Fucking-"Nam??? It was suppose to be a ninety day TDY but when I arrived in Binh Thuy I had my TDY orders pulled and I was there for a year. The 1st Sgt who was on his way home, had never heard of me or Black Gold Investments or Executive International Airlines or Global Cargo Air Freight informed me that now I was earning combat pay it should make it easier for the wife to pay the bills. Pay what bills you fucking cracker? I had enough money to buy this stink hole country and sink it into the South China Sea! I was about ready to have the boys in the North End get out a contract and blow General Rosa away!

"You're what?" Donna exclaimed looking up from her desk.

"Orders Honey, I'm going back to Vietnam," I said sitting on the corner her desk. "But it's only a ninety day TDY."

"What? I don't fucking believe it!" She was really pissed because I had never heard Donna drop the "F" before in anger but she wasn't mad at me but she was pissed at General Rosa. "You got out of the regulars so you wouldn't have to go back to that shit hole, you joined the reserves and now they're sending you back to Viet FUCKING Nam!" There goes the "F" bomb again,

"I'll desert," I joked.

"Right! Then instead of going back to 'Nam you'd end up in the Fort Belvoir Slammer!"

"The guard house would only be for a year and nobody would be shooting at me."

"I'm sorry, Honey," She said as she took my head in her hands and pressed me into her warm, soft, breasts. "When are you due in country?"

"January 23rd," I replied trying to sound calm but I was more pissed than she was. "They're sending me to Bhin Thuy."

"Where in hell is Bhin Thuy?"

"South of Saigon in the Soc Trang Province area on the banks of the lovely Mekong River."

"Have you told Billy and CJ yet?" She asked.

"No, not yet,

"This should go over like a fart in a space suit," She groaned. "And Billy's really going to go through the roof! He'll probably try to get a contract out on Rocco Rosa,"

"He'll get over it." I said as I caressed her soft breasts.

I phoned CJ in New York City then Billy Toye out in California and explained the situation to both of them, CJ took the news in his usual calm demeanor but Billy went ballistic. "How in the fuck can they send you back to 'Nam, Stevie? How much more blood does the Air Force want from you? You got out of the regulars to avoid 'Nam and they're sending you back anyway?"

"Yeah I know Billy but what in hell can I do about it, but it's only a ninety day TDY," I said trying to placate him.

"Yeah right and as soon as you get over there they change your orders and keep you there for a whole fucking year!"

"Yeah Billy. It's possible but I doubt it." I hoped the hot headed Dago was wrong.

I said my good by's to Curtis and Barbara, Benny and Roger and their families, then Donna and I flew down to Hollywood, Florida and bid my folks a fond farewell, then on to Harrisburg, to say good-bye to Donna's folks, then to New York City and I said good bye to Charley and Karen then Donna and I flew out to L.A. stayed with Billy and Lee Ann for three days then we flew up to San Francisco and I caught military flight out of Travis and seventeen hours later, with a refueling stop and a quick sandwich at base ops on Wake Island the C-141 touched down at Ton Son Nhut. From TSN I caught a quick flight on a C-123 into Bhin Thuy's 23rd Ariel Port Squadron where an Air Force pickup was waiting for me with a gook driver who drove me to the 211 Operations Squadron's orderly room. It took ten minutes and I was processed in. I'm glad that I held onto my four sets of jungle fatigues, two pairs of jungle boots and my boonie hat. The new Squadron 1st Sgt, Master Sgt. Ray Saccoccio was a tall thin, tanned, nice looking pisian from Providence, Rhode Island. He told me that base supply was about out of everything and the base was going to be turned over to the Vietnamese forces and there was not much being flown in.

"What am I doing here 1st Sgt?" I asked sitting down beside his desk. "I was totally taken by surprise when I received my orders."

"Call me Ray, Steve. We're pretty much informal around here, except for the officers. They still like being called sir and still expected to be saluted."

"Except on the flight line, right?"

Ray looked at me and chuckled. "You call that a flight line?" He said as we both looked out of the window.

"I wouldn't want to be a fighter pilot and try to land with all those pot holes stretched across the flight line,"

"Want another surprise?" He asked me handing me new orders.

"No, not really," I said looking over the papers. "Aw shit. I'm here for a year," I said shaking my head as threw the orders on the 1st Sgt's desk.

"Come on, Stevie, I'll show you where you're staying and you're really gonna love it. They're ten of us NCOs living in a hootch that if it was stateside it would be condemned and burned to the ground. No shit Steve, this place is an incredible rat hole. Once the fighter jocks moved out the place went right down the toilet."

"Then what's the game plan, Ray?" I asked picking up my two B-4 bags and following him down the dusty street.

"Red Horse and the See Bees will be flying in with heavy equipment and construction materials," He said opening the door of the hooch and introduced me to some of the guys.

"How soon, Ray?" I asked.

"Last week," he chuckled. "You know, Stevie? I have no idea why the military is still fucking around with this dump. We have absolutely no reason to even be here. If the gooks want the shit hole, turn it over to them and fly us the fuck out! Did you check out the flight line when you flew in? We don't even have a fuckin tower or lights!"

"Where can you get a drink around here?" I said.

"That's one thing we have plenty of. If you want to dine in the mess hall that's up to you but most of us eat "K" rations or eat downtown, because the swill they serve in the mess hall really sucks, and there's not much in the way of supplies either, It's a good thing that you held onto your jungle fatigues and boots and kept your weight down or you'd walking around the base in your underwear. And there are hookers that hang around the main gate but I wouldn't recommend that you avail yourself of their charms and services. They're nothing but a bunch of douche bags; but we have lots and lots of booze. Come on Sgt Dyer, I'll show you around the compound."

The walk took about ten minutes because there wasn't much to see. There was the mess tent, and a bar tent and you were your own bartender. You brought in your own bottle put your name onto it and placed it on a shelf. The beer was kept cold in a large cooler that the motor pool guys took from the NCO club when the joint was mortared. The beer was bought at the Base Exchange and sold at the bargain price of ten cents a can. The hard stuff was sold out of a conex box that was large enough to drive a tank through. The forty ounce bottles went from Crown Royal at $2.25 a bottle to a forty ounce of rot gut gin that sold for $.65 cents. That was about the same price it was selling for the last time I was in 'Nam.

"No ration card? 1stSgt?" I joked as we walked into the dispatch office tent. All our electricity was supplied by a ten kilowatt diesel generator that ran twenty four a day seven days a week. When I first arrived on the base the generator was annoying, especially at night but it didn't long to get used to it and the only time that you were aware that it was there was when it ran out of fuel and or shit the bed, Sgt Saccoccio introduced me to the head dispatcher and the assistant dispatcher who was the same person. A1C Roscoe Clark, a tall skinny black kid from Mobile, Alabama. Roscoe looked and talked just like Bill Cosby. And he was just as funny.

"What the fuck is a lily white millionaire like you doing back in Vietnam?" He asked shaking my hand. "But I'm glad you're here. Where you gonna be working?"

"Who told you I was a millionaire Roscoe?"

"The tooth fairy," He grinned showing me a mouth full of lily white teeth.

"I have no idea. Maybe the 1st Sgt knows," I said looking at Ray Saccoccio.

"How about we start him off in the mess hall Ray, opening up cans of "K" rations?" Roscoe Clark suggested sitting back down.

"Naw…let's start him off with something simple."

A week after my arrival on base, Red Horse and the See Bees finally showed up, the construction began and the heavy equipment began to resurface the runways, rebuild the barracks and the base infrastructure. The VNAF (Vietnamese Air Force) pilots got the barracks while we were still living in tents.

My duties were simple but interesting, coordinating the construction efforts between the Sea Bees and Red Horse. The Sea Bees resurfaced the runways and Red Horse built a new flight line tower and strung light up and down the flight line. All I really had to do was show up in the morning and meet with a Navy Chief and go over what had to be done and to make sure that all the supplies were in place then we spent the rest of the day at the construction sites.

Chief Petty Officer Bobby Ray Leonard and I became fast friends. Bobby and some of the Seabee petty officers moved into the Air Force tents because we were closer to the heavy equipment and when our duty day was finished we would usually end up in the booze tent with the card board containers carrying our dinners, a can of franks and beans, a tin of crackers, a package of soluble coffee, sugar power milk and three Pall Mall cigarettes. Two or three times a week I would go into the village and have dinner and a couple of drinks and play cards at The Play Boy Club Bar (There was a Play Boy Club Bar in Bien Hoa when I was stationed there; it must be a chain.) with Bobby Ray Leonard, Ray Saccoccio and Roscoe Clark.

On Friday and Saturday nights they had a Vietnamese rock and roll band that showed up at the Play Boy Club and they were pretty good. The band drove down from Bien Hoa in an old Air Force bus that was so beat up that no stateside junk yard would ever consider scraping. The four boys called themselves The Bien Hoa Beatles. They knew more Beatles song than the Beatles did and although they couldn't speak ten words of English they knew all the words and the music. When the Bien Hoa Beatles came to town you would have thought it was the real thing. The place was mobbed with the part of crowd spilling out into the street. There was more V.C. in the crowd than town's people. They even had pictures taken of themselves and they would autograph them, "John; Paul; George and Ringo."

In later years I often wondered what happened to the four mop-headed Vietnamese singers. I hope that they got out of Vietnam before the US media made sure their country got it's ass kicked. They were that good.

SIX MONTHS LATER

Roscoe finally made Staff Sgt (E-5) and his promotion meant we were going to let him let him pay for dinner. The Playboy Club Bar was where we were eating when a little VC Gook fuck walked into the restaurant carrying a shoe shine box placed it in the shithouse set the timer and hauled his ass out. We didn't have a chance. The place was leveled and when we finally got our heads back on straight the four of us were in the hospital at Ton Son Nhut Air Base. We were lucky. Ten of the patrons plus the bar tender and three hookers were killed outright and another five died from their wounds. All the dead were Vietnamese.

I don't remember all what happened that night. I saw a bright light heard a loud blast then all the lights went out including my mine. All four of us were taken by meat wagon back to the base our conditions were evaluated and med evacuated by an Air Force Rescue and Recovery chopper up to Tan Son Nhut and dropped off at the base hospital. It took almost a week before Roscoe and I could get out of bed without the help of a medic. I never liked anyone looking at me while I was taking a leak but a medic had to hold me up while I pissed and had to help me off the toilet following my bowel movement. The medics were great.

"Are we all still alive?" Roscoe Clark asked as medics tried to get us out of bed and onto our feet. "Any of you guys named Jesus?" He asked looking at the medic's one at a time. Roscoe was your typical Southern Baptist. We were really sore from having the building fall on top of us. The poor bastards that were working behind the bar or working the kitchen got the worst of it. Thank God the blast happened the day before payday and before the Bien Hoa Beatles arrived so the restaurant was almost empty of American troops. If the dumb gook only waited another day he would have wiped out a shit load of the good guys. The little Gook fuck got his dates mixed up.

"Yeah we are Roscoe," I said as I sat on the side of my bed, my legs and feet dangling over the edge. "How are you feeling?"

"The same as you, Stevie," He smiled as he shook his head. "I can hardly hear a fucking thing."

"Yeah I know. My ears are still ringing, but have you heard anything about how Bobby and Ray are doing?" I asked looking at the bandages wrapped around my back and chest and hands and arms. All we were wearing was olive drab boxer skivvies and slippers with a robe placed at the foot of our beds.

"No but I pray God every morning and every night that they're alright."

"Have you seen them?"

"No but the medics said that were going to be okay and resting comfortably but they both are in tough shape."

"Wanna take a walk, Roscoe?" I said as I tried to stand erect on shaky legs.

"Yeah, let's try to find the NCO Club, I need a drink." He said as attempted to stand up and walk around the ward.

"Good idea my friend, but first let's see if we can find out where Ray and Bobby are," I said as we put on our robes, held on to each other as we approached the door that led out of the ward. "Then we'll try to find the NCO Club."

Just as we finally began moving toward the end of the ward a huge black medic came down the hallway and hurried up to us back to our beds. "Just what in the name of Sweet Baby Jesus are you two fools doing?" He asked in a deep baritone voice. "Do you know how badly you two fools are hurt?"

"We just want to visit Sgt Saccoccio and Chief Leonard. We only want see how they're getting along."

"They are doing just fine and they're gonna live, alright?"

"So they're still here," I said

"Yeah in another ward, but if you want to explore the hospital let me know and I'll get you wheel chairs, alright?"

"How about now?" Roscoe asked.

"All the wheelchairs are being used so how about you crips going back to bed before the Doc shows up and checks all of us for hemorrhoids?"

"Yeah alright." Roscoe said chuckled as the medic left the ward.

"Hey Stevie," Roscoe said as he hobble over to my bed and sat down beside me.

"Hey what?"

"You think the black medic's a faggot?" Roscoe asked.

"Well the next time he comes back drop your skivvies and show him your baby's arm with an apple in its fist dick and see what happens under his green medic outfit."

"Hey that's a good one Stevie," Roscoe laughed. "You make it up?"

"No, I read it in a Lenny Bruce book, "How To Talk Dirty and Influence People"."

"Stevie, you think they'll be sending us home?" Roscoe asked as he slid off my bed and sat down on a chair that was facing me. "We almost got fuckin' killed you know!"

"It would be nice if they did send us home, Buddy. Hell I have only six months to go before I'm outa this shit hole country."

"And Ray and I have about the same."

"What about the chief?" I asked.

"Bout the same as you, Ray and me I guess," He said looking at me. "This is all our second tour so they'll probably give us a ticket to home," Roscoe reasoned.

"Roscoe?"

"Yeah?"

"Think we'll get the Purple Heart?" I asked looking into his
·dark wise eyes.

"We fuckin' better! If asshole Kerry can suck ass for his Silver
Star, Bronze Stars and three Purple Heart with only four months in
country we all should get fuckin' Medals of Honor!"

Ray Saccoccio and Bobby Leonard were worse off than Roscoe
and I so they were med evacuated to the Clark Air Force Base
Hospital in the Philippines. Roscoe and I were held at Ton Son Nhut
until the Docs were sure that we were fit to travel then we were put
on a C-141 and with about fifty other litters with wounded GI's and
flown back to the states

General Rosa got the word that I had been wounded and was
going to be sent home when I was able to travel. Then he called on
Donna and gently let her know about the explosion and my wounds
but I was going to be alright. She was worried because she got a letter
from me every day, now it was over a week and she hadn't heard from
me and she was bouncing off the walls.

The General drove over to Washington National Airport and
paid her a visit at The Executive Airlines Corporate offices. When
she saw him walk into her office she about fainted. "Hello General,"
She said her legs shaking as she climbed to her feet.

"Good morning Donna, everything's fine," The General said
getting right to the point. "Steve's in the Tan Son Nhut hospital
recovering from injuries suffered in an explosion. He and some of
his friends were having dinner down town when someone from the
other side planted a bomb in the restaurant's bathroom. He has some
bumps and bruises and some stitches on his back and his arms. He
also suffered a slight concussion but I got the word from Seventh Air
Force that he will be on his way home in a week or so."

"Thank you so much for coming by, General. You could have
phoned." Donna said as she tried to stop shaking. "I know you're
busy."

"I'm never too busy not to make a personnel visit to my two favorite people. And besides your husband has friends in lower places, one is a very close friend of mine…"

"I know; Fudgie Iaconio," Donna said

"Yeah, Fudgie and he would have put out a contract on me if I phoned you instead of visiting you in person," The General joked. "And I feel somewhat responsible for his injuries. I talked him into going into the reserves. If he had stayed in the regulars he was going back to Bien Hoa which is considered fairly secure and he would have been stuck in an office for a year."

"Has Steve's family been notified?" Donna asked.

"Yes they have. Stevie's brother phone and let them know Steve's was alright."

"Exactly what happened, Sir?" Donna asked as she invited the general to have a seat on the sofa and she sat down beside him.

General Rosa filled her in with all the gory details of the explosion. "The restaurant was totally leveled, Donna. If that building came up to stateside codes nobody would have been killed, but the roof made out of thin, cheap, corrugated tin, and instead of the roof crashing down on them it was blown all too hell and landed outside of the building. What injured the guys were the nails and ball bearings that were packed inside the ordinance and if the Vietnamese weren't sitting between the bomb and the guys they would have all been killed."

"I don't understand the war and the people that we're fighting to save," She cried looking at General Rosa. "They think nothing of slaughtering their own people!"

"The military job is to fight this impossible to win war and the politician's and the media's job is to make sure that we lose this impossible to win war." He said as he climbed to his feet.

"You're serious!" Donna exclaimed as she stood up and faced him.

"Yes I am my Dear. Now let's get your husband home and get him well shall we? I'll stay in touch," He said as he warmly hugged her gently kissed her cheek and walked out of her office.

Roscoe and I were wheeled out of the TSN hospital and wheeled aboard an Air Force C-141 with about fifty ambulatory patients and flown to Clark AFB where we picked up Ray Saccoccio and Bobby Leonard then flew to Guam to drop off a couple of wounded natives then too Hawaii then onto Travis. Donna was waiting at the Travis hospital when we were wheeled into admissions. So were Billy Toye and CJ Wilson. "Now listening to me fuck head," Billy said as he walked over to my gurney and whispered in my ear. "Are you ready to run the airline or are you still looking to be a hero?"

"The Air Force is giving me the Purple Heart," I whispered into his ear.

"Good," He smiled kissing my cheek.

I spent ten days with Roscoe, Ray and Bobby in the Travis Hospital going through physical therapy. Donna was staying on base in one of the visiting family apartments. Ray Saccoccio and Bobby Leonard had more extensive injuries, so they were stuck at Travis going through physical theropy. Ray had a broken leg and a fractured pelvis, Bobby had a five fractured vertebras in his back and a broken shoulder. I lost touch with Ray and Bobby but I assume that they were both given medical discharges, but I stayed in touch with Roscoe. He had a desk job at Eglin Air Force Base, Florida. He got the Purple Heart and the Bronze Star too.

When I was able to travel I was wheeled out of the Travis Hospital with Donna, driven to the small regional airport and loaded onto the an Executive Airlines C-140 Jet Star with sleeping quarters and a small head in the rear of the plane that comfortably slept two little people (midgets). I had never given that much thought to the size plane's bedrooms. I wasn't in the 140 long enough to go to the back of the aircraft and see what was there. I knew there was a bed room in the back but I never had an opportunity use it.

This was the first time in more than seven months that Donna and I had the opportunity to be alone and we took advantage of the privacy of the plane and hospitality of Executive Air. They should treat me well I was awarded the Purple Heart and more than that: I owned the airline.

There was a well stocked mini bar in the cabin a large platter filled with the best food that Executive had to offer.

I hadn't had a drink since the blast but I wasn't on pain killers, sedatives or any other opiates so what the hell, "Come on Donna let's have a drink," I smiled looking over the platter filled with lobster salad, shrimp, sliced roast beef, sliced ham, sliced Monterey Jack cheese and a Cesar salad. I grabbed a lobster salad sandwich and plate full of cooked shrimp and sat down on the small couch.

"Can you have a drink, Honey, with your wounds?" She said as she opened four Grey Goose nips, looked around the bar and picked out the largest glasses she could find. They looked like jelly glasses.

"Yeah, I'm no longer on medication."

"On the way," She smiled as she poured the top shelf vodka over the ice from the small refrigerator that was under the bar. I can't believe all the shit they built into the custom built Jet Star. The plane wasn't all that big but it would blow the wings off most of the air limos.

"My wounds are not very pretty, Honey, but the stitches are out and most of the wounds are healed,"

I said as I slowly climbed to my feet, removed all my clothes and stood naked in front of my wife. Donna finished making my drink with ice, vodka and a lime, then turned faced me and handed me my high octane cocktail then she removed her clothes. God she was beautiful "You're not as bad as I had imagined, Honey," She smiled as she examined my manhood it then turned and mixed herself a Grey Goose Martini in a glass that was as large as mine. "I'm glad none of your important parts were injured. Shall we take our food, drinks into the bedroom and get comfortable. I want to make sure that all your goodies intact and in good working order. God, Stevie I've missed you so God damned much and when General Rosa walked into my office and told me what happened to you I thought I was going to pass out. Stevie, if anything ever happened to you I wouldn't want to go on living I love you that much," She cried as we walked to the back of aircraft opened the door and entered small bedroom. There was a small table at the foot of the bed where she placed the platter and the drinks.

When she showed up at the hospital she was wearing shorts, a short sleeve sweat shirt and sandals, her hair was done up in a pony tail and she was wearing very little make up it was early evening and since she had been up since early morning she looked incredibly beautiful as she walked into the room hospital that I was sharing with Roscoe and four other GIs. All five of us couldn't take our eyes off Donna. "That's your wife, Stevie?" Roscoe asked as Donna approached my bed.

"Yeah, Roscoe," I answered as I sat up in bed. "That's Donna, my wife."

"She's a beautiful woman, my man. You're one lucky dude."

After a medic pulled the curtain around my bed Donna fell into my arms. She was trying to hold back her tears as she kissed me all over my face, my nose, my eyes and my lips. "Oh God Stevie I was so scared on the flight out here. My imagination was running wild. How badly you were wounded, if you could walk…"

"I'm fine Honey just a little stiff from the stitches spread all over my back chest and arms, but we were lucky, Honey, we all could have been killed."

"Yes I know General Rosa visited me at my office and told me what happen and he didn't spare any of the gory details," She said as she climbed into bed with me. "And he said that he regretted talking you into signing up for the reserves."

I don't know if it was against regulations to have my wife crawl into bed with me while I was recovering from my wounds in a military hospital but what are they gonna do, send me back to 'Nam?

"God Stevie you feel so good. I could eat you up."

"Let's wait until I get out of the hospital. Let's not start something we may not be able to finish."

We were both sleeping when the Jet Star approached National. The pilots didn't want to bother us with fasten your seat belts place your seats in an upright position. The greased the runway landing woke us up. We rolled out of bed, we were both still nude. We brushed our teeth, I shaved and we both took a whore's bath. There was a clean uniform for me hung up in the head so we dressed then opened the tiny bedroom door and walked up the aisle. I was doing much better, I could almost stand upright.

"Well good morning, Steve, good morning Donna" The two pilots grinned as they squeezed out of the Flight deck and into the cabin. "How are you feeling, Steve? And welcome home."

"Thanks Jimmy." Jimmy Brody and Billy Norris were my two best pilots. They both flew cargo in the Air Force Reserves and the both had spent time flying in and out of Vietnam and Thailand. "There is nothing like a couple of drinks, good food, making love then getting a few hours sleep to bring you back to the world."

"Is the chief still on medication, Donna?" The Billy asked. We're very informal here at Executive Airlines.

"Why yes he is, Billy, the medication was three or four glasses, of Grey Goose vodka on the rocks, a complete body massage by me, some sleep and that is what's helping him to recover." She smiled as she patted Billy Norris and Jimmy Brody on their Rosie red cheeks.

"There's a car waiting to take you over to Andrew's Air Force Base Hospital, Steve. The docs want to check you out before they let you go home. You're still on active duty you know?" Jimmy reminded me.

"Thanks for reminding me, shithead," I said as I gave him a sarcastic smile.

"Thanks fellas," Donna said as Billy open the cabin door and helped me down the five steps and over to one of the corporate Lincoln Limousines and the corporate chauffeur drove us to the Andrew's base hospital. I was checked in, wheeled to the elevator transported up to the second floor showed me my bed on the ward where a medic handed me a jonnie and ordered to remove all my clothes. They could have saved me some trouble if they hung the jonnie in the Jet star latrine and had me put it on there. Donna wheeled me to the head where I stripped out of my summer tans, put them on a hanger, handed Donna my underwear, put on my Johnny, Donna tied up the back then reach around the front, patted my dick then wheeled me back to my bed and helped me up and pulled the curtain around the bed: Shit, the bed in the Jet Star was bigger the beds on the ward.

The next morning following breakfast in bed I was wheeled into X-ray had a few shot taken, then back to the ward, Donna was waiting when the doctor came in, told me he liked what he had seen on the X-rays, my wounds were healing fine so why don't you get dressed and get the hell of here. You do not need to tell me twice Doc I said. Donna wheeled me back into the head, I dressed into my summer tans and Donna drove us home. My 68 Lincoln Mark 111 was parked in the hospital lot. One of the guys from Executive dropped it off.

It was nice sitting in the front seat of our Lincoln. I wanted to drive the Mark 111 home but Donna thought better of it. "You'll have plenty of time to get behind the wheel of you classics but for now, Stevie, I'm in charge! You got that?"

"You don't love me no more," I whined laying my head on her shoulder while I acted like a spoiled little kid.

"That's anymore, Stevie" She corrected me.

"Anymore." I sniffled as I caressed her right breast.

"Will you cut the shit, Stevie," She laughed as she reached down and rubbed my crotch. "And I love you, you asshole! And that's forever. You got that?"

"Oh God…I just got home and we're fighting already," I said while I continued caressing her right breast.

"Not now, Honey, I don't want to crash us into a tree." She said as the speedometer approached seventy miles an hour.

"You crash us into a tree while you're playing with my nuts?" I yelled feigning anger. "We could get killed, Honey."

""Then you had better stop playing with my tits," She said as she put her hand down the front of my loose fitting trousers. I lost a few pounds while I was in the hospital.

Now we were having fun. While were dating we would we would have fun bouncing off each other the same as a comic bouncing off the audience. "When we get home let's go right to bed."

"God, Honey, you must be exhausted," She said as she took a left off the Wilson Bridge and merged onto Route 1.

"No, nothing like that, but except for the small bedroom in the Jet Star I really haven't seen you in the nude since before I left for 'Nam," I said.

"You know, Stevie, when you told me that you were going back to Vietnam I had an incredible feeling of…whatever you call it."

"A premonition?"

"For Christ sake, Stevie," She said as she signaled attempting to break into the traffic that was always heavy on Route 1. "What was the Air Force thinking? With all the lay about, fucked up, drugged up assholes that could care less about whether our country survives or not, why would the Air Force want to send a…"

"Millionaire?" I said.

"No Stevie, my husband, a husband that I cherish, love and a husband that I almost lost." She said referring to me in the third person. "A man that so many depend on and so many love and respect you and you know when the people at Executive Airlines heard that you were going back to 'Nam I had never seen so many sad faces in my life. Josh Kaplan was beside himself when he found out. He didn't even try to flirt with me."

"Josh the horny Hebe?" I said looking at her while she looked straight ahead. She was really upset at General Rosa and the whole Air Force.

"Yeah, him. I wish he would get married. There has to be a million nice looking young ladies down town, ready to satisfy everyone even the horny Jew."

"How are Suzanne and Dianne doing?"

"Oh God, Stevie, when I told them what happened they both totally fell apart. You know how sensitive they are, so when I flew out to Travis I had to call them every day and give them updates. Suzanne said that when you finally come home they want to nurse you wearing white costumes, aprons and hats."

I had to laugh, what sounds like cheep theatrics to most people but with the girls it wasn't play acting. They actually meant it.

"Come on Honey," I gently kneading her breasts while she still looked straight ahead down the road "I'm home now, alive and Vietnam is history. So let's stop feeling sorry for each other and go on home, okay?"

"Yeah let's," She smiled looking over at me and while she continued to massage my crotch. "The girls said that they would have a chilled pitcher of Grey Goose and tonic on the ready and you know that while you were back in "Nam" they were so incredible supportive. I hardly had to raise a hand. When I came downstairs ready for work they had coffee ready, toast all buttered and when I came out of the shower they had my clothes laid out on the bed. And when I got home the house was cleaned, the bathroom ready for my morning shower."

"They didn't try to, yeah know...?" I said winking at her.

"Bite your tongue, Steven!"

"Well they are cute couple," I joked.

"Yeah they are, Honey," She said as turned the big Mark 111 off Route 1 and drove the back roads to our house. "But they don't have what I really need."

"Oh and what's that, Sweet thing?"

"It's the love of a dear sweet husband whom I love more than my own life."

When Donna pulled onto the big Mark 111 into the driveway where I spied four of my eight classic cars parked in the driveway waiting for us to arrive, my 40 Ford Coupe, my 51 Mercury Monterey, my 67 Corvette and my favorite of all time, my 1940 Lincoln Continental Cabriolet Convertible. That was Benny's idea.

Suzanne and Dianne were waiting on the deck with a pitcher my favorite libations and when they spied the Lincoln come up the driveway they were both, dressed in nurses uniforms, came running towards the big Mark 111, Dianne's hands clapping, Suzanne's arms out stretched. "Oh Christ, Donna, they're dress like fucking nurses," I groaned looking as the girls as ran up to the Lincoln opened the door, undid my seat belt and helped me out of the front seat and were hugging me as though I just returned from the grave.

"Oh God, Stevie, when Donna told us what happened to you," Suzanne cried. "I thought that we were going to die. We all love you so much because you are so good and so kind and so generous and every night before going to bed, Dianne and I dropped to our knees and prayed and prayed for your safe return." Dianne said as they helped me from the car to deck and helped me into one of the lounge chairs. Donna followed us.

"Really? You prayed for me?" I was touched.

"Yes we did, Steve. We would do anything to get you home safe and well."

Suzanne poured the drinks while Dianne baked pizza on the grill. I never even heard of cooking pizza on the grill but it was good. The charcoal was place in the back of the grill and the five four inch in diameter dough with all the toppings including cheese, tomato sauce, onions, peppers and pineapples was positioned in the front.

"These are great," I said tearing into the treat. "How did you know that you could grill pizza on the grill?"

"Donna thought it up," Dianne said. "Your beautiful wife is very creative." Dianne said while she and Suzanne looked at Donna with love and admiration written all over their faces.

We didn't spent a lot of time on the deck, once the vodka and tonic was gone and the grilled pizzas was finished, I was finished too. I was knocked out. Donna and I bid good night to Suzanne and Dianne and a heartfelt thank you and Donna and I turned down there generous offer to help me upstairs and get me into the shower. "That's my job Ladies," Donna said as she hugged them both then we retired to our bedroom. Donna helped me out of my clothes and into the bathroom.

I was in the shower sitting on lawn chair, (Donna was afraid that I was going to fall on my head if I tried to shower standing), the first since I left the hospital at Travis, when she walked into the bathroom in all her naked glory carrying a tray with Cognac, ice and glasses. "How are you doing Honey?" She asked as she put the tray on the makeup table beside the john and helped up from the chair and out of the shower. I glanced at myself in the mirror. It looked like I had large measles scars all over my chest, stomach and right arm.

"I'm alright but I look like something right out of a Frankenstein flick," I said trying to look at my back. "I'm glad my dick was spared,"

"Wow, Honey! You really took a few hits. You even took one in the ass."

"I'm happy that I didn't take one up my ass," I said. "I may look perfectly normal but if I did take a hit up my rectum I wouldn't be standing in middle of the bathroom with an erection so hard a cat couldn't scratch it."

"That's cute, Stevie, real cute," Donna giggled while poured the drinks then climbed into the shower. I watched her while she soaping her body spending a lot time washing her breasts and between her legs, and she knew that I was watching her. Making love in the back of a Jet Star was nice but nothing like making love in the privacy of your bedroom. Donna looked at me and smiled while she was washing her beautiful body.

Later on while we were laying in bed watching television Donna turned on her side, faced me, and while she was massaging my stomach she said, "Stevie, were not getting any younger you know..."

I turned on my side and faced her and placed my hand on her thigh. "What do you want a boy or a girl?"

A year later, Donna presented us with identical twin girls Kathleen Charlotte and Jacqueline Louise.

God they are beautiful I thought to myself as I gazed lovingly at my gifts from God. They both had strawberry blond hair, hazel blue eyes and they looked exactly like their mother.

Dianne and Suzanne were waiting for us when we brought the twins from the hospital. They were with Donna from the time that we learned that she was expecting twins and right up to the time that Donna delivered our girls. We all were in the waiting room Dianne and Suzanne were with me as we paced the waiting room floor, waiting for the nurse to give us good news. I wanted to sit down and watch television but they wouldn't hear of it. "Come on Stevie," Suzanne scolded me as she took my hand and yanked me to my feet. "You either pace the room with us or we'll beat the shit out of you!"

I jumped to my feet and began the waiting room stroll. How could two of my best friends threaten me, but I wasn't about to challenge them.

"God Steve," Dianne whined both of their arms around me walking me around the waiting room like I was a cripple. "Suzanne and I love you both so much not only what you have done for us but for being our special friends. You both know how much Suzanne and I love each other and you never held it against us. You embraced our life style without condition and without your love and support we never would never had been able to accomplish what we had been able to do. Thank you Stevie."

Dianne and Suzanne with a loan from Black Gold Investments and Executive Airlines Inc, helped the girls open an extremely successful garden and flower shop in Newport, Rhode Island. When Donna and I drove up to Boston to look in on my Mom and Aunt Louise we stopped off in New York City, to look in on CJ and Karen, Donna presented the Suzanne and Dianne's proposal to C.J., he looked it over then gazed up and at her and said, "No sweat, Donna. Hang around and I'll have a check cut."

The girls found a one hundred fifty year old house and barn and when the house and barn was restored to their former perfection it was going to become "Dianne and Suzanne's Narragansett Bay Gardens and Nursery".

The half a million dollars Black Gold had advanced them was paid back in less than five years and their corporation was worth five million dollars. Donna and I would drop in from time to time to visit and see if there was anything they needed. It was always an adventure seeing Dianne and Suzanne and spending time with them. They were two of the happiest girls that Donna and I had ever had known.

As the twins grew older they had no trouble fooling their old man. Donna could tell them apart because when they were born they were connected at the ear, Jackie had a small scar on her right ear lobe and Kathy had a small scar on her left ear lobe. Donna could tell the twins apart but I had trouble and of course too really screw with my head Donna dressed them in identical clothes. My little ladies thought up all kinds of shit to screw with their old man and they thought it was the funniest thing in the world. They both looked the same talked the same and when they walked into the living room together; they were always together, they would be wearing the same clothes holding hands and wearing shit eating grins. Donna would smile and tell me that the twins each had a small scare on their ear lobes and I should try to remember which twin had the scare which ear. Then I suggested, why not take them into D.C. and have their initials tattooed on their knuckles

28 JULY 1982:

Donna the girls and I arrived at the hospital but we were too late. My Dad had died an hour earlier. He hadn't been feeling well and was having trouble breathing so Mom and Aunt Louise drove him over to Saint Luke's Hospital outside of Hollywood to see what the problem was. He was admitted right away and was sent down to x-ray. His lungs were filling with fluid and upon a biopsy the doctors discovered that he had lung cancer and it was terminal. So terminal that in three days Dad was gone. Mom called me Thursday evening to let me know about Dad's condition and I said that we all would be down as soon as possible. It never occurred to anyone, not even the doctor who was treating Dad that he had only two or three days before it was over.

We arrived in Tampa and Tom who was stationed at Pensacola Naval Air Base was at the airport with Joan picked us up and drove us to the hospital. "We had better hurry Steve, Dad has only an hour or so to hours to live." The hour or so turned out to minutes and when we all arrived at the hospital he was gone. Tommy drove us to down to the folk's house to make arrangements for Dad's funeral and I had Executive Airlines flew Dad's body back to Waltham for the wake and funeral.

When the folk's moved to Florida they both insisted that when it was their time they both including Aunt Louise were going to be buried in their family plot at Calvary Cemetery.

As soon as we got back to the folks house I called Curtis Blakely who was now retired from the military and working for the airline. I let him what I wanted him to do but by the time we hung up he was telling me what he was going to do for my Dad and my family. He was the best of the best. He said that he and Barbara would fly up from D.C to attend the wake and funeral. Thank you my friend.

A local funeral home went to the hospital and picked up Dad. Tommy and I with Donna picked out his casket, Joan, stayed with Mom and Aunt Louise. The next evening Dad's body was loaded aboard the Executive Airlines Boeing 737 and flown north to Hanscom Air Force Base civilian terminal where Bobby Joyce and Eddie Cronin pick up Dad's body, transported him to the funeral home and two days later he was waked and buried from St. Jude Church. Mom and Aunt Louise were incredible. So were Charly's Mom and Step Father. Ann and Jack met the plane at the base and stayed with Mom, Aunt Louise, Tommy, me and our families through the whole celebration of his life. Ann treated Donna and the twins just like they were part of her family. Barbara and Billy Flynn who were now married were there, so was Richie, Paulie and their families and Frankie, Rosie Ianotti and their daughter Charlotte Louise along with the Coyle Brothers. We had them flown in from Los Angles.

Following the Mass and funeral we had a luncheon at the Three Sons. The Nardone Brothers closed the place and said we had the Three Sons Restaurant for the day, there was no rush. Cosmo "Fudgie" Iaconio was paying for everything.

I phoned Fudgie when I got to the hospital and said that my father was had passed away and if he wanted to come north I'd send down my best aircraft. He and Frankie Rosa arrived on the day of the wake. Fudgie looked the same as he did the last time I had seen him. Still tall, slim but now well tanned from his summers and winters spent on the Florida's beaches.

I was standing in the hallway of the funeral parlor talking to Eddie Cronin and Bobby Joyce when Fudgie and Frankie walked through the door. I couldn't restrain myself. While I hugging them I totally fell apart. Fudgie maintained his composure but Frankie fell all too pieces. "Oh God Stevie, I'm so sorry," He wept as he held me tight. Fudgie placed his arm around my shoulder and told me how proud he was of me and what I had accomplished. "Stevie, you are the son I never had and what you have achieved in your life leaves me speechless. Now please lead Frankie and me in and introduce me to your beautiful wife and your twin girls. Rocco told me you have a beautiful family."

"The General told you the truth, Fudgie, I do have a beautiful family. God has been generous."

I led Fudgie to the head of the line both he and Frankie knelt in front of my Dad's casket, said a prayer in Italian and when they had finished with their prayers I introduced Fudgie and Frankie to Donna and my girls. He and Frankie had already met everybody else at Sharly's funeral.

"Donna, I would like to introduce you to Cosmo Iaconio "Fudgie" and Frankie Rosa, General Rosa's cousin," I said introducing them both to my wife, "And my twins girls Jackie and Kathy."

"You are right, Stevie, God has been good to all of us and your Father's life we're celebrating, your father a great man and his ascension to Heaven will be a celebration of his life on earth. God is smiling on you and your family Stevie."

"Mom, I know that you met Mr. Iaconio at Sharly's funeral but I want you to say hello again."

Mom with a rare display of affection toward people that are not family hugged both of them and thanked them for my education. "I want you gentlemen to know that you had done more to teach my son his values than he could ever learn in school. Thanks to you and to Mr. Rosa my son has become successful beyond anyone's wildest dreams."

"Come on Mom, I just lucked out. I was in the right place at time."

"Do you believe that's how it all happened, my young friend? Listen to your mother's words," Fudgie voice filled with deep emotion as he put his arm Donna and embraced her then put his arms around the twins, "Why were you in the right place at the right time, Stevie? Because you were suppose to be and what about your two friends that you met while you were in basic training? The right place at the right time again? And the pictures that you took at the oil fields; the right place at the right time again? And your beautiful wife and family; the right place at the right time again?"

God, he had me there, I didn't have an answer. "I don't know Fudgie. I don't have an answer."

"Of course you don't and I don't have an answer for you either Stevie. Maybe your father in time will talk to God and then your father will let us all know. I love you Stevie," Fudgie said as he embrace me. "Now go and never forget the lessons you learned in school and the lessons your mother and father taught you. It was I that was in the right place at the right time."

Fudgie and Frankie stayed with friends in Boston, returned for my Dad's funeral and burial, the family dinner at The Three Sons then Exec Airlines flew them back to Florida.

Donna, me and the twins stayed with my mother for a week to make sure she was alright then we returned to Washington DC. Mom wasn't interested in returning Florida, Waltham was her home and all her friends and family were here.

I asked Mom if she would mind signing her home and golf course over to me. I offered her a million dollars for the property. She looked at me as if I had lost what little sense I had been born with. "Now what in God's name will I do with a million dollars?"

"Well I want to give you something, Mom," I said. "You own some valuable property down there."

"Steven my dear, I'm three years away from my eightieth birthday," She smiled her blue eyes glistening. "Your father; God rest his soul and I have done well through his business and your generosity your Aunt Louise and I have more money than we could ever spend. Now put your money in the bank and invest it for Jackie and Cathy, for their future."

"I suppose I could split the money with Tommy," I mused.

"How about a nice cup of tea Steven?" Mom said ignoring what I had suggested then pushed back her chair got to her feet and lit the burner under the tea pot.

Curtis Blakely had finally retired from the Air Force following twenty four years of active duty, Curtis called it quits retiring with the rank of Chief Master Sgt. While he was in the service we stayed in touch and his last two years was spent at Bolling. Donna and Barbara were very close especially when Curtis and I were in Vietnam. Curtis always came up choice state side assignments. He had that type of personality. Everybody liked him and his easy going ways. Dover Air Force Base, Delaware, Andrews Air Force Base, Maryland, Lackland Air Force Base as a TI, Technical Instructor. I couldn't picture Blake being an in your face screaming at a "boot": "WHAT'S YOUR MAJOR MALFUNCTION NUMB NUTS!!!" He was too laid back.

Two years later after being the most inept Technical Instructor in Lackland's history he was assigned to Eglin Air Force Base. I asked how he got a tit job like that. He was the Non- Commissioned Officer in Charge of the NCO club. "How in hell did you get a gig like that?" I asked as we sat beside the NCO club swimming pool having an Absolut and tonic. "You had to have kissed a lot of ass old buddy," I said. Donna the girls and I was visited Barbara and Curtis on our way to Pensicola to look in on Tommy and Joan. Curtis spent more time on the beach then he spent at the NCO club. He was very good at delegating.

"You must have spent a lot of time working on your tan, Curtis," I joked. Donna reached across the table and gave me a slap upside my head.

I told Curtis that when he retired and if he was interested I had a position for him with Black Gold Investments. He would let me know. "Let him know fool? Steve is offering you a job with a Fortune 500 Company!" Barbara said looking at him in total disbelief.

Donna and I went to Curtis' retirement ceremony, had lunch at the base NCO Club. While we were having after lunch we were sipping Courvoisier Curtis asked me when he could start. "I want to start at the top and go up," He chided me.

"Okay, but on your first day come to work in overalls and brogans shoes, we'll supply the hat." I said winking at Barbara. "It has the company logo sowed onto the front."

"You mean to tell me that my man's gonna be a janitor, fool?" Barbara asked looking first at Donna than at me.

"Yeah," I grinned looking at Curtis.

"I'll see that he gets his black ass to work on time?" Barbara Blakely was a treasure with a love of life. She would have loved to have children but it wasn't to be.

I offered Curtis a position in charge of the day to day operation and he took to the job like he had been running the airline business all of his life. Some of the more senior employees would bitch to me about Curtis being hired to run the company and I let them know that I realized and understood why they were upset but I wanted Curtis to be in charge of the operation because I knew Curtis well and I knew he was the best person for the job. I want you all give him a chance to prove himself. And if he can't then I'll be back in charge but don't count on it.

Donna the girls and I were still living in our colonial house in Northern Virginia. We would fly up to Massachusetts and look in on Mom, Aunt Louise and Anne and Jack Furey, Billy and Joan Flynn, Richie and Patty, and Paulie and Lilly. They were all still living in the Bleachery going to Mass at Saint Jude's Church and visiting the cemetery on Memorial Day. Uncle Eddie and Aunt Mandy had passed away so did Richie and Paulie folks.

Then we would fly into Harrisburg and visit Donna's folks. Her Dad had long retired from flying and they were spending their leisure time between Pennsylvania and Florida. And every month or so they would come up to D.C. stay with us visit with their granddaughters, Donna and I would let Jack fly co-pilot on one of our C-140 Sabreliners. He was as good now as he was when he was flying fighters in WW Two.

Executive Airlines was the third largest private charter airline in the United Sates serving every major city in the U.S. and Canada. Curtis Blakely was promoted from Vice President in charge of operations 1984 to President of Executive Airlines. He was the best corporate officer in the private airlines business. He earned the respect and admiration of his fellow employees and if the any malcontents had a problem because he was black, Curtis would give them the option to get over it or move on. They all stayed. The money was excellent and the perks were outstanding. If the members of the military needed a ride and a charter was going your way and if there was room you got to fly for free and the drinks were on the airline. Just don't say anything to the paying customers. That was a Curtis Blakely perk. He came up with more incentives for his "military friends" then I could have ever imagined and Curtis had a lot of retired military friends and connections.

"Good morning Donna. Steve, I have a great promotional idea," Curtis announced as he hurried into my office. Donna and I were enjoying an early morning cup of coffee and an English muffin.

"How much?"

"Pardon?" He asked helping to a cup of coffee.

"How much is the airline going to get for reamed this time Mr. Executive Airlines?" I said as I got up grabbed mine and Donnas empty coffee cups and walked over to the desk that held the coffee pot and the English muffins.

"It won't cost the airline much and I will be great Public Relations."

"Okay Buddy, what you got in mind?"

"Well since we put on twenty-five new Boeing 727's and ten D.C. 9's usually the flights go out with a few empty seats so what say we let the military, in uniforms of course, fly for no." He smiled.

I looked first at Donna and then back at Curtis. "We do fly out of all the major airports, Steve. And we have our own check-in terminals, and if we haven't filled the seats let's do something for the troops."

"What do you think?" I said looking at Donna. She raised her eyebrows and nodded her head in the affirmative.

"Okay but we're going to need to get permission from the people that contract the charter flights."

"I'm way ahead of you, partner…"

"What's this partner shit?"

"One thing at a time, alright, Steve…"

"Ah… what about this partner shit, Curtis?" I said folding my arms across my chest tapping my foot on the floor like Wiley Coyote would do while he snorted through his nose.

"I already checked it out with all of our charter contracts and they all loved the concept. In fact Digital Equipment Corporation said that they would if there was enough troops going to the same city they would charter the planes. All expenses paid for by Digital."

"How long have you been with Exec, Curtis?" I asked looking at him dead in the eyes.

"Six years four months and three days." He said giving me the concise account of his service. That was a military thing.

"Alright Curtis, I'm going to have to get the Okay from CJ and Billy and if they go along with my recommendation you're in as a partner."

"I already have, Steve," Donna said. "They both agreed that with the success that Curtis had brought the company, well let's make him a partner."

"Do I still have a position here?" I lamented shaking Curtis hand. "Welcome to Black Gold Investment and Executive Airlines."

"Thanks boss," He smiled at Donna then me.

"Save it Curtis. Now you're going to really begin to earn your salary," I said. "How much are we paying you?" I asked.

"Two fifty a year."

"Beginning next month you're up to three seventy five?" I smiled.

"That's all Mr. Scrooge?" He said winking at Donna. As long as Curtis and I had know each we never had a cross word. We were good friends

"Take it or leave it Cratchet." I said.

"Does that include a company car?" Curtis asked pouring himself a cup of coffee. He already had a classic car collection that almost matched mine. He wanted to buy my '40 Lincoln Continental but that was a definite no.

"And a driver." Donna chimed in with a shit eating grin on her face.

"Who says?" I asked taking a bite from my English muffin.

"CJ and Billy and now you," Donna said sitting down behind my desk.

"Now me," I grinned looking down at the floor shaking my head.

"You sho is a good massa." Curtis smiled showing a mouthful of beautiful white teeth. He had the gold cap on his front tooth removed.

31 DECEMBER 1999
NEW YEARS EVE

Donna and I had planned to spend the evening home, alone enjoying a few drinks some Chinese food, take in some TV, watch the ball fall in Times Square then go to bed. We were both in our mid fifties. The twins were married. Jackie was married to an Air Force Jet jockey. They were stationed at Hickam Air Force Base, Hawaii. She has two boys. Kathy married one of our Executive Airline Pilots and they were living in Tampa Florida. She also had two boys.

This was the first New Year's evening we spent alone. It was always a party going on somewhere, New York, Washington DC, Boston, Florida, but this year Donna and I wanted to be alone. We were still living in Northern Virginia, Mom and Aunt Louise had passed away, Tommy was retired from the Navy and he Debbie was living in Charlestown, South Carolina. They bought a house that was owned by a long lost uncle who had fought in the Civil War and retired from the Army. He died in Texas was buried in Waltham, his wife died in 1935 was buried next to my long lost uncle and their son William who they called Billy had settled in California. It was reported that he and his family was extremely wealthy.

Donna and I were stretch out on the living room floor, a thick blanket under us and a thick blanked thrown over us, pillows behind our heads and a glass of VSQ in hand. We were watching the Marx Brothers when a knock reverberated from the back door. "Who in hell could be knocking on our door on New Year's Eve?" I grumbled pulling on my BVDs. We were "au natural".

"Now, Stevie," Donna scolded as I climbed to my feet, slipped into my robe and began walking to the back door.

"Wait until I get something on," She said, she was nude too.

I watched her as she pulled on her panties, put on her robe and stood up. "Okay, Honey. Go see who's out there."

I put on the back door light, unlocked the door opened it and standing in the deck smiling through the door glass was Dianne McCarthy and Suzanne Williamson. What in the name if God were they doing here?

"Who is it, Steven?" Donna asked as she walked into the kitchen holding her robe closed.

"You'll never guess, Honey," I said as I opened the door and let Dianne and Suzanne in. They both had been celebrating.

"Donna…Stevie," Dianne croaked as she and Suzanne pulled us close and embraced us. I do believe that they will be spending the night with us.

"What in hell bring you ladies to our humble abode?" Donna laughed as we all were caught up in a group hug. "It's so nice to see you again!"

"Well we were at the Fort Meyer's NCO Club for a New Year's party, it was boring as hell so Suzanne came up with the suggestion that we drop in on Donna and Stevie. You guys always have a bitching party so where is everybody, Huh?" Dianne asked.

"You're looking at it, Dianne. We thought a nice quiet evening, a few drinks, some slope food and an early night."

"So what are you guys drinking?" I asked. "You guys hungry? We have a shit load of left over Chinese food."

"I'll have a Beefeater and tonic," Suzanne said.

"How about you, Dianne?" Donna asked as she invited Suzanne and Dianne into the den.

"I would love a VO and ginger, Honey," Suzanne said. Both girls were a little unsteady on their feet. "You think you could put us up for the evening…Huh?"

"Yeah. Your apartment over the barn is still there, I'll give you the keys, the heat is on and whenever you're ready to hit the sack; it's up to you." I would keep the heat on low for my car collection. I had to enlarge the barn to make room for my 1913 Model "T" Ford, my '32 Deuce coupe' my '40 Ford deluxe coupe Tommy's '56 Ford Crown Victoria and last but not least my '51 Mercury Monterey.

I had to kiss a lot of ass and grease a lot of palms to get permits for the construction but money talks and bull shit walks.

"Whatcha got for Chinese food?" Dianne asked.

"Any egg foo young?" Suzanne asked.

"Yup, we got egg foo young." I replied.

"How is the egg foo fucking young?" Dianne said. Suzanne clapped her hands as she broke out laughing.

I replied. "Egg foo young velly fucking good."

Now everybody was laughing. Donna removed our epicurean delight from the micro-wave oven and spooned out the reheated egg foo young, fried rice, and what was left of the poo, poo plater on paper plates.

While we were eating I wanted to ask the girls what brought them down here to DC. Not to party at the Fort Meyer NCO club then show at our house. It was at least a seven hour drive from Newport Rhode Island. But knowing Dianne and Suzanne for almost forty years Donna and I had come to expect the unusual from lovely, happy, giggling lovers. And in the almost forty years that we had been friends they look as young, fresh and pretty and the day I had met them on our flight to basic training. No if I could just get them to quit smoking.

We finished off the Chinese food, the girls had another drink, bid us a happy New Year and climbed the barn steps, unlocked the door entered their former dig and went to bed. They weren't in their apartment for five minutes before the lights went out.

Donna and I cleaned up the kitchen got naked and had a VSQ brandy night cap at the bar then went on to bed. "Steven?"

"Donna?" I replied my womb broom buried deep in her crotch. I grew a mustache a few years back and Donna loved it. She thought that it a sensational sex toy.

"Our night guest drove up from Rhode Island spent half the evening partying at the Fort Meyer's NCO Club then drove across the river and showed up at our back door."

"Yeah I know. Why didn't they make reservations at a hotel in DC or a motel in the DC area? They just didn't drive down here, get loaded at the NCO Club and show up here to wish us a Happy New Year."

"You know Honey, I wouldn't put it past them. They have done dopey things since we have known them. Remember when I returned from my second tour in 'Nam with wounds all over my back and chest? There they were dressed up as nurses wearing mini-skirts and white panty hose. I almost broke out laughing. Good thing I didn't, I would have blown out all my stitches."

"Yeah, they are a couple of characters."

"Remember the dildo incendent...?

"Don't go there, Stevie," Donna said as she put her hands over her face and mouth to keep from laughing out loud.

"I didn't know a rubber dildo could fall apart that easily," I said.

"Steven!"

"It was so funny, Donna. You gotta admit it."

"They are up to something," Donna stated while she observed my action. She loved to watch.

"I know," I said kissing her wet spot then looking up into her eyes. "Usually before they'd drive all the way down for visit they would call us."

"Come on big guy," Donna said as she smiling. "Let's bring 2000 in, in style."

"Yeah, let's," I said as I crawled over her still beautiful body and kissed her gently on her lips.

"Your mustache smells like me," She said as she turned me over and slid down my still rock hard body and placed her full ruby red lips over my erection. "Now I want my breath to taste like you."

1 JANUARY 2000:

Donna and I slept in later than usual and we were in the kitchen having coffee and bacon and egg sandwiches. We had our robes on instead of the usual walking about the house in the nude. Suzanne and Dianne we imagined were still in bed. They were pretty much on the way when they hit the sack so we thought it would be better to let them sleep in. Donna and I had no plans for the day and Black Gold/Executive Airlines were both going great guns. I went to my office every morning and spent my afternoons working on my car collection. Donna was busy working for Veterans Affairs. She left her job at Executive Air ten years ago. She was bored not having that much to do at Ex Air so she applied for a position with Veteran's Affairs Office and was hired. She put in more hours working for the Vets than I did with EX Air. She was happy working downtown, she loved DC and had her hefty salary was deferred to Veterans programs.

"What in hell are those two doing?" I asked no one in particular. "Christ it's almost ten thirty."

"I don't know Honey, but close your robe will you please," She ordered. "I'm the only one that's allowed to look at your jewels."

I closed my robe then went into the master bathroom to shave, brush my teeth and take a shower. Donna stayed out in the kitchen if by chance the girls came down from the apartment and graced us with their presents. They were most likely either sleeping off New Year's Eve or enjoying breakfast in bed. I looked out of the bathroom window and their "pink" F-150 Ford Pick-up was still parked in the driveway. The truck was red when the girls bought it but they took it a body shop and had the truck painted pink. You gotta love the alternate life style.

Donna walked into the bathroom while I was drying myself off and announced that Dianne and Suzanne were on their way. I finished drying myself off, donned my robe and Donna and I walked out into the kitchen just as the ladies knocked on the door. I open the door while Donna poured coffee for Dianne and Suzanne.

"Happy New Year!" They both shouted out as I swung open the door and let them in. They both had on the same clothes that they were wearing last night.

"And the same to you," I said as I hugged them both. Although they were wearing the same clothes that they showed up in last night, they both looked fresh as a daisy. No sign of a hangover, no red eyes, no headache, no booze or crotch odder on their breaths, just two lovely ladies who enjoyed their New Year's Eve, a good night's sleep and no broken dildo's.

"Happy New Year," Donna smiled as she hugged the girls. She was still in her robe so let's not linger too long with the salutations,

Sweetheart. Dianne and Suzanne told me many times that they thought Donna was incredibly beautiful. They were right about that.

"Now, ladies," I said. "What brings you to our humble abode? You didn't drive down here just to wish us Happy New Year, now did you?"

"Yes we did, Stevie," Dianne said. "We had the best year since we started out and we have CJ, Billy, Curtis and you and Donna to thank. You all have accepted Suzanne and me, regardless of our lifestyle, no prejudices, no laughing behind our backs, only love and friendship and although we had paid back EX Air and Black gold for you trusting us and made it possible for us to make our business an unbelievable success, so Suzanne and I knew we had to do something to show our appreciation so have a small check for the Vietnam Veteran's Fund for the disabled troops."

Dianne handed Donna the envelope holding the check. I thought her eyes were going to fall out of her head as she opened the envelope. "Oh my God!" She cried as she handed me the check. It was a cashier's check for two hundred and fifty thousand dollars. "I don't believe it! Are you sure you want to donate this much money?"

"Yeah we do, Donna, it's the least we can do." Dianne said with a sad smile.

"When Stevie came back from his second tour cut to ribbons Dianne and I thought we were going to die. You and Stevie are the family we've always wanted. Our families and who we thought were our friends never accepted us and our relationship. We were called dykes, queers, muff divers and any other nasty comments that they could think up but when we met Stevie on the plane going to basic he knew that were together but never questioned our relationship. He just accepted us and we always loved him for kindness and support."

"But I did giggle behind your back when I knew you couldn't hear me." I kidded my robe accidently falling open exposing the family jewels. I snapped it closed but not before both girls got an eyeful.

"No you didn't, Stevie," Dianne cut in. "You and Donna always treated us with love and respect and when we had moved back to Rhode Island to start our business you always stayed in touch and whenever you had the time you would stop in and say hello. So did Curtis and Barbara, and we will never forget CJ, Billy, for their kindness and their support and all your generosity."

"Thank you so much," Donna cried while she hugged them and kissed them both on the lips.

I followed Donna with a warm hug and kiss them on their lips too. God they tasted good!

We sat in the kitchen drinking coffee Dianne and Suzanne were making bacon, cheese omelets, hash browns in the toaster and toast baking in the oven. Donna and I had breakfast a little earlier but these babes put on a breakfast that was fit for the Whitehouse.

When we asked the ladies if they would want to stay with us and head home in the morning, they agreed, finished breakfast and went up to the apartment, undressed donned some old wool robes that were hung in one of the closets; they smell like cotton balls; brought down their dirty clothes and did their laundry. We had another cup of coffee laced with Bacardi rum then another…hell it was New Year's Day none of us were going anywhere so let's relax, enjoy, have a few drinks, and keep our robes closed.

That after noon, laundry done, all of us dressed and we all watched the Rose Bowl parade then later the Rose Bowl game, Dianne had the deck grill fired up and was Suzanne cooking "T" bone steaks, while Dianne made a salad. There were dinner rolls in the oven. It was a good thing that we had the deck covered because the weather had turned cold, windy and it had begun to rain.

Donna had always kept the fridge loaded. We never knew who was going to drop by, Curtis and Barbara, Benny Polly and his wife, Roger Hicks and his Korean wife Suzi, and three or four times a year Bob Shadley and his wife Laura would fly down from Minnesota for a visit. Bob and Laura along with their son Gordie owned a fishing and hunting lodge a few miles north of International Falls. That's one cold mother in the winter. Josh Kaplan, now retired from the military, he had made bird colonel, would show up with whomever he was dating at the time but he never dated a Jewish American Princess. He would say that Jewish girls were too pushy and wanted to be lavishly entertained. Tight ass Josh was not your guy, so he always dated a shiksa. Josh was worth millions thanks to Black Gold, Digital Equipment Corp and his other investments, but whenever he showed up at our door; he was always welcome as were all the others invested in the company; had a different girl tattooed to his to his arm. "Josh, you're pushing sixty. When are you gonna settled down?"

"As soon my dick stops working Stevie," He laughed punching me on the shoulder then handing me a bag with a bottle of Johnny Walker Black. Josh was the only guest that brought his own bottle. I told him that I'd supply his favorite libation but he said with everything that Black Gold had done for him to allow him to financial freedom well the least he could do was supply my own booze. Thanks a bunch Josh.

Most our friends were invested in Black Gold, EX Airlines, Digital Equipment Corp, AT&T, and most of the other major airlines. Our only other friend that couldn't make it was CWO Richardson. He passed away a year ago and he was buried in a National Cemetery outside of Creed, Colorado. We were all there for his wake, funeral and burial with honors full military. He said that he always wanted to be buried in a gold plated casket. I made sure that he got his wish.

Fudgie Iaconio was now seventy-eight years old and had a beach front home in Hawaii. Donna the twins and I visited him and Frankie Rosa a from time to time and Fudgie had not changed. I asked him why he had left Florida and He said that Florida was over loaded with Cubans, Latinos and other reprobates and although Spanish would be an easy language to learn ("Hell," he would say, "If the spicks could learn to speak Spanish it had to be simple.") but I would much rather live where English was the spoken language.

Frannie Rosa was still there him. At seventy-five Frankie was still bartending. He had a part time job at a plush private golf course outside of Honolulu. The old canvas back could lay back and retire to the beach and look at the girls if he wanted to but he would say, "Who was gonna pay the rent, buy the food, light Fudgie's Guinea Stogies and make sure that fudgie didn't spend us out of house and home!"

That's why they lived in a million dollar home overlooking the Pacific Ocean facing Diamond Head.

When Benny retired from the military in 1986, he and his wife Roseanne moved back to Bogalusa. Benny opened a finance consulting firm in New Orleans. We taught him well because he would say, "I was getting tired of getting my ass hammered by the IRS for taxes. I had to spend some money." He is maybe one of the richest men in the state.

Roger and Suzi were living the good life in Carmel, California. They owned a charter boat company that booked party boats for rich business men and woman from all over the world. At last count Executive Charters owned and operated ten multi-million dollar boats. EXs Boats offered gourmet meals, free drinks and once they were 20 miles off the California coast the slot machines, the crap tables and the roulette wheels were fired up. Roger and Suzi along with their three boys had done very well thanks to Black Gold Investments.

Frankie and Rosie resided in Gainsville, Florida with their two sons and one daughter. Artie and Philly had since moved back to California. They were all still involved in drag racing. They were also invested in construction of world class drag racing facilities. "There is nothing more important when it comes to safety for our drivers," Rosie said at a NHRA convention. She was the spokes woman for the NHRA Safety Safari. She had come a long way from waitressing at Harrigan's restaurant. It was the first time that her breast size and her age matched. They were both forty-four.

Frankie and Rosie also designed computer software for building racing engines. Frankie could thank Rosie for all of her computer expertise. She made it all look so easy.

Then we would stop by and look in on Tommy, Debbie and my niece and nephew. Nancy was working on Wall Street and Richie was a pilot for Ex Air. He joined the Air Force when he graduated from Boston College, went to flight school, flew cargo; he wanted to fly fighters but the Air Force thought he would do better flying cargo. He loved it, and when his obligation was finished Curtis offered him a position with Ex Air, he joined the Air Force Reserves and came flying with us.

Richie took after his father he was tall, slim with a great smile and large, dark, mischievous eyes. He had Tommy's sense of humor and his love of practical jokes. I just wish he would not get comically creative while flying our planes. He and his best friend and Air Force buddy and co-pilot Bobby MacAbee would leave the cabin mike open and would pretend that they were mixing drinks. Richie would take a glass filled with ice and water put a cover over the glass and shake the shit out of it. "Hey Bobby, you made the Martinis too weak. Here take the wheel and I'll show you how to make the perfect martini. And when we finish drinking the martinis I'll show you the best way to put together the perfect Manhattan.

"Too bad we don't have a blender up here, Richie," Bobby said the mike still alive. "Then we could make up some frozen Margaritas."

"I'll pick one up when we get into D.C."

"Good, it'll give us something to drink on the flight back to Tampa."

"I have a great idea, Bobby," Richie said swirling glass of his ice water.

"Go ahead," Bobby said.

"Let's go to BARTENDING SCHOOL!"

"Ready for another?" Richie asked shaking a water and ice filled glass.

"Yup, you can't fly on one wing."

Most of the passengers knew that they were just screwing around but there was always one or two that took these two clowns seriously and posted complaints so I had Curtis call them into his office and tell them to knock off the drunken bullshit act.

Another one of their gems and this was a good one. When they climbed out of company car that dropped them off, they entered the aircraft both wearing dark glasses and had a golden retriever on a leash. Although everyone on the flight broke out laughing no one on the aircraft bought the comedy act. It brought about lots of laughs but no complaints.

TIME TO GO HOME

28 OCTOBER 2012

The past ten years went by quicker than the blink of an eye. Donna passed away a victim of breast cancer. She went through hell with the chemotherapy treatments, the radiation treatments but nothing would save her life. When she died she had wasted away to almost nothing. He beautiful body was a shell of her former self. Kathy, Jackie and I were with her when she passed away. So were Suzanne and Dianne. They took Donna's death as badly as the family did because they were our family.

Black Gold, Executive Airlines and the rest of our investments were all doing very well. CJ and Billy were still at the top of their game making investments all over the world. Curtis Blakely now was running Executive Airlines. After Donna's death I lost all interest in our Corporations, sold the colonial and moved down to Florida. I had more money than my great grand kids could spend. I just wanted to lay back on the beach, enjoying a cocktail and ogling the young ladies in their bikinis while they sashayed in front of my appreciative eyes. I had just turned seventy-five but I still appreciated female beauty and there was a lot of it down here in.

But none of those beautiful ladies could hold a candle to Rose Lyn (Rosie Beanbags) Donna Marie Dyer or Charlotte Louise O'Sullivan when it came to their beauty or their kindness of heart.

STEVE AND SHARLY TOGETHER AGAIN

Steve caught a flight out of Tampa for a quick trip up to DC. He had planned to stop in and visit with Curtis and the rest of his friends that worked for Executive. Then he bordered another flight to New York City to visit CJ and Karen. Stevie had been out of the company loop for ten years but he had kept in touch with all of his friends.

He always had taken care of himself, never smoked, never did drugs, but he love a cocktail or a glass of Courvoisier before retiring for the night but he never had a problem with booze and always made sure that he could get out of bed first thing in the morning, but today he had a pain in his chest which he had never had experienced before, and a pain in his left shoulder going down his left arm. Should he tell Richie and Bobby, they were his pilots and could call ahead to Boston for an ambulance? Maybe he would mix a vodka and tonic. Yeah why not, a drink may make him feel better, he thought to himself. He wasn't driving. He undid his seat belt slid out of his seat and walked to the rear of the Saber liner opened the door that hid the bar and looked over the array of liquor. He was amazed at the choices.

"Hi Stevie," Came the silky, soft voice that he recognized from the time he was twelve years old. She was dressed in light blue shorts, a white short-sleeve blouse and white sneakers. That's how he remembered her, her long blond hair the way it rested on her shoulders, her full red lips so sensual even without lipstick...she was the Charlotte he knew before she was taken from him and more beautiful than ever. But what was she doing here?

"It is Stevie and we're all waiting to for you."

"Sharly?" He said gazing into her beautiful violet blue eyes. "I must be dreaming. You were killed while I was in Vietnam." He said.

"Yes and now I'm here to take you home." She smiled mixing him vodka and tonic with a lime.

"I'm not ready to come home yet Sharly. I still have Jackie, Kathy and to care for. And now that Donna is gone they need me more than ever, and I still have a few responsibilities with our companies and to CJ and Billy. I can't just walk out on them."

"That's what I've always loved about you, Stevie," Sharly said smiling as she handed Stevie his drink. "You have been loyal to your friends, family and me and you always make it a point to visit my grave whenever you come back to Waltham. So does Rosie, Frankie and before Fudgie and Franny passed away they would visit me too. And Pauly and Richy and their wives and kids, even Kuckie and his wife would drop by whenever they were in the Bleachery."

"Gonna join me, Sharly?" Stevie smiled as he sipped his drink.

"Yes I will," She said while Stevie watched her clothes melt away from her body and stood before him with a white robe thrown over her shoulders that was opened all the way down to the aircraft floor.

"Tell me Sharly, what's it like in Heaven?" He asked looking at her beautiful body while she mixed her cocktail. She was stunning.

"Go into the restroom and see yourself in the looking glass."

He walked into the small, cramped head and looked in the mirror. Holy God! He exclaimed as he watched all of his clothes melt away and a white robe was also draped over his new body. God he thought, he had to have dropped forty five years. He looked the same as he did when he was in Vietnam. Then he walked back out to the cabin, his eyes wide open, and smiled shaking his head back and forth. "I guess there's no going back now."

"Come on Stevie, let's finish our drinks and I'll take you home."

"You know Honey?" Steve said smiling into her eyes as he caressed her cheek. "I really missed you."

"I really missed you too," She smiled loving the gentle caress of his tender touch.

"Maybe we can make love when we get there," He said. "Is that allowed in Heaven, Sharly?"

"It was God that thought it up, Honey. It was all his idea," Sharly chuckled.

"Does that go for girlfriends too?"

"We're already there, look around, Stevie and yes we are allowed to show each other love and affection. That's what it means to be with God and the Holy Family."

"I love you Sharly," He said still wrapped his arm around her waist. "I always have loved you, even while I was married to Donna."

"I know, Stevie, she told me."

"She was a beautiful woman and I love her very much and when she died I lost the two women that I had ever loved and I just about told God to get out of my life…"

"But you didn't because Donna and me with our guidance kept you close to our Lord, your Mother, Father, and your Aunt Louise also helped," Sharly smiled as she removed her robe and helped him off with his. "But let's not forget Rosie Leonardi, you were pretty hung up on her too as I remember."

"Yeah, she was fun to be with," Stevie smiled back at her. "And her physical attributes were nice too."

"She and Frankie are doing well they still live in Florida."

"Will we be seeing them soon?"

"In God's good time," Sharly answered.

"My Grandfather would repeat that cliché from time to time," Stevie said as he lovingly admired Sharly's grace and beauty.

"It's not meant to be a cliché Stevie," Sharly admonished Stevie with a smile. "A cliché is a trite phrase. God doesn't deal in trite phrases."

"I beg God's pardon," He said then asked Sharl, "You wouldn't have my '51 Mercury Monterey up here would you?"

"It can be arranged," She smiled patting his cheek. "And maybe we can get your 40 coupe' up here too, we had a lot of fun riding about in those two cars didn't we?"

"Yeah we did and maybe we can go parking?" He asked while taking her into his arms. "Or making out at the old Natick Drive-in that's not there anymore?"

"Just like old times, Stevie," She said as she took him into her arms kissed him passionately and led him into heaven's bedroom where they would spend eternity in each other's arms never to grow old.

And of course let's not forget Dianne McCarthy and Suzanne Williamson. They too share there love in God's arms too.

"Sharly?" He asked as he looked at his new home in total awe.

"Yes Stevie," She said as she turned and faced him her arms wrapped around his waist.

"I do believe I'm gonna like it up here," Stevie smiled as her looked into her grey blue eyes. "Yeah, I think I'm gonna like hanging around for a while."

THE END

This Book is dedicated to the all the military that served honorably, the MIA's, POW's and the 58,247 names inscribed on the VIETNAM WALL.

And for Judy, Jackie, Kathy, Joe, Patrick, Christopher and Mason: I love you all.

Printed in the United States
By Bookmasters